Price to Pay

Dedication

For anyone who has been told it is a sin to be sick.

Part One

"Man is not what he thinks he is, he is what he hides."
~ Andre Malraux

"History is made as humans all over the world react to tonight's events. Dozens of mermaids and humans gathered at Arthur's Aquarium to stand in support of merpeople gaining their rights back. Leader of the Rebellion – Amy Wilson – stood front and center with her followers. Police quickly arrived and attempted to shut down the protest, only to be interrupted by a shocking announcement.

"The Supreme Court has just voted to restore basic civil rights to all merpeople after discovering that these shape-shifting sea creatures are simply humans infected with a virus.

"Soon after the announcement, famous mermaid catcher, Morris Falcon, attempted to open fire on Amy Wilson and his own nephew, Tom Falcon. Morris was apprehended by another merman and died on the scene. Both teenagers and many others are still alive and being treated in the hospital for their injuries. Humans around the world are waiting anxiously for their release. I think we all have questions we would like to ask them."

~ XYZ Nightly News.

MERCER

The air conditioning on my damp skin after months of being at sea felt icy and unfamiliar. The carpet beneath my bare feet felt even stranger. But I stared straight ahead at the man in front of me, slightly enjoying the shocked expression on his face. Or was that repulsion?

I sniffed the air. Definitely repulsion. This was not one of the humans who had wanted to free my kind.

"How did you get back here?" he asked, shutting his office door behind him. I glanced over to the open window. He really should have locked that.

"I have a proposition for you," I said. The man reached for his phone, but I grabbed it before he did, sliding it out of his reach. I could smell the sweat beading on the back of his bulbous neck.

"I'll call the police," he warned.

"And I'll kill you before they get here," I hissed. "Now are you going to listen to my proposition or not?"

The man swallowed, his Adam's apple bobbing up and down. "Fine. What do you want?"

I leaned forward in the mayor's padded leather chair and folded my hands on his thick mahogany desk, a blade carved of whalebone dangling from my left hand. The mayor sunk into the chair on the opposite side of his desk and white-knuckled the armrests.

"I don't want merfolk to be free any more than you do," I said quietly.

He raised his eyebrow. "Why? Aren't you one of them?"

I stiffened. "The ones living here on land? The ones from the Sanctuary? They are not real merfolk," I spat. "They have abandoned our traditions, made a mockery of our history, and defiled themselves by working together with humans. I want nothing to do with them. They do not deserve to be called merfolk."

His eyebrow remained raised. "Your traditions?" he echoed.

"The legends that have been passed down for centuries," I said.

The mayor crossed his arms. "I thought those legends were false? That your kind was secretly gentle and peaceful this entire time?" he asked.

I scoffed. "Do I *seem* gentle and peaceful?" The light streaming in through the window made the blade of my knife gleam. The man swallowed once more.

"Forgive me for not assuming the idiosyncrasies of your species," he deadpanned. "All I know is that your kind are apparently just humans who got sick, and therefore have to be treated as such."

"We are not remotely human!" I hissed. "And any supposed merfolk who believes that deserves to be -" I stopped myself, forcing myself to inhale.

"The remaining *true* merfolk live with me, in the sea. We have no need of human laws protecting us," I continued. "And I would imagine that your life would become much easier if all the merfolk here were to return to their ancestral homes in the ocean."

At this, the man leaned forward. Sweat still beaded on the back of his neck, but it smelled like excitement instead of fear. "What are you saying?"

"Make it as difficult as possible for merfolk to integrate back into society. You may not be able to capture and sell us anymore, but as mayor, you can shape how the humans here will treat them. And over time, these merfolk will realize that it will be easier to come back to me than to stay."

The man raised his eyebrow. "I thought you wanted *nothing to do with them?*" he quoted. "What about the ones who won't leave no matter what? Your species is a stubborn one - after all."

At this, I hesitated. I knew he was right - Amy and her group of insolent friends would never submit to my rule in the ocean - not after all they had fought for. But then again, did I really want the likes of those with me? Cursed was Cursed. No amount of teaching or training could get rid of that. They would be better off gone.

"Once they realize life on land will never be the same, I'm sure they'll be begging to return home with me. As for the stubborn ones – let me worry about them," I said.

The man leaned back in his chair, chewing on his lower lip. "So, to be clear . . . you want me to treat the mermaids here so badly that they want to leave and go join your tribe or whatever you call it?"

I nodded. Our species was at a precarious point. In the beginning, I had seen the logic of integrating back into a free society. But Amy Wilson had ruined everything.

She let herself be captured by the enemy to protect that worthless merfolk hunter. She recruited humans to help her cause – as though merfolk weren't strong enough to fight for themselves. She didn't flinch when she took aim and killed one of my men – all because she wanted to spare that pathetic excuse for a merman from being Removed. She cared more about her precious friends than her actual species.

Real merfolk were loyal to their traditions. Real merfolk stayed with their mates. Real merfolk defended themselves against humans *without* cavorting with them. If things kept going the way she wanted, our species would be corrupted to the point of no return. Merfolk would become the very humans we had sworn to abhor. Freedom at the cost of integration wasn't freedom.

Unless someone like me took a stand. Protected the ones that were left. Rescued the ones who weren't brainwashed.

"You have a deal," the man said.

EMANUEL

Norman lurked in the corner of my hospital room and didn't try to hide his bemused smirk as a nurse attempted to push my nose back in place. I swore very loudly as she finally did it. She winced on my behalf and started taping a thick bandage over it.

"It'll heal in about three weeks. Keep this on it to keep the swelling down. Try not to touch it," she said, handing me an ice pack. I gingerly pressed it against my face.

"What if I have to blow my nose?" I asked, earning another snigger from Norman.

"Try not to - it'll hurt." The nurse vanished.

11

"You look great with a nose the size of Texas," Norman teased, plopping himself down on the arm of my chair. I rolled my eyes and shoved him.

"At least my head isn't the size of Texas," I retorted, cringing as my words came out with a nasal twang. He giggled again, and the sound made my heart melt. I let my hand rest over his, glad for a moment that some angry human had decided to punch me in the face during the protest. My embarrassing injury seemed to be making Norman forget about the reason merfolk had been freed.

We're not fucking sick, he had spat, clenching his fists and pacing.

I could understand his frustration. Queer people like us had been labeled as *sick* for decades, which only served to encourage public hate, but society came around eventually. Surely they would for merfolk too. If being labeled as *sick* meant he was going to be treated as a human instead of an animal to be captured and sold, I would take it.

"So, were Tom and Amy making out by the time you left?" I asked. He shrugged.

"I dunno. I just told her what was going on and the nurse said she could go see Tom. I've never seen her hobble so fast."

I sniggered, and we lapsed back into silence.

He's free, I thought, instinctively squeezing his hand. *He's free, and he's all mine. That night on the boat wasn't our last kiss, after all.* Norman turned red beside me as if he could tell exactly what I was thinking about. I let myself blush, for once, trying not to tamper my feelings. We were free. We were alive. I was allowed to have a crush on Norman - different species or not.

Norman opened his mouth but was interrupted by the pounding of footsteps before he could speak. The curtain to my room was thrown open, and I found myself squished in a familiar embrace.

"Mom?" I pushed her back only for her to squish me against her once again, body wracked with sobs as she stroked my hair.

"Mi Nino, I'm so glad you're safe," she cried. Over her shoulder, I could see Norman had shied away to the corner of the room, frozen as my two little siblings tried their best to climb him like a tree. My dad watched the scene with his arms crossed, his mustache hiding his lips. *Since when does Dad have a mustache?* I wondered.

My mom finally pulled away, and my dad walked over. I tensed, waiting for him to call me irresponsible and reckless, but all he did was pull me into another hug that almost broke my nose again. He didn't cry, but his strong arms felt like iron manacles, and I might've let a tear or two slip as I breathed in his familiar scent.

"I missed you guys," I whispered. Stealing a police boat to abandon my educational camping trip in a rash decision to help protect merpeople seemed like eons ago. Exactly how long had it been since I had seen my parents? My brain was too overwhelmed to crunch the numbers and figure it out. Meanwhile, my mom had pushed my siblings aside and attacked Norman in his own rib-crunching hug. His big brown eyes went wide with shock, but he stood there and let her cry into his hair as she muttered in Spanish. My siblings threw their arms around me from the other side of the chair as they peppered me with questions.

"What's it like swimming with mermaids?"

"Are you gonna get sick too?"

"Dad, is Emanuel grounded for running away?"

My dad finally let go and gently scraped my siblings off me. "We'll talk about that stuff later," he said gently. "Right now, I'm just glad that your brother is safe." My mom dragged Norman over to the rest of us, beaming like she had just found buried treasure.

"Boys, this is Norman, the young merfolk who helped keep your brother safe and rescue all those people!" she said. "You owe him a very big thank you." Norman's face turned unfathomable shades of red as my siblings showered him with praise. I returned his bemused smirk from earlier as he floundered under the attention.

I can't believe they're not upset. I thought. Shouldn't they be mad at me for running away with zero warning or explanation? Maybe they were just secretly okay with merpeople the entire time and they're proud of me for taking a stand? That thought seemed pretty believable as my family swarmed Norman.

They're just happy to have me back. And they seem okay with Norman too. Thank god. It would be hard enough to tell my parents I was gay. It would be even worse if they hated merfolk.

They sure got here fast, I thought. When are Norman's parents going to show up? Have they been released yet?

Based on Norman's past stories about them, I wasn't sure if that would be a good thing or a bad thing.

ADAM

The world felt fuzzy. I could vaguely overhear voices whispering around me. My stomach hurt. Whenever I tried to lift my arms, they flailed like someone else was controlling them. Words came jumbled out of my mouth. It was easier to linger in the darkness of sleep.

Until the nightmares started.

My face was sticky. My hands were tacky with blood. The humid air smelled like copper. People screamed around me, but all I could see was the end of my sword buried in another person's body.

I would never hurt another human.

I tried to rewind the scene - do something - anything else other than kill the man in front of me. No matter how I replayed it, no matter

15

what I said or threatened, my sword ended up piercing the man's heart, leaving me drenched in the last dregs of his life.

I would never hurt another human.

The next time I opened my eyes, the world was in focus. I gasped for breath, clutching my heart as a machine next to me beeped wildly. Instantly, there were people gathered around me. I blinked, trying to process all the different faces and remember what had happened.

Oh my god.

The events of the previous day hurled through my head. Humans shooting at us with tranquilizers. Dogs barking. Rebels clutching signs and fighting for their lives. Injured merpeople bleeding on the ground. The bandages on my stomach holding back a gaping wound.

Morris had a gun pointed at Amy and Tom. He was shooting. And I stabbed him.

Oh my god, I killed Morris.

Someone reached down and touched my hand, sending a wave of calm over me. I focused on his face and realized it was Emanuel with a thick bandage over his nose. Norman stood next to him and grinned. *They're still alive.*

I turned my head to see faces I feared I would never see again.

"Mom? Dad? Ethan?" I whispered. I remembered Ethan barging past crowds of protestors to hug me before the chaos erupted. I remembered him falling to the ground and blood leaking through his white shirt. I grabbed at him, trying to inspect his body for wounds.

"Ethan! Are you okay?"

He laughed and gently pushed my arms away. "I am fine, brother. A bullet only grazed me. They already patched it up."

I allowed myself a little sigh of relief and then turned to the two adults at the end of my bed. Tears shone in both of their eyes.

"Hi . . ." I whispered. My dad strode forward and threw his arms around me, hugging me the best he could. His body heaved with sobs. I froze as his relief and sadness poured into me, so thick I could hardly breathe.

"I'm so glad you're safe," he said, finally pulling away and wiping his eyes. My mother smiled sadly and held my hand, stroking my thumb like how she used to do when I was little.

How mad are they? I wondered. *Are they upset I was never honest with them? Are they upset I got their biological son hurt? Are they wishing they never adopted me?*

"Dude, don't look so horrified. You're fine. It just took you a thousand years to wake up from surgery," Emanuel said, his voice slightly nasally.

"Surgery?" I asked.

"Yeah. Turns out Tom didn't get the entire bullet out of you, so they had to go back in for the rest of it." Norman held up a little glass bottle and shook it - sending little fragments of metal clinking on the sides. "They said you could keep it," he said, winking. I looked down at my torso and noticed that it was wrapped in bandages. *That's why my stomach hurts,* I thought. I tried to force a smile, but it felt broken. It felt like I had been shot by that sailor years ago. So much had happened. I didn't remember anything after . . .

I stopped breathing, and the machine beeped angrily. A nurse pushed through the crowd and checked my heartbeat.

"Are you feeling okay?" she asked. I nodded, forcing air into my lungs. I clenched the edges of my bed, the entire world suddenly feeling lopsided. My hands started to tremble. The world was spinning too much for me to see if anyone had noticed. My heart felt like it was the thing that had been stabbed. Was this what dying felt like?

Oh my gosh, I must be in so much trouble, I thought. I vandalized countless ships. I murdered someone. When are the cops going to show up and arrest me? Can my parents afford a lawyer? Do I even deserve a lawyer?

I would never hurt another human.

"You should probably try to eat something," Ethan said, pushing a tray of food onto my lap. *Why is no one else freaking out?* I thought. *I'm a liar. I'm a murderer. Why is everyone being so nice to me?*

Emanuel squeezed my hand one more time. "We'll let you rest and hang out with your family. We'll be back in a little bit, okay?" he said. I nodded and watched as my two friends left my room. Guilt clawed its way through my insides. The machine started beeping more frantically.

"I'm so sorry," I whispered. My mom frowned as she grabbed my hand.

"Sorry for what, baby?" she asked. My throat closed.

I'm a murderer.

9:45 PM: Bro I can't believe our freaking classmate was the leader of the rebellion

9:46 PM: Ikr. She was always so quiet

9:46: But can you believe that tom was in on it all too? Guy used to be such a prick

9:47: and markus too. I wonder if he was in that big fight

9:48: You think theyll come back to school

9:49: Idk man. I heard they offered mr johns a teaching job

9:49: I mean half the school ditched to go rescue him. Its the least they could do. Man deserves a raise for what he did

AMY

I stayed with Tom until I was politely but firmly redirected back to my hospital room.

"You're still dehydrated and not in super great shape. You need to rest. And then my friend, Dr. Hartzfield, wants to talk to you for a minute," the nurse said, holding back the curtain to my room. I sat back down, eyeing the newcomer as he walked in with a beaming smile and clipboard.

"Hi, I'm Dr. Hartzfield, head of psychology," he said. *Great, a shrink*, I thought. I probably needed a lot of therapy, but after Cindy's involuntary experience in the mental hospital - the thought of talking to a psychologist didn't exactly make me feel any more at ease.

I nodded and grudgingly let the nurse hook me into another IV as two more people walked into the room. The hair rose on my arms. I clenched my fists, nearly tearing holes into the cheap blanket. The two strangers awkwardly turned to face me. I held their gaze. No - they didn't deserve eye contact. I broke my stare and turned to Dr. Hartzfield.

"What are my parents doing here?" I asked, fighting to keep my voice level.

He cleared his throat. "Well, you're still a minor, so legally, they are still your guardians. I figured it would be best to have a meeting together and figure out things moving forward."

Moving forward. I swallowed, my stomach turning. My priorities had been winning my rights back and keeping my friends alive. I had never once imagined what I would do *after* those things had happened.

This so *does not count as resting,* I thought. *I guess we need to make sure all the merpeople from the Rebellion got home safely. And that the merfolk from the Sanctuary get back to the sea. Are they even still here?*

My dad cleared his throat. "We're glad you're okay, Sweetie."

I almost laughed. I wanted nothing more than to tear out the IV and run back to Tom's room. How dare they? They had told the entire world over the radio that I was never their biological daughter. They had adopted me out of the kindness of their hearts only to realize I was a monster. And now, they just wanted to waltz in and pretend like that had never happened. That they were glad I was *okay?*

"Once you've had a few more days of recovery - we'll discharge you and you'll be able to go home with your folks," Dr. Hartzfield said.

My stomach twisted. "I don't want to leave with them," I whispered. *I don't want to sleep by myself. I need to sleep on the beach surrounded by dozens of other people.*

"Your room is still the way you left it," my mom said. *You didn't turn it into an office once you decided I was a freak?*

"What about Tom, where is he going after he's discharged?" I demanded.

"Tom is eighteen, so that is entirely up to him," Dr. Hartzfield said. It took me a minute to realize both of our birthdays had passed when we were living as refugees in the ocean. Tom had been seventeen; I had been sixteen when merfolk were revealed to the world. *Damn it, why couldn't my birthday be a few months earlier?*

"Mr. and Mrs. Wilson, how do you feel about your daughter returning home?" he asked. The air rang with silence.

"I'll have to buy more groceries," my mom finally said after a moment. *That's all you can think of?* I thought. *You sure had some strong feelings about me on the radio when you told the world I was a dangerous creature that couldn't be trusted. Your adopted mistake.*

"Amy, how do you feel?" Dr. Hartzfield asked. I curled my arms around myself. Was I even safe with them? Legally, they couldn't hand me over to any mad scientists or aquariums, but they were still cops. They had guns at the house. What if they had all their cop friends pitted against me? Who exactly would I call for help if they still thought I was a dangerous monster that needed to be contained?

Or put down?

There's no way they would just shoot me, I thought. *Surely they don't hate me that much?* But if they did, they would have to answer to Tom and the rest of them.

"I'll be fine," I muttered. *I'll play nice*, I told myself. Maybe they were brainwashed by Arthur. Once I show them that I'm the same daughter they've always had, they'll calm down. They'll accept me again. Things will go back to normal.

Dr. Hartzfield cleared his throat and consulted his clipboard. "Well - there's also her medical needs to consider. Her leg has technically healed a little - but there is extensive damage. Depending on whether surgery would help - there will be a recovery period for that. I'm assuming they'll at least want you in physical therapy for a while. And of course - your daughter will need time to swim to stay healthy now that she can phase again."

The way my mom's nose twitched like she smelled something awful did not escape my attention. My mind swam. *Surgery? Physical therapy? What happened to drink more water and take a nap?* I clutched my stomach. I was definitely not okay with being unconscious while a doctor operated on me. Were there any merfolk doctors left?

"I also am going to recommend regular counseling appointments - not just for her - for all of these young people. They have been through a lot the past year."

"I thought her leg was already healed?" my dad asked, ignoring the therapy comment. I resisted the urge to hit him with my new cane.

"Barely," I muttered. Dr. Hartzfield motioned towards my cane leaning against my leg, where my parents seemed to notice it for the first time.

"She requires the use of the cane to move more than a few steps," Dr. Hartzfield said. "But hopefully with surgery, she'll be able to improve her mobility."

"How much is all this medical stuff going to cost?" my dad muttered. Dr. Hartzfield forced a smile and stood up.

"Talk to your insurance company about that. Why don't we give Amy some time to rest?" He stood up and held the door open as my parents walked out. My dad hesitated and turned towards me. As our eyes met, the smell of disappointment filled my nostrils like I had just dove into a septic tank.

TOM

I tried not to cry as Amy was guided back to her room. I wanted to hold her in my arms and never let go again. *This wound better heal up quick so we can all go home*, I thought.

Home.

The word tasted weird on my tongue. What was our home? Had the others already been discharged? It dawned on me that I had no clue where Norman, Emanuel, or Adam were even from.

Or Sam.

My heart clenched all over again. I should have never let those girls go off to Baldwin by themselves. Sam could've discovered the virus at the Sanctuary, protected by the others. Now it was too late. Morris' lackeys

25

had killed Terri in cold blood and no amount of regret would bring her back.

What would even happen to Sam? She was living in a group home before the world fell apart. Would CPS try to take her back? *There's no fucking way they're taking her,* I thought. She's too smart to rot in a group home waiting for some random family to adopt her. She's staying with me. We can live on my boat. That's basically what I did before anyway. I'll pay for her to go to college. I'll protect her this time. We'll make our own home – together.

Suddenly, I remembered I technically had family and a home left on shore. My hands hardened into fists as I thought of the bloated man living in that run-down shack of a house. Had he seen the news? Was he sober enough to understand what had happened if he had seen it? Was he even aware I had been missing for months? That his brother was gone?

I can't believe Adam killed him, I thought. But thank god he did. Otherwise, we would all be dead.

My thoughts were interrupted as Mr. Duncan walked through the curtain. I cracked a smile and attempted to sit up.

"So you did make it," I said, shaking his hand. He grinned and pulled up a chair next to my bed.

"I did, yes, and Marisol is safe too, thank goodness. You kids pulled off a miracle yesterday," he said. *Had it only been yesterday?* I wondered.

"Don't thank me. It was all Amy. And all Sam," I whispered. Mr. Duncan's smile faded.

"Yes, poor girl. She's doing okay - physically at least. I'm afraid you kids are going to need some time to heal."

At least we have time now, I thought.

"However, there are next steps to consider," he continued. "According to Amy's first video she posted, she promised she would be truthful about everything upon receiving her freedom back. I know it hasn't been very long, but the press is demanding she make true to her promise."

"Didn't Sam already explain how the Curse works?" I asked.

"Scientifically - yes - but humans still want to know the exact story. They want to know how everything went down - and I mean *everything*. How you managed to outsmart government agencies to rescue people, how Amy was Cursed, where you all were hiding - everything."

I sighed. The last thing I wanted to do was make my friends spill their guts on live TV, especially after the last interview had gone. Images of Morris descending out of the sky and taking Amy away flashed through my head.

He's gone, I reminded myself. *He's not coming back.*

"The news wants to do a press conference with all six of you as soon as everyone is discharged, which according to the doctors, may be in a matter of days. Do you think it's something you'll be able to handle?" Mr. Duncan asked. I chuckled. After having survived so many guns pointed at my head, answering some questions on TV should be a piece of cake. But the thought of spilling everything made my gut turn.

The next three days passed in a blur. Adam recovered quietly surrounded by his biological family. Amy spent as much time as she could in my room, avoiding her therapist and parents. Emanuel's family practically made camp and refused to let their son or Norman out of their sight. Sam hung around listlessly, eyes hollow, quieter than normal, but shrugged off any condolences or attempts to make her feel better. Mr. Duncan flitted around between all our rooms like a stressed butterfly, making sure we were being taken care of and managing paperwork and the adult stuff.

We were discharged on a Friday. Mr. Duncan had arranged for transport to a local news station. Several long limos waited for us right outside the doors. We only had twenty feet to walk, but those twenty feet were swarmed with reporters and cameras. The writhing mass screamed questions.

"Amy Wilson, what was it like getting infected with this virus?"

"Would you consider doing an underwater photoshoot?"

"Do you think more humans are going to become infected?"

"How do you feel about your uncle's death, Tom?"

The merfolk behind me winced from the noise, covering their ears and shying backward. Policemen shouted at the crowd, forcing them away and leaving us a path. I grabbed Sam and Amy's free hands and all but carried them to the limo. Adam and his family weren't far behind.

Emanuel's mom glared at the reporters as she held Norman and Emanuel by the shoulders.

I slammed the limo door shut and resisted the urge to tell the driver to run the cameramen over. The crowd slowly dissipated and the car lurched forward, carrying us out into the new world we had created.

I wanted to throw up, but I couldn't, not with Amy and Sam beside me. Someone had to be there for them. I wasn't going to let anyone down - not this time.

AMY

My heart thudded in my ears as the limo pulled to a stop in front of the news station, where more reporters congregated. All I could see was the flash of cameras. A hand in front of me pulled me forward, fingers tight as chains. I could feel the anxiety radiating through them - like acid burning my skin. But I held on, trying to breathe. Somewhere in the distance, I could hear shouting – some curious questions, others angry comments. My feet finally touched the carpet and doors shut behind us, canceling the bright lights and shouting.

Tom turned around, eyes dark with worry. I forced a fake smile, which I knew he didn't buy. In front of him, the three boys held hands, scanning the room. Sam stood in front, following a man in a suit like she was being pulled along on strings.

We were ushered into another room filled with mirrors and people armed with makeup brushes. I fumbled my cane as I maneuvered myself into a hydraulic chair. The human behind me smiled shyly before spinning me around. I winced as I made eye contact with the girl in the mirror.

She didn't look great. Bruises still decorated her right cheekbone. Her eyes were too wide and suspicious. She still looked a little too skinny. Her haircut looked like it had been done in the bathroom of a boat with a pair of rusty scissors - oh wait - it had.

I tensed, gripping the arms of the chair as I realized this stranger would have to touch my face and hair. I hadn't let a stranger touch me on purpose in months.

You're fine. You're free. This person is legally not allowed to hurt you.

People do illegal shit all the time.

"Chin up, darling," the stylist said. I tried to watch the others through the mirror as my face was cleaned with a makeup wipe. Tom sat with his ankle on his knee as his stylist gave him a long overdue haircut. Norman squirmed as his stylist tried to rub foundation into his face, avoiding his vibrant blue markings. Sam was the only one looking somewhat composed, sitting up straight as her stylist fixed her braids.

Someone who looked like a supervisor glanced over my shoulder.

"Don't cover up those bruises too much. But god, fix that hair."
Without a word, a cape was placed over me, and I watched my dirty
blonde hair fall to the floor.

After I was deemed camera-worthy, I was pulled into a room filled
with racks and racks of outfits. I hadn't worn my own clothes in months.
When I had been rescued, I had resorted to wearing Cindy's old clothes,
and then Tom's when hers fell apart. The stylist held up a pantsuit in one
hand and a blouse with a pencil skirt in the other.

"What's your style, sweetheart? Masc or femme?"

I opened my mouth, but no sound came out. My style had been
pretending to be a human biological female - which meant wearing
leggings with hoodies in high school. I had no clue what my style was or if
I wanted to be *masc* or *femme*.

The stylist's grin faltered, and they lowered the options. "How
about you try both on, and then we'll decide from there, okay? What's
your bra size, honey?"

I swallowed. "Um . . . I don't have boobs."

"Oh honey, don't say that! Even if they're small -"

"Merfolk don't develop breasts until they breastfeed," I muttered.
The stylist turned red and apologized for what felt like hours before
leaving in a flustered mess. I sighed and considered the two outfits.

I took the top from the femme outfit and the pants from the masc
outfit, trying to cover as many scars as possible. Although, according to the
supervisor, they *wanted* me to look a little banged up. I guess it would add
to the drama. I buttoned up the dark blue shirt and tucked it into the

black pants. The girl in the mirror looked ready for a job interview in a fancy corporate office - clean, polished, normal. I resisted the urge to laugh.

I ventured back out to see the others. Sam was the only one who looked comfortable in her outfit. She wore a white button-up tucked into black pants - the cuffs rolled up to her elbows. Her braids were piled up on top of her head, and gold eyeshadow shimmered in the lights. For a split second - she almost looked like a scientist from the lab. Tom looked like he was ready for his fraternity initiation in a collared shirt and khaki pants. Norman, Emanuel, and Adam looked no better.

I squared my shoulders and attempted to look brave.

You're free now. No one is legally allowed to hurt you.

I followed Sam out into the conference room. I settled into a plush chair, the lights from the stage searing my skin. A guy in the rafters cradled a boom mic above my head, and I wondered if he had ever accidentally hit someone with it.

A tall human in a suit to match his fashionable streak of gray hair smiled at us and leaned back in his chair like he got to interview the leaders of civil rights movements every afternoon.

He waited patiently for us to get settled before he clasped his hands together, staring directly at me. I forced myself to match his eye contact. *He's not Arthur. Look at him.*

He grinned for the cameras and motioned to all of us in a wide sweep. "Good evening, America. Welcome to this very special live broadcast. I'm your host - David Winchester." He turned his gaze to me.

"Amy Wilson. How does it feel knowing your very existence started a revolution?"

I thought of all the people who had died because of me.

"To be honest . . . I wish there hadn't been a need to start one, sir."

The questions kept coming for what felt like hours. Each one seemed to tear open an old wound or memory. I remembered everything in vivid detail - accidentally revealing my species to the world. Falling into that tank of water in Arthur's secret lab. Learning to walk on a leg with shredded muscles. My best friend dying for marks on her face that matched mine. Revealing secrets I had sworn never to reveal. Giving myself up to save an island of merfolk. Watching my repressed crush bleed out underneath me. Waking up in a hospital only to learn I had never been a different species, to begin with. That I was a creature out of storybooks because of a virus.

Emanuel and Tom answered questions about what it was like as a human to risk losing everything to help the rest of us. Adam answered questions about vandalizing countless ships and rescuing merfolk. At the mention of Morris' impromptu ending - every ounce of color drained from his already pale face. For a moment, I thought his freckles would fall off.

Sam was the only one who answered questions without a shaky voice or nervous ticks. She calmly and methodically explained how she and Karen had figured out how to Curse a normal human to become merfolk.

I processed new details as she explained. It would only work if the blood types matched and if the human was young - probably not past the age of puberty. It would only work if enough blood was injected straight into the human's flesh. It made my meeting with that trap seem even more incredible. I wondered whose blood had accidentally been injected into my body.

"So, the last question I have for all of you is - what's next? What do you do now that you can return to your normal lives?"

What *do* I do next? What do I want to be when I grow up? For so long, the answer had been free. Alive. Safe. Now that all of those things were true . . .

We all exchanged glances, silence echoing on set.

No one answered.

Mom Against Mermaids

I can't believe they set those creatures free. I'll tell you what - they better not be going to the same school as my kid. My family's not about to get sick.

3 People liked your post

OG Soccer Mom <3

I'm with you. These things have advanced senses - they're going to take over athletics! I don't want my baby having to compete against one of those freaks. It's not fair.

7 People liked your post

Turing Machine

~~You guys are so fucking racist. Merpeople are people too. They're not out here trying to take over everything.~~

Comment has been removed by admin

NORMAN

I changed out of my stupid preppy clothes as soon as they would let me, wishing I could take a shower to scrub all of the nervous stress away. Emanuel looked just as relieved to have survived the interview. Adam looked moments away from passing out.

We rejoined the parents in the lobby. Amy folded her arms and stared at the carpet with enough vitriol to singe the fibers instead of looking at her parents - which I could hardly blame her for. Tom had Sam's hand clamped in his as if he was daring anyone to try and take her away.

This is where we would separate. This is where we would get into different cars and go into different houses to lead different lives. There would be no getting back on the boat to sneak away to the Sanctuary and eat raw fish while singing campfire songs.

The thought made me want to cry.

Mr. Duncan walked around to all of us, shaking our hands and looking very pleased with our performance, like a proud soccer coach. He pressed something into my palm.

"I got all of you cell phones so you can stay in contact with each other," he said. "I'm sure your folks will get you nicer ones eventually, but just for now." I flipped it open and saw my friend's numbers had already been programmed in. To Mr. Duncan's shock, I threw my arms around him in a tight hug before sneaking off to fire a text.

Sup loser.

Across the room, Adam opened his phone and attempted to laugh before slipping his phone back into his pocket. His parents had been staying at a local condo for the time being, but what would they do now that we were all out of the hospital? He lived farther away from everyone else. How often would we see him? Emanuel was in the next school district over from me - we had lived half an hour away from each other our whole lives and never known.

A small hand tugged on my pants, and I looked down to see one of Emanuel's siblings staring up at me. He had Emanuel's same thick, dark, curly hair, but his mother's round innocent face. I was sure I had been told his name over the past several days, but I couldn't remember it for the life of me.

"Mom, can he come home with us? Emanuel told me to ask you," he shouted to his mom, running his fingers over the blue markings on my legs. I instantly blushed.

"I - You don't have to let me stay with you," I stammered.

She waved me off, grabbing my arm and steering me back towards the others. "Nonsense. Your parents aren't here yet, and you need a place to stay until they come for you."

I swallowed. It had been almost a week since the court's decision. My parents had definitely been released by now, but I had yet to hear anything from them even though I wasn't exactly hard to find. The implications of their silence made my stomach churn, but I buried it as I realized I had a more imminent problem:

Living with my crush's family.

I barely had time to panic before I was shoved into their minivan and driven away. Contained in the car, I focused on committing the siblings to memory. The one who had tugged on my shorts seemed to be about five years old, the other about ten. The older one's name was Isaiah and the younger one's name was David.

Emanuel's house was in the middle of a cookie-cutter suburban neighborhood. All the houses looked like clones - the only difference being the outside paint. The flower beds were weeded, and the garages were cluttered with tools. Sidewalks laced the streets. It looked like the place where kids would beg to go trick-or-treating to get the *good* candy.

We piled out of the car, and the siblings dragged me through every room in the house, explaining what belonged to who. They decided I would sleep in Emanuel's bed while he took the floor - because that's what friends do at sleepovers - until Isaiah pointed out I might have to go sleep in the bathtub. I realized they were probably right - their house was too far away to walk to the beach in a timely manner. At least Emanuel had a bathroom attached to his room.

The whole time, Emanuel reeked of embarrassment, refusing to meet my gaze, which I found secretly adorable. The tour finished off with dinner, which consisted of the best enchiladas I had ever eaten. Emanuel and I scarfed down an ungodly amount, his mom beaming every time she plopped another helping on our plates. As Emanuel bantered with his siblings, his dad quietly interrogated me at the end of the table.

"So Norman, what do you like to do for fun?" he asked. I froze with my fork halfway to my mouth. No one had asked me that question in so long. What *did* I like to do for fun? I struggled to remember my life before.

"Um . . . I like to watch movies I guess," I said.

"What's your favorite?"

I chewed thoughtfully. "Spirited Away." I flushed, wondering if that choice sounded weird.

His dad cracked a smile. "Emanuel enjoys those kinds of movies as well."

Did he? I had never heard him talk about what he liked to do in his spare time. We had been too busy trying to survive and rescue Merfolk. *What else did I not know about him?* I wondered. *What do I do if he likes really stupid movies, like Sharknado?*

I snuck a glance at him, hoping my body language hadn't been betraying me. Emanuel wasn't out to his parents yet - and though they seemed nice - I didn't want to take any chances. *There's no way a science geek like him likes Sharknado, I decided. He would spend the entire time complaining about the lack of physics.*

After dinner, his dad winked as he handed me the remote. I nearly cried as I scrolled through Disney Plus. It felt like *years* since I had seen a movie or scrolled Instagram or listened to actual music and not just refugees singing around a campfire. I stared into the bright colors until they started to flicker in my vision. Emanuel sat next to me as the rest of the family cleaned up the kitchen.

"I don't remember what watching TV feels like," Emanuel said, yanking the remote from my grip and scrolling through the list. "We've missed so much."

"There's a live-action *Mulan* movie? And a second *Trolls*? What the heck is *Onward?*" I sputtered. We settled on *Mulan* and watched in silence, fascinated by the colors flashing across the screen. The family joined us with bowls of popcorn, which I scarfed down despite how full I was from dinner. They all cheered as the movie ended – which was super cheesy and cute. Just like Emanuel. *Jeez, get ahold of yourself.*

"Okay, time for bed," Emanuel's mom declared, shooing the small kids up the stairs. David avoided her sweep. He stood in front of me, his arms crossed, dark eyes boring into my soul. His gaze flitted between me and Emanuel, his lips pursed.

"Are you dating my brother?" he asked. Emanuel choked on his water as my jaw hit the floor.

"Nino! You know better than to ask those questions! Leave them alone!" Emanuel's mom came around the corner, her eyes ten times more dangerous than David's. He quickly skittered off and she sighed as she stood in front of us.

His dad rubbed his temple. "I apologize, Norman," he said.

"He can be a bit of a snoop sometimes," the mom added, shaking her head.

I closed my mouth and nodded. "Don't worry about it, ma'am."

She scoffed and waved her spoon at Emanuel. "Tell your boyfriend not to call me ma'am."

Emanuel choked on his water again. "*What?*"

She turned, hand on her hip. "Is it supposed to be a secret? I thought you two were good at keeping secrets! It's a miracle you weren't caught - either one of you!" The parents shared a grin before disappearing back into the kitchen.

"Oh my god . . . does everyone see it?" I demanded, feeling the enchiladas turn in my stomach. *So much for trying to act normal.*

"I think I'm going to throw up," Emanuel muttered, clutching his gut. He scrambled off the couch and booked it towards the bathroom. I sat there, stunned, as the door shut. After a few exasperated moments, I walked over and knocked.

"You can come in," he said. I opened the door to see him leaning against the toilet.

"Being gay makes you that nauseous, huh?" I said, allowing myself to sound a little hurt. He sighed.

"It's not like that. I just wanted to . . . you know . . . *actually* come out. Not have everyone magically read it on me," he muttered. "I mean, my god. How long have we been home, three hours?" I closed the door and sat on the sink, fiddling with my fingers.

"Yeah, I guess I get that. I was so little when I came out. I barely remember it to be honest. It's always just been a part of me."

"I thought they would be pissed," Emanuel said. "About everything – me running away – us. But they don't seem to care."

"They're probably just glad to have you back safe," I said. "Be happy about it." Thoughts of my parents flashed through my head.

He chuckled. "Yeah."

We stewed in the awkward silence, avoiding eye contact.

"Listen," Emanuel began, "I know it's been a minute since . . . you know . . . that night."

I instantly stiffened. *No, no,* I thought. *I'm not ready to have this conversation.* Suddenly, I felt like I was the one who needed to be kneeling over the toilet.

"And . . . I'm not sure how you feel exactly . . . I know you know how I feel," he said, forcing a laugh. "But um . . . you know . . . if you still feel the same way . . . and I'm apparently out of the closet, so . . . would you want to um . . ." Blood roared through my ears, stealing away his last words. I stood up, the floor wobbling under my feet.

"I'm not ready for this," I said, sweat gathering on my brow. "I'm sorry. That night was one thing but . . ." I swallowed. "I can't . . . I can't date you. Not right now." I could feel Emanuel's heart collapsing under its weight from across the bathroom. His adorable cheesy, cute energy faded to dust. The few feet between us suddenly felt like a wasteland.

"Oh. Okay," he whispered.

I stood frozen for a moment, waiting for him to get mad and yell. I flinched as he shifted and braced myself for whatever onslaught awaited me.

"It's okay. I get it. I mean, I don't get it but . . . if you're not ready that's okay," he said, thickly, wiping his eyes.

My heart lurched. "Are you okay?" I asked.

He shook his head. "I'm not mad at you, I just need some time alone."

I nodded and slid out of the bathroom door, clutching my fingers into fists so they wouldn't tremble. I made my way up to his room, where I curled up in a ball on the carpet.

You're such an idiot, I thought. *Why don't you just date him?*

Memories from my past relationship tore through my head. Keeping it a secret from my parents because I knew how they would react. Trying to protect him while all he did was abuse and hurt me. Realizing he never cared about me. Escaping capture by the skin of my teeth to curl up in a cave miles away to mourn the loss of my body and my family. Almost getting my fins sliced away for the sin of *finally* getting the courage to leave him. The triumphant joy of realizing that I could protect myself from my former mate despite all the stories telling me it was impossible.

I *knew* I was no longer mated to that bastard. But the thought of having a second mate made my stomach drop. Had it ever been done before? What if it ended badly again? What if it just *ended*? It wasn't strange for merfolk to mate young, but Emanuel was human. Did he understand what he would be getting himself into? Making a permanent commitment? Of course, if mating wasn't permanent, there would be no issue.

Everything I thought I knew about how mates worked was up in the air. It was *supposed* to be that mates were permanent. A couple engages in *coitus* as Sam had so politely put it, the girl gets the ability to cry healing tears; the guy grows poisonous fins that can be used against anyone but his mate. They all live happily ever after except the ones who mate with humans (whoops) and the ones who leave their mates (double whoops). I shivered as I remembered the cold blade pressed against my fin. Emanuel screaming bloody murder in the background.

Amy had cried for Tom even though they weren't mated. Or did that mean they were mated? Maybe it worked differently with mixed-species couples? Then again, according to science, we weren't different species. Maybe the whole concept of mating was fake, to begin with – there was no permanent bond, there was no *coitus* required, and you could use your new abilities for anyone.

And then there were my parents to think about. How exactly would they react to finding out their son had been cavorting with humans for the past several months? How would they react to find out that their son was not only a divorcee but had *another* human boyfriend? If they were still as traditional as they were before being captured - my odds were not good. They would take me back to Dr. Mercer and make me get Removed, no matter what I told them about how mates worked.

There was no way I was going to stick Emanuel in that crossfire. And there was no way I was sticking myself in it either. Not again.

TOM

Sam and I were the only ones who didn't have a set of parents to take us home. Mr. Duncan offered to give us a ride back to my boat, the only thing left that could almost resemble a *home*, and we sat in silence in the backseat as he drove towards the docks. A thousand questions raced through my head.

CPS hadn't reached out, so for now, Sam was safe. It remained to see for how long. I still hadn't heard anything from my father, which made me picture his rotting corpse stuck to our couch - a beer can still clutched in his skeleton fingers.

I noticed Sam white-knuckling the seat beside me, and I immediately shut down my thoughts. The poor kid had already been through enough - she didn't need to pick up on my stress and feel even worse.

My plan to remain calm failed almost immediately as we were dropped off and started walking down the dock.

"What the?" Sam muttered. "Why is everyone still here?" I broke into a run down to the *Lazy River*. At least fifty merfolk lingered on the deck or the surrounding docks, bags under their eyes and frowns marring their faces. I caught the eye of a boy who looked somewhat familiar and walked up to him. He forced a smile as I sat down next to him.

"Hey kid, what's going on?"

He shrugged. "Someone else is living in our house, so we came back here," he said.

My stomach dropped. I had just assumed all the refugee merfolk would just go back to their homes and normal lives after they were freed. But it had been months since they vanished. The banks had probably foreclosed on all these people's houses and sold them off while they were gone. I should've known they wouldn't be able to go back to normal just like that.

"Where are your parents now?" I asked.

"Trying to find a job," the kid said. "They lost those too. And their old bosses don't want them back."

My blood boiled. *It's illegal to discriminate against someone based on any illnesses or disabilities they may have!* I wanted to scream. Don't they know they can't do that?

I kept my mouth shut. *Don't make the kid even more upset.*

"Well . . . I'm sure they'll be able to find jobs soon," I said, trying to sound like I believed it. *Even if they do find jobs, where are they going to live? Do they still have money in the bank, or were those accounts deleted too? I* thought. Were all these peoples' lives erased when they fled? Do they have anything left? I was suddenly very glad I had kept my money in cash hidden on the boat.

I got up and left the boy sitting on the dock. I made my rounds around the other lingering merfolk and had almost the same conversation with many of them.

I lost my house, my job, my car.

I don't know what we're going to do.

I ended up pulling my motorcycle out of the boat's living room and sped down to the nearest Walmart. I filled a cart with sandwiches and snacks. *The least I can do is feed these people for a night,* I thought. *I should've left the hospital sooner.*

I made it back and distributed the food. Small smiles softened their faces as they took sandwiches and ate together in groups. I searched the crowd for Sam and found her with another teenager and two other kids.

"How are you guys doing?" I asked. The gangly teenager next to Sam shrugged.

"Do you have a phone?" the teenager asked. I nodded. "Can I borrow it?"

"Sure, why?"

He hesitated. "I need to try to call my parents. My human parents," he clarified. "I ran away right at the beginning of things and well . . . I haven't heard back from them yet . . . so." *Oh shit, I forgot about the adopted ones too,* I thought. I handed him my phone and watched out of the corner of my eye as he walked away.

"Do you two need to call your parents too?" I asked. The two little girls nodded. For a startling moment, they reminded me so much of Sam and Terri the day I rescued them from the aquarium. They couldn't have been any older than ten. *How could these parents not even bother trying to find their kids?* I thought. My throat closed up, and I tried to discreetly wipe away my eyes.

The teenager returned with my phone. I could feel his fingers trembling as he pressed it back into my hand.

"What did they say?" I asked. All he did was shake his head before turning and walking down the dock, shoving his hands into his pockets. I turned back towards the girls and forced a smile.

"Would you like me to call your mom and dad for you?" I asked. They nodded and the older one rattled off a phone number. I walked away and dialed it, praying as it rang.

"Hello?" a feminine voice on the other end answered.

"Hi! Hello. My name is . . . this is Tom Falcon," I said, wincing at my awkwardness. The woman sucked in a breath on the other end.

"Hi, listen, your two little girls are here. They're excited to see you again. They've missed you a lot -" The line went dead. I took my phone away from my ear, shocked. *Maybe the line just disconnected*, I thought. I dialed again, but it went straight to voicemail. I tried again. Voicemail.

It took a lot of energy to not chuck the phone into the ocean.

How are parents doing this? I thought. *How can they just abandon their kids? How can they not even bother to say goodbye or give an excuse?*

I forced myself to walk back over to the girls and didn't bother faking a smile. I took both of their hands and took a deep breath.

"Your parents don't want to talk right now. But I'll keep trying," I promised. The younger one's eyes widened.

"Why don't they want to talk to us?" she asked. The older one snorted and crossed her arms.

"Because they're assholes," she muttered. She didn't seem surprised at all at the outcome. But she held on to the edge of the dock in an attempt to hide her shaking fingers.

"What's going to happen to us if our parents don't want us back?" the younger one asked. My heart fractured into a thousand more pieces. I squeezed their hands.

"I don't know. But we'll figure something out," I said.

AMY

Stepping back into my parent's small beach house felt nightmarish. It looked exactly the same, just like my parents had said. It felt fake. Shouldn't it have changed at least a little bit?

We ate dinner in silence, except for my dad commenting on how much I was scarfing down. I washed the dishes and used being tired as an excuse to go avoid them in my room. I groaned inwardly at the stairs I had forgotten. I shuffled up and limped into the doorway.

I felt like a ghost. Everything was covered in a fine layer of dust. The clothes I had left at the foot of my bed still lay there, not smelling great. Candy wrappers grew mysterious things in the trash can. Rings around the bathtub from my late-night baths remained.

I sat down on the bed, releasing a little poof of dust as I texted Tom on the new burner phone.

He called in response. "Amy? Can you hear me?"

I winced at the cacophony of noise on the other end of the floor. I held the phone away from my ear.

"Kinda?" A few moments passed, and the noise grew quieter. He sighed.

"Things . . . things are messy," he said. "There's like fifty merfolk sleeping in, on, or under my boat. They've been here for days."

"Why aren't they going home?" I asked.

"Most of their houses have different families living in them now," Tom said. "Everything these poor people have worked for is completely gone. I don't know what to tell them. I bought some food for tonight but . . . there's a lot of people here with nothing."

I bit my lip. With everything going on over the past few days, I had barely thought about the other merfolk that had fled the Sanctuary.

"There are kids here without families to go to either," Tom said. "We tried calling their parents and they just . . . hung up."

I wished my parents had just not bothered to show up. Even as the thought crossed my head, I felt guilty about it. I at least had a roof over my head. I had some semblance of family left.

"Surely the government is going to do something to help?" I said.

Tom scoffed. "I doubt it. And frankly, I don't want their help. I can handle this."

Really, you can handle housing and basic care for fifty families, including a handful of orphans? I thought.

"I mean . . . you are kinda rich," I joked.

Tom laughed. "Listen, I gotta go. Sleep tight. I love you." My eyes went wide as he hung up, not even bothering to wait to see if I would say it back or not.

I mean, it hadn't been the first time we had said the L-word. But the previous time had been when he was bleeding out underneath me. Saying it now felt . . . weird. *I guess he's my boyfriend,* I thought. Surely saying the *L-word* and saving each other's life makes that official? Technically according to Merfolk law - we were Mated. Even though we had never done anything except hold hands.

Processing all the possible terminology made my head swim. I had never allowed myself to dream of having a partner. But in the span of a few months, I had grown from hating Tom Falcon to loving him, even though I barely knew anything about him. He was kind and I would trust him with absolutely everything, but I didn't even know what his favorite color was.

How could you say you loved someone when you barely knew them?

Whatever I feel, I can figure it out later, I thought, my eyes growing heavy. I'll have enough chaos to deal with in the meantime. I can figure out how to be in love when the refugees have a place to live.

. . .

I woke up the next morning in a panic, reaching for a body that wasn't there. The ground beneath me was soft instead of gritty. I smelled paint instead of salt.

I remembered where I was and groaned. I reached for my phone to see I had a missed call and text from an unknown number.

Amy, it's me, Mr. Duncan. I need to have a meeting with all of you and your parents. ASAP preferably. ˜ Mr. Duncan

What a dad, I thought. I sent a text to Tom asking him to give me a ride and headed downstairs. The kitchen was empty. I wandered around, opening the cupboards and scanning for food. After months of eating whatever seafood could be caught, having hotdogs, sliced cheese, and frozen chicken nuggets seemed like a miracle.

I smiled to myself as I watched the food whirl around in the microwave and ate in silence at the kitchen table. My dad strolled in a little while later, headed straight for the coffee machine. I watched him out of the corner of my eye as he drained his mug.

"Good morning," I said. He grumbled a reply before shuffling back towards the bedroom. I told myself that this wasn't a slight at me - he was always that grumpy in the morning.

His coffee mug stood empty by the sink. *Be a good daughter,* I told myself. *Make peace. Show them you're not the monster Arthur told them you were.*

I crutched over to the sink and washed his mug before putting it on the drying rack. I took out the empty K-cup and threw it away. I emptied the garbage. By the time I had finished, Tom had texted me back.

Be ready outside we are meeting at Emanuels place with Duncan

Half an hour later, we gathered in Emanuel's living room. The first thing I noticed was that Emanuel and Norman were not sitting next to each other. Norman sat curled up in a ball in a chair as Emanuel sat by himself on the couch. The air was thick enough to cut with a knife. Tom and I exchanged a brief look before finding seats. Mr. Duncan stood in front of the TV with another stranger.

"Hey everyone, thanks for meeting with me today. I just wanted to gather you all together to figure out our next steps here. This is Mr. Yule, the superintendent of schools for this school district," Mr. Duncan said. The stranger waved.

"First of all, housing. Emanuel, and Amy, you guys are with your parents. Adam, I understand you're here for now. As far as Sam goes . . ." Mr. Duncan trailed off.

Tom crossed his arms. "Sam's not going anywhere" he muttered.

"I understand that is what you would both like, but the fact of the matter is that it's up to CPS at this point. She's a minor," Mr. Duncan said.

"The fact of the matter is that CPS hasn't even bothered to reach out to me about Sam or any of the other refugees living on my boat," Tom said curtly. "And even if they had, I'm the closest thing she's got for family right now, and I'm not shipping her across the country to go live with some stranger." Sam buried her head in her knees, radiating embarrassment.

"We'll continue that discussion later. Norman . . ." Mr. Duncan hesitated. "Perhaps we should save that bit for later too."

Norman sat up. "Um, no. What's going on?" he demanded.

Mr. Duncan sighed. "Your parents were freed from the aquarium they were being held at. They're fine - healthy. We reached out to them . . . updated them on some things and well . . . they aren't pleased," Duncan said.

Norman paled. "And by not pleased, you mean . . ."

Duncan looked like he was trying to swallow nails. "Pleased with . . . you. Your behavior. Your activism. Your . . . friends," he said. Norman didn't look surprised, but his eyelid still twitched. "They've gone AWOL. We think they went back to the ocean," Duncan finished. The tension in the room grew thicker. Norman slumped against his chair.

"Cool," he muttered.

"Which means we also need to find you a place to stay," Duncan added. Emanuel sat up.

"He's staying with me," Emanuel growled. Norman flushed as Emanuel's mom put a protective hand on his shoulder.

"Tell CPS we will foster him if need be," she said coolly. Mr. Duncan sighed. *Do they know foster siblings can't date each other?* I wondered.

"Okay, let's switch tracks here. There is also the matter of school to discuss." Mr. Yule cleared his throat and stepped up.

"First of all, I know you all have been through a lot, and my goal today is to help you figure out how to move on with the rest of your lives - and a big part of that is going to be finishing your education." He looked at me and Tom.

"You two were just shy of completing your junior year and missed a few months of your senior year, so that will be where you start back up." He turned to look at Norman, Emanuel, and Adam. "You three had almost wrapped up your sophomore, so you'll be going into your junior year." He turned to Sam. "Not sure what to do with you, yet," he admitted. Sam rolled her eyes.

"Now, there is the question of placement. Online school is an option here, or you could choose to go back to school in person. How do we feel about that?"

We all exchanged glances. Online school sounded easier, but it also meant I would have to spend more time with my parents alone at the house.

"I want to go back in person," I blurted. Tom raised his eyebrow.

"Are you sure?" Mr. Yule asked. "You . . . uh . . . you know how high schoolers can be. And you're a household name now. Are you sure you want all that attention?"

I nodded. I would rather be stared at by strangers than trapped in my parents' stupid house.

"Well . . . what about the rest of you?" Mr. Yule asked.

"If Amy's going back, I'll go back with her," Tom said.

"I'll go back too," Emanuel said. Adam and Norman nodded.

"Throw us all in, coach," Norman muttered.

"Very well. Now, of course, this arrangement will depend on where you are living. Tom, Amy, Emanuel, you were originally zoned here, so you won't be a problem. You'll go back to your original schools. As far as Norman and Adam are concerned . . . I can enroll you temporarily and we can switch over your records if need be. I want to help make this journey as painless as possible, so just let me know if you need anything. School starts Monday," Mr. Yale said.

"Sam, let's talk for a second before you leave," Mr. Duncan said. Sam got up and walked over to the men. Tom stood behind her as the others filtered out. I stayed on the couch.

"Sam, you are a very smart young lady as I understand it," Mr. Yule said. She nodded.

"Mr. Duncan has told me he is willing to pay for your college, and that he's extended an opportunity for you to work at his biotech company as an apprentice," Mr. Yule said. The smell of Sam's embarrassment quickly turned to guilt. *That was news she chose not to share with us,* I thought. Mr. Duncan's words the first time we met flashed back through my head.

Merfolk are valuable to the scientific community. We can use you to figure out how to cure diseases.

I went tense. If it was Sam's idea to go work for this guy - that was her choice - but this guy wasn't about to bully this girl into doing anything she didn't want to.

"I was going to pay for her college," Tom said, crossing his arms.

"How am I supposed to apply for college when I never officially graduated high school?" Sam asked.

"Given your reputation, I'm sure you'll have your pick of what college you would like to attend," Mr. Yule said. "And we'll help you with whatever you need help with. We just have to get your guardianship figured out first. In the meantime, think about where you would like to go."

Sam nodded, and I paused by Duncan on the way out the door.

"She's not your lab rat," I growled under my breath. The sharp scent of Duncan's sweat flooded my nostrils.

"I have no intentions of making her my lab rat," he whispered. I looked up to glare at him.

"Good. Make sure it stays that way."

SAM

I was quiet on the ride home after we dropped off Amy, my head full of colleges and my heart full of dread. I hadn't told the others about Duncan's offer for an internship for . . . obvious reasons, but Tom and Amy knew now – and neither seemed happy with the surprise revelation.

I made a beeline for the back bedroom on the boat, but Tom snagged me by the sleeve before I could get the door shut.

"Talk to me, what's going on? Do you actually want to go off to college? Work for that Duncan guy? Be honest with me," Tom said. I sighed. No getting around it now.

"Yeah . . . and yeah," I whispered. Tom's eyebrows furrowed and he motioned for me to sit next to him. He folded his hands on his lap and stared at them for a moment.

"When did he offer that to you?" he asked finally. *Thank god Amy's not here*, I thought, sweat running down the small of my back. *She would smell the guilt on me in a second.*

I flashed back to the promise Duncan had made me at the hospital, mere hours after I found out my sister had been murdered. The pleading in his eyes, the urgency in his voice.

I want you to work for my biotech company . . . I'll get you whatever you need . . . study whatever you want . . . just consider . . . a vaccine. A cure.

I had agreed despite the grief in my heart and the voice in my head screaming at me that merpeople didn't need a cure. Duncan wasn't trying to trick me – he was trying to help me – help my species. But the others wouldn't understand that – not yet. I shook my head.

"It doesn't matter. I want to do it," I said, sitting up straight.

"Why?" he asked.

"He said he'll let me study whatever I want. I'll have unlimited funding. In the science world – that's a miracle. He just wants me to study merfolk. Ethically – of course," I added.

"But do *you* want to study merfolk?" Tom asked.

I nodded. "I know it'll make other merfolk upset. But I want to understand how our bodies work. Who knows what things we could learn from the virus? I could help people. He's not pressuring me. I just really want to do it. And I don't want to be judged for it," I muttered. Tom's shoulders finally softened, and he took my hands in his.

"Sam, if studying merfolk is what you want, I'm perfectly okay with that. I just don't want this guy to pressure you into doing anything you don't want to do," he said. I let out a tiny breath of relief.

"Thank you," I said.

"Also - I'm the one paying for your college. Not him," Tom said.

"It does seem fitting that you pay for my college seeing you only have that money because of me," I smirked. "But you also realize that I'm smart enough to get a full-ride scholarship, right?"

Tom rolled his eyes. "Well, at least let me buy you a college sweatshirt then, okay?"

I smiled and let Tom hug me. I could feel his Adam's apple bobbing and his chest shuddering. *He's such a sap*, I thought.

"What would you say if I wanted to adopt you?" he whispered. *What? Where on Earth did that idea come from?* I stiffened and pulled away as Tom blabbered on.

"I know . . . I know I'll never be your *dad* dad. You had one of those and lost him too soon. But I don't want you living in some group home or with some random family who-knows-where," he said. *There's no way he wants to adopt me*, I thought. *He just feels bad for me.*

"You don't need to take care of me out of guilt," I said.

Tom winced. "No, no, it's not just guilt," he protested.

I narrowed my eyes. "It's mostly guilt."

Tom deflated. "I never should have let you and Terri go off by yourselves," he said. "I should have protected you both." His guilt tasted sour. Grief settled in my heart all over again, making it feel like it weighed a thousand pounds. *I fucking miss her.*

"You're not the one who shot her," I said. "And adopting me won't bring her back."

"I know. But it's better than nothing," he said. *I guess he's got a point. I don't want to end up somewhere random, I thought. And Tom likes me. He doesn't think my love of science is weird like the other merfolk do. Keeping him close could protect me in more ways than one.*

"I *suppose* I would rather be stuck with you than some other random human," I said through a smile. "But don't you have to be married and like . . . an actual adult?"

"I am an actual adult!" he protested. "I'm eighteen!"

"An entire five years older than me," I pointed out.

Tom pouted. "If only you knew a rich, influential, scientist adult who could maybe vouch for me being a good parent . . . pull some strings for us . . ." he suggested.

I raised my eyebrows. "So let me get this straight - you don't want me to be pressured by Duncan. But you want me to pressure *him* by saying that I'll only be his apprentice if he pulls some government strings so you can adopt me?" I asked.

"Exactly!"

Clever boy, I thought, pursing my lips.

"Why don't you just pull some strings to start an entire group home for all the poor little orphaned merfolk while you're at it?" I asked. I meant it as a joke, but Tom's eyes were already lighting up.

"Wait . . . that's not a bad idea."

TOM

The next morning, I was awoken by a shoe in my ribcage. I coughed and rolled over to see Sam looking down at me.

"Why'd you kick me?" I croaked.

"I tried waking you up nicely first." Sam held her phone in front of my face. "Duncan wants to meet with you this morning."

I woke up immediately. "Holy shit, really?" I dashed into my room, pulling on some fresh clothes as Sam smirked. My phone buzzed, and I nearly tripped over my shoelaces as I tried to see who it was.

Hey, if you're not busy can you take me somewhere today?

My heart warmed as I saw it was Amy who had messaged. I texted her back.

I finished pulling on my shoes and ran outside. The sun was barely peeking over the horizon. At least a dozen merfolk – mostly kids – still lay sprawled out asleep on the deck. By the time I navigated around them, Amy had shown up on the docks. Her short hair and sweatpants made it look like she had just rolled out of bed. It was cute.

"So, who do you have a meeting with this early?" she asked, yawning.

"Sam got me a meeting with Duncan to talk about . . . you know what, I'll tell you all about it later," I said. "Where am I taking you?"

She hesitated. "The cemetery."

For a moment, I forgot to walk. She flushed as she looked down at her feet.

"Nothing's wrong," she said quickly. "I just want to go visit . . . Cindy." I reached over and gently squeezed her hand.

"Of course. I can go with you if you want?" I offered. She shook her head.

"No, I need to do this alone. You do . . . whatever you're doing with Duncan," she said. I smiled and tried to bury my nerves. We rode towards the town's cemetery, and Amy hopped off, taking a deep breath before approaching the gates. I offered her a tentative smile before speeding off towards Ducan's biotech company.

The building was surprisingly close to the beach. I could've walked there. As I pulled into the parking lot, the gigantic logo registered in my head for the first time after having passed it a thousand times.

The building looked like one scientists would be doing high-tech experiments in, with glowing white walls that curved in unique slopes, as if it was trying to portray how fancy and elegant it was. The white double doors parted soundlessly for me, and a security guard the size of a bear automatically apprehended me.

"What's your business here?" he asked, settling his hands on his thick belt, adorned with what looked like several tasers and a gun. I smiled, suddenly feeling very unprofessional in my board shorts and worn tennis shoes.

"I'm Tom . . . I have a meeting with Duncan?" I said, my voice rising to make my statement sound like a question. The man made a guttural noise with his throat as he pulled out a walkie-talkie and muttered into it. We waited in silence for a few minutes before Duncan rounded the corner. He had exchanged his normal Hawaiian shirt for a button-up and suitcoat. He grinned as he shook my hand and led me down a hallway.

I peeked through the windows we passed and saw rooms full of test tubes and robots alike. Scientists in white lab coats roamed like ants, staring intently at whatever they were working on. If Sam were with me, she would probably be able to explain everything they were doing without hesitation. *Sam really would love to work here*, I thought.

"Come inside, have a seat."

I settled myself in a swivel office chair across from his desk. He leaned over and folded his hands.

"So . . . Sam said you wanted to meet with me?"

"Yes. I want to adopt her," I blurted. Duncan raised an eyebrow. *Jeez man, slow down. Give him some context,* I thought.

"That's not the main thing," I said, my brain feeling like an anthill that just got kicked. "Look - all of the merfolk from the Sanctuary are currently living on, under, or around my boat. I'm buying them food every day. They can't find jobs, go back to their old houses, and parents aren't coming back for their kids. It's a mess. And the cops or government or CPS haven't done anything about it. I want to adopt Sam so she has an official place to call home. And something needs to be done about the refugees. They can't just stay homeless forever. I want to build some sort of a place for them where they can stay until things get back to normal."

Duncan frowned. "Tom . . . you know I'm not like . . . a government agent, right? What makes you think I have any control over all of this?"

"Sam said you have rich friends in powerful places," I admitted. "She was under the impression there could be some . . . convincing."

Duncan laughed. "Oh that kid . . . she's too smart for her own good," he muttered.

"So, she was right then? You do have rich friends in powerful places that could pull some strings for me?" I asked.

Duncan sighed. "Have you talked to Amy about any of this?"

I blinked, taken aback by his question. The look on my face was all Duncan needed to know the answer to that question.

"Tom, as a married man, let me give you some life advice. Your marriage will go a lot smoother if you talk to your wife about life-altering decisions such as this."

I flushed. "We're not married."

"But you are Mated according to Merfolk standards, and that's a really big deal. Even if Amy hasn't said anything about it."

I sat back in my seat, suddenly embarrassed. *I probably should have asked her how she felt about me doing this stuff*, I thought. We had barely had time to talk with everything going on, never mind talk about what we wanted with our futures. I was ready to devote my life to helping Merfolk, but what if she wasn't wanting to do the same thing? What if she just wanted a normal life?

"Yeah, you're probably right," I said. Duncan folded his hands back under his chin.

"Assuming she is okay with doing all of this . . . are you sure you want to? I know you kids have been through a lot. I know you feel responsible for what's happened. But you're only eighteen, Tom. Are you sure you want to devote your entire life to this?"

I clenched my fingers. "No one else is going to help. CPS hasn't even so much as called to see where Sam is. The other adopted kids have parents who are completely ignoring them, and no one's doing anything about it. No one else cares. Amy and I might be the only ones who do care and have the resources to do something about it," I said.

Duncan nodded. "Go talk to Amy. And I'll see what I can do on my end. But I make no promises," he warned. I smiled and got up to shake his hand.

"And, Sam works for me as promised, correct?" he asked. I nodded. As I headed out the door, he called out after me.

"Also, Tom, I know that the government is a lot more likely to let a young person adopt if they're married. Might want to talk to Amy about making that Mating thing official in the human world too."

I flushed again. The thought of proposing to Amy made my heart flutter and my stomach heave.

Wait, are we even dating?

I had told her *I love you* on the phone last night. We had held hands a few times – but merpeople did that all the time anyway. Had we ever actually established that we were in a relationship? Had I ever asked her out, taken her on a date?

How can we be Mates but not be dating? Dang, I'm really bad at this, I thought.

"I'll talk to her," I promised.

And figure out what the hell we even are.

AMY

I entered the cemetery carrying a small handful of flowers I had picked by the gates. A quick Google search during my sleepless night was all it took to figure out what had happened to my best friend's body. Her plot was on the right side next to a lonely tree. I sat down in the shade, fiddling with the petals of the flower.

"I don't even know why I brought these," I muttered. "You were never one for flowers." The gravestone didn't respond.

In the movies, they never show what happens to the bodies of murdered people. It just shows them being dissected in an autopsy and shoved in a refrigerator. But here she was, buried like any other normal person who had died of disease or old age.

It was a sad family reunion. Her mom was buried on the right, Cindy in the middle, and her father on the left, the dirt over his grave still smelling fresh. I finally put the flowers down by Cindy's headstone.

I had a million things I wanted to say, but now that I was here, I couldn't remember any of them.

I could think of a few choice things for her father, but even then, the hatred was quick to sputter out. He had died trying to make things right. I felt like that gave him some credit, but it still didn't go back in time and erase what he had done to me and my species.

"I'm still mad at you," I whispered to his headstone. If Arthur had never tortured me, I would have never been scared of my best friend. We would have never fought. She would have never felt the need to leave. She would have never been shot.

"I guess it doesn't matter whose fault it is," I said. "You're still gone." My fingers started to shake. I hadn't had time to grieve her death at The Sanctuary. I thought I was ready to tackle all my unleashed sadness and anger, but it hurt so much worse than I thought it would.

I could almost hear her in my head, making fun of me for being such a mess. *I just want to have one more conversation with her*, I thought. *I want to tell her that I'm so sorry.*

But she wouldn't want to hear it. She would want to hear about all the drama that had happened since she left.

"So . . . a lot's happened since you've been gone," I choked out. "My parents hate me - which I'm sure is shocking. I think Tom and I are dating now?" She cackled in my head.

It took you this long to find a boyfriend, and it's Tom fucking Falcon? Girl, why would you ever stoop so low?

I chuckled. "He's not bad. He's changed a lot. Has a god-complex, though. Thinks it's his job to save the entire world. He's got like fifty refugees living on his boat."

Damn. And let me guess, you want to help him save the world?

"Someone has to fix it," I said. I clenched my fists. Tom shouldn't have to be fixing shit. The government should be stepping in to get the refugees housing. Why were teenagers the only ones doing anything?

I'm never going to rest again, I thought. *We were dumb to think the battle was over.*

"We shouldn't have to step up, but if we don't, no one else is going to," I said. *But if the next generation of merpeople can grow up in a world that's safe, it'll be worth it,* I thought. If Cindy could die for us, I could give the rest of my life.

"I'm so sorry I never said goodbye," I said.

It's not your fault. I should've believed you when you told me how awful my dad had been.

My hands trembled. "I hope you have peace," I whispered. "I will make sure no one ever forgets what you did."

You better.

I stood up and brushed off my jeans, taking a deep breath. I held my hand over my heart.

"Through hell or high water," I whispered. I walked back over to the gates as I heard the familiar rumble of Tom's motorcycle. I wordlessly hopped on the back and he drove us towards the docks. Refugees milled around, staring into space or kicking their ankles in the water. I followed Tom aboard as he walked to the living room. Sam sat sprawled out on his bed, scrolling on the laptop, her brow furrowed.

"Hey Sam," I said. "How's the college hunt going?" She didn't take her eyes off the screen.

"I think I've narrowed it down to two," she said. I couldn't help but smile. Smart girl.

"How'd your meeting with Duncan go?" Sam asked. Tom ran his fingers through his hair.

"Actually, Amy, I want to talk to you about it first . . . privately . . . if that's okay?" he said. I raised my eyebrow but nodded. As Sam got up to give us a moment, shouting sounded outside. We all frowned and hurried out.

A pair of parents were shouting at who appeared to be their children. A little boy was hunched behind a taller version of him. I vaguely recognized them as some of the first kids Norman, Adam, and Emanuel had rescued from the school raids. The teenager was beet red as he shouted at his parents.

"Whoa, whoa, what's going on?" Tom asked.

"They want to leave. They want to go back to the Sanctuary!" the teenager shouted. I blinked in surprise.

"Why?" I demanded. The dad sighed.

"We've lost everything. I've spent days trying to find a job, and no one will hire me back. There's nothing here for us."

"All of my friends are here!" the teenager protested. "I don't want to live on some random island in the middle of the ocean for the rest of my life!"

"This isn't up for debate," the mom said, crossing her arms. "Several other families are doing the same thing." Tom and I exchanged a look. I had never considered that it would be easier for them to go back to the ocean. *Is that even allowed?* I wondered. *What would the government do if a bunch of their citizens just went back to the ocean? Would they even be considered citizens at that point? Would it matter if they were?*

"You know that if you go back, the US can't protect you," Sam said. "You'd be on your own, and no other countries have passed protections for merfolk." *Shit, she's right,* I thought. Merfolk were only free in America. *I guess being a citizen is important.*

"We're still American citizens even if we're in international waters," the dad snapped. "We are perfectly within our rights to leave and still be protected." *Good luck thinking the US will sail out to the Bermuda Triangle to protect a couple of families,* I thought. What are the odds that people from other places would sail out to The Sanctuary to capture them? Sell them and dissect them in their own countries?

"Why don't you just give it some more time? I'm sure you'll be able to find a job soon," Tom pleaded.

"It is already decided," the dad said.

"Well, we're not going!" the teenager snapped, holding his brother behind him.

"You'd rather stay with humans than your own family?" the mom asked, narrowing her eyes. I resisted the urge to roll my own. *When are these stupid creatures going to realize that not all humans are awful?* I thought. The teenager held his ground, and the parents stomped off down the deck. As soon as they were out of view, they both deflated. It should've shocked and infuriated me to see parents abandoning their kids, but at this point, all I felt was familiar numbness. Tom placed his hand on the teenager's shoulder.

"What's your name, kid?" he asked.

"I'm Will. This is my brother, Grayson." Grayson smiled shyly from behind Will's legs.

"Why don't you guys go hang out on my boat for a while? I'm sure your parents will change their minds," Tom said. The two walked off, leaving me feeling a thousand times more exhausted.

"It's not safe for them to go back there," Tom said, running his fingers through his hair. I shrugged.

"I don't know if there's anything we can do. They technically have the right to go back. I think it's stupid to leave all this behind after we just got it back, but it's their lives I guess."

"Yeah, their lives except for the kids they're willing to leave behind," Tom muttered. Footsteps sounded behind me. I turned around to see little Caspian and his dad. His dad smiled apologetically.

"Tom, I believe we should talk," Caspian's father said. "Will's parents have told me of their wishes to go back to the Sanctuary. I know that's probably not what you were expecting or hoping for. But if it will make you feel better, I will lead them back and offer them as much protection as I can. Our family has lived there for generations in safety. Our location remains difficult to find. And we can defend ourselves. The only thing we lack is a Protector," he said, turning his gaze to me. I immediately shook my head.

"There's no way I'm going back to be your Protector," I said. My days of being a figurehead and calling the shots for an entire marginalized community were over. Someone else could make that their issue to worry about.

"Of course not, I was simply implying that it is within your rights to choose who should be the next Protector," he said. I debated for a moment before pointing back at him.

"You seem like a decent enough guy for the job. You do it."

Caspian grinned ear to ear as he stared up at his dad, who flushed.

"I - well - thank you," his dad stammered. I sighed. I still didn't want the merfolk to go back and hide away from their problems, but I knew I couldn't stop them. At least if they went with Caspian's family - they would have some added measure of protection.

"No offense man, but I'm not ready to give up on them yet. Wait a few more days. Then, you can take whoever wants to go," Tom said. Caspian's father nodded.

"As you wish." He led his son back down the docks. Tom and I sat together in silence as the sun rose further into the sky. After a while, I tentatively put my hand in his, which made him smile like a complete idiot despite the horrible circumstances.

"When do you turn eighteen?" Tom asked. I raised my eyebrow, and Tom flushed.

"Not for like . . . *that* . . . but you know. When are you legally not your parent's problem anymore?" he asked sheepishly.

I scoffed. "Calling me their responsibility is a stretch right now," I muttered.

"How are they treating you?" he asked.

"Weird . . . I'm trying to do everything I can to keep the peace. Washing dishes, cleaning my room, doing my laundry. But they won't talk about what happened."

"Well, you're welcome to stay here whenever," he said. "If you can find any room."

"Thanks."

"Listen, I know things are . . . crazy right now. But I want to spend as much time with you as I can. I want to make sure you're doing okay," he said. The tension in my shoulders drained as if the sudden emotion flowing through his voice was carrying it away.

"I know. We . . . we are dating, right?" I asked. Tom sniggered, and I shoved him.

"I'm laughing because I was asking myself that same question earlier," he admitted.

I grinned. "Dang, we kinda suck at this," I joked.

He smiled. "Listen . . . I really like you. And I do want to date you. I just want to make sure you feel the same way," he said. I squeezed his hand. We had been through a lot together. We had saved each other's lives countless times. I couldn't imagine going forward in life without him – no matter what direction that was.

"I do want to be with you," I said. "I just feel like . . . I don't know anything about you. We've been too busy fighting for our lives to get to know each other. I mean . . . have we ever hung out? Like . . . *just* hung out?"

Tom laughed. "Well, we've got the rest of today before school tomorrow. We could go to the Winter Formal dance that the seniors always host," he said. "Maybe things will have calmed down by then. We can go on an official boyfriend-girlfriend-no-stress-date."

I laughed. "You want me to dance? In a dress?"

He smirked. "Come on, it'll be fun."

"Maybe fun-*ny*. But sure."

He smiled and squeezed my hand. "I also need to tell you about my meeting with Duncan," he said, twisting his fingers. "I – I know it probably sounds like a lot. But I want to adopt Sam, and I want to build some sort of place for all the refugees to stay until they get back on their feet."

Dang, we've only been home for a day and a half and he's already got way more ideas on how to help these people than I do, I thought.

"That's a lot of responsibility," I said. "Are you sure you want to take all of that on?"

He swallowed. "I mean . . . in all honesty, I would like to have a normal life. Not have to worry about refugees or abandoned kids. But if no one else is going to do it . . ."

"Then we have to," I finished. "I get it."

"I just want to make sure you're okay with that," Tom said. "You don't have to help me if you don't want to, but if we're . . . boyfriend-girlfriend . . . then I don't want to make major decisions without you."

Sudden heat blossomed in my gut. *He's asking me for permission like we're an old married couple*, I thought. I swallowed my nerves and leaned over, gently kissing him on the cheek. Such a move seemed elementary and childish, but the smell of adrenaline increased tenfold as my lips touched Tom's cheek.

"Tom, we're Mates," I said. "And I don't know exactly what that means, but I know I love you. And I know we can't just leave these people to figure it out by themselves. We can't do this without each other. Through hell or high water, remember?"

Tears glimmered in Tom's eyes. He smelled like determination. "Thank you," he whispered, squeezing my hand.

No kid is ever going to be afraid for their life again, I thought. *They will have a place to live, food to eat. They'll never be afraid of being locked in a cage or experimented on. They will have some sort of a parent who cares about them - even if it's just me or Tom.*

ADAM

I stared at the floor of my parent's rented condo as I tried to convince myself I deserved what I was asking for.

"You don't want to go back home?" My mom's voice rang with hurt. I could feel her trying not to tear up, which only made me shove my hands deeper into my pockets.

"It's not that I don't want to go home," I whispered. "It's just that . . . it's not home anymore. My friends are here, and I don't think . . ." the words got stuck in my throat. "I can't be away from them. I don't know what I'll do." I was putting my feelings as delicately as I could. My parents didn't know I hadn't slept a wink last night because I was all by myself in a room that didn't have a sand floor or waves a few feet away. They didn't

82

know I was shaking because I was too afraid to sleep and relive my memories. The thought of moving away from my friends was enough to make me stop breathing. They had been through my side, protecting me through thick and thin for months. They saved my life. What was I supposed to do without them?

My parents exchanged concerned glances.

"Son, if you're worried about something bad happening to your friends, you shouldn't. You're all safe now."

You don't know that, I thought.

"I just can't be alone right now, okay?" I said. "Please? You guys don't have to stay here - I can live with Emanuel and Norman."

"It's rude to invite yourself to live at someone else's house, you know," Ethan teased. I rolled my eyes.

"Why don't we do this - you and mom go back home. I'll get an apartment up here - and Adam will live with me," Ethan said. Our parents exchanged glances.

"I mean . . . that's not a bad idea," my mom said. "He already has to find a job and apartment anyway."

My brother clapped his hands together. "Then it is decided! We will live here!"

I cracked a smile. He winked at me.

"Are you sure you'll be okay without us here?" my mom asked, sounding upset again. *I've been okay without you for months,* I thought. I nodded.

I knew I was hurting them. I figured Norman was wishing his parents had even bothered to show up for just a moment. Any kid in my situation should be grateful to have parents who love him and want to be with him.

I was being selfish. But I couldn't handle being away from my friends.

"I'll be fine. I'll call you every day. We'll come visit on the weekends." *I'll go to school like a normal kid with my friends and grow up to be a normal, functioning adult.* My parents exchanged another look before nodding.

"If that's what you want, we'll give it a try for a few weeks," my dad said. I sighed, relief taking some of the tension out of my shoulders. My hands quit trembling.

"Before we go, would you like a blessing?" my mom asked. My shoulders went tense again. *I don't deserve a blessing,* I thought. But if I didn't accept it, they would be even more worried. I nodded.

I tried to block out most of it. I could feel how much my dad cared and wanted the best for me as he laid his hands on my head and began to pray. All it did was remind me that I was selfish. A liar. A murderer. I didn't deserve any blessings or mercy.

We spent our last day together watching movies and laughing like nothing was wrong. They took me shopping for school supplies and new clothes. As they loaded up the car and drove away, I faked a smile and told myself that everything was going to be fine. I would go to school the next day and be a normal person and start making up for everything wrong I had done.

I kept telling myself that as Emanuel's mom picked me up Monday morning to take me to school. The air in the car was tense. Emanuel sat in the front seat, leaving Norman and me in the back. He refused to turn around to look at us. *Okay, they're being awkward*, I thought. I opened my mouth to ask them if everything was okay and then shut it. If they were having relationship problems, they probably didn't want me pestering them in front of Emanuel's mom. Besides, if they wanted me to know they would've brought it up. I didn't need to bother them.

"Now boys, if anyone gives you trouble at school, ignore them, okay? You are all safe and protected. Focus on your studies. Bring home good grades, understand?" Emanuel's mom commanded as she pulled into the drop-off line. We all nodded.

Normal, I chanted. *Be normal.*

Whispers and stares accompanied us as we walked down the hallway. My markings might as well have been flashing neon signs attached to an ambulance siren. Halfway down the hallway, we exchanged wide-eyed glances, the tension from the car vanishing. Nerves wafted off of Emanuel like smoke off a fire. He seemed poised to throw hands at a moment's notice in case anyone tried to mess with us. Norman carefully surveyed the area around us as if he were plotting an escape strategy.

We're not here to rescue anyone or be shot at! I wanted to remind them. *We're safe.*

I instinctively grabbed their hands in mine, hoping to comfort them, until I remembered that humans thought that sort of thing was very gay. I mean, my friends *were* gay, but they didn't need hate for that as well. I dropped their hands like they had burned me and shuffled on, keeping my eyes on the floor, which did not feel very brave.

You are fine, I chanted in my head. *No one here is going to mess with you. You can handle your first day of junior year.*

I nearly screamed as a water bottle hit me on the back of my head. I spun around to find a chortling human laughing at me from his locker.

"What? Scared of water, freak?"

I reached for a sword that wasn't there. It wasn't until Norman put a hand on my shoulder that I realized how tense I was. My heart was pounding. I could hear blood rushing through my head. My breathing was quick and shallow. My ears - which still refused to go back to their human form - were pressed flat against my head.

You knew this would happen, I told myself. *You know everyone wasn't on your side. You can deal with some merphobes.*

"Leave him alone, asshole!" someone else shouted from the crowd. I took a deep breath. *See, some people are being nice! Turn the other cheek and let it go.* I shouldered my bookbag and continued down the hallway.

"Dude, are you okay?" Emanuel whispered. I nodded, trying to force my body to relax. *This will be fine. I will survive my first day.*

EMANUEL

I successfully obtained my schedule from the front office, found my locker, and sat in my first class without passing out. The teacher introduced me - which was dumb because everyone already knew damn well who I was. I waved awkwardly and kept my head down throughout the day. Unfortunately, I didn't share any classes with my friends. I guess the front office thought the regular kids couldn't handle more than one famous person in their classes at a time. But I heard comments.

"That Adam guy is super awkward."

"I have Norman in history. He looks like such a badass!"

"Do you think he'll show us his fins if we ask him nicely?"

He's not a toy, I wanted to scream. As hurt as I was that he wasn't ready to date me, I still curled up my fists in preparation to punch the kid's lights out. I could handle being heartbroken, but I could not handle anyone else hurting him.

Thankfully, the conversation moved away as the crowds dispersed for lunch - the only thing we did have together. I found them at a corner table and sat down, breathing out a sigh of relief. Judging by their faces - they weren't having a great first day either. Norman picked at his food, and Adam had his head buried in his arms.

"How's it going?" I asked, trying to sound cheerful. Norman dropped his fork on his plate and folded his arms.

"Well, one girl touched my markings *on my face*. Another guy asked if I have clamshells covering my chest like Ariel. And one guy told me that he thinks mermaids aren't real and that I'm faking it. So . . . great," he said, picking up a fork and stabbing at the chicken nuggets on his plate. I winced on his behalf. I had figured the day would be rough for all of us, but no one had tried to touch me or tell me I wasn't real. I reached across the table and grabbed both of their hands.

"We can go home if we need to," I reminded them. "If this is too much."

"I'm not a wimp," Norman muttered, squeezing my hand back. Adam stayed silent. *Great*, I thought. *I should've signed up for online school.*

"Hey, look at the lovebirds."

I glanced up to see a mammoth of a senior sniggering down at us. "They're holding hands!" I rolled my eyes. Let them judge us for holding hands - it was perfectly normal - and if it made my merfolk friends feel better - then screw whatever they thought.

Adam lifted his head from the table, mouth twisted with rage. His body coiled like a panther before he jumped over the table, tackling the senior and shoving him against the wall. All commotion in the cafeteria came to a standstill.

"What the fuck did you just say about my friends?" he growled. The color drained from the senior's face. He held his hands up.

"Calm down man, it was just a joke!" he sputtered. Norman vaulted over the table and grabbed Adam.

"Dude, cool it!" he hissed. Adam shoved him away, balling his hands into fists. He reached for a sword that wasn't there and gave chase as the senior ran for it. I helped Norman grab Adam and pull him back as the senior bolted for safety.

"Adam, calm down!" I pleaded. He shouted as he thrashed against our grip, his chest heaving. The other students stared, slack-jawed. Sweat poured down Norman's face. His fins began to grow from his arms.

"We need to get him out of here before I poison his ass," Norman grit through his teeth. Still kicking and screaming, we dragged Adam out of the cafeteria and into the nearest bathroom, where he finally deflated. He collapsed to the floor, curling his knees up to his chest, fingers pulling at his hair. I dropped to my knees and pried his face up to look at me. His eyes were wide and unblinking, ears bent back.

"Dude, what is wrong?" I asked. He pressed his clammy hands over mine.

"It's too much. There's too many people here - too many emotions. I can't take it. I - I need to go home," he whimpered.

"Okay, okay. Stay right here, I'm going to call my mom from the front office, okay?"

Norman grabbed my arm, eyes also wide. "I want to go home too," he whispered. I nodded.

"Stay with him, I'll be back." I ran out the door and raced to the office. The secretary gave me a look as I burst in and handed me the phone without a word.

"Hey, um, we all three need to come home," I muttered to my mom.

"I'm on the way."

AMY

I couldn't help but smile as Tom pulled up on his motorcycle on Monday morning. He flipped the visor on his helmet down. "Hey, pretty lady. Need a ride?"

I chuckled as I crutched over to him, straddling the bike behind him. He handed me a helmet, and I wrapped my arms around him as we sped off towards school. "You know we could have just walked," I shouted over the wind.

"This is cooler!" he shouted back.

People stopped to stare as we pulled into the parking lot. I blushed as we walked up to the front. Tom squeezed my hand as he opened the door for me.

Streamers and balloons filled the corridor. Everyone lining the hallway stopped their conversations and clapped, smiles beaming. My jaw hit the floor.

"What's all this?" I asked. Out of the crowd rolled a familiar teacher. I handed my crutch to Tom and leaned down to hug him.

"What are you still doing here? What is all this?" I asked. Mr. Johns smiled up at me from his wheelchair.

"I might have suggested that we throw you and Tom a little welcome party," he said. A smile broke over my face. The crowd started chanting.

"Merpeople, merpeople, merpeople!"

Tom wiped his eyes as the cheers filled the hallway. He pointed over to the row of lockers - where one was noticeably different. My throat closed up as I walked over to it - running my fingers over the metal.

In Memoriam - Cindy Johnson - The First Martyr

They had painted her old locker white and stenciled the words. My hands shook as I turned to Mr. Johns. "Thank you," I whispered. He smiled at me.

The rest of the day went just as smoothly. Everywhere I turned, people came up to me, offering their thanks. Seats were vacated so I could sit in the most accessible spot in class. And most different of all - Mr. Johns did not ignore me like he had the year before.

My first day of senior year went better than I ever thought it would, and Tom seemed equally as happy, though the teachers still warned he had to do his homework if he wanted to pass. The day was almost over when my phone buzzed. I opened up a text from Emanuel and groaned.

First day went bad. We're all back home now. Come over when you get out.

. . .

"Adam did *what?*" I hissed. Norman and Emanuel shushed me as we sat down on their couch.

"He's upstairs, be quiet!"

"He attacked a senior? Why?" Tom demanded. "Did he threaten you?"

"He didn't threaten us - he just made a stupid comment. Adam overreacted," Norman said. *Jeez, even Norman thought he overreacted?* I thought.

"Did he get in trouble?" Tom asked.

"The front office is calling his parents. It technically wasn't a fight seeing as the senior ran off before it could become one, but still. Didn't look good," Emanuel said. Tom groaned. I racked my brain for any signs Adam was acting weird over the past few days. I mean . . . technically we had all been acting weird with everything going on, but Adam tended to be the stable one out of us. *I should've been paying more attention, I thought. I should've noticed he was on edge and talked to him.*

"What about you guys? Did your day go okay?" I asked. Norman and Emanuel winced.

"Everyone kept asking me a bunch of weird questions," Norman said. "Normally I'm down with being the center of attention, but things just felt . . . bad."

"Should've picked homeschool," Emanuel muttered.

"I'm sure they can switch you over," Tom said. "Or maybe things just need time to cool off." *Yeah, but how long is that going to take?* I wondered.

"I thought everyone would be cool with us, seeing that we literally risked our lives to protect kids like them, but apparently not," Emanuel muttered. "Anyways, how was your day?"

Tom and I exchanged glances. "It was . . . okay," I said. Norman crossed his arms and narrowed his eyes. I sighed. "Fine. It was great. They had a welcome party for us. Everyone was super nice. They even turned Cindy's locker into a memorial."

The boy's jaws went slack. "Are you kidding me? They threw you a fucking party?" Norman gasped.

"Our school was one of the ones attacked by the MCA. Yours wasn't. Maybe that's the difference," Tom pointed out. *Nothing like trauma bonding*, I thought. Emanuel's mom paced in the kitchen, speaking rapidly in Spanish to someone on the phone. Emanuel winced.

"What's she saying?" Tom asked.

"She's yelling at the principal for not controlling her students and giving us a warmer welcome. Home school here I come," Emanuel muttered.

"Maybe it'll be for the best," I said. The looks on their faces didn't match my sentiment.

"It feels like giving up," Norman said.

2:23: Dude did you hear about the
fight at the other high school today?
That adam guy apparently went
off on some merphobic senior

2:24: Yeah I was just telling my
mom about it. Shes pissed. I
asked her why when I dont even
go to school there and she said
that merpeople shouldnt be at
school with the rest of us

2:24: Bro why theyre not
dangerous
2:24: well I guess they can be

2:25: Whatever man I just know if
any show up at our school they better
not mess with me. If I was that senior I
wouldve fucked him up for real

2:25: Or you could just not be
an ass and they'll leave you alone

ADAM

"Are you *serious?*" my mom shouted. I held the phone away from my ear, biting my lip as my parents yelled. "On your first day back you attack another student? What has gotten into you?"

My protests died on my tongue. "I'm sorry," I whispered.

"You need to go back and apologize to that young man! Him making a rude comment is not an excuse to act like that!"

"I know, mom."

"Do you? Because . . ."

I turned as the bedroom door opened slightly. Norman's eyes went wide at the noise coming from the phone. *Are you okay?* he mouthed. I offered a weak smile and a thumbs up.

"Your brother is here to pick you up," he whispered, closing the door behind him. I braved interrupting my mom's yelling.

"Mom, I gotta go, Ethan is here to pick me up."

She sighed. "This conversation isn't over, young man. I know we said you could stay there and go to school with your friends but after this . . . we'll talk later." She hung up, and I trudged downstairs. Amy and Tom offered an awkward wave as I walked to the door. Emanuel's mom grabbed me in a tight hug.

"Text us if you need anything," Norman said. I nodded silently and walked to Ethan's car, bracing myself for the second round of yelling. He drove off without a word. *This is it*, I thought. This is exactly what I deserve for making such a selfish decision. My parents are going to make me move back home and never let me see my friends again, and I deserve it.

We rode in silence for a few minutes before Ethan pulled into a Dairy Queen drive-through.

"What do you want?" he asked. I stared at him in shock. "Come on man, there's people behind us," he said.

"Why the hell are you buying me ice cream right now?" I snapped. Ethan raised his eyebrows as I slapped my hands over my mouth. "I'm so sorry, I didn't mean to swear."

He sighed and pulled into a parking space. He tentatively reached out a hand. "You guys hold hands to feel better, right?"

I nodded slowly, and he grabbed my hand in his. He leaned back against the seat, closing his eyes. "Brother, am I angry right now?" I looked down at my feet. The most I felt was a hint of exasperation, but mostly the soothing calm that my brother usually radiated.

"No . . ."

"Exactly. So, relax. I understand why you went after that guy today. I can't technically condone it because violence, blah, blah, whatever. But you won by not finishing that fight, so I am buying you ice cream."

I wondered if he knew the only reason I didn't finish the fight was because my friends dragged me away. I had been more than ready to tear that senior's throat out.

"Mom and Dad are upset," I whispered. "I think they're going to make me move back home."

"Of course they're upset! They are your parents. They want what's best for you, and what's best for you is making friends, not enemies. But they forget that Jesus also flipped tables in the temple."

I chuckled. *But Jesus never killed anybody*, I thought.

"If you feel the need to fight, fight me," Ethan continued. "You have to keep your mind and body busy. I don't need to be a mermaid to know you're very stressed right now. I'll talk to Mom and Dad and try to cool them down. Now - what flavor of ice cream do you want?"

Mom Against Mermaids

So I just got off the phone with the principal at the high school. My baby came home inconsolable because he was attacked by one of those creatures today! Poor baby has bruises all over him, and the district is refusing to do anything about it!"

53 People liked your post

OG Soccer Mom <3

I would sue. I can recommend a good lawyer if you want one

34 People liked your post

Student Against Mom Against Mermaids

Yeah lady i saw the fight your son totally deserved it tbh

104 People liked your post

Another Student Against Mom Against Mermaids

Yeah fr get wrecked your homophobic son started it

109 People liked your post

Mom Against Mermaids

I demand to know your real names! This is a group for concerned parents!

87 People liked your post

Mom Against Mom Against Mermaids

Hi - parents of a merfolk student here. Mess with my kid and I'll drown you for him <3

134 People liked your post

EMANUEL

Norman and I sat in silence at the kitchen table after Adam left with his brother. My mom continued to mutter under her breath as she made dinner. I almost offered to help – but the speed at which she was chopping tomatoes made me worry I would get sliced instead. I stared down at the table instead, wondering how hard it would be to build a time machine to stop this from happening. She got mad all over again as my dad got home from work and she explained what happened.

"I can't believe the school would let those kids talk to you like that," she fumed as she set the table. "Even if you are gay, what does it matter to them?" Norman and I both blushed.

"It's fine, Mom," I muttered, pushing rice around on my plate. She opened her mouth - probably to tell us that it was most definitely *not* fine when my dad interrupted her.

"Why don't you boys take tomorrow off? Let things cool off for a day. Go do something fun," he said. *What on Earth would we do for fun?* I thought. Norman chewed thoughtfully.

"I have something we could do," Norman said, holding up his phone. "I've been texting some friends I had at my old school. We could try to hang out with them tomorrow?" Norman asked. *Norman had friends?*

Of course he had friends, I scolded myself. What kind of loser didn't have friends?

Me, I thought.

I mean, people were generally nice to me, but I had been a nerdy wallflower before the Rebellion. I certainly didn't know anyone well enough from my past life to shoot them a text and ask to hang out.

Part of me became instantly jealous, and Norman looked up from his phone to raise his eyebrow at me. I instantly flushed and looked away, embarrassment replacing the jealousy. I hated that he could feel my emotions.

"Yeah, that sounds fun. We can invite Adam too if his parents haven't killed him yet," I said. Norman smiled. After dinner, we headed up to my room like normal. Despite the awkward tension that had been following us ever since he told me he wasn't ready to date, he hopped up next to me in bed as we scrolled through Netflix. I resisted the urge to hold his hand as he slowly drifted off beside me. I knew I should wake him up and tell him to go soak in the kiddy pool we had put up in the bathroom, but he looked so adorable asleep. He looked adorable every night he had fallen asleep in my bed.

A more socially adept person would have assumed he was doing it on purpose, even though we were awkward as hell around each other in the daylight, but I refused to let my brain jump to that conclusion. Norman said he wasn't ready to date - and I was okay with that. Perfectly okay with that. He definitely wasn't falling asleep in my bed on purpose. And just because he wanted to hang out with old friends didn't mean he was sick of me.

. . .

By the next morning, Adam still hadn't texted back, so we set off to go hang out with Norman's friends by ourselves.

"It's pretty cool that your friends get to ditch school to hang out with us," I said. Norman nodded, surprisingly quiet. I wondered if he was nervous to see them after everything that had happened. Heaven knew I was nervous enough.

Be normal, I chanted. *Be not socially awkward.* We turned a corner and arrived at a playground centered in a grassy field. A few moms with strollers loitered around the benches, chatting with their friends. They stared and whispered as we walked past them. I was tempted to turn and stick my tongue out, but I didn't have a chance before Norman spun around, eyes narrowed.

"Take a picture, it'll last longer!" he snapped. The moms gasped and quickly vacated their seats, leaving us alone in the park. Norman triumphantly plopped down on the bench, and we scrolled on our phones until two figures came into view. One waved, jumping up and down. Norman's face broke into a grin as he ran towards them. I stayed on the bench, unsure what to do as Norman's friends threw their arms around him, laughing.

"Guys, this is Emanuel. Emanuel, this is Raymond and Camden." Camden flipped their neon blue hair out of their face and grinned at me.

"Yeah, we know who you are," Camden said dryly, sticking out a hand. "My pronouns are they and them, by the way." I shook it, already feeling my face burn. How was I supposed to pretend to be normal when my face had been plastered all over social media and the news?

"So, how did you guys meet?" I asked. Raymond sniggered, and I blushed, mentally slapping myself. *How did you guys meet? That was something a mom would ask their child's significant other! They obviously met at school, idiot.*

"We've been friends going way back. We were all in a play together back in elementary school," Raymond said. I raised my eyebrow as Norman blushed.

"Norman was in a play? What play was it?" I asked.

"*Wizard of Oz*. He was the dog," Camden smirked. I burst out laughing as Norman's flush grew redder.

"Oh my god, please tell me you have pictures," I laughed. Norman lunged as Camden took out their phone. Raymond held Norman back as

Camden and I bolted. We chased each other around the park for a while until Norman eventually wrestled the phone away. I lay on the grass, panting between gut-wrenching laughs. Camden wiped tears from their eyes.

"Damn, Norman. You merpeople really do have some super strength, huh?" they said. Norman sank on the grass.

"No. Just faster reflexes," he gasped. For the first time, I realized that Norman's friends hadn't asked any questions about the Rebellion or about Norman's true nature. They had accepted him back as their friend with open arms - no questions asked. It felt strange to hang out with other teenagers and not feel a need to explain things.

The second thing I realized was that I absolutely had to get a picture of a little Norman dressed up as Toto.

"So, how do you like your new school?" Raymond asked. "It sucks that you can't come back with us." Norman and I exchanged a weary glance.

"It's . . . okay," Norman said. "Could be better, could be worse. Anything interesting going on back at Ridgemont?"

"Nothing too crazy . . . Mackenzie is still a bitch to everyone. Oh - you remember that hot football player? What was his name . . . John or something?" *Oh, no, are they talking about Jason?* I thought. Norman went stiff. I subconsciously reached out and grabbed his hand, which Camden definitely noticed.

"No, I think his name was Justin. Anyway, he *totally* got arrested the other day. He sexually assaulted someone at his college," Raymond continued. "It's all over the news because it was the dean's son he went after. People are freaking out about it." Camden handed over their phone, and Norman's face drained of color.

His ex's mugshot shone back at us. The caption matched the other's gossip. *Oh my god*, I thought, my stomach turning.

"Oh," Norman managed.

"Other people are coming forward too. It's turning into a hashtag me-too thing except for like . . . gay guys," Camden said.

"Never would've pegged that guy as a queer. He screamed straight guy vibes," Raymond said. "Haha, get it? *Pegged?*" Norman faked a laugh and handed back the phone. Only I noticed that his fingers were trembling. I opened my mouth to ask him if he was okay, but he shot me a warning look, and I shut my mouth.

"What about that crazy math teacher? Did she get fired yet?" Norman asked. We continued to talk about schools as the sun sank lower in the sky. Norman eventually yawned and stretched, saying that we should probably head back home. We all hugged and said goodbyes, and I waited until we were out of sight to open my mouth.

"Norman -"

"Don't," he warned, shoving his hands in his pockets.

. . . *are you okay?* The rest of the words died on my tongue. We walked the rest of the way in silence as a thousand worries ran through my mind. *Why doesn't he want to talk to me?*

ADAM

That night, I tossed and turned like normal. I had been suspended for the next two days, so it wasn't like I had to wake up early for school anyway. I watched the glowing clock on my nightstand change numbers until sunlight streamed through the curtains. My phone buzzed, and I glanced at it to see that Norman was asking if I wanted to hang out that day. I swiped his message away and went back to staring at the clock. Surely if I stared at it for long enough it would lull me into a dreamless sleep.

Not that I deserved a dreamless sleep.

"Hey Adam, come downstairs, we have a visitor!" my brother shouted. I sighed and rolled out of my bed, making a sad attempt to pat down my hair before walking downstairs.

My brother was grinning like the sun was shining through his teeth. Beside him stood an older man with salt and pepper hair. He stood with his back straight, his lips pursed in a thin line. He eyed me up and down like I was a specimen strapped to a table. I scowled and shoved my hands in my pockets.

"What's going on?" I muttered. My brother flushed and motioned towards the stranger as if I hadn't noticed he was standing there.

"Adam, this is Mateo DeSilva . . ." he trailed off, and when I didn't jump up and down or gasp in awe, he continued, ". . . the Olympic Coach for the American fencing team."

Why my brother was so excited suddenly made perfect sense. My dad had worked with the team for several years before becoming a teacher. He was probably good friends with DeSilva, but my sleep-deprived brain was still struggling to compute why the man was standing in my living room.

I waited for one of them to enlighten me, but they just stared as if I should be bowing. I finally shrugged. "Well, hi."

My brother's eyelid twitched. DeSilva's face stayed stoic.

"I've seen videos and heard tales of your fighting skills," DeSilva said. "I have to say, it is quite impressive that a teenager as reckless as you is still alive." *Is he trying to compliment me?* "Though others think it's stupid of me - I would like to offer you a spot on the team. Of course - I'm not even sure you would ever have the chance to compete in the future . . ."

The rest of his words turned to mush in my head. My hands clenched to fists in my pockets. My webbed ears pressed flat against my head. My brother's excitement felt like a thorn digging into my cornea.

How dare he? Did he know what had happened the last time I touched a blade? Was my dad behind this? Did he spend all yesterday yelling at me knowing that today, his old friend would waltz in and invite me to take part in more violence? What was wrong with them?

"No," I said, cutting off whatever DeSilva was saying.

My brother's jaw dropped. DeSilva leaned back and crossed his arms as if I was a roach scuttling across the carpet. "Very well then." He clapped his hands on his knees and stood up to leave, but my brother practically shoved him back down on the couch.

"Wait, wait just a minute, please!" he pleaded. "Just, just give us a sec!" He grabbed my arm and dragged me into the kitchen, his eyes wide. "What are you thinking?" he hissed. "That's the Olympic fencing coach offering you a golden ticket!"

"I said no, okay? Drop it!"

"Dude, will you please talk to me? What's going on?" he pleaded. "You love to swordfight."

I saw myself grabbing him by the throat and holding him against the wall. I saw myself grabbing the nearest knife and showing my brother just how skilled I was with a blade. Maybe then he would believe me when I said that no one should trust me with a weapon ever again.

"I don't want to talk about it," I muttered, shoving my way past him and running up the stairs. I ducked into the bathroom, slamming the door shut behind me and locking it. I leaned against the sink, hands trembling, my head pounding. It had been less than 48 hours since my first day of school ended with me attacking a human, but it felt like years. My vision was beginning to blur. My brain felt caged inside my skull. Exactly how long had it been since I had slept?

I just want to sleep.

I clawed open the mirror and found an orange bottle. I knew my brother had been diagnosed with insomnia as a kid and had gotten medicine for it. Funny how I was having the same problem even though we weren't even related.

I unscrewed the safety cap, tilted the bottle back, and forced myself to swallow whatever fell in my mouth.

I just want to sleep.

I just want to sleep.

I just want . . .

EMANUEL

Norman woke me up early the next morning. He was already dressed.

"Get up. I need you to come with me somewhere." *Guess we're not going to school today either*, I thought. I asked no questions as I hurriedly got dressed and followed him outside. Norman had Google Maps pulled up on his phone, and practically jogged on the blue line. I hurried after him, wondering where on Earth he could be taking me at six am on a Wednesday morning. I shot my mom a text to let her know we had left the house.

Maybe we're going to the beach, I thought. That guess was proved wrong as Norman took us downtown, scanning the buildings as we walked. Above us, dark storm clouds circled, growing heavier and heavier.

He eventually stopped in front of an office building, white-knuckling his phone. I finally caught up to him, panting.

"Dude . . . what's going on? Where are we?" I asked.

"Just come with me," he muttered, pushing his way through the front doors. A lady with slicked-back hair and an expensive suit eyed us over her half-moon glasses as we walked in. It smelled like coffee and stale carpet. Norman held up his phone.

"I have a meeting with Mr. Thomas," he said. We were escorted down a dark hallway. The secretary knocked on a thick mahogany door and left us. It opened, revealing a tall white man with graying hair. He nodded and ushered us in. Norman shook silently as we sat down across the lawyer's desk. *Why on Earth are we talking to a lawyer right now?* I wondered.

"Emanuel, Norman. My name is Martin Thomas. What can I help you with, Norman?"

Norman took a deep breath. "I heard about the Jason case on the internet. I . . . I want to add my testimony against him," he said quietly.

My heart leaped in my chest. I instantly reached across the chairs and grabbed his hand. I squeezed hard, trying to feel as confident as I could for him. *Yes, get his ass in even more trouble.* Mr. Thomas nodded and laced his fingers together.

"You are not the first to come to me with allegations," he said. "Right now - it's Jason's word against four people and a decent pile of evidence. So, what's your story?"

Norman took a deep breath. He opened and closed his mouth several times before words came out.

"It - it was almost a year ago. Jason and I were dating. He wasn't - he claimed he wasn't ready to come out of the closet yet, so we kept our relationship a secret."

I squeezed Norman's hand, and he squeezed back.

"He was . . . pushy. He pressured me into doing things I wasn't comfortable with. And . . . one night I was at his place during a party. He was drunk. He wanted to go upstairs and once we got there . . . he locked the door and said that if I didn't sleep with him, he was going to kill himself."

My chest grew tight. I didn't know whether to cry or punch the wall. *How fucking dare he. How could someone do something so horrible?*

"Do you have any solid evidence?" Mr. Thomas asked. Norman shook his head. Mr. Thomas sighed and leaned back in his chair.

"You things can tell if I'm lying right?" he asked. Norman stiffened slightly at being called a *thing* but nodded.

"Then allow me to be frank. I appreciate you coming forward, I really do. But right now, we've got a really strong case. Four testimonies, physical evidence, powerful people. People, other people will believe in the trial." He motioned at Norman's markings. "Humans other humans will believe in the trial."

It was my turn to stiffen. "What are you saying?" I asked. Punching the wall was beginning to sound like a better option.

"I'm saying that right now, this case is a shoe-in - which is lucky to begin with. Predators - especially men attacking other men - very rarely get prosecuted. That bastard will go to prison for a long time where he'll get a taste of his own medicine. If I bring a merperson into this - it'll become about just you. And the humans on a jury might not see past that," Mr. Thomas explained. I squeezed down on Norman's fingers so hard he winced.

"Just because he's merfolk doesn't mean that his testimony doesn't count!" I protested.

"Right now, this is a case about sexual assault between men. If I bring a merperson into this - this becomes a case about sexual assault between merpeople and humans. And people will have their opinions I won't be able to change no matter how good of a lawyer I am. It's too early. And it's too risky. I can't risk jeopardizing this case. I'm sorry."

My mouth felt glued shut. I waited for Norman to leap out of his seat, screaming and swearing, but he stayed just as quiet as I was.

"Honestly boys, I wish it could be different. But if I stick with what I've got - he will end up in prison for sure. If I bring you in - I lose that confidence."

I tried to pry my mouth open to say something - anything, but Norman stopped me.

"It's fine, I understand," he said quietly. I stared at him, my jaw slack. *He's just going to give up?* I thought. *What the hell is wrong with him?* He stood up, dragging me with him. "Let's go." He pulled me behind him as he marched quickly to the door.

"Norman, I-"

"I don't want to talk about it," he snapped. He took off running down the street, and this time, I didn't chase after him. *Fine. If he doesn't want to talk to me, then I won't force him,* I thought. I walked slowly home. The clouds above me broke, drenching me. By the time I made it back, I was soaking wet and my teeth were sore from being clenched. I wanted nothing more than to go back in time and save Norman from his ex, but even if I could, he probably wouldn't let me.

I knew I shouldn't be angry with him, but I couldn't help it. I had never done a damn thing to hurt him, and he still acted like he couldn't trust me as far as he could throw me. Never mind that he was sleeping in my bed at night. Never mind that my mom cooked all his meals. At the end of the day, we were just humans. Humans who he wasn't allowed to trust or confide in.

Or fall in love with.

I lingered on the porch, not trusting myself to go inside. I paced back and forth as the rain crashed down around me, clenching and unclenching my fists.

I jumped as the door creaked open. My mami poked her head out, her brows furrowed.

"Norman got back a little bit ago and just ran upstairs to your room. Is he okay? I thought you guys were going to try going to school today?" She paused as she closed the door behind her.

"Are you okay?" she added. Sudden tears pushed against my eyes. She held out her arms and I fell into them, shaking as sobs escaped me. We sat down on the steps.

"Mijo, what's wrong? Are you two fighting?"

I took a deep shuddering breath. How did I even begin to explain what was going on without spilling Norman's traumatic past?

"He . . . he doesn't trust me," I whispered. She frowned, running her fingers through my hair as I blubbered on.

"He has a lot of issues with humans. And I get it - believe me - I would too if I went through what he has. But . . ." I swallowed. "I know he can read my emotions. He knows . . . he knows I'm not like the others. He knows . . ." *He has to know I'm in love with him,* I thought. *How could he not?*

"But he still doesn't trust me," I said. "He won't confide in me. And I'm trying hard to be patient but . . ." *How long am I supposed to wait? What if he never gets over it? I want to be able to have a life, fall in love, and get married. Be able to talk to my spouse if I'm upset. My spouse talk to me if they're upset.*

My mom wrapped an arm around my shoulder. "Do you love him?" she asked. I hesitated before nodding. "You know what they say above love. Love is patient, love is kind."

I scoffed. Norman was not a particularly patient person.

"Once he becomes brave enough, he will come to you, mijo. He is just scared," she said.

"Scared of me?" I asked bitterly.

"Not scared of you. Scared of love. Scared of what he feels for you," she crooned. "He still has some healing to do, but once he is ready, he will realize he must conquer fear to enjoy love."

I swallowed, wiping my eyes.

"Thanks, Mom," I said, my tears finally coming to a stop.

"You know, when you disappeared, the last thing I was expecting was for you to bring back a merman you had fallen in love with."

I blushed. "Does that upset you?"

"I just want you to be happy. *Safe* and happy," she clarified.

"I meant about being gay, Mom. And the boy being not-human."

She sighed and hugged me close. "In another timeline . . . yes maybe, I would be upset. You know how badly I want grandchildren. And you are far too handsome to not have your own kids." I blushed. I wondered if now was a bad time to mention that Norman claimed he hated kids.

"And in the beginning, I believed what the people on the news said about the merpeople. I suspect I still would if you hadn't run away to help them. But you are an incredibly smart and kind boy. I know that if these creatures were important enough for you to run away and be away from my cooking for that long - the people on the news must be wrong," she said. I managed a smile.

"I did miss your cooking. And maybe we'll adopt," I muttered. She smiled.

"Be patient with him, nino. Even though this Norman boy is fearful, I know he would do anything to keep you safe." She stood up.

"Take the day to chill out. Let Norman calm down. But tomorrow, you have to go back to school. Your brothers are starting to get jealous."

I nodded, and she patted my head one last time before going back inside. I sighed and leaned against the steps, wondering how long I would have to be patient before my beloved mustered enough courage to love me back.

DUNCAN

The sun had set hours ago. My eyes were beginning to burn from staring at my computer screen. I had never been one for government rules or politics, and the laws and policies concerning refugees and adoptions and citizenship were blurring in my head.

I wanted to help Tom out, I truly did, but the more I read, the less likely it seemed possible. I had already contacted my lawyer friends, but there was little they could do.

I sighed and turned on the small TV in my room. Immediately, the news popped up with a reporter wandering around one of the local neighborhoods. She seemed to have a line of irate humans wanting to talk to her.

"I'll tell you what now, these damn mermaids been sleeping on my docks for weeks now, and I'm sick of it!"

"They're running wild! My boy goes to *school* with one of them. How can they even let these creatures in the building? They're *sick*."

"I mean, they seem pretty nice, but I'm not trying to turn into one of them. Something needs to be done to make sure the rest of us don't get infected."

I know, I thought.

I knew the odds of a human getting infected were minuscule. But I had figured from the beginning that humans would be terrified of the virus spreading. Humans were good at causing riots and much worse because of irrational fears. Selling such a vaccine would not only provide funding for Biosyn for decades to come but it would put a stop to the fearmongering. Humans would have no reason to attack merpeople if they had nothing to be afraid of.

And Sam had already technically promised me. If anyone was smart enough to make a vaccine - it would be her.

It wasn't like making a vaccine would take away from the merfolk population. Vaccines couldn't cure something if the host was already infected. But if we could show that humans would be protected, they would leave the merfolk alone to their own devices. True - there would be no more Cursed - but that seemed to be in everyone's favor. If I could convince Sam to do it . . .

My phone rang suddenly, making me jump as the noise shattered my train of thought. I picked it up and rubbed my temples.

"Hello?"

"Hello, Mr. Duncan. This is Mayor Lawson."

I took a deep breath. He was the last contact on my list of powerful rich friends, as Tom had put it. We had grown up together. I had voted for the man and kept voting for him as the years passed. We rarely had time to chat, but I was praying the old familiar bonds would do me some favors.

"Hey there. I . . . I have a request to make." I briefly reiterated Tom's proposal of opening a group home and adopting Sam. By the time I was done, the mayor sounded like he was in tears, laughing.

"You can't be serious."

I deflated. "Listen - I know it's a lot. I know it sounds ridiculous but -"

"It *is* ridiculous. I may be mayor but that doesn't mean I can give this eighteen-year-old kid all the college education and certifications to run a group home. There are rules and laws and actual qualifications for this sort of thing."

"But surely you can agree that something needs to be done," I protested. "There are dozens of homeless merfolk right now, jobless and penniless. Where are they supposed to go?"

"To be frank, I don't care. They belong in the ocean, do they not?"

I sucked in a breath. *I know which side of the debate you were on,* I thought. *Is that why the government hasn't been offering a lick of help? Because they just want the merfolk to give up and go back to the ocean?* I glanced over at the TV, at the crowd of angry humans surrounding the reporter.

"Well . . . your human constituents seem to care," I said. "Have you been watching the news?"

"I have."

"Don't you think your voters would be happy if you got these homeless merfolk off the street at least?"

"To have them take over our schools?"

The merfolk population is tiny, I thought. *They're not about to take over anything.*

"Look – I don't understand why you've been so insistent on helping these things out to begin with. But regardless, I've got to think about the greater good here. And the truth is - most humans, myself included, are simply not interested in having these creatures anywhere close to them," he said. *You mean the humans who can vote,* I thought.

"However," he took a breath. "There might be a deal we can come to." I leaned forward, tapping my foot on the floor.

"First of all, humans are very uncomfortable with the idea of living with these creatures and not knowing who is what. I think it would be fair to ask these creatures to personally identify themselves whenever they're in public. Make them pay a fine if they refuse."

"You mean showing their markings? Most of them already do that."

"Then it shouldn't be a problem. Second thing, many humans, even the CDC have expressed concerns about the virus spreading. I'm sure I'm not the only one who has mentioned the creation of a vaccine to you."

My heart echoed in my chest. *This is my chance.* "You are not," I said.

"Then surely it won't surprise you if I ask you to create a vaccine."

I threw my fist in the air but forced my voice to remain calm.

"Sir, the idea of creating a vaccine for this isn't as simple as you think. It will take years of research to even begin -"

"Then you better start soon. I'm not saying it will even be released, but, if things ever do get out of hand with these creatures, I want it on standby."

I stared at the ceiling, grinning. Now Sam would have no choice. I was getting exactly what I wanted.

"Would this vaccine become mandatory?" I asked.

"That depends on the creatures. If no one ever gets infected, there won't be a need to release it or make it mandatory."

"So, we have a deal then?" I asked.

"One more thing. Tom needs to thin out the herd, or the school, I suppose. I don't have enough resources to take care of every mermaid that washes up on our shores."

You definitely do, I thought. *All the refugees could live in one corner of your mansion without you even noticing.*

"So, you want Tom to pick and choose who gets assistance? And do what with the others?"

124

"Send them back to where they came from."

I resisted the urge to laugh. "So, let me get this straight. You're offering to help but only if merpeople agree to show their markings, send half of them back to the ocean, and make a vaccine?"

"Well, technically I don't need anyone's permission to make the mermaids show their markings. But yes, you need to make me a vaccine. And Tom needs to send some of them back to the ocean. Let me remind you that you're asking an awful lot of me here," Lawson said. "You're asking me to let an eighteen-year-old run a group home with absolutely no qualifications. Which is illegal."

"So is discrimination based on medical history," I muttered under my breath.

"This is the most I can offer. This way, my humans see that I am helping but still keeping them under control."

My stomach twisted. "I'll make your vaccine. But I'll need to talk to Tom about the rest of it."

"Tell him he has twenty-four hours to decide. After that - you and the mermaids get nothing."

NORMAN

The rest of the day was quiet. I hid in the bathroom and lay awake for hours before my body finally succumbed to sleep. The next morning, I maneuvered around Emanuel in silence, part of me too embarrassed to speak, the other part certain I would burst into tears the moment I did.

He ignored me just as harshly as I ignored him. I could feel the turmoil of emotions radiating off of him like a lightbulb burning my skin. He was furious. And hurt.

I'm such an asshole, I thought. *Why can't I just talk to him?*

The question plagued me as we got in the car to go to school. Emanuel hopped out to rap on Adam's door. Emanuel's mom hummed along to the radio as we waited. *Please don't talk to me,* I thought. I looked out the window to see Emanuel holding his phone up to his ear. His anger and frustration were beginning to smell like worry.

I took a deep breath and steeled myself to talk. I opened the door.

"Dude, what's taking so long?" I yelled.

"He's not answering," Emanuel snapped back. I frowned. It wasn't like Adam to sleep in. Even at The Sanctuary, he was always up by dawn. I walked to the door. His brother's car was missing from the driveway.

"I tried calling him, but he won't answer," Emanuel said. I pounded my fists against the door.

"Wake up fuckface!" I shouted. The house remained silent. Something turned in my gut. *This doesn't feel right*, I thought.

"He probably just overslept. Let's just go." Emanuel turned to walk back towards the car, but I stayed by the door

"He wouldn't oversleep," I muttered under my breath. Emanuel yelped in alarm as I raised my foot and slammed it against the handle, blowing the door in.

"You're breaking in? What the hell man?" Emanuel demanded. I ignored him as I stepped over the threshold and walked inside.

"Adam? You alive?" I shouted. No one answered. I climbed up the stairs only to freeze in the narrow hallway.

Adam's arm stuck out past the bathroom door, limp. The blood drained from my body as I ran to him, almost slipping on a stray orange bottle that had fallen to the floor.

He groaned as I grabbed his shoulders, chest rising in shallow breaths. His eyelids fluttered as he tried to focus his gaze on me.

"Hi guysss," he mumbled, his words slurred.

"Dude, are you high?" Emanuel demanded.

"I don't . . . think . . . so." Each word was punctuated by a breathy gasp.

I reached over to the bottle I had almost slipped on and read the inscription. *Ambien.*

"What is Ambien?" I asked. "Did you . . . did you take this whole bottle?" Adam's head lolled to the side, his eyelids fluttering closed again.

"I just Googled it. It's a sleeping medication. Why would he take a bunch of sleeping pills?" Emanuel sputtered.

I snapped my fingers in front of his face, but he didn't flinch. "I don't know, but let's get him on the couch at least."

I grabbed him under the arms as Emanuel grabbed his legs and we lugged him down to the couch, plopping him down like a bag of potatoes.

"He's not gonna like . . . die is he? What's the worst that can happen if you overdose on Ambien?" I asked.

"I mean other than trouble breathing or a coma . . . should be fine," Emanuel said. "You guys are like . . . immune to human medicine, right?"

I rolled my eyes. "It still affects us, idiot."

We stared down at Adam's body. His chest continued to rise in hesitant, shallow breaths.

"I don't think he's gonna die. But I don't want to leave him here. We should call his brother," Emanuel said. I nodded in agreement. Emanuel stepped outside to call the brother and tell his mom that school wasn't happening today as I sat down on the floor in front of the couch, playing with the loose threads on the carpet. Emanuel returned after a few moments and sat down on the carpet next to me, avoiding eye contact.

"Why would he overdose on sleeping pills?" I whispered.

"We don't know that he overdosed on purpose," he muttered back.

I scoffed. "He's not stupid. Do you know how hard it would be for merfolk to overdose on accident? He did this on purpose."

Emanuel sniffed, eyes welling up with tears. "Why would he try to hurt himself?"

I shrugged. I could think of a million reasons to hurt myself - but I knew I wasn't upset enough to act on any of them. Adam had always been the chill, collected one of all of us. Why was he losing it?

We should've been paying more attention, I thought. *If he was trying to hurt himself on purpose - it's our fault.*

Emanuel reached out a hand, and I shied away from him.

"Will you just fucking talk to me?" he shouted. My mouth fell open, and Emanuel immediately recoiled as if he could snatch his words out of the air. *Oh my god, did Emanuel just yell at me?* I thought. *I don't think he's ever yelled at anyone.*

I was such a disaster. This was all my fault. I made Emanuel mad. I had been so caught up in my drama that I had been ignoring everyone around me.

"Norman - I'm so sorry - I didn't mean -" he sputtered. I stood up, intending to pace around the room like I always did when I was nervous but found myself slamming my fists into the wall instead. Emanuel's mouth fell open as I beat the wall until the bones in my knuckles felt like dust. I slid to the floor, my entire body shaking.

"I'm so selfish," I whispered. "This is my fault."

"What?" Emanuel asked.

"I should've been paying more attention. I've been so worried about myself that I forgot about him," I said.

"We both could have been paying more attention -" he stammered. I slammed my fists against the wall again.

"You don't understand!" I shouted. "I'm the empath here. Why didn't I notice anything? What the hell is wrong with me?"

"This isn't your fault. You didn't make him swallow those -"

"THIS IS MY FAULT. EVERYTHING IS MY FAULT!" My chest heaved.

"What are you talking about?" Emanuel demanded. I clenched my jaw shut, not trusting myself to talk. Emanuel got to his feet, hands clenched.

"You are not going quiet on me again!" he said. "You're going to tell me exactly what you are feeling and thinking right now you Little Fuck or I swear to god you can go fuck off to the Sanctuary!"

Oh my god, he just yelled at me again.

Fucking talk to him, you idiot.

"It's my fault that college guy got attacked. If I had just spoken up when it happened . . ." My fingers trembled. "If I had just reported him to begin with . . . that other people wouldn't have gotten hurt." Every ounce of anger radiating off Emanuel promptly evaporated.

"Norman." He sank next to me, and this time I didn't shy away as he wrapped his arms around me. I let myself sink into him.

"Is that what's been going on? This whole time, I thought you were mad that the lawyer didn't take your case," he said. I shook my head.

"The lawyer was right. I can't risk him getting away with it. That would make me even more selfish," I said.

"It's not selfish for you to want justice," he said. I scoffed.

"I am selfish. I want to go back to my old school. I want my parents to come back. And I want to fucking have you but . . ." I swallowed. "I'm such a mess. You probably hate me. You deserve someone so much better than me."

"I mean . . . I've been super pissed at you. But I don't think I could ever hate you," Emanuel whispered. I trembled harder, wanting nothing more than to rewind the clock and go back to that night when we weren't mad at each other. Where we had kissed with no fear or insecurity.

"Look - we kinda forgot about Adam. But that's on both of us - not just you. We'll do better," Emanuel said. "We'll make sure we're spending more time with him. We'll make sure he feels supported. As for you . . ." He leaned back and grabbed my face in my hands, forcing me to look up at him.

"You've got to talk to me when you're upset. I can't help you if you don't open up to me," he pleaded. "I-" He took a deep breath and shut his eyes. "I love you. And I know you're not ready to love me yet. But if something bad ever happened to you, I would never forgive myself."

Holy fuck, Emanuel just told me he loves me. I stroked his cheekbone with my thumb.

"I love you too," I admitted. "And that scares me a lot. I don't know what kind of relationship I want. I don't know if I want to be mated again. I don't know if I want to date the human way. I just don't know."

A smile broke across Emanuel's face. "I just want to be with you in whatever capacity you'll have me," he said.

I scoffed. "You're not scared of being biologically linked with a mythical creature forever at sixteen? Or being murdered by their parents if they ever found out?"

Emanuel shrugged. "I mean . . . kinda used to the murder thing by now." I punched him in the chest.

"There's no rush to decide," he said, rocking me back and forth. "Everything's going to be okay. Everything's going to be okay."

We were interrupted by the door slamming open. Adam's brother raced over to the couch, face pale and eyebrows furrowed. He pressed a finger against Adam's throat and breathed a small sigh of relief.

"Was the bottle empty? There weren't any pills on the floor or anything?" he asked. We shook our heads.

"Thanks, boys, but you can leave. I'll let you know when he wakes up."

AMY

Marisol held up a gold dress covered in sequins that were almost blinding in the fluorescent lights.

"Ooh, what about this one?" she asked, holding it up to herself and swirling it around. My mom looked up and frowned.

"Are you trying to match the disco ball?" she asked cynically, going back to her phone. *Oh dear god, why did I agree to go to a dance with Tom? And why did I agree to let Marisol of all people help me shop?*

Because she's the closest thing to a female friend you have, Tom had argued. And before you say it - Sam doesn't count. She hates dresses. And you have to take your mom too. Maybe it'll help the two of you bond.

I looked down at the floor as the smile faded from Marisol's face. She whipped it away in an instant and put it back on the rack, dragging me down the aisle and thumbing through the dresses. I winced and sank further into despair at the sight of most of them. They were all low-cut or chopped off at the stomach or slit up the side. It was as if the designers had all my insecurities specifically in mind when creating their flashy masterpieces.

I finally agreed to try a red one with spaghetti straps. I wiggled into it too easily - the dress droopy around my chest where my breasts should have been to fill it up. I stepped outside and Marisol oohed, straightening out the dress around me as my mom stared, expressionless.

I tried to feign excitement and held my arms out. "What do you think?" I asked. My mom was silent for a moment more before shrugging.

"I think you should find something with sleeves. Your markings clash too much."

I sucked in a breath as Marisol froze around my ankles. I forced myself to breathe and not clench my fists. I turned and marched back into the dressing room but instead of tearing the dress off, I sat down on the pedestal, dragging my fingers through my choppy hair.

Marisol came in through the curtain and sat next to me, putting a hand on my shoulder.

"I don't suppose it would make you feel better if I told you to ignore her?" she asked hopefully. I looked up at myself in the mirror and held back a laugh of scorn.

"I mean, she's right." My collarbones and sternum stuck out against my skin, making me look like a ten-year-old boy playing dress up in his sister's closet. My blue markings clashing with the red lowkey made me look like Spiderman, or some special-effects makeup gone wrong. *They're going to clash no matter what because they're on my face!*

Marisol got in my face; eyebrows furrowed. She took me by the shoulders and forced me to look at her.

"This sucks, I know. You wish Cindy were here instead of me, and you wish your mom wasn't being a bitch." I raised my eyebrows at her bluntness. "I know it sucks. But Cindy wouldn't want you sulking here, thinking you're ugly and not good enough to go to this stupid dance. So, I'm going to tell your mom to get us some coffee; I'm going to find you a new dress to try on, and you are going to tell yourself you look beautiful in it because you will be." I swallowed back a wave of emotion and nodded. She grinned at me and leaped up, running back into the racks.

She returned a few moments later, a dark navy blue dress draped over her shoulder. Her grin was brighter than the overhead lights as she handed it to me.

"I had to convince the sales guy to take it off the mannequin." She winked before closing the curtains. I sighed and stepped into it. Marisol walked back in and gasped. I fidgeted in front of the mirror, trying to make eye contact with the girl in the mirror.

The dress was so dark blue it was almost black. My thorny markings popped out as if I had installed a backlight behind them. It had one strap, which just so happened to be the one that didn't cover them.

The slit up to my thigh only revealed the stripes and scars even more. The fabric glittered ever so slightly in the light, making me look like a shimmery mirage.

It was a dress meant for a girl with big breasts and wide hips. It was a dress for a girl who knew she was confident and beautiful and sexy.

It was not a dress meant for someone like me.

"Well, what do you think?" I asked, already going after the zipper. Marisol stood in front of me.

"You almost look gorgeous in it; it's just missing one little thing."

"Like what? A smile?"

She rolled her eyes. "Okay Wilson, if you can't wear it with confidence, wear it with spite."

I blinked. "What?"

"Don't wear it because it makes you look pretty. Wear it because there will be people out there who don't want you to wear it. Who don't want to see your markings and scars on display. Wear it to spite everyone who thinks you're nothing but a human with a weird disease."

I involuntarily curled my hands into fists as I contemplated her words. Wearing a dress to feel beautiful? Totally out of my realm. Even as good of a liar as I was - I could never convince myself I looked beautiful in this dress.

But spite? Spite I could always do.

By the time my mom returned with coffee, we had already bought the dress and secured it in a bag. Marisol said it was a surprise for dance night.

We drove back home in awkward silence, my whole body tingly with nerves and excitement. I texted Tom to break the shocking news that I had found a dress, and he appeared at the doorway about thirty seconds later.

"Can I see it?" he asked. I crossed my arms.

"Absolutely not. No one gets to see it. I might lose my nerve to wear it if they do."

He chuckled. "Can we hang out?" he asked, almost sounding shy. "I'm waiting to hear back from Duncan, and I am very nervous about it." *Right, hanging out is one of the things we said we would do as a normal boyfriend-girlfriend couple.*

"Do you guys mind if Tom hangs out for a while?" I asked. My dad grunted a reply, which I chose to take as a yes. We sat down across from him at the kitchen table as my mom turned around, her hands on her hips.

"Is it too hard to ask you to put your bowl in the dishwasher?" my mom snapped. Tom's head flew up. I grabbed his hand to prevent whatever words were about to fly out of his mouth.

"Sorry, I'll get it." I grabbed my crutch and walked over to the dishwasher. My mom scoffed.

"Don't you think you use that thing a little too much? Your leg will get stronger if you stop using it."

My grip on the bowl tightened. *Why don't I slice the muscles in your leg and see how well you can walk afterward?*

"She needs it to walk," Tom said through gritted teeth. My mom sighed in exasperation.

"So, how is school going?" my dad asked, flipping through his newspaper. "You guys working on homework?"

"Not at the moment, sir. I'm trying to figure out a way to open a group home for the merfolk refugees here," Tom said. My dad frowned.

"Find good homes? Why don't they just go back to their families? Isn't everybody off that island or whatever now?"

"Well, a lot of them can't go back to their families because their parents don't want them. Or because they lost their jobs." Tom cleared his throat. "Anyways, I'm trying to adopt Sam as well."

My dad choked on his coffee. "You want to *adopt* her? Aren't you a little young to be a dad?" *Tom would be twice the father you've been,* I thought. "I mean, haven't you done enough? You're already dating one of them."

I froze with the bowl halfway to the dishwasher. Tom's jaw was hanging off his face.

"Sorry?" Tom asked.

My dad playfully shoved Tom's shoulder. "I'm just teasing you. After all - I know what it's like to have one of them as a daughter. It's harder than you think."

The bowl hit the floor, shattering into a million loud pieces. My mom gasped.

"Honey - that was an expensive bowl-"

"One of *them*?" I hissed.

Everyone in the room froze. The only sound I could hear was the blood rushing in my ears and my heavy breathing. I very slowly limped forward and slammed my hands on the table.

"One of *them?*"

My dad lifted his hands. "Honey - it was a joke." He smelled of nerves. It almost made me want to smile. Maybe I was trying to earn respect in all the wrong ways. Maybe the only way they could learn respect was to be afraid.

"I know it was. Because you don't know the first thing about being the parent of merfolk," I hissed. My dad's mouth fell open. Tom hid his smirk behind his hand. My mom walked over and tried to put her hand on my shoulder.

"Amy. Calm down. You're getting out of hand."

I jerked away from her, and she flinched as my gaze landed on her.

"First of all - you do not have permission to touch me! Second of all - *I'm* getting out of hand? Just like how I was out of hand when I wouldn't turn myself back in? When I started telling the truth? When I almost died to prove the merfolk deserve just as many rights as you?"

My dad stood up. "Calm dow-"

"NO!" I screamed, slamming my cane against the ground. "It's my turn to talk! I've tried so hard to be nice. To be understanding. I've been walking on eggshells around you - trying to keep my room clean and put the dishes away - to be your *normal* daughter - and none of it is good enough for you. You thought I was a freak back then and you still do. You lied in front of everyone. You told the world I was adopted! You're ashamed of me." They gawked at me, mouths hanging open.

"Forget it. I'm done." I limped towards the door. My dad tried to grab my crutch.

"Now wait." I yanked it out of his hand, nearly sending him to the floor.

"You never even *apologized*. And I sure as hell have nothing to apologize for. I'm not the human daughter you thought you had, and I'm done pretending to be. I am merfolk - and I'm proud to be. And if that makes you ashamed, you can be ashamed without me here." I burst through the door and limped as quickly as I could through the thick sand.

"Amy, wait." Tom caught up to me. I let myself fall into his arms, shaking.

"I tried. I tried," I whispered. He slowly stroked my hair, holding me tight.

"You did. Let's go." We ended up in his room on the boat. He snuggled in next to me and held me until my shaking stopped.

"So, you're waiting to hear from Duncan?" I asked, trying to distract myself.

"Yeah, I told him you were on board and he said he would get back to me ASAP after talking to some people." Tom's phone buzzed, interrupting him. Instead of looking relieved or excited, he swore as he looked at the screen.

"Adam did *what*?"

TOM

Despite our many requests, Ethan wouldn't let any of us see him until further notice. Norman and Emanuel didn't know anything other than their theories about why he would try to overdose. The rest of us went to school like normal, trying not to worry about him.

We were all worrying.

I racked my brain over how he could've gotten to such a point without any of us noticing. He had had a lot on his plate during the Rebellion, rescuing kids and getting shot, but why wouldn't he have been fine after we were freed? I mean, we were all dealing with our stressors, but the worst part was over. Had it all just built up over time? What pushed him over the edge?

Meanwhile, Amy refused to go back to her place, not even to get her stuff. Which meant I had to.

I took a deep breath before knocking on the door. Her father opened it with a frown and crossed his arms.

"I'm here to get Amy's stuff for her," I said. He scoffed.

"Tell her she can come get it after she apologizes." He went to shut the door, but I blocked it with my foot. *Ow.* He glared at me.

"Son, I suggest you get off this property before I arrest you for trespassing," he threatened.

"You can arrest me after we talk," I snapped back. "Look, I get it. I thought merfolk were dangerous too, but your daughter showed me that they're not. The difference between you and me is that I admitted I was wrong and tried to fix it. If I was her father, I would be ashamed of myself."

His face turned purple, eyes bulging. "Listen here -"

"I'm done listening to adults who don't care," I said coldly. "And so is she. So, whenever you get the balls to apologize, you know where to find us." I removed my foot from the door and stalked off. *I'll buy her some new clothes*, I thought. I stormed back on the boat.

"I take it that didn't go very well?" she asked. I shook my head. She walked up and hugged me.

"Don't worry about my stuff. It doesn't matter."

I sighed and buried my head in her hair. "I'm sorry," I whispered. "You deserve better."

"So do you. We can't always get what we want."

I might not end up being the best dad in the world, but at least I won't be drunk or ignorant, I thought.

Our moment was interrupted by my phone buzzing. I took it out of my pocket and took a deep breath.

"It's Duncan. Let me go talk to him." I walked back out onto the deck and answered it.

"This entire situation is stressing me out, Tom."

I winced at Mr. Duncan's tone. He did not sound happy.

"I'm sorry - I know it's a lot," I said. He sighed. The line went silent. For a moment, I thought he had hung up on me.

"Hello?"

"Yes, I'm still here. Look - the town as a whole is not thrilled that there are a bunch of infected people wanting refuge in this country at all."

I stiffened. "They're not *infected.*"

"We understand that - but that's not how a lot of people are seeing it right now. Even though they have legal protection, a lot of humans are hoping they'll just go back to the ocean." My blood ran cold. *Is that why the government hasn't been doing anything to help? They're hoping this problem will solve itself. Those bastards.*

"Well fuck that. I'm allowed to let them live on my boat as long as I want," I said.

"You are, but how long will that be feasible? They need jobs, they need healthcare. I know you think you're rich, but that money will disappear very soon at the rate you're using it."

My heart fell even further. *It can't just end like this,* I thought.

"However . . . I received a call from the mayor earlier. He has a compromise for us, if you will." I held my breath. "It will be required that merfolk always show their markings in public places – so humans can be aware of potential infection. And he is willing to let you adopt Sam *and* fund a group home for the refugees. But . . . he doesn't have enough funding for all of them. Some will have to go back to the ocean."

The fuck? I hadn't realized I said the words out loud until Duncan kept talking.

"I know but hear me out. You said that a lot of the merfolk are already willing to give up. Let them. Let them go back to the Sanctuary. Focus on helping the kids – the ones who want to stay."

I ran my fingers through my hair. The whole markings thing sounded a bit Holocaust-y, but that wasn't what concerned me the most. Sending merfolk away defeated the entire point of a group home!

"What about the adults who want to stay?" I protested.

"Thin them out. I know this isn't ideal, but it's better than nothing. Without this deal . . ." He trailed off, but I could very well imagine what he was thinking.

Without this, no one gets a roof over their head. Without this, Sam and all the other kids end up with strangers or stay homeless.

I paced back and forth again, digging my fingers into my scalp.

Amy would never go for this, I thought. *She wants to save everyone.*

Duncan's previous lecture about being honest with the wife replayed in my head. She was distrustful enough of Duncan from the beginning. This would just confirm her worst fears. She would never agree to it, and then we would be back to square one.

I thought of all the homeless and parentless kids living on the docks. The hope vanishing from their faces as the days passed. I couldn't keep watching them give up.

Merfolk couldn't afford to be back at square one.

If I agree to this, I'll have to keep it a secret from her forever, I thought. *Amy can never know. And who knows, maybe when public opinion is better in a few years, more people will be able to come back. This doesn't have to be permanent.*

"Fine," I whispered.

ADAM

Turns out, a side-effect of taking 27 Ambien pills was a massive headache. A lesser-known side-effect was being cornered by your brother and forced to talk about why you decided to take 27 Ambien pills.

I had woken up early the next morning with my brother standing over me, his eyes red and puffy. As soon as I could sit up and form coherent sentences, he started yelling at me.

"What the hell were you thinking? I was so worried about you! Do you realize what you could have done? What could've happened to you?"

I swallowed, the guilt finally seeping through my veins and into my bones.

"I wasn't trying to kill myself," I whispered, realizing that's exactly what it looked like. "I just . . . I just wanted to sleep."

"So you couldn't have taken some melatonin? Or at least asked me before you decided to take twenty-seven of my prescription sleep meds?"

I threw my hands down on the couch, gritting my teeth. "I haven't slept in days, okay?" I snapped. "Or if I have - then I've woken up every five minutes screaming from nightmares!"

Ethan blinked and leaned back. "What? Why didn't you tell me you were having nightmares?"

I almost laughed. How could I not be having nightmares after what I did?

"It doesn't matter," I muttered, attempting to stand up and wobbling on my feet as I did so. "I'm going upstairs."

Ethan pushed me back onto the couch.

"Oh no, you're not leaving this spot until you tell me exactly what's going on!" he demanded. The guilt boiled into anger.

"Fine, you wanna know what's wrong?" I growled. I balled my hands into fists. My webbed ears pressed flat against my head. "God hates me!" I shouted. "I broke every single fucking commandment I possibly could. I lied to you guys for years. I destroyed people's property. I stole things. I *killed* someone. Why the hell would God or anyone still want me around? I was trying to do the right thing. I swore that I was only doing things to help protect other people. I promised I would never hurt anyone and look what happened!" I flung my head back against the pillows. Maybe if I hit my it hard enough, I would black out again.

Ethan stood slack-jawed, his dark eyes filled with tears. "Adam . . . it's not your fault that Morris died."

I almost laughed. He made it seem like Morris had keeled over in old age, not that he had been stabbed to death.

"I *killed* him," I said. "I killed him after I swore to myself that I would never hurt anyone."

"You had to! He was going to kill you, kill all of your friends!"

"I should've found a different way!" I protested. "If I had just tried harder . . ." My anger finally bled out, leaving my voice pale and scratchy. I lifted my knees to my chest, my fingers trembling as they wrapped themselves around my legs. "In the beginning, I justified running away and all the attacks by saying that I was helping people. That I wasn't doing any permanent damage to anything important. That I had to. But . . . it just spiraled." I buried my head down into my knees, squeezing my eyes shut. For several moments, all I could hear was my own heart pounding against my skull and the weight of Ethan's silence.

"Adam." Ethan lifted my chin. Tears were running down his face. "Do you honestly think God is mad at you for killing that bastard? Without you . . . several of your friends would've died - probably you included. Do you understand that?"

"It's still a sin," I muttered.

"Then I guess you've never read scriptures before because God makes *plenty* of exceptions for murder depending on the circumstances." Ethan took my hands in his.

"I never told you about what happened when mom and dad called me on the mission to tell me that you had run away," he said. "They were so scared. And confused. But I was just angry. I felt like you had betrayed me. A part of me almost wished you had been caught. But -" His voice cracked. More tears ran down his face. "But I decided to pray about it first. So I did. And without a doubt . . . the Spirit told me that you had done the right thing. I didn't know what that meant at the time, but when I saw news of you rescuing other merfolk . . . risking your life to help complete strangers . . . I knew that you weren't a monster. I knew that Heavenly Father was proud of you. And so was I."

I swallowed, stunned. "Really?"

Ethan nodded. "I promise, Adam."

I wasn't sure if I could believe him.

"Look, obviously you're not feeling okay. Will you please let me schedule an appointment with a therapist? Someone who can help you with your nightmares? Maybe get you your own prescription of sleeping meds?"

I took a deep breath. "Are you going to tell mom and dad?"

"I mean, you're on their insurance, so they'll find out. But I promise they won't be mad. Will you please trust me on this?"

Every cell in my body wanted to tell him no - that I deserved the pain I felt. But I couldn't deny the love I could feel through my brother's fingers - like a warm tide pool.

Maybe God doesn't want me to suffer.

I nodded. "Okay."

SAM

My cell phone rang, interrupting me from my college search.

"It's me," Duncan said. I made sure the bedroom door was shut.

"What's going on?" I asked. "What did you just tell Tom?"

Duncan sighed. "Are you alone?" he asked.

"Just tell me," I said, worry prickling in my gut.

"The mayor is willing to make a compromise to let Tom open a group home for the refugees. Merfolk will be required to show their markings in public and Tom cannot provide for all the refugees, some will have to go back to the ocean. But I didn't tell him everything. And I suspect you're not going to want to tell him or Amy either."

I swallowed. "What did you do?"

"You have to make the vaccine," he said.

I white-knuckled the phone. *I guess you're not smarter than Eve after all.*

"Listen - it's for the best. The vaccine will only serve to protect the human population from getting Cursed - it won't affect merfolk at all. And the mayor said it will only be released if Cursing becomes a problem. But it must be on standby."

I ran my fingers through my braids. "And you didn't tell Tom about this part, why?" I asked.

"Do you want him to know that you already promised me you would consider making a vaccine?"

I clenched my jaw, hating that he was right. Tom might see reason for creating a vaccine, but Amy never would. She would go ballistic. She would never trust me again.

"Making a vaccine implies that there's something wrong with us, that we need to be cured," I said.

"You and I both know that's not true. But it will give the humans peace of mind. They'll leave you alone. You'll be safer."

Safer. I chewed my lip. "But it won't be released until it has to be - right? So as long as no one else gets Cursed . . . it'll be fine?" I asked.

"That's correct."

I sighed, feeling like I was selling my soul for a second time. *I can trust this guy, right? I thought. He risked a lot to help us during the Rebellion. He's never lied . . . well . . . he's never lied to me, anyway. This is still in our best interest. What ulterior motives could he possibly have?*

"Fine. Count me in," I said.

"Hey, Sam?"

Shit. I fumbled to hang up on Duncan as Tom poked his head into the back bedroom. "We have some visitors."

I followed him into the living room to see Amy, Norman, and Emanuel gathered on the benches.

"We kinda have an update on Adam," Emanuel said, holding up his cell phone. "He said his brother finally gave his phone back, but he still doesn't want to talk about what happened yet."

"But his brother thinks he's either got PTSD or depression or something," Norman interjected. "So there's that." Norman glanced out the window. "Soo, what's going on with all the homeless people on your boat? I thought you guys had a scheme for that?"

Oh if only you knew, I thought.

Tom summarized his plans for the group home but left out the deal Duncan had proposed. *Interesting,* I thought. *Tom hasn't broken the news yet.*

"I bought a dress," Amy muttered. The small crowd collectively gasped. Norman pretended to faint, and everyone burst out laughing. Amy blushed. "It's not *that* shocking," she muttered.

"It is," Emanuel said. "Also, why are you buying a dress?" Tom beamed and reached over to hold her hand.

"We're going on our first official date in a few days!" he said proudly. "To Winter Formal!" The crowd awed, which only made Amy blush harder.

"You know what, we all deserve something fun to go do," Tom said. "Why don't you guys come too? And make Adam come. Maybe it'll cheer him up a bit."

"We don't go to your school," Norman said.

Tom shrugged. "So? Crash the party. We deserve a night off with everything that's going on. Besides, don't you want to see Amy in a dress?" Amy punched him in the shoulder, but she smiled as she did it.

"I'm not a fan of dances," I said, "but you guys knock yourselves out." Norman and Emanuel exchanged a shy look that reeked of unrequited love.

NORMAN

Whoever was on the dance committee did a great job of decorating the place. Blue and silver streamers fell like rain from the ceiling, sprinkled with twinkle lights. A huge table of snacks and desserts stood on the opposite side. A crowd danced in front of the DJ, laughing and spilling their drinks on the floor.

Adam was doing a good job of looking solemn as he munched on a cookie. Per his request - we didn't ask him what was wrong. Tom shifted, glancing back at the door every five seconds. I sighed.

"I'm sure your date will be here soon," I muttered, taking a sip from my cup.

"I'm just nervous," Tom admitted. "She was hesitant about coming. I just don't want her to wimp out."

"Haha, look at Emanuel trying to dance," Adam laughed, pointing across the room. I looked up, instantly regretting coming.

Emanuel of course looked amazing in his suit and bowtie. What a nerd. He had looked so amazing that another guy had immediately asked him to dance as soon as the music started. Too polite to say no, Emanuel had joined him out on the dance floor. Without me. And even though he had no rhythm and flailed around like a toddler – he still looked adorable.

"Hold on, why is Emanuel dancing with another guy?" Tom asked.

"We aren't dating," I muttered, crushing my drink in my fingers. Tom gently plucked it from my fingers.

"I mean this in the politest way possible . . . but why the hell not?"

I swallowed. "It's complicated," I admitted. "I don't know if I want to have another Mate."

Tom shrugged. "Okay, so just regular-human date him then."

I sighed. *My question exactly*, I thought. *If I don't want to risk messing up with another Mate, why not just slap the boyfriend label on him and call it good?*

Deep down, I think I knew the answer.

I wanted to call him my Mate. I wanted to have a biological bond that wound us together. But I also wanted the freedom to leave if he turned out to be like my ex.

"I mean, not to bust your bubble, but you know that Amy and Tom are Mated even though they didn't . . . you know," Adam whispered. "And if you love Emanuel, and he loves you . . . aren't you two basically already Mated?"

"Should I go stab him with my fins and find out?" I muttered.

"Maybe it's not about whether or not you *could* poison him. Maybe it's about whether or not you *would*," Adam said. I swallowed, a lump forming in my throat. I couldn't imagine hurting Emanuel - at least not on purpose. I had already had my fair share of screw-ups that had hurt his feelings. Hell - I made him yell - and Emanuel never yelled.

"I mean, I love Emanuel too, but if he turned out to be like your ex - and you literally couldn't poison him - I would rip his balls off for you. And all you would have to do is ask," Adam said calmly.

"Go on man. You'll regret it if you never take the chance," Tom said. "You know he loves you too. And he's been super patient and not pushy. Isn't that like . . . the greenest flag ever?"

I watched him dance with his mystery guy. He was so awkward, and borderline looked like he was having a seizure, but he owned it. His partner was in tears laughing.

"He's literally dancing with another guy," I said flatly.

"And that is, literally, your own fault," Tom said. I sighed. A very decent chunk of me wanted to march across the floor and scoop Em into my arms. I wanted to hear him giggle over me like that night several weeks ago. I wanted him to hold my hand and smile and fill me with that sense of peace and protection.

The song changed. Soft music drifted out of the speakers, and the dance mobs separated into couples. Emanuel and the guy drifted off to the food table. *At least they aren't slow dancing together*, I thought.

Tom gasped. I turned around to see Amy and Marisol walking through the doors. A decent number of people stopped to stare. Tom shoved his cup in my hand and all but bolted to her. Even as a gay guy, I could understand how gorgeous she looked. She wore a dress so blue it was almost black that purposely revealed her markings on her left shoulder and arm. It was cinched tight around her body except for where it flowed out around her legs. She didn't look like your traditional model - but damn she sure oozed attitude like she was.

I turned my head before Tom reached her, staring across the floor at Emanuel. *He does look adorable in that stupid bowtie*, I thought.

I closed my eyes. My ex towered above me, eyes cruel and cold. A group of men held me still as they held a knife to my fin, disgust flowing through their veins.

I hate you, I thought. *I hate who you turned me into. I hate that you made me afraid of love. I hate that you made me ashamed to protect myself.*

Fuck it.

I opened my eyes and forced myself to walk across the dance floor. I tapped Emanuel on the shoulder, whose eyes got big as he turned around, half a cookie sticking out of his mouth. I tangled my fingers together, trying to keep them still.

"Um . . . would you maybe want to dance with me?"

Emanuel practically spat the rest of his cookie out and followed me onto the dance floor, abandoning the other boy. We fumbled for a second, trying to figure out who was leading until we settled and started drifting in the crowd.

"You know before I came here . . . I Googled how gay guys figure out who leads and who follows," he whispered.

I sniggered. "Oh yeah? What did you find out?"

"It's the more assertive, leadership-type who leads. Or whoever's taller."

"Guess that means you should be the leader," I said.

"Do you want me to lead?"

"I want you to be my Mate," I blurted out, staring down at the floor, my face burning. Emanuel stopped us and gently lifted my face, his eyes shining.

"Are you ready?" he whispered.

I cupped my hands around his. "I want to be, so . . ."

He grinned and rested his forehead on mine, pulling me closer.

"Just so we're clear - we're the new progressive version of Mated - not the traditional kind," I said. "I'm definitely not ready to . . . you know."

Emanuel giggled. "Okay then, Progressive Mate of mine. What about kissing?"

I slammed my lips against his and the dancers around us stopped to cheer. Emanuel laughed through his kisses like before but held strong. He tasted like a half-eaten cookie and like a huge burden was finally lifted off my back.

AMY

Tom and I hooped and hollered as Emanuel and Norman kissed on the dance floor. *It's about freaking time*, I thought.

As they parted, Tom and I went back to our dance. I had given Adam my cane for safekeeping, and Tom was doing a pretty job of supporting me without it.

"You look gorgeous," he whispered.

I flushed. "Thank you."

He spun me, making the dress sparkle in the lights. We danced until the sound changed to something more upbeat, and then I retired to the snack table. Adam and I laughed as Tom made a spectacular fool of himself dancing out on the floor. He returned as the song changed to another slow one.

"So, I've got news," Tom said, suddenly smelling of nerves. I raised my eyebrow.

"What's up?" He looked up at the other people around us, swallowing.

"Um . . . can we go talk where it's quieter?" Mystified, I let him lead me out into the hallway. He paced, running his fingers through his hair, his nerves smelling worse and worse. *Oh my gosh, is he breaking up with me?* I thought.

He faced me and grabbed my hands.

"So, you know I've been waiting to hear from Duncan. He finally got back to me, and the mayor made me a deal. There's an old hotel on the beach a few miles away from here. He offered to buy it so I can turn it into a group home for the refugee families."

I covered my hands with my mouth.

"And he's also on board with helping me to get my social worker certifications so I can run it. This way, the kids won't have to go into foster homes all over the place. We can keep them all here. I'm also going to ask Sam if she wants me to officially adopt her. If you're okay with that."

"Why wouldn't I be okay with it?" I asked. "They're actually going to let you?"

"Well, normally, no. But this mayor guy is pulling a lot of strings for me. There is one string attached though," Tom admitted, running his hands through his hair. "Duncan kept preaching about how kids should grow up in a household with two parents, so . . ." I blinked as he trailed off.

"Tom, are you proposing to me right now?" I asked. He swallowed once. Then again.

"I think so," he whispered. I couldn't help but laugh.

"You know this is technically our first date, right?" I asked.

"I know," he said. "I don't even have a ring. And I know we're still getting to know each other but . . . maybe in a few years? Duncan said I had to at least ask," he said.

"You are the most awkward person on the planet, you know that right?" I said.

"So . . . is that a yes?" he whispered, sweat running down his face.

I never thought I would get married. How could I get married if no merfolk wanted to be with a Cursed? If I wasn't allowed to love humans? Then again, I never thought I would be at my senior Winter Formal Dance with my markings displayed either. I never thought I would have the opportunity to be a mom - biologically or otherwise. I never thought I would survive the lab. I never thought I would survive the Rebellion. I had my whole, wonderful life ahead of me to live to the fullest as a free merfolk.

All with the annoying twerp from next door.

"Yeah," I whispered. "Sure. Eventually – I mean." Tom's nervous smell changed to joy and relief as a boyish grin lit up his face. It made him smell like flowers.

We returned to the dance without anyone noticing we had been gone. The night passed by like a dream, a blur of awkward dancing and stolen happy smiles. Emanuel and Norman were inseparable. Adam stayed calm from the sidelines. Tom wouldn't shut up about all the plans he had for the group home - saltwater pools and dozens of rooms - a huge kitchen - quarters for the workers if they wanted to live there - it was going to be incredible.

We still had a lot of work to do. There were still plenty of people who hated merfolk. There were lots of homeless merfolk. The group home would take a while to build. But we were one step closer to making the world right again. I was technically engaged to a human who loved me for the merfolk I was. And more importantly, I was learning to love the merfolk I was.

We may have started the mess, but we fixed it. And thousands of merfolk all over the world were better off for it.

Getting stuck in that trap was the best thing that had ever happened to me.

After the dance, Tom offered to take us all back to his boat for old time's sake. We arrived at the docks in chaos. A figure I hoped I'd never see again stood in the middle of the chaos, nose to nose with a tiny Caspian holding the Protector's staff like a javelin. The rest of the merfolk stood behind him, shouting and pointing.

"Oh fuck no," Norman growled, rolling up his suit sleeves and diving into the crowd. The rest of us followed him. His poisonous spines grew out of his arms and back, ripping through his suit. He threw himself in front of Caspian, baring his teeth. The figure smirked as the rest of us caught up.

"What are you doing here, Mercer?" I demanded. Emanuel planted himself next to Norman, hands balled into fists. Caspian's father appeared from the crowd, yanking the staff from his son's grasp.

"Speak," Caspian's father demanded.

"Why the cold welcome?" Dr. Mercer asked.

"You don't belong here," Caspian hissed from behind Norman. "You spread lies. You hurt members of your species."

Dr. Mercer narrowed his eyes at Norman and his new Mate. "Surprised to see you show your face again," he said.

"Get fucked," Norman spat. Mercer's sharp teeth flashed in the light, and he took a step forward. Before I could blink, Adam had planted himself between his friend and Mercer, poised, ready to fight.

"You're missing your sword," Mercer taunted.

"I don't need one to fuck you up," Adam hissed. Despite the tension, my heart swelled with pride. My boys were back to normal.

"I'll ask one more time - what are you doing here?" I shouted. Dr. Mercer turned his cold eyes to me.

"I want to offer your little crowd of refugees a choice," he said. Whispers raced through the crowd. Tom blinked.

"I know all of you think the battle is over," Dr. Mercer continued. "But it has barely begun. Just because you are free on paper doesn't mean the humans are going to treat you any better. Many of you have lost your

166

homes, your jobs, your savings. These humans are making you start completely over in the name of freedom." He pointed out to sea.

"There are more merfolk in the sea than you think. *True* merfolk, who uphold our sacred traditions and beliefs." He took a moment to glare at me and Norman in turn.

"You will only be free if humans are far away from us. I am offering you a different sanctuary - a place where humans really will never find you. You'll be safe from them. Forever."

What the hell? I wondered. *There are other groups of merfolk in the ocean? They have an even better hiding place than the Sanctuary?* I exchanged glances with Tom. He remained silent, but I could feel the turmoil of emotions in his gut. Behind us, whispers spread through the crowd. Some of them sounded intrigued.

"These merfolk are welcome to return with us to the Sanctuary," Caspian's father said.

"Are they? How long have they been wanting to leave? How long have you been telling them to wait?" Dr. Mercer sneered. "I'll take them to their new homes *tonight*."

The whispers increased. *What psychos would want to join him?* I thought. *These merfolk all know they've been lied to. That their history wasn't really what Dr. Mercer said it was.*

"I will also remind you that your town's mayor has now made it mandatory for you to show your markings in public," Mercer said. "I'm sure that will go well for everyone."

Wait, the mayor did what? I thought. I turned to Tom, who had paled. The sour smell of his guilt washed over me.

"You knew about this?" I asked. He flinched as if I burned him.

"I saw it on the news earlier, but I didn't want to upset you," he said. *Most of us show our markings anyway,* I thought. After years of hiding, it was a relief to not have to hide them. But there were probably still merfolk in hiding who don't feel the same way. *And if humans can see our markings, they can decide how to treat us before even getting to know us,* I thought. That doesn't bode well.

"Are you ashamed to show your markings?" I asked Mercer.

"Are you free if you're required to identify yourselves?" Mercer demanded. The concerned whispers turned angry.

"This is your only chance. Come with me now, and I can promise that your family will be safe and hidden from humans and Cursed. Our history and traditional morals will be upheld." Dr. Mercer said to the crowd. All across the deck, eyes flitted back and forth.

Mercer slowly made his way to the edge of the deck. As he did so, merfolk trickled out of the crowd, following him. Caspian's father looked on with large eyes as more merfolk joined the flow. I grabbed Tom's arm.

"We need to do something," I whispered. "Tell them about the group home. Tell them they'll have a place to stay!"

Tom locked his jaw. "It'll be a long time before it's ready," he muttered. "It's their choice. If they don't want to be here, let them go."

Mercer smirked at Caspian's father, whose face had fallen. "Got a problem with this, Protector?"

"These people are free to go wherever they please. But only one of us here is upholding any true traditions," Capsian's father said.

Mercer narrowed his eyes. "We'll see about that." With that, he turned around and dove back into the water. Others jumped in after him. By the time movement had ceased, less than half of the crowd remained. Many of them were children. Tom turned to face the crowd.

"Don't worry," he said. "I know things seem bleak, but I promise you all will be taken care of."

"Where the fuck are we supposed to go?" a teenager spat. Tom reached over and grabbed my hand.

"We'll create our own Sanctuary," Tom said. "Right here on land."

Part Two

Five Years Later

"Among the monsters, I am well hidden; who looks for a leaf in a forest?"
~ Angela Carter

Department of Health and Human Services 126 - 254

All humans infected with the merfolk virus must make their markings visible in public spaces.

Department of Health and Human Services 126 - 257

Any human guardians of minor children infected with the mermaid virus maintain the right to relinquish custody until the age of adulthood without consequence.

Department of Health and Human Services 126 - 258

No human infected with the merfolk virus may intentionally infect another human.

GRAYSON

"Why are your brake lights on? This is the *school carpool* lane. You drop off your kid and go! What the fuck are you doing?" Norman slammed his hand against the horn, and the mom in the car ahead of us turned to give us a disgruntled look. Norman responded with a middle finger.

"You are aware that I got detention for flipping someone off the other day, and you yelled at me for it," I reminded him.

"You are the exact reason I hate kids." The car in front of us finally moved, and Norman pulled forward.

"You should've let me get shot, then," I retorted. He smirked as I gathered my stuff and stepped out of the car. As usual, a thousand smells and feelings registered, none of them particularly pleasant. Body odor masked by axe, sickly sweet perfume, angst from kids nervous about a test or talking to a crush, and teachers filled with dread all marinated together in the heat.

"Have a good day. Don't you dare get in trouble," he said. I slammed the door shut and began my walk towards class. *Only one more year of this place*, I reminded myself. *Then I'll be off to high school. Things will be better then. I hope.*

The girl who had gotten out of the car in front of me turned to give me a dirty look similar to her mom's.

"Tell your stupid freak dad to learn some patience!" she spat before vanishing into the crowd.

"He's not my dad!" I shouted. *My dad is in the middle of the freaking ocean with my mom because they lost everything.*

It had been five years since the Supreme Court had realized my kind was technically human, and therefore deserved human rights. It had been five years since a teenage Norman had broken into my elementary school and carried me out in his arms as MCA officers shot tranq darts at us. It had been five years since my parents decided it was easier to follow a crazy stranger to live in the middle of the ocean than start completely over. It had been five years since my older brother had refused to spend his life counting fish and begged Amy and Tom to let us stay with them. It had been five years since my brother became my dad, along with Norman, Emanuel, and the others.

I made it to my homeroom without pissing off any other strangers and started doodling in my notebook. My best friend flounced down beside me, smelling like salt.

"Why are you irritated?" they asked, pulling their brown curls out of their eyes. Delicate blue markings framed their dark eyes almost like glasses.

"Nothing. Drama in the carpool lane," I said. Another familiar figure walked by my desk, taking a moment to flick my pencil onto the floor. I resisted the urge to trip him, remembering Norman's hypocritical admonishment. Avery sent the boy a glare on my behalf. Reed turned around and stuck a middle finger up at us - which of course the teacher didn't see.

"Asshole," Avery muttered under their breath as the final bell rang. Our teacher, a portly grandmotherly figure with the smile of a bulldog, snapped her head up.

"What did I just hear?" she asked. Avery sunk in their seat.

"Nothing, ma'am," they muttered. Mrs. Hall harrumphed and turned around to write something on the board. I had considered complaining and requesting to switch classes a million times, but knowing how relieved she would be to get rid of me stopped me every time. Mrs. Hall would not win this battle. She was going to put up with me whether I liked it or not.

Thankfully, most of the other kids were nice to us - if not a bit clueless. You would think humans would be curious enough to do their research, but Avery and I got stupid questions on the regular.

Do you grow a tail when it rains on you?

You can't eat fish - that's like cannibalism - right?

Can you read my mind?

Are all merfolk nonbinary?

Whenever I complained, everyone else just told me to kill them like kindness, which I knew they didn't believe because merfolk can't be lied to. In truth - there was nothing to do other than suck it up and avoid them. It seemed there were as many humans willing to actively stand up for us as there were bullies. Any standing up would have to be done carefully and away from teachers lest my reputation get any worse.

I survived my merphobic math teacher and made it to my second class with my science teacher. As I walked in, she winked at me, which made me flush. *I just want normal teachers, is that too much to ask?* I thought as I sank into my front-row seat. As usual, she made a point of calling on me and praising my answers as the other human students sniggered behind their palms.

At one point, something hit me on the back of the head. I turned around to see stupid Reed grinning at me from his spot in the back corner. I opened the paper football that had fallen to the floor and gritted my teeth.

Fish freak

My blood boiled. The insult had grown in popularity over the years, which bothered me for several reasons.

1. I wasn't a fish. I was a mammal (if you're gonna insult me, at least be accurate)

2.   I wasn't a freak either. There was absolutely nothing wrong with being merfolk.

Screw it, I want to be petty.

"Ow, Reed. Stop throwing stuff at me!"

His grin morphed into a glare as Mrs. Miller turned on her heel and shot him a dirty look.

"Reed, do we have a problem?" she asked.

"No, ma'am," he muttered, sinking in his desk. As Mrs. Miller faced the board, I sent him a sweet smile. Reed never got in trouble. Most kids were afraid to mess with him because the teachers liked him so much.

I managed to avoid Reed's wrath and survive the rest of the day without incident. The weather was nice, so I sent a text to Norman to not bother picking me up so I could walk home to Atlantis.

Okay, it wasn't Atlantis out of the myths, but it might as well have been. After we had been freed, Amy and Tom had worked together to transform an old hotel into a gigantic group home for all the orphaned or abandoned merpeople. Atlantis was her official nickname.

Norman waved at me from his position in the guard tower by the water as I walked up the sidewalk. The front door opened into a huge lobby, chairs, and couches scattered about. To the left, the famous Amy Wilson paced in her office, rubbing her temple as she held up her phone to her ear.

"Ma'am, your home did not pass inspection. End of story. You cannot foster any merfolk if your home does not meet regulations . . . no ma'am, a bathtub does not count as a pool. Ma'am, I'm not going in circles with you anymore, goodbye." Amy tore the phone from her ear and white-knuckled it in her fist. For a moment, I thought she would chuck it through the window, but she took a deep breath and put it back in her pocket. I leaned against the doorway.

"I take it that family didn't work out?" I asked. She sighed, and I could practically taste the frustration on her breath.

Amy Wilson didn't look like someone who had sparked a civil rights revolution. The documentaries about her portrayed her as a wild teenager with fire in her eyes and a perfect physique. In reality, she had the vibe of a tired mom with the body of a teenage boy, which didn't at all match the cane she used to walk around the house. She often wore joggers and long sleeves, which she claimed were more comfortable, but I knew she did it to hide her scars from the little kids.

"All these people want to foster the little kids because they're so *cute*, and think they'll be just fine sleeping in a bathtub," she muttered. I bit back a smile, knowing that every soul here, save the humans, had probably slept in a bathtub at least once.

"Speaking of bathtubs, I'm going to go swim." I headed for the staircase and trotted down the steps to the basement level. On my way down, I spotted my brother, Will, vacuuming the carpet.

Like many merfolk, he had trouble finding a good-paying job. Amy had offered to let him become a part of the staff by working as a custodian. It wasn't a glamorous job, but he was saving for a future apartment so we wouldn't have to live off of handouts for the rest of our lives. He smiled at me as I ran past.

As usual, the basement was pretty empty at this time of day. Most of the residents here used the pool at night.

Calling it a pool was a bit of an injustice. When Amy and Tom renovated this place, their first priority was making sure everyone would have a safe place to swim - actually swim - not just soak. The floor had been ripped up and dug down to turn almost the entire basement into a gigantic saltwater pool. At the end of the steps was a sidewalk of concrete that extended around the perimeter. At the deepest end, it was forty feet down. Artificial caves had been planted on the walls, providing private spaces to hide. The caves even came with night lights.

I set my bookbag down by the laminator in the far-left corner and took out the notes I had taken earlier. Most merpeople would come down at night to sleep in one of the caves, but I preferred to be awake and use my time wisely by studying. Tom had bought the laminator a few years ago that let me laminate my notes so I could study underwater.

My brother was insistent I do well in school. He had had a difficult time adjusting after our parents left and dropped out with a GED. Instead of attempting to go to college, he started working right away and dumped all the pressure on me to get good grades so I could get into college and get a job good enough for the both of us.

With my notes laminated, I dove in, swimming to my usual cave. I ducked inside the entrance and let myself float until my back was pressed against the ceiling. I turned on the nightlight with the edge of my fin and started reading.

A little while later, more people began to filter in. I clamored out and ventured towards the gigantic living room. A few elementary schoolers lingered on the couch, staring up at one of the TVs. I raised my eyebrow as I came up behind them. The TV featured a merperson swimming through a cloud of reeds, their markings helping them blend in.

"As we can see, merpeople have incredible markings that help them blend in with their surroundings. They aren't the fastest creatures in the sea - but their incredible eyesight gives them plenty of quick reflexes." The merperson lashed out and snagged a fish from its swim before swimming out of frame with their prize.

"Why are you guys watching a documentary about us?" I asked. The boy shrugged.

"I want to see how accurate it is," he said. I chuckled as I walked away. *I wonder how much money merpeople get paid to be in documentaries like that,* I thought. I picked a couch and scrolled on my phone until the dinner bell rang.

It was literally a bell. I let the little kids run ahead of me as they raced for the cafeteria. Again, calling it a cafeteria didn't give it much justice. Amy and Tom made sure to have actual chefs on staff, and the food they prepared was ten times better than anything from the school cafeteria or anything my brother could cook in our little apartment.

That night was breakfast night. I loaded my plate with bacon and cheesy grits. I looked around for my brother, but he was nowhere to be seen. He often got stuck working late and missed dinner. Along with me.

I grabbed him a to-go plate and shuffled up to my apartment on the third floor. Amy and Tom had renovated it to make mini apartments for the few kids lucky enough to have family. I shoved the plate of leftovers in the fridge, ignoring the previous night's to-go plate, and curled up in my bed, scrolling on my phone. A notification from Avery popped up.

Did you hear about this?

I clicked on a link that opened up an article to another familiar face. He still looked the same as the day he had fought off the MCA guards – boyish and covered in freckles. He smiled at the camera, fully decked out in his fencer's outfit - whatever that was called. The caption read: *Will this merperson finally have a chance to compete?* I skimmed over the article. It was the same as others that had popped up over the years.

After Adam had graduated high school and learned to function with his PTSD, he had finally decided to join the Olympic fencing team. Although, his chance to officially compete was still being debated. Merpeople's safety was only guaranteed in the USA, so until the Games were held here, he was definitely out of luck. And whenever the USA did host them again, the ethics committee was still debating how fair it would be for him to compete.

They had tried a variety of things to make it "fair", including giving him a helmet and earmuffs to dull his senses. But no matter what they tried, the humans always claimed his victories were unfair. *Maybe one day*, I thought.

The door creaked open, and I jumped up. My brother dragged himself through the doorway, offering a weak smile as he plopped down at the table.

"I grabbed you a plate of leftovers," I said.

"Thanks, man, but I'm probably just going to go to bed," he said. "You get your homework done?"

I tried not to let my smile falter and nodded. "Yeah." He shut himself in his room and the light flickered off. I sighed.

He's trying to support you, I told myself. *Don't be ungrateful. He's sacrificing a lot for you. That's why you need to keep your act together and get good grades. So you don't have to stay in this tiny apartment for the rest of your lives. Besides, he's the only real family you have left.*

The next morning a knock on my door woke me up. I opened it to see Emanuel. He grinned and ruffled my hair. "Hey buddy, you look bored. Want to come out with me today?"

I instantly perked up. I definitely wouldn't be doing anything fun with my brother today, and I had nothing else to do but scroll on TikTok.

"Uh - duh." I quickly got dressed and followed Emanuel outside. Like usual, he wore a green vest with a thousand pockets filled with who-knows-what. If Norman was here, he would have called his Mate a nerd and then kissed him when he thought I wasn't looking.

After the Rebellion, Emanuel had graduated from high school and then college to become an environmental scientist. He ended up working for Mr. Duncan's biotech company - Biosyn. His research had something to do with tracking invasive fish species. On my lucky days, Emanuel sent me down with a spear and let me stab all the invasives I could find.

"Is Norman coming with us?" I asked.

Emanuel shook his head, motioning out to the dark water. "He's on guard duty all day."

While Emanuel had been off doing nerd stuff, Norman had graduated with no clue of what to do and plenty of pent-up rage and energy. Amy and Tom had offered to help him get a license to be an additional security guard for Atlantis, and he now spent most of his time patrolling the beach in his uniform and pistol to protect us from any potential threats.

Norman didn't exactly seem like the security guard type at a whopping five foot four and soft brown eyes, but I knew from experience he would fuck up anyone who dared mess with Atlantis. The only question that remained was why Amy even bothered with security guards. No human in their right mind would dare venture near Atlantis. Yet, she remained paranoid. *Just in case.* Whatever that meant. I mean sure, people at school could be mean, but it wasn't like they were lunging after me with nets or chains. Amy was probably a little bit too traumatized from the Rebellion.

Whatever, with Emanuel, I was free, at least for a little bit.

We climbed aboard his research vessel and chugged out to the open ocean. The farther we went out, the more tense Emanuel got. He tapped his fingers on the steering wheel, constantly scanning the horizon.

"Am I diving today?" I asked. He shook his head, and I deflated slightly.

"Nope, just fishing the old-fashioned way today." He brought the boat to a stop and started getting a drop net ready.

"After I pull up the net, I'm going to need your help sorting the invasives from the others. You see - I'm trying this new technique where you . . ." I tuned him out as he dropped the net into the sea. Five minutes later, he was still talking as he maneuvered the crane to pull up the catch. Only the sound of a violin from his pocket interrupted him. He groaned as he fished out his cell and held it up to his ear with his shoulder. His mom's voice came through the speaker of the phone. She didn't live far away and was currently fostering two merfolk toddlers along with her two other sons who were about my age.

"Hola mi nino, como estas?"

"Bien, mami. I'm kinda busy right now-"

I waded into the pile of wriggling fish, snagging one to eat as I started to scoop the invasive ones into a bucket.

"I know, I know, but have you talked to Norman about my *proposal* yet?" she asked. Emanuel's face immediately went white, and he promptly let his phone fall into the pile of fish. I raised my eyebrow as he smiled sheepishly at me.

"What was that about?" I asked.

"Nothing," he lied. "Don't worry about it."

"Yeah, okay." I didn't have time to think about what his mom's proposal could be about before something in the pile caught my attention. I waded through the fish and pushed others out of my way to reveal a large white tail.

A merfolk lay partially tangled in the net, eyes lidded. His entire body was white - from his tail to his eyebrows. The only color that showed up was a slight pink tinge to his irises.

"Whoa," I whispered. "I didn't know we could be albino."

Emanuel ran up behind me. "Hey kid, are you okay?" he asked. The merperson, probably not much older than me, shifted in the net.

"The sun," he slurred. His head swayed on his head like it was too heavy for him to lift. Emanuel and I exchanged a glance.

"Sorry?" Emanuel asked.

"The sun. It's . . . kinda hurting me." He shielded his face, and I noticed that the backs of his arms were burned.

"Let's get him out of the net and into the shade," Emanuel said, stooping down to untangle the ropes. I grabbed the merperson's shoulders and lifted him. His tail dragged awkwardly behind him as I pulled him into the shade.

"Thanks," he muttered, collapsing to the deck as I released him. He lay on his back, eyes closed, breathing heavily. *Where the hell did he come from?* I wondered. *He wasn't from Atlantis, maybe a kid who wandered too far from the Sanctuary? Or from Mercer's Tribe? I feel like I would have remembered an albino merperson.* I couldn't help but stare at his scales - almost translucent. You could see the web of delicate arteries through his tailfin. There was no hint of markings anywhere on him. Even his eyebrows were snow white.

"Is he okay?" I whispered.

Emanuel shrugged and bent down by his side. "Hey kid, what's your name?"

"Daniel."

"Are you hurt?" Emanuel asked. *Why isn't he phasing?* I wondered.

"Probably," Daniel said as his body started to melt back. I yelped as he did so, quickly averting my eyes.

Emanuel looked away as well. "Daniel, did you know you're naked?"

Daniel looked down at himself in mild surprise. "Am I? My bad."

I quickly grabbed a towel and threw it over him as the crease in Emanuel's eyes grew deeper.

"Can you sit for me, Daniel? I just want to make sure you're not injured." Daniel pushed himself up with some considerable effort. His ribs poked out from his pale skin a little too much, but other than that and the sunburn, he looked perfectly fine. As Emanuel knelt behind his back, the color drained from his face. The sour smell of fear stung my nostrils.

"Dammit, we need to go back to shore. Now."

I furrowed my brows. I walked around and stared at what made Emanuel so terrified. A black barcode had been tattooed onto Daniel's shoulder.

"What is that?" I asked.

Emanuel ignored me as he ran for the controls. "Call Amy, and tell her to call the police," he shouted.

Back on shore, Daniel sat on the edge of an ambulance as a cop interrogated him. Off in the distance, Emanuel and Amy talked in hushed tones, but I could feel the rage radiating off Amy. It made her smell like Sour Patch Kids.

I tried my best to eavesdrop on the interrogation without looking nosy. Emanuel had refused to elaborate on what the black barcode could be for - and the albino kid had been way too out of it to explain on the ride to shore.

"Where are you from, kid?" the cop asked.

Daniel shrugged, leaning heavily on the side of the ambulance. "I dunno. The last thing I remember was swimming and getting caught in something. When I woke up, my head hurt, and I was in a tank."

The cop frowned. The medic ran his fingers through Daniel's long hair, feeling along his skull.

"Don't see any visible wounds or swelling. How long were you in that tank?" the medic asked.

"Maybe a few months?"

"Do you remember anything about where you were being held?" the cop asked.

"No one ever talked to me, but I remember hearing different voices. They opened the tank every day to feed me. I think the food was drugged because it always made me tired. A few days ago, they didn't latch the lid shut, so I ran for it."

I could smell his spike of guilt from across the beach. *He's hiding something,* I thought.

"Where were you being kept? What did it look like?"

Daniel shrugged. "I dunno. I'm blind."

Wait, he's blind? I wondered. The medic checking him over immediately looked into his eyes.

"I was born blind," he clarified. "You're not going to be fixing that anytime soon."

"Still, we'll need to check your head for internal injuries. It's probably the cause of your memory loss," the medic said.

"Were you ever harmed by anyone?" the cop asked. Daniel shook his head. The cop closed his notepad.

"Alright, go ahead and take him to the hospital. We can ask more questions later." The cop stood up and walked over to Amy and Emanuel as the ambulance sped off in the distance.

"Well?" Amy demanded.

"Kid's got amnesia. They're going to check out his head at the hospital, but I don't know if that's something that can be fixed. Other than that, he seems to be alright given the circumstances."

"Do you think he's from land?"

"Seems to be. Are you sure he wasn't reported missing?"

"I think I would've remembered an albino merfolk going missing," Amy muttered under her breath. "But I've never heard of one existing, let alone a missing one."

"Makes sense why he was trafficked. Rare one like that?" the officer said. Amy narrowed her eyes at the officer, who flushed in embarrassment. *Trafficking? What are they talking about? I wondered.*

"No offense," the officer said sheepishly. Amy rolled her eyes.

"I'm going to go to the hospital. Can you stay here and tell Tom what happened?" she asked. Emanuel nodded. I put on my best smile and tilted my head.

"Can I come with?" I asked.

"Sure. You can keep him company," Amy said. *Who cares about keeping him company, I just want to know what's going on. If Emanuel or Amy won't tell me what's going on, maybe I can get Daniel to talk.*

DANIEL

I let the doctors and nurses poke and prod me. Part of me felt like I should be more resistant, but my body still felt like it was swimming through concrete. It was all I could to keep my head from wobbling on my neck.

They didn't bother to explain what they were doing. They could have been pumping me full of more sedatives. They could've been the ones who kidnapped me to begin with, and I would have no idea. The thought was almost enough to jump-start my heart back to its regular rhythm.

Eventually, whatever they were injecting me must've been helpful because my head stopped wobbling, and my senses sharpened once again.

I could smell the cleaning products they cleaned the room with. I could smell the fabric softener on the doctor's scrubs. I could hear the beeping of machines echoing off the walls of the room, painting an outline for me.

I took a deep breath of relief. *I survived. I made it. I escaped.*

I refused to let myself think of why I had escaped.

Instead, I felt for the edge of my bed and gently lowered my feet to the floor, making sure I wasn't tugging at the IV in my arm. I shivered as I pressed my bare feet against the cold tile and slowly stood up.

I collapsed almost immediately.

"Legs out of use?"

My head snapped up as the source of noise moved in front of me. I wasn't sure, but it sounded like the kid who had found me tangled in the net on the boat. I nodded and heard his shirt rustle.

"If you're holding your hands out, I can't see them," I said. I held back a snigger as a flash of embarrassment radiated off the kid.

"Sorry, forgot." He tentatively brushed the top of my knuckles with his fingers, and I held onto his hands. I wobbled as he tried to help me up. I managed to balance for a few moments before falling back down on the bed.

"Thank you," I said. "Sorry, you had to see my junk earlier."

"I'm sorry you got kidnapped and put on display as a pet for months and lost your memory," he said. I shrugged, not entirely surprised he had listened to the cops interrogate me. I wondered who else already knew about what had happened.

"At least I don't remember most of it," I said. *That's not true,* I thought.

"But you remember more than what you told the cop," the boy said. *Dang it, he felt that.* "Relax, I won't tell anyone unless you want me to. But you're probably coming home with us, and you definitely can't lie to Amy," he said.

More nerves shot through me. I had heard tales of the gigantic safe haven for refugees run by the leader of the Rebellion. I had never imagined I would end up in her care. I wasn't keen to be on her bad side.

Unpleasant memories rolled through my head. For most others, being freed had been a relief. It hadn't mattered much to us who still had to hide.

"I was in foster care before I was kidnapped. I was pretending to be human, which is pretty easy when you have a disability like mine. Humans think we can't have disabilities," I said.

He sucked in a breath. "You know that's illegal - right? Well, I don't know about where you're from. In this town, you're required to show your markings in public places."

"I know. But I literally can't show my markings," I said. "What am I supposed to do - paint them on?"

"Fair enough. Do you think it might have been your foster family that figured it out and sold you?"

I shrugged. He asked the question with a sting in his words that made me think he hadn't had the best experiences with humans either. Then again, who had?

"I barely knew them before I was taken. And I don't remember much."

"Well, if they didn't, your foster family would have reported a missing human - not a merperson," he pointed out. "Maybe they have been looking for you."

I softened. "Maybe you're right," I admitted.

"You should tell Amy. She'll get to the bottom of it - believe me. And she won't let anyone else hurt you."

I smiled and nodded. "Thank you."

"My name is Grayson, by the way."

I waited a moment and smirked. "You're holding out your hand again, aren't you?"

"Damn it."

A few more hours of the doctors pumping me with fluids and a brain scan later, I was discharged. One of the nurses held my hand and pulled me to the parking lot like a dog on a leash, which I chose to put up with. Hopefully, I would never be around her again.

An unfamiliar person opened the door for me. Grayson hopped in as the car took off. Almost instantly, my stomach turned. *How long has it been since I've ridden in a car?* I thought. *I hope this person is a safe driver.*

"My name is Amy," the driver said casually. I instantly perked up. *The* Amy? She was the one chauffeuring me?

"Nice to meet you," I said. A short time later, I stepped out of the car, tasting the air. I could hear waves crashing in the distance. Grayson grabbed my hand like the nurse had, and I shook it off as politely as possible. This person I would be stuck with for a while – he needed to know.

"I can get around just fine," I said, wiggling my webbed ears. I wore my hair longer than most merfolk to obscure them. It helped me hear better.

"Do you use a cane?" Amy asked.

"It makes life easier, but I can get by fine without one," I said. I followed the sound of their footsteps to the house. Once inside, Amy pressed something to my palm.

"It's not a perfect cane, but you can use it until I find something better," she said. I nodded, chuckling silently. It felt like a cane that old men used to look sophisticated. I experimentally ran it over the floor in front of me, then decided it would be easier to focus on using my ears for the time being.

"So, you echolocate like a bat?" Grayson asked. I responded by thwacking him in the shin with the cane. I smirked as he yelped.

"Grayson! Be nice and show him around the house. Pick a room for him. Help him get settled and find some clothes. Dinner is in an hour," Amy said. I followed Grayson as he gave me a tour of the group home. I tried to keep track of all the turns, but the place was so massive I quickly lost track. It didn't help that Grayson was blabbering a mile a minute about all the other people who lived here. I recognized some other famous names, but it all jumbled together after a while.

We finally stopped in a room that smelled like a Goodwill.

"Do you care what clothes you wear?" Grayson asked.

"I go more by texture, believe it or not," I said.

"Well, start feeling some clothes then."

I ran my fingers along racks that lined the walls, searching for soft fabrics. I pulled one off a hanger and held it up.

"How's this look on me?" I asked.

Grayson chuckled. "Well . . . it may or may not have a picture of a fish on a hook that says *master baiter* on it."

I groaned. "Why do you even have that here?" I muttered, putting it back on the hanger.

Grayson laughed. "We get a lot of donations. They don't always get checked as well as they should. Let me help."

A few moments later, I had a pile of soft T-shirts and a few pairs of jeans. Grayson walked me back to my room and showed me around. I was shocked at how stocked the room was. There was a queen-size bed and even a mini-fridge in the corner. I had my own TV and bathroom too.

This is way better than anything I got in foster care. I should've quit pretending to be human years ago, I thought.

"Thank you," I said. "Do you know how long I'll be allowed to stay here?"

Grayson chuckled. "Um . . . forever? I mean, the goal is to get adopted by some sympathetic human family that's willing to put up with you. A lot more people are willing to adopt the older kids because we don't require as much babysitting. But I'll be honest, you're blind, so that lowers your odds."

"How many kids live here?" I asked.

"Right now? Maybe ten, and they're all little. Like I said, it's easier to take care of an older merperson than a younger one. And Amy is protective of where they go."

"Why aren't you adopted yet?" I asked.

"Don't need to be. My brother is an adult, and he's my legal guardian. We live in one of the apartments on the next floor up."

I detected a hint of resentment in his voice. "What happened to your parents?" I asked. The resentment intensified.

"Fucked back off to the ocean instead of starting over with us. Haven't seen them in years. You?" he asked.

"My mom went back. Never met my dad."

Grayson cleared his throat. "Well, I'll let you get settled. I'll come grab you for dinner in a little bit." He shut the door behind him, and I sank into my new bed. *Finally*, I thought. *I can relax.*

That hope was shattered a second later as someone knocked. I held back a groan.

"Come in," I said. An unfamiliar set of footsteps walked in, shutting the door behind him. I sniffed the air. The newcomer was human.

"Hi, Daniel. My name is Tom."

Wow, another famous person, I thought. I waited and then smiled. "Are you holding out your hand?"

"Oops. Sorry, guess handshakes aren't your thing, huh?" Tom said. The mattress shifted as he sat down next to me.

"Well, I just wanted to introduce myself. We're happy to have you here," he said. I nodded.

"Thank you for helping me," I said. Something lingered in the air that told me Tom wasn't only here for a warm welcome.

"I wanted to ask you a favor," he said, stretching out his words. "And just know I'm asking Grayson the same thing."

"Okay?"

"Can you keep the story of how you got here . . . PG? And not mention the whole . . .", he trailed off, and I debated whether to feel disrespected or relieved. *He doesn't want anyone to know I was kidnapped*, I thought.

"Amy just doesn't want to scare the younger kids that are here," Tom said. I nodded, leaning towards feeling relieved.

"I understand. To be honest, I don't want to talk about it a whole lot either," I admitted. *I don't want to talk about how I escaped.* Tom breathed a sigh of relief.

"Good. I appreciate it. We can get that tattoo removed. We have counselors working on staff if you ever decide you do want to talk about it - okay? We'll make sure you're safe here. And we're going to get to the bottom of who did this to you."

I shivered and nodded. Secretly, I hoped they would never find who caught me. They couldn't find out about what I did - if I had even done what I thought I had.

It could ruin everything.

Data Log 12:39 AM

Brain scans from the volunteers have shown that merfolk have ten times the connections in the amygdala - explaining the ability we have to sense emotions from other people.

Further tests have shown the amygdala is closely linked to the olfactory bulb and parietal lobe, explaining why many merfolk describe others' emotions as smells rather than feeling, and why they are more easily able to sense other emotions through physical touch. It's like a sort of synesthesia.

Such an ability would make merpeople excellent candidates for policemen, interrogators, judges . . . not that humans would be freaked out by us any less . . . it's hard enough for many of us to get normal jobs. But just think of how useful we could be if we were just given the chance.

GRAYSON

Tom had taken a seat across from me in the cafeteria and he was trying awfully hard to look more sympathetic than he deserved after what he had dared just ask me. I crossed my arms as he stuck out his bottom lip in an attempt to appease me.

"You're telling me that merpeople getting kidnapped and used for personal zoos have been a thing for a while now?" I echoed.

He winced. "Yes."

"And you and Amy have been keeping it on the down-low this entire time?"

He winced again. ". . . Yes"

"I'm sorry, but if merpeople being trafficked is this big of an issue - then shouldn't everyone know?" I asked. Amy's paranoia and insistence on keeping security guards suddenly made perfect sense. How long had this been going on? How many kids had been kidnapped that she had neglected to tell us about?

Tom shushed me, looking around the cafeteria for anyone who might be listening in. He sighed like the burden of explaining this to me might crush him.

"I don't want to scare the little kids. Knowing won't help them be any safer than they already are. This is why we have guards on duty and keep the doors locked."

"So, you want me to *lie*?"

"It's not lying. It's just not talking about it."

This is some BS, I thought. If Tom wants me to fib the truth about how bad the trafficking problem is, what else could he be lying about?

"Please, Grayson. Daniel said he didn't want people to know what happened to him either. If you won't do it for me - do it for him."

I held back a groan. Tom was great at delivering perfect doses of guilt trips.

"Fine. But you and Amy need to be honest," I said. "Especially if this gets worse."

Tom smiled, but I could feel the lie radiating off of his teeth. "We will."

. . .

The next Monday, I escorted Daniel through the middle school doors. More than one person stopped to stare – eyebrows raised. Most glances went to his white hair or his new cane tapping on the floor. *At least he can't see everyone looking at him*, I thought.

We stopped by the lockers, and I realized the one they had assigned to Daniel was useless as Avery walked up.

"Avery, this is Daniel. He just . . . moved in," I said, hoping they wouldn't ask any probing questions. I waited for Avery to extend their hand and get laughed at, but they just stood there.

"Hi Daniel," they said, lacking the usual cheer to their voice. The bell rang, disrupting the awkward silence.

"Can you show me to my class?" Daniel asked. He followed me down the hallway through the whispers of the other kids. Avery grabbed my arm as soon as I made it back. I winced as their sharp nails dug into my skin.

"Ow," I complained.

"What's wrong with him?" they demanded.

"Daniel? I mean . . . he's blind and albino but -"

They waved me off. "Not *that*. He smells weird."

I blinked, not comprehending the venom in their voice. I mean, I supposed he smelled a little different than a typical merperson. But that was probably from being held captive for who knew how long or being in the hospital. Avery groaned as I stared at them.

"Seriously? You haven't noticed anything off about him?"

I couldn't exactly explain how his origins made him smell different without breaking a lot of promises.

"No? I mean, he seems pretty normal to me," I said.

"Something just seems weird," they said. "He doesn't smell like a typical merperson. Be careful around him."

Mrs. Hall rapped on the board, and the class went silent. As I chugged my way through math problems, Avery's warning replayed in my head on repeat.

There's not something off about him, right? Given the circumstances, he seems shockingly normal, I thought. *They're just being paranoid. Daniel's fine.*

I survived first period but unfortunately, Reed found Daniel in the hallway before I did. Daniel had tucked his hair behind his webbed ear – which was gathering much more attention than his lack of pigment or cane. Reed sniggered to his friends as he walked up behind him. I groaned and started walking in their direction.

Just as Reed was about to reach for Daniel's ear, Daniel turned and firmly planted the tip of his cane on Reed's chest. All motion in the hallway stopped as students' jaws dropped. Daniel stared right at Reed's frozen face, a smile playing on his lips.

"I can hear you," he said, slowly lowering his cane to the floor. *Ha, take that loser,* I thought. *Teach you to mess with the blind kid.*

Reed quickly backed off. We survived the rest of the day without incident and made it back to Atlantis. No sooner had we sat down on one of the couches than a knock sounded on the front door. Only one visitor knocked like that.

I got up and opened it to reveal a darkly tanned blond, eyes wide and full of wonder like they always were. He grinned and waved vigorously.

"Hey Caspian," I said. *I wonder what he's doing back here,* I thought.

After Mercer had taken the "traditional" merfolk back to god-knows-where in the sea, Caspian's father and the rest of their group returned to the Sanctuary. Caspian occasionally traveled back to bring news and catch up. He never ceased to be enthralled with human stuff. He was like a blond Ariel. One time, Amy had scolded me for convincing him forks were used for combing hair.

"Hello, Grayson!" He stepped inside, and Amy poked her head out of her office.

"Who is it?" Daniel asked.

"Caspian, this is my friend Daniel. He just . . . he just got here. Daniel, this is Caspian. He's the Protector's son from out at the Sanctuary," I explained. I had originally become acquainted with Caspian when I was rescued. He was a few years older than me and had been busy trying to comfort all the kids who had been rescued - most in rougher shape than I was. Now, he was seventeen - the same age Amy had been when merpeople were given their rights back.

I had been assigned the job of being his unspoken babysitter whenever he visited after that one time he went on a walk by himself and almost got hit by a car. He stared at Daniel sitting on the couch and walked up to him.

"You smell funny," Caspian said. Daniel tensed, and I rubbed the bridge of my nose. *That's two merpeople who have said Daniel smells weird,* I thought.

"He can't see," I said, as if that was an excuse.

"Oh!" Caspian waved his hand in front of Daniel's face and giggled when Daniel didn't react. "Why can't you see?" Caspian asked. "Is there something wrong with your eyes?"

"I was just born with it," Daniel said. "It's common for albino people to have vision problems."

"What's albino?"

"It just means I don't have any color in my skin. That's why my markings don't show up," Daniel said. Caspian reached out and touched Daniel's hair, a puzzled expression on his face.

"Interesting," he murmured. I gently removed his hand as Daniel tried to smother a laugh.

"What are you doing back so soon?" I asked. At this, Caspian's smile faded. He turned to Amy.

"Just . . . wanted to visit," he said. *Sanctuary merpeople are the worst liars,* I thought. *They've barely had any practice.* He placed his hand on Amy's shoulder and mouthed something. I frowned. Amy nodded and they walked to her office. Caspian clasped his hands behind his back, his knuckles white. He smelled tenser than he normally did.

I knew it was difficult making the trip back and forth, and his visits had become more frequent. The swim alone took almost a week, and it was risky swimming in international waters. I wondered more than once why his parents let him travel by himself, but whenever I tried to ask, he deflected with a smile that didn't hide his stress.

They disappeared into her office and shut the door. Tiptoeing, I sidled up against the wall and pressed my ear against it, straining to hear their hushed conversation.

"The . . . worse . . . not sure . . . time."

"Why . . . here?"

"Stubborn."

I pursed my lips, wondering if they could be talking about the trafficking problem when the door suddenly opened, toppling me to the ground. I yelped, rubbing the side of my ear as Amy glared down at me.

"Scram or learn how to sneak around better," she growled, slamming the door shut behind her. I sulked back to the couch, where Daniel sniggered.

"You're not very quiet, you know," he teased.

"Shut up. You have supersonic ears. You should go eavesdrop," I muttered.

"And why do you want to eavesdrop?" he asked.

I hesitated. "It's weird that he's been showing up more often. He seems worried. I wonder if there's problems going on out there."

Daniel shrugged. "I don't know man, but I'm sure if it's bad enough, they'll tell us what's going on," he said. *Yeah, right,* I thought.

A few hours later, they both emerged from the office. Amy gave me a knowing look.

"Grayson, why don't you take Caspian and Daniel out to do something fun?" she asked. At this, Caspian clapped and jumped like an excited little kid. I sighed.

"You'll need some human clothes if we go out in public," I said. I led him to the Goodwill room and convinced him to change out his skirt of reeds for a pair of blue jeans, a t-shirt, and flip-flops. He ran his fingers over the new clothes as we walked towards downtown, the tapping of Daniel's cane setting a beat to our footsteps. Caspian quickly lost interest in his clothes as he gawked at the passing cars and street signs. I tried to think of something fun to do that would be manageable for a merfolk who had barely seen land and a merfolk who had never seen anything. Daniel mercifully gave a suggestion.

"I could use a haircut, to be honest," Daniel said.

"That's a wonderful idea!" I said. "Caspian, have you ever gotten your hair cut before?"

"I cut it with a knife when it gets too long," Capsian said. *That's a no*, I thought. We turned a corner and entered a salon that smelled like Sweet Pea. A skinny blonde girl smiled and welcomed us in.

"Haircuts?" she asked.

I nodded. "Just them. This one has never had one before," I said, motioning to Capsian. He smiled and waved.

"So, you have trained to cut hair?" he asked. The stylist nodded, seeming to have connected the dots that this overly excited merfolk in front of her wasn't from land. Thankfully, she smiled and showed him her different pairs of scissors instead of telling us to beat it. Caspian oohed as he ran his fingers over them.

"I can make your hair look like anything. I can even dye it different colors," she said.

"You can make my hair change colors?" Caspian gasped.

The stylist chuckled and nodded. "Hop on up, hun. Let's get you started. Katie will get you in a minute," she said to Daniel. We sat down in the waiting room and watched the performance.

"What are your pronouns?" the stylist asked. Caspian blinked in confusion as I smirked. It was common for merpeople to look androgynous to the point of confusion, and Caspian was no exception.

"My pronouns?"

"She wants to know if you're a boy or a girl," I said.

"Why?" he asked.

"Humans care a lot about gender," I said. "She's just trying to be polite by not calling you a girl when you're a boy, or vice versa."

"Oh! I understand. I am male. But you can call me whatever."

The stylist seemed just as confused. "So, are you like . . . gender fluid?" she asked.

Caspian raised his eyebrow. "What's gender fluid?"

I sighed. "He's a guy; his name's Caspian. What he means is that it doesn't bother him if you accidentally call him a girl instead of a boy. Not because he's gender fluid or nonbinary or whatever - it's just that merfolk like him don't care if they get misgendered," I explained. The stylist blinked, still seeming confused.

"Why don't you guys care?" she asked.

"There's nothing wrong with being a girl," Caspian said. "Why would I be upset if you thought I was one?"

Daniel chuckled. "He's adorable," he whispered. "He's just like a little kid."

"Tell me about it," I said.

"Humans just see it as respectful if you call someone what they've asked you to," the hairstylist explained.

Caspian nodded. "So . . . what are you?"

The hairstylist shared an amused look with her coworker. "I'm a girl, so I go by she and her."

Caspian grinned. "I guessed right!"

They continued to chat as another white, blonde girl appeared and took Daniel for his haircut. I flipped through the magazines in the waiting area until Daniel returned, and with nothing else to do, we watched Caspian get his hair dyed.

An hour later, Caspian gawked at himself in the mirror. He turned around, giggling and pointing at his hair.

"Look! She turned my hair pink!" Indeed, the fringes of his blond hair were now a hot magenta-pink. I smiled, not wanting to crush his enthusiasm by pointing out that the salt water was going to ruin that color significantly once he returned to the Sanctuary. Oh well - might as well let him have his fun while he could.

We returned to Atlantis, and Amy gave me a look upon seeing Caspian's new hairdo. I just grinned and shrugged.

"You said to keep him entertained," I pointed out.

"I love it!" Caspian said. A smile broke over Amy's face.

"Well, I'm glad," she said. Caspian changed out of his human clothes and back into his skirt of reeds. He shook our hands before disappearing back into the ocean.

As we watched him swim away, Amy's shoulders grew tenser and tenser. I crossed my arms.

"Afraid he's going to get kidnapped and trafficked?" I asked.

"No. I mean . . . a little."

Liar, I thought. So, they weren't talking about the trafficking problem in her office. There was something else going on in the seas.

DANIEL

In some ways, living at Atlantis was the best thing that had ever happened to me. I was well fed, someone came and cleaned my room once a week, my laundry was done, and I had unlimited access to a luxury pool.

But the air tasted like a bomb about to go off.

Amy was always tense - which was understandable with all she had to worry about. But it had grown noticeably worse after Caspian's visit. I was pretty sure Grayson had noticed too, but he hadn't brought it up to me. I wasn't sure if he considered me a close enough friend to talk to about stuff like that - especially considering we had been told not to discuss the dirty secret that had brought me here in the first place.

Tom occasionally kept me posted on the investigation concerning my disappearance, but the questions only seemed to multiply. There was no sign of my foster family. The only records that existed of me in the group home were that of fake human me. All leads had gone dead, and the investigators didn't think it was worth much energy to keep pursuing it. Which was fine by me. If they never found out who took me or who sold me - they would never learn how I escaped.

Which was good because some people had already noticed there was something off about me. Caspian had pointed it out point blank, and I was pretty sure Grayson had noticed something too but chose not to say it out of the kindness of his heart. Maybe that's why he wasn't confiding in me about Amy's odd behavior.

I wandered around the hotel, trying to keep my mind off my paranoid questions by memorizing the layout. I traced my fingers along the plaques of the rooms, but most of the braille had been covered up by paper - probably with the occupant's name on it. If only my fingers were sensitive enough to read ink.

My paranoia suddenly came to a halt, a cold wave of resentment washing over me like ice water. I shivered and rubbed the goosebumps on my arms. Pleading voices trickled out from a closed door, and I recognized them as Norman and Emanuel.

"Norman, can we talk about this?" Emanuel asked, his voice strained. Norman breathed a huffy sigh. I could practically hear him cross his arms.

"I don't see why it's important," he muttered. I could feel Emanuel deflate from across the room.

"You don't see why us getting married is important? Why not?"

I winced on Norman's behalf. His pacing stopped.

"We're basically already married," Norman said. "We're Mated, which is like being married on steroids. We have been for years. Why do we need to get married on top of that? Is this really something you care about, or is it just your mom pressuring you?"

"I mean . . . I would like to be able to call you my husband too," Emanuel muttered.

"Is being my Mate not enough?" Norman asked.

Emanuel groaned. "You know it's not about that! Getting married would mean a lot to me. A lot to my family. It's a way to celebrate. To show that we're official. It's not like the government acknowledges Mates!"

"The government didn't acknowledge gay people for a long time either," Norman said. "Why do we care what the government thinks?"

"Fine. Never mind then."

Rapid footsteps sounded on the carpet, and I hurriedly backed down the hallway and back the way I came as the door slammed open and shut.

Cool, more stress, I thought. Whoever had stormed out of the room was headed in the same direction I was, so I hurriedly found a stairwell and booked it down to the main floor.

I pretended to play it cool and sat on a couch, fiddling with the new phone Tom had got me. Others milled around, watching what sounded like a merfolk documentary on the big TV screens. Whoever had left the room behind me walked out from the stairwell, and I desperately hoped I didn't smell guilty. *I'll just stay here for a bit and then go back up to my room, and no one will know I was eavesdropping,* I decided.

"Oh, hey Sam," Emanuel's voice said. "What are you doing here?" *The* Sam? I thought. *The smart one?*

"Just wanted to come by and see you guys," she said. "Where's Norman?" Emanuel sucked in a breath.

"Taking a nap upstairs," he said through his teeth. "Does Amy know you're here?" Sam's energy quickly shifted.

"I haven't said hi to her yet," she admitted.

"Uh-huh. Look, Sam, you know how things are right now. I wouldn't push it."

"I'm not pushing anything. I just want to talk to the new kid for a minute," she protested. I perked my head up.

"Are you guys talking about me?" I asked. They both jumped as if they had just now noticed me sitting on the couch a few yards away from them.

"You must be Daniel," Sam said.

"If you're sticking your hand out, I can't see it," I said, trying not to sound irritated.

"I know." *Surprising,* I thought. "My name is Sam," the stranger said. "I was wondering if I could ask you a few questions."

In the background, Emanuel's footsteps faded away. I wondered if he was grabbing Amy so he could tattle that Sam was here. *Why would Sam wanting to ask me some questions be a bad thing? Why would Amy be upset that she was here? Wasn't Sam her adopted daughter?*

"Sure," I said. The couch settled beside me, and I heard the scratch of a pen on paper.

"Were you born blind?" she asked. I raised an eyebrow in surprise again. I had expected her to ask questions about my captivity.

"Um . . . yeah."

"Any vision at all?"

I shook my head.

"Would you say that being blind has enhanced your hearing at all? How do you navigate underwater?" She continued to pester me, all the while taking notes. She reminded me of the doctors who had interviewed me after my rescue.

A new pair of footsteps sounded as she asked me one final question.

"Would you mind if I took a blood sample? I would be interested in studying your genetic differences."

The footsteps suddenly stopped.

"Sam."

The couch shifted again as she turned towards the source of the steps. Sam suddenly smelled like she had been caught in a bear trap.

"Hey, Amy," she said, quickly standing up. *Ah, so Emanuel was tattling*, I thought. I felt a hand press down on my shoulder, the nails dangerously close to digging into my skin.

"Daniel, why don't you hang out with Grayson for a bit," Amy said, nearly shoving me off the couch. Mystified, but relieved to have an excuse to not answer Sam's question, I nearly ran from the room. I used my memory of the twisted hallways to find Grayson's apartment. He laughed as I told him what had happened.

"Yeah, that sounds about right. Tom legally adopted Sam, which technically makes her Amy's adopted daughter too - but things have been tense between them for a while. Sam works for Duncan at Biosyn and she exclusively studies merpeople. But that's a little hard to do without willing participants or bodies."

"Bodies?" I echoed.

"Yeah. Sam goes around to every merperson she can find, asking for blood samples, skin samples, scale samples. She's even gone to people asking them to donate their loved ones' bodies or skeletons after they've died," Grayson whispered.

My skin prickled. "That's . . . kinda gross."

"It is. I mean - I kinda get it because how is she supposed to study merpeople without merpeople to study - but it makes a lot of merpeople uncomfortable. Especially when she asks kids *here* to donate."

"Do they?" I asked.

"I mean, some of the older kids have signed up to donate blood or go in for an examination, but they keep it under wraps because it makes

Amy upset. Hell - it kinda makes everyone upset. A lot of merpeople see Sam as this sort of traitor against us because she experiments on us like the humans used to."

"But I mean - she's not like dissecting us against our will or anything. She's not like the humans," I said.

"*We* know that. The older merfolk don't, though," Grayson said.

I shrugged. "Yeah, I guess that makes sense."

"So, what did she ask you to donate?"

I went tense again, then tried to relax so Grayson wouldn't notice. "A blood sample. And she asked me a bunch of questions about being blind and albino."

"Makes sense. Your genetics must be even weirder than the rest of ours. No wonder she wants to study you."

I laughed, but the sound was uncomfortable. I didn't know if what was wrong with me lurked in my genes, but I wasn't keen to find out. If Sam had been smart enough to figure out the merfolk virus as a thirteen-year-old kid, I knew she would be able to spot whatever lurked in my DNA. It wasn't worth the risk.

Grayson hesitated a beat and then reached out and grabbed my hand. I jumped in surprise. Merfolk holding hands to help one another regulate emotions was normal, but no one had offered to hold my hand the entire time I had been there.

"Seriously, if it bothers you, don't let her. She'll get over it," he said. I nodded and squeezed his hand back.

"Thanks," I said. A beat passed. *If we're friends enough to hold hands, surely we're friends enough to confide in each other about stuff, right?* I wondered.

"Hey, you're close with Emanuel and Norman, right?" I asked.

"Yeah. They're like brothers. Or dads. Somewhere in between there," Grayson said. "Why?"

"Well, I was wandering earlier and heard them fighting. I was just wondering if you knew anything about what's going on with them?"

"What were they fighting about?"

I hesitated, wondering too late if this wasn't my business to spill. "About getting married," I said.

"Married? Wait . . . proposal . . . *ohhh.*" Grayson let go of my hand to fling himself on his back, and I could hear him pulling at his hair. "That's what that phone call was about," he muttered.

"What phone call?"

He sat back up. "The day we found you, Emanuel was talking to his mom on the phone, and I overheard her saying something about a proposal. I didn't know what that meant until just now."

"Seems like Emanuel's mom wants them to get married," I said.

"And Norman didn't take that well," Grayson finished. "Dang it, I should go talk to them." He moved to get up, but I held onto his shoulder.

"Maybe let them both cool off a little first? Emanuel seemed hurt, and Norman was just offended by the whole thing. I also definitely do not want them knowing I ratted them out," I said sheepishly. Grayson sat back down.

"*Fine*. But those two are basically my family. They're not splitting up under my watch."

Data Log 5:59 AM

Today I watched the brain scans of the volunteers as they were lied to. As long as the human was aware that what they were saying was a lie - the merpeople could tell. If the human wasn't aware that they were lying, the merpeople couldn't tell. It seems possible that merpeople can be fooled into believing the truth if the human believes they are telling the truth - like beating a polygraph test.

Turns out we can be lied to after all. I hope Duncan doesn't know that.

GRAYSON

The next day in the carpool line, I took my time getting my bookbag on and let Daniel get out of the car first before crossing my arms and staring at Norman.

"So . . . you gonna propose to your boyfriend or not?" I asked. Norman's fingers turned white on the steering wheel.

"How the fuck do you know about that?" he demanded.

"Because you and Emanuel are usually all over each other and this morning at breakfast, you barely looked at each other," I said. *And not because Daniel overheard you arguing,* I thought. Norman sighed.

"Do we have to do this right now?" he whined.

"Respectfully, I'm not getting out of the car until you talk to me."

Norman swore and pulled off to the side so the other cars could pass him. He hesitated a moment before his angry expression melted.

"Am I the asshole here?" he asked.

I shrugged. "Does it matter? If it would make Emanuel happy?"

He groaned, hitting his head against the steering wheel. "Wanting a wedding is so *easy* for him. He has someone to walk him down the aisle and pay for everything!"

"Is that what this is all about? You're butthurt that your parents wouldn't be here to support you?" I asked.

"So what if I am?" Norman retorted.

I rolled my eyes. "Fine, have Emanuel's mom walk you down the aisle, and Emanuel's dad can walk him down the aisle. Case closed. Or better yet - walk each other down the aisle! It's not that hard."

Norman chewed on his bottom lip. "I just want being Mated to be enough for him," he said.

"I mean, I would say he feels that way considering that you've lived together and been Mated since you were sixteen. He's been with you for five years. He's not going to leave you over this, even if you are being an asshole."

Norman huffed. "Fine then. *If* we get married, how the fuck am I supposed to propose?" he asked.

"On the beach at sunset?" I suggested.

He crossed his arms. "That's like . . . the most stereotypical way for a merperson to propose ever," he pointed out.

"Well, you're merfolk aren't you?" I shot back. His gaze was withering. "Fine then, take him to his favorite restaurant. Put the ring in the dessert or glass of champagne or whatever," I said.

"That's even more cliche!"

"Then you come up with something!"

"Get out of my car!"

I finally got out of the car. "Seriously, man. Just think about it." I slammed the door shut and walked into the school where Daniel was waiting for me by the entrance.

"So, how did the ambush go?" he asked. I shrugged, then remembered he couldn't see me.

"I guess about as well as I expected it to go," I said. "We'll see how it plays out." We walked down the hall, and I settled myself on my desk. My phone vibrated, and I checked to make sure Mrs. Hall wasn't looking before taking it out, expecting a begrudging apology text from Norman.

It wasn't from Norman, it was from my brother, who I had barely seen for the past week since rescuing Daniel.

Sorry ive been gone so much bud but i just got another job

I grinned, rapidly texting back.

No way congrats! What is it?

Lifeguarding at that swim park uptown. Ill be gone a lot but it pays a lot better too and we get benefits. Wont need to be a janitor anymore

I quietly fist-pumped the air and turned around to Avery.

"My brother got a job!" I said. "Like, a real job."

They grinned and high-fived me. "It's about time! Doing what?"

"Lifeguarding down at that popular swim park. I guess their pools are saltwater, so it works out!"

Someone scoffed in the back of the room. "Sounds unfair to me." Against my better judgment, I turned around to face Reed, who sat with his arms crossed.

"I'm sorry? Did you just say it's unfair to hire someone who can breathe underwater to be a lifeguard?" Avery snapped.

"What if a human wanted that job? What if the people going there don't want to be rescued by a freak of nature?"

Don't sink to his level, I told myself as blood rushed through my ears. *He's ignorant, he doesn't understand, it's not worth it.*

"Do you know how long it's taken my brother to find any job because of humans like you?" I growled. *Oops.*

"It's discrimination to only hire a certain group of people," Reed shot back.

"You hire the person who's best for the job. And for any job that involves swimming, you hire the best swimmer. And I'm sorry, but merpeople are the best swimmers!"

"It's still discrimination. You're only giving jobs to a specific group of people because of how they were born. It's not fair!" he retorted. I slammed my hands down on the table.

"You want to know what's not fair? My brother has been begging for a real job for months, and no one will hire him because he's merfolk! What about the discrimination *against* merpeople? How many of you have had a merperson waiter? Or a merperson receptionist?"

The class fell silent. All I could hear was my heaving breathing.

"Exactly. Most companies don't like to hire merpeople to interact directly with other humans. Because we freak you guys out apparently. Merpeople only get jobs that allow them to do behind-the-scenes stuff. We're good enough to cook your food but not serve it. Or talk to you over the phone but not face-to-face."

Mrs. Hall crossed her arms. "Grayson, that is quite enough," she said.

"Technically, merpeople are a lot more likely to end up being cops or working for the FBI because they can tell if people are lying," another student piped up.

"That sounds like a conspiracy theory. I've never seen a merfolk cop," Avery said.

"It's because they all work behind the scenes!" the student argued.

"Prove it!" they shouted.

"There's literally a *real* merperson teaching at the high school," Reed said. "No conspiracy theory there."

"Oh wow, you come up with *one* example. The only reason he's there is because he got *shot* protecting one of his students during a MCA raid. He's paralyzed now, remember? They let him come back and teach because he's a hero. And still, there's one merperson teacher for how many merperson students? It's still not exactly a fair ratio," I said.

"Well, I'm sure the district would hire more merpeople teachers if they would just apply," Reed said.

"How are they supposed to apply when they can't go to college because their house and jobs were stolen during the Rebellion when they didn't have any rights?"

"And that's our fault?" he shouted.

"Yeah, maybe it is because if there were less humans like you who thought we were freaks of nature, my brother could afford to put food on our fucking table!"

Mrs. Hall slammed her hands against her desk. "Grayson. Office. Now," she growled. Reed smirked at me as I grabbed my stuff and stomped towards the door. *Good going, Grayson. Way to be cool about things.*

"Screw all of you," I muttered as I slammed the door behind me.

I spent the rest of the day in ISS and unfortunately, ran into Amy as soon as I walked in the door.

"I got another call from your school," she said, crossing her arms. I tuned her out as she yelled, keeping my eyes on the floor, the tightness in my chest building more and more. The Amy I watched in documentaries wasn't the one who yelled at me when I got in trouble at school. Documentary Amy had been just as likely to lose it on merphobic assholes, if not more. She never apologized for putting someone in their place. So why did she expect me to plaster a fake smile on my face and pretend being called a fish freak wasn't a big deal?

I nodded periodically until she was done talking and trudged back to my room, wishing it had been Norman who had been waiting for me. He might chastise me out loud, but at least I could tell he didn't mean it. He would just as soon go off on a merphobe and never apologize for it. At *least he still had the balls to stand up for himself.* I crawled into bed, part of me wishing I could go back in time and undo what I said, part of me happy I did it.

A little while later, someone knocked. I groaned, covering my face with a pillow.

"I said I'm sorry. Leave me alone," I muttered. The door creaked open, and Avery poked their head in, wiggling their eyebrows. I scoffed.

"Amy let you in here?" I asked.

"Norman let me in here," they clarified. "Why don't we have some fun with Reed and his buddies tonight?" I had no clue what Avery was planning, but it involved revenge, I wasn't going to question it. A few minutes of sneaking later, we were diving into the cold ocean water as the sunset. We stole through the dark, dodging dock supports and other sunken trash until we heard voices and distorted laughter.

I could see little feet hanging over the edge of a kayak, kicking and splashing in the water. I immediately recognized the smell of Reed and his friends. I grabbed Avery's arm.

How did you know they would be out here tonight? I mouthed.

Heard them talking about it at school, they mouthed back. Avery motioned for me to stay put and swam up to the surface. They delicately trailed half of their tailfin above the water, slowly circling the boat. It took the teenagers a few moments to notice.

"Hey, what is that?" Avery quickly ducked back under the surface, bubbles floating up from their mouth as they giggled. They swam to the other side of the boat and stuck their tailfin up again, this time leaving it up as the teenagers took notice again.

"Is that a shark?"

"No way man, shark fins don't look like that."

Smirking, I swam up and slammed myself into the bottom of their kayak. The confused comments turned to screams as it teetered dangerously.

"What the fuck man, something's coming after us!"

"It is a shark!"

"Go back to shore!"

I moved out of the way as paddles hit the water. Maneuvering carefully, I reached up and snagged one, nearly pulling the teenager into the water as I yanked it from his grip.

"Dude, something just stole my paddle!"

Avery swam to the other side and stole the remaining one, and we dissolved into laughter as the humans panicked above.

If only we had a camera, they mouthed. I handed them the paddle before slamming myself into the bottom of the boat one last time. The teenagers screamed, and I finally swam up to the surface, howling with laughter. Avery surfaced beside me, holding up the paddles.

"Looking for these?" they teased.

Two of the boys stopped crying to gawk. The look on Reed's face was priceless. His mouth dangled open before slamming shut, a vein pulsing on his temple.

"What the hell are you freaks doing out here?" he shouted. "Give us back our paddles!" I swam closer and held it out only to yank it back at the last second.

"Sorry, I don't feel like giving it back after what you called me at school today," I said with a big smile. The vein on Reed's forehead pulsed more.

"Well, that's exactly what you are! A fish freak!" he hissed. One of his friends tugged at his shoulder.

"Dude, just apologize so we can get the paddles back. My dad's going to kill me if we lose them," he whined.

I held the paddle by the edge of its handle. "Last chance. Apologize or paddles go bye-bye."

Reed scowled, white-knuckling the edge of the kayak. "You're gonna regret this," he growled. I let the paddle fall, and Reed's friend whimpered as he watched it sink into the inky depths.

"Then I guess you're swimming home. If only there was a human lifeguard to rescue you," I said.

Norman eyed us with suspicion when we got back, stupid grins stuck on our faces, but one glare from me was all that was needed to remind him he didn't have an excuse to push me. I went back to school feeling like I had finally grown a backbone, consequences be damned.

I could feel Reed's eyes on me during all of math and science. I finally got a break during lunch but had to face him again during gym. Our gym coach had a sub. We all waited impatiently as he stumbled through the attendance list. The sub finished calling roll and shooed us off to the locker rooms. I settled myself on the bleachers and opened a book. The sub walked over and crossed his arms.

"And why aren't you going in the locker room to get dressed with the others?" he asked. I blinked, not sure if this guy was messing with me or not.

"Um . . . I'm excused from the swim lessons."

He barked with laughter. "Excused? What, you're telling me that you can't swim?"

I tried not to laugh. "I can swim sir . . . but this is a chlorine pool."

"You can't handle a little chlorine?"

I sighed. *Why are humans so dumb?* I thought.

"He's trying to pull a fast one on you, sir. He's been swimming with us every day."

I looked up to see Reed poking his head out of the locker room, a twisted smile on his face. *What does he think he's doing?* I thought. *Everyone in class knows I can't swim in chlorine.* The sub harrumphed and pulled me to my feet.

"Nice try son, go get dressed."

I stumbled forward, nearly dropping my book in the water. "Sir, he's lying. I cannot swim in chlorinated water - it'll burn me!" I protested. "How do you not know that?"

"Don't tell me what I know! You go get changed right now or I'll call the Principal down here!" the sub threatened.

"Go right ahead!" I said. The sub's face turned a dark shade of purple as he walked away, muttering something into his walkie-talkie. I turned my glare to Reed, who looked like Christmas had come early.

"You know you're going to be the one in trouble when the principal comes down here, and I tell her that you were the one who lied to the sub," I said. Reed walked over to me, crossing his arms. Other kids filtered out from the locker room, taking turns staring at me and the angry sub. Their eyes reminded me of a crowd of spectators at a boxing match. A shiver traveled down my spine.

"You and your little fish freak friend nearly killed me last night!" Reed hissed, shoving me backward. I gasped as I narrowly avoided falling into the pool.

"Stop. Calling. Me. That." I shoved him back, and the small crowd of students oohed.

"Or what?" Reed demanded. "That's exactly what you are." I tried to shove him once more, but he blocked me and pushed me away. I yelped as his foot landed on my chest. I flailed backward, hitting the cold water behind me with a splash. I phased instantly, choking as the chlorine burned my gills.

Ow, ow, ow, *ow*.

The others around the pool laughed as I scrambled to pull myself up, gasping for breath and shaking. Reed was bent over at the knees, wiping tears from his eyes. I heaved myself out of the water, wincing as I phased back. I looked down at my arms and legs to see angry red marks. It felt like my skin had just been introduced to an air fryer. Everything stung, but not nearly as much as my pride.

"I'm going to freaking drown you!" I shouted, lunging for Reed's ankles. He hit the concrete with a thud as I clawed at his hair.

"HEY, HEY, HEY, SEPARATE NOW!"

Strong hands ripped us apart, yanking us to our feet. The cold eyes of the principal stared down at me.

"My office, now!" she snarled.

. . .

The nurse muttered under her breath as she applied cream to the burns on my skin. Bandages covered the worst ones, but they didn't erase the burning sensation trapped under my skin. I swallowed some pills she gave me.

"Who should I call?" she asked. I winced at the question. I knew that whoever she called was going to have a conniption. *Except Amy,* I thought bitterly. *She would probably tell me to apologize for falling into the pool.*

"My . . . call my brother." I gave her the phone number and after a few moments, she shook her head.

"Not answering. Anyone else?" *Of course he wouldn't answer,* I thought, instantly feeling guilty for thinking that way. He probably wasn't answering because he was at his new job.

"Call Norman," I muttered. The nurse muttered under her breath and crossed herself before dialing the number. I could hear him shouting over the other end. She motioned for me to leave the room, and I ducked out into the principal's office.

Reed sat in a chair across from her desk, looking rather pleased with himself. Principal Jones narrowed her dark eyes on me.

"Take a seat."

I sat down next to Reed and braced myself.

"Reed, why did you push Grayson in the pool?" Principal Jones asked calmly.

"Because he and his stupid fish friend attacked me and my friends in a kayak last night. They were trying to drown us," he said matter-of-factly. I threw my hands up.

"We weren't trying to drown you; we were just trying to scare you!" I retorted. "Believe me, if we wanted to drown you, we would have."

He pointed an accusing finger at me. "See!"

Principal Jones massaged the bridge of her nose. If she rubbed any harder, it would probably fall right off.

"Grayson, why did you and your friend pretend like you were going to drown Reed?" she asked.

"Because he keeps calling us fish freaks," I said.

She blinked. "And?"

"*And*? It's offensive!" I sputtered.

"How is it offensive? Aren't you half fish?" she asked. I could feel Reed's smirk burning beside me as I clenched my fists, forcing myself not to shake. They didn't deserve to see me cry. I wasn't half fish any more than they were half monkey. How did humans still not understand?

Thankfully, Norman chose that moment to barge into the office. His jaw was clenched so hard I thought it might fall off. He pointed at Principal Jones, chest heaving.

"Forgive me if I'm mistaken, but did you just tell my son that a human calling him a *fish freak* isn't a big deal?" he growled. Principal Jones put her hands up.

"And are you telling me that this same human student pushed my son into a chlorine-treated pool? A pool with chemicals that could have severely burned him?" Norman was shaking, and not afraid to point his trembling finger in her face.

"I don't know what kind of a show you're running here, but as soon as I'm done yelling at you, I'm taking my son to the hospital, and *you* are paying for his medical bills. And then I'm going to tell the school board about this and demand they make every damn employee in this district learn what counts as a slur." Principal Jones finally had the common sense to go pale and shut her mouth. Norman grabbed my shoulder and pushed me out of the office. We marched out to the car.

"I don't need to go to the hospital," I muttered. "The nurse already fixed me up." Norman spun and started checking under my bandages. His fingers were still trembling.

"If it starts to get worse, you tell me right away," he said. I nodded.

Norman swore the entire car ride home. He swore as he relayed the story to Amy. And then Amy swore under her breath.

"That was assault!" Norman seethed. "We need to press charges."
Amy turned her gaze on me.

"Grayson, do you want to press charges?" she asked. I swallowed. In truth, I had no idea if pressing charges would even do anything. What were the odds a lawyer would even look twice at my case? What were the odds that it would even deter Reed from messing with me in the future? I technically had been the one to threaten him first. Maybe Principal Jones couldn't punish me for trying to scare Reed off school property, but a lawyer definitely could.

I found myself shaking my head. "No," I muttered.

Norman's eye twitched, and Amy nodded. "Okay, then it's done. Go upstairs and get some rest, okay?"

I nodded and dragged my feet to my apartment. I could hear Norman and Amy arguing behind me. A little while later, Emanuel came up to my room. He sat down beside me on my bed and ruffled my hair like he normally did.

"Hey buddy, how are you feeling?"

I shrugged. "Itchy." I sat up and leaned against Emanuel. "I think Norman is mad at me," I said. Emanuel frowned and turned to look into my eyes.

"He's not upset with you at all. You know the both of us think of you as a son, right?" he asked. I nodded, remembering how Norman had called me his son in the principal's office. "Norman is very . . . sensitive . . . when it comes to humans hurting merfolk and not getting justice. I think he wishes that you would try to press charges."

"I don't think it would help," I said. *Or work*, I thought silently.

Emanuel nodded. "It's your decision. As long as it's what you want. Norman will get over it. Don't feel guilty, okay?"

"I think Amy's mad at me too," I whispered. "I mean . . . she literally started the Rebellion and wasn't afraid to tell humans or merfolk exactly what she thought, but now I'm not allowed to stand up for myself when people are being assholes."

Emanuel sighed. "Amy is . . . Amy has a lot of pressure on her shoulders," he said. "She's the only Cursed on the planet, and that makes her this sort of bridge between humans and merfolk. She tries very hard to keep that peace. And sometimes to keep peace, you have to bite your tongue and pretend that things don't bother you."

"So, I'm making her look bad," I muttered.

"Yup." Emanuel grinned, and I chuckled.

"I don't want to give our species a bad name," I said. "But I don't want to be walked all over either."

"I don't want you to be walked over, either. Being called slurs and pushed into pools is not okay. But . . . maybe leaving people stranded out at sea isn't the best way to make things better either."

"So how do I make it better?" I asked.

"Be patient. This Reed fellow sounds like someone who was raised in a household full of biased people. But people can change. I've told you how Norman and Tom used to be." I had a hard time imagining Reed suddenly being tolerant of merpeople, but I supposed crazier things had happened.

"Yeah, okay. As long as I don't have to marry the guy."

Emanuel laughed and then promptly stopped, a pained expression on his face. I winced.

"I know about the whole . . . proposal thing," I said. Emanuel ran his fingers through his hair.

"Has it been worrying you?" he asked.

I snorted. "Who cares about me? It's obviously been worrying *you*," I said.

"It shouldn't be. I know we're Mates but . . ." he motioned to his arms. "It's not like I can biologically adjust to him like he can to me. There's no physical sign on me that we are Mated, but a wedding ring could be."

"Did you tell him that?" I asked.

He shifted. "No . . . I just wanted him to want it because I wanted it. I guess that's pretty stupid, huh?" he asked.

"I mean, I'm only thirteen and know that communication with a romantic partner is important," I said dryly. Emanuel cracked a smile and ruffled my hair.

"We'll get it sorted out," he promised. "In the meantime, try to get some rest, okay?"

I was allowed to skip school the next day. I spent all afternoon alternating from lying in bed to trying to scrub the burning sensation out of my skin in the shower. I slathered myself in aloe vera, which helped more than whatever cream the nurse had used on me.

My brother came in when he could to check on me, but I could tell he was distracted with his new job. I didn't have enough energy to care. I made myself ramen noodles in the microwave and avoided everyone else as much as I could. I didn't want another lecture on making better choices or face Norman's disappointment.

The next night, the burning was finally fading, and I desperately wanted ice cream. I knew Amy kept her stash hidden in the freezer in the gigantic kitchen. I found myself slinking down around midnight and made off with the carton when I heard voices coming from Amy's office.

I paused and looked down the hallway. The air was heavy with tension as if a thunderstorm was about to break out. I raised my eyebrow and slunk closer to the door. When I saw who was inside, I forgot to breathe.

Sitting in Amy's office chair was Reed. He held his knees up to his chest and we locked eyes across the hall. He was surrounded by Amy, Tom, Norman, and Emanuel, all looking very worried.

What the heck is he doing here? I wondered. For a moment, I was convinced the others had kidnapped him and were torturing him on my behalf, but the look of worry on their faces made me pause. Norman noticed Reed staring at me and turned to see me in the hallway. I opened my mouth to ask what on Earth was going on but Norman grabbed me by the shoulder and pushed me away from the door.

"He's going to be living here," Norman said. My mouth fell open. I balled up my fists. Norman silenced me with a glare.

"I know it doesn't make sense, but he has to. And you're going to keep your mouth shut about it, got me?" he whispered. I couldn't help but gulp and take an involuntary step back. *What happened?* I wondered. *Wasn't Norman inches away from tearing this kid's head off just a day ago?*

"What is going on?" I demanded.

"Don't worry about it, okay?"

Don't worry about it? I wanted to scream. *He attacked me a few days ago! Why on Earth would anyone like him be allowed in a safe haven for merfolk?* Before I could protest anymore, Norman vanished back inside the office and shut the door.

I knew he would kill me if I meddled, but by God, I was going to figure out why that asshole was living in my house.

8:45: Bro . . . youre not gonna
believe what happened to my
little sister

8:45: Bro what

8:46: actually nvm its personal
she dont want me to tell. Forget
about it

8:47: lol ok then

DANIEL

"We need to figure out what's going on," Grayson said. I rubbed my arm where he had latched on and practically dragged me to the side of the school building after we were dropped off. Avery joined us a few moments later. With my permission, Grayson had spilled everything about why I was really there - the trafficking up to Reed's odd arrival at Atlantis. I was tense enough from Grayson's frantic stress wafting off him, but I couldn't shake the feeling that Avery was glaring at me.

You're being paranoid, I told myself. *You're here to figure out all the mysteries going on right now, and for once, those questions aren't centered around you. Be grateful.*

"And how exactly do you propose we do that?" I asked. There was a moment of silence, which usually meant the others were exchanging facial expressions I couldn't see.

"Well?" I demanded.

"I don't know where to start," Grayson admitted. "Maybe we can hack onto Amy's computer and see if there's anything in there?"

"Oh yeah, I'll be a ton of help looking at a computer," I said.

"Sorry. I don't know what to do. And it's driving me nuts that they won't tell me!" Grayson muttered. Something thumped, and he swore.

"I don't think punching the wall is going to help," I said.

"Okay, let's think about what we know," Avery said. "Amy's been acting more paranoid for a while now. Tom and Amy asked you both to cover up the whole trafficking thing with Daniel. And now merphobic Reed is living in your house and they refuse to explain why," they said. "Maybe it's all connected?"

"The only way Reed could be connected to trafficking merpeople was if he was the one doing it," Grayson muttered.

"How would a thirteen-year-old kid be involved with trafficking?" Avery asked.

"Why don't we try following him around at school? See what he's up to? Old-fashioned spy on the kid?" I suggested. The others were quiet.

"We'll need to be careful about it," Grayson said. "I don't want him knowing that we're onto him."

"Make him do it," Avery said. I could only assume they were talking about me.

"Why me?" I asked.

"Because you're blind, and he wouldn't suspect you of being a spy," they said like it was obvious.

I crossed my arms. "You think blind people can't be spies?" I asked.

"No, they're right. He's already underestimated you once. And we've already established that you're good at eavesdropping," Grayson pointed out.

I rolled my eyes. "Fine."

We walked back into school right as the bell rang. I took my time tapping down the hallway, sniffing for his familiar scent, but couldn't find it. I eventually gave up and made my way to my homeroom. Grayson was stuck with him for most of the day, but we all shared lunch. I would begin my spying then.

Even though I pretended like being compared to a bloodhound bothered me, I knew it was true. I had gotten a good whiff of the kid the first time he had tried to accost me in the hallway, but for the life of me, I couldn't find his scent in the cafeteria. I must've wandered around for ten minutes before I gave up and finally sat down with the others.

"Is he absent today?" I asked. My skin prickled under their invisible gazes.

"Are you kidding me? You passed by him like five times. He's over there on the left sitting with his loser friends," Avery snapped.

I furrowed my brow. "Wait, really?" *Why didn't I smell him?* "What's he doing right now?" I asked.

"Just sitting there with his friends, like normal," Grayson said.

"He's not eating anything," Avery said.

"I'm going to walk by him," Grayson said, standing up. "See if I can overhear what they're talking about." He left the table, I heard Avery lean toward me.

"I know you're not normal," they whispered. I stopped breathing. Goosebumps rose on my arms.

"What?" My voice barely escaped my throat.

"You smell funny," they said. "And you give me a bad gut feeling. And my bad gut feelings are never wrong. Grayson may think you're fine, but I know something's wrong."

I smelled Grayson returning and forced myself to relax. "I don't know what you're talking about," I said. "And I don't think Grayson would appreciate you telling him how weird you think I am at a time like this." I felt them recoil across the table right as Grayson sat back down.

"You hear anything?" I asked.

"He threw a french fry at me," Grayson muttered. "So, all appears normal."

"We'll just have to keep trying," I muttered. The rest of the day proved equally as useless. At pickup, Norman remained silent on the car ride home. Grayson followed me to my room.

"What are we doing now?" I asked.

"Watching to see when he gets home," Grayson said. A few moments later, another car drove up.

"Amy brought him home," Grayson said. "They're getting out now. Go into the hallway and see where he goes. Look inconspicuous." I dashed out into the hallway, pretending like I was heading to the kitchen. As I walked down the hallway, I caught a whiff of an unfamiliar scent. *Is that Reed?* I wondered. *Why does he smell so different now?* I listened to his footsteps, and after waiting a few moments, returned to my room.

"He went up the staircase. I think he's on the third floor," I said.

"Why would he be on the third floor? That's where the families live," Grayson muttered. "We need to do more stalking."

The next day, we waited outside for Avery, but they never showed up.

"Maybe they're sick?" Grayson mused. *Who cares*, I thought. *If they're not here, they can't interrogate me on my weird vibes and threaten me.*

"Let's just go look for Reed," I said.

"I haven't seen him get out of the car rider line," Grayson said. "What if he doesn't come to school?"

"I don't think Amy would let him skip school," I said. "If he's at home - there's probably a reason." I pulled out my cell phone and dialed Norman. I walked away from Grayson, guilt settling deep into my chest. *This is for a good cause*, I told myself. *Just do it.*

"Hey . . . I'm sorry I didn't say anything earlier, but I'm not feeling well. I think I might throw up," I said.

"Okay, I can turn around and come get you. Just wait out front."

I walked back to Grayson. "I'll see if he's at home," I said. Grayson didn't ask about how I was able to lie without Norman noticing. I clutched my stomach on the ride home to sell the narrative and thanked Norman again as he dropped me off at my room. As soon as it was quiet, I snuck out.

I tried the third floor first, searching for Reed's new scent, but found nothing. I tried the lobby next and heard voices from Amy's office.

"Yes, I'm taking him to the hospital later today . . . no he's not doing any better." *Taking who to the hospital?* I wondered.

"Any word about his parents?" Tom asked.

"Nope."

Are they talking about Reed? I wondered. I got out my phone and ran back to my room. I used my voice to text to message Grayson.

"Is anyone at the Sanctuary sick or anything?" I spoke to the speaker. A few seconds later, my phone read his reply.

"No, why?"

"I think they might be taking Reed to the hospital," I said.

"Cool. We're going to follow them."

True to his word, Grayson appeared in my room less than a half hour later, smelling like sweat and adrenaline.

"Have they left yet?" he gasped. "I ran all the way here."

I crossed my arms. "No, but how are we supposed to follow them? Are you secretly sixteen with a driver's license?" I asked.

"No, but there are bikes downstairs. Can you ride a bike?"

"Oh sure, my mom definitely made sure I knew how to ride a bike before she left."

"Fine, then you're riding on my handlebars," Grayson said.

"How are we going to sneak into a hospital?" I asked. "I don't exactly blend in very well."

"Leave that to me."

A heart-stopping bike ride on a set of handlebars later, we arrived outside the hospital.

"We're going to look sketchy as hell, man," I complained. "Are you sure this is going to work?"

"Just trust me, okay?" Grayson said. I unfolded my cane and followed him into the lobby. The place stank of bleach and blood. I instantly flashed back to the day I was transported here after my head injury. For a moment, I could still feel the sunburn on my skin and the pounding in my skull.

"Hello boys, can I help you?" someone asked.

"My friend here isn't feeling well," Grayson said, shoving me forward. I could smell the nurse's skepticism. It smelled like lemons.

"Where are his parents?" she asked.

"Oh, right behind us," Grayson said. "But they've seriously been puking everywhere . . . can we at least point us towards your gender-neutral bathroom? My friend is nonbinary," he whispered. He squeezed my arm, and I bent over, clutching my stomach. The nurse's skepticism turned to repulsion.

"Yeah, yeah, the family bathroom is over there."

Grayson dragged me over to where the nurse pointed and locked the door behind us.

"You are a terrible person," I said.

"I have a real nonbinary friend, it's fine," he said. "Now we just wait until they get busy and see where they stuck Reed."

I huffed and sat down on the floor. "I hope you know that if you ever drag me around like that again, I'll shove this cane up your ass," I threatened. The door clicked open, and we stood in silence as Grayson watched through the crack. Just when I was afraid that the nurse was going to come searching for us, he grabbed my arm.

"He's here! He's being escorted to a room . . . come on, let's go."

Despite my warning, Grayson pulled me up a hallway and down to my knees. I found myself huddling against what felt like a desk.

"Where are we?" I hissed.

"We're hiding behind the nurse's station across from his room," Grayson whispered.

"Tell me what's going on," I demanded.

"Hold your horses, I'll narrate in a second," Grayson snapped. "He's in a hospital bed. A nurse is hooking an IV into his arm. He looks . . . he looks kinda awful, to be honest."

"Describe awful," I said.

"Like . . . bags under his eyes. Skinny. Well, he was already skinny, but skinner than normal. Pale. Tired. He's shivering."

"What's in his IV bag?"

"I think it's just fluids. Fluids are clear, right?"

He must be sick, I thought. *But why are they just giving him fluids?*

"Damn it, they closed the door. I can't see him anymore. Wait . . . Amy and another doctor just walked in. Can you hear them talking?"

I strained to listen, but the sound was quiet and muffled. I shook my head, and we waited in silence for the door to open again.

Someone started screaming. I jumped to attention as blood-curdling wails echoed through the hallway. Grayson jerked as I covered my ears with my hands. Running footsteps sounded down the hall. The screams slowly subsided to whimpers. More footsteps sounded out from behind the door. Grayson held my hand, and I could feel the worry coursing through his veins.

"This isn't getting better," someone said. "Why isn't it getting better?"

"It only took me a day to get used to it," Amy muttered. "This shouldn't be happening. It can't keep happening. He's staying dehydrated."

"We need to run more tests. Amy, I strongly recommend you talk to Sam."

There was a moment of silence, and the tension doubled.

"No," Amy said. "We can't go there yet. I won't allow it."

The doctor sighed. "Very well. But if this doesn't get better soon, you might not have a choice." The footsteps continued down the hall. We waited until they were gone and relaxed.

"Did you see anything?" I asked.

"No. But what the hell?" Grayson whispered. "What's wrong with him?"

I took a deep breath. "Grayson . . . do you think he got . . ." I made an injecting motion on my arm. I could feel him go pale beside me.

"There's no way," he said. "How could he have gotten Cursed? There's no freaking way. It's got to be something else."

"Well, go look."

Grayson disappeared for a moment and came back rejected. "I can't. The door's locked and the window is covered up."

More footsteps sounded.

"Well, let's get out of here while we still can," I said. As we made our way back home, a thousand questions filtered through my head. If Reed was Cursed, how did it happen? It was illegal to Curse people on purpose. If news got out, humans would be furious. Norman's insistence on secrecy suddenly made perfect sense. Who knows what would happen if a merfolk was found out to have Cursed Reed? The humans would probably run every single one of us back to the ocean.

But why was it making him so sick? Why was he at Atlantis instead of with his family?

Maybe Grayson Cursed him. He hates the guy. Maybe he did it to get revenge.

The thought made me sick.

There's no way, I thought. *Grayson wouldn't do that. He couldn't do that. He's not that good of a liar.*

Unless he's someone like you. Then he would be able to lie without anybody knowing the truth.

GRAYSON

We made it back to the house before anyone noticed we were gone. We watched from Daniel's window, but it took Reed hours to get back home with Amy. When he stepped out of the car, he walked as if his legs were made of Jello.

Daniel's hypothesis ran through my head on a loop. *There's no way he's Cursed,* I thought. Amy is the only Cursed merfolk on the planet, and Cursing doesn't happen by accident. It's got to be something else.

I pulled out my phone and texted Avery an update, but they didn't respond. *Dang, maybe they're sick too,* I thought. *Maybe this is all just some freak disease going around.*

Except merpeople can't get viruses. We're already sick.

"Got any other theories?" Daniel asked.

"I'm more confused than I was yesterday," I admitted. "We just need to keep following him, I guess."

"We're going to get caught eventually," Daniel said. "What if we . . . you know . . . just talk to him? Ask him what's going on. Maybe he'll be honest."

I scoffed. Reed wasn't about to do me a favor anytime soon. "Not happening," I muttered. We sat there in silence until dinner and pushed food around on our plates as the other kids and adults ate like nothing was wrong. Daniel suddenly grabbed my arm and jerked his head towards the living room.

"Is that him?" he whispered. I turned to see Reed sneaking out the front door. Whoever the guard was that night must've not been paying that much attention.

"It is," I said. "Let's go." We slipped through the front door and followed Reed's skinny figure down the sidewalk and onto the main road. He stumbled, his legs still slightly wobbly, but walked like he was in a hurry, hands shoved in his pockets. Daniel held onto the back of my shirt as I followed him so the tapping of his cane wouldn't gather any attention. *Where are you going?* I wondered.

Reed turned down a street, and we found ourselves amid a nice neighborhood. The bushes lining the brick houses were all trimmed without a leaf out of place. Reed picked up his pace and practically ran up to one of the houses. He knocked softly on the door, breathing hard. I could see his Adam's apple moving up and down as he swallowed.

"What's he doing?" Daniel asked.

"He's knocking on some house," I whispered. Reed waited a few moments and then knocked again, harder this time. He paced on the porch, his breathing growing more and more labored. He turned and slammed his hands against the door, digging his nails into the wood.

"I know you're in there!" he shouted. "Talk to me!" I turned to stare at Daniel even though I knew he couldn't see me. *Whose house is he knocking on?*

Police sirens sounded in the distance, and the color drained from Reed's face. He swore and turned tail, running down the street. Daniel and I stayed in our hidden spot as the officer cruised down the neighborhood, shining a flashlight out of one of the windows. It did several more laps before it disappeared.

"Can you track him?" I whispered.

"Yeah, yeah, what else am I good for," Daniel grumbled. I let him lead me out of the bush as he sniffed the air and followed his nose in the same direction Reed had vanished.

We found him half an hour later, sitting by himself at a bus stop by Atlantis, his arms wrapped around himself. He shivered into his hoodie, looking quite small.

"What do we do? He's just sitting there," I said.

"Here's a novel idea - let's *talk* to him instead of just stalking him," Daniel said. I rolled my eyes and slid back into the shadows as another car passed down the road. Beside me, Daniel went rigid. He stared after the car, his fingers a vice on my shirt.

"Daniel, you okay?" I asked.

"That car. It smells familiar." He stepped out into the light as the van drove closer and closer to Reed. It screeched to a halt by the bus stop.

"REED RUN!" Daniel screamed, letting go of my shirt and booking it down the street. Reed's head snapped up as a hooded figure jumped out of the van and lunged for him. I pounded after Daniel, adrenaline lighting my heels on fire. All of Amy's paranoia flashed through my head.

Oh my god, Reed's about to be kidnapped.

Reed tripped over his own feet in his attempt to scramble away and the hooded figure grabbed his arms, dragging him towards the van. Daniel screamed and hit the figure with his cane.

"Hey, stop!" I shouted. I skidded to a halt, helpless as I watched the hooded figure fight Daniel for Reed. The figure kicked out at Daniel, and he doubled over, wheezing as he hit the ground.

I looked around, suddenly desperate for that cop to come back. *What the hell am I supposed to do?* I thought. *I don't have any fins or weapons.*

But the van door was open. And the keys were still in the ignition.

I jumped up into the driver's seat and floored it. In the rearview mirror, the fight came to a standstill as I drove away.

Hah, good luck kidnapping anyone without your van, I thought.

My elation was promptly cut short as another van rounded the corner. *Fuck.* I screeched to a halt and looked around for anything I could as a weapon.

"Come on, come on, *come on*." I tore the glove box open and found a gun.

Was it loaded? No idea. Had I ever used a gun before? Nope. But I yanked the van around back towards the fight and rolled down the window to point it at the hooded figure's face.

"Let them go!" I shouted. Reed's jaw fell open as Daniel felt along the ground for his cane. The other van pulled up beside me, and very unfortunately, the other driver was also holding a gun. He glared at me through his mask.

Damn it, I'm actually going to have to use this thing, I thought. I nearly dropped it as I tried to hold it still in my hands.

"Let them go! I'll shoot you - I swear!" I shouted. The hooded figure laughed. Reed sank his teeth into his captor's arm, and he let go, howling. Reed booked it towards the van, leaving Daniel on the pavement.

Oh come on, I thought. I jumped out of the driver's seat, shoving the gun into Reed's hands as I grabbed Daniel and dragged him towards the van. He was bleeding from where his head had hit the pavement. *Guess that's another traumatic head injury to add to the list*, I thought.

"What the fuck is going on?" he asked, his speech slightly slurred. I shoved him into the van and slid the sliding door shut.

"DRIVE!" I shouted. Reed floored it and the van jerked forward, sending me and Daniel right into the back doors. Reed looked in the rearview mirror, sweat pouring down his face.

"They're following us!" he shouted.

"Shoot them!" I yelled. I clawed my way up to the front and sat in the passenger's seat. Reed's hands were trembling on the steering wheel, his eyes wide and unblinking.

"Do you know how to shoot a gun?" I asked. He nodded. I put a hand on his, trying as hard as I could to feel calm.

"Then do it! You're a better shot than you think!" *Assuming you're merfolk, that is.*

The van suddenly swerved. Reed struggled to keep us going in a straight line as the other van rear-ended us. Pops sounded around us.

"It's either us or them!" I shouted. "Do it!" I slid over, grabbing the wheel and keeping my foot on the gas. Reed stuck his head out the window, the gun clenched in his hands. He took a deep breath and aimed.

The sound of the shots echoed in my ears. I nearly crashed the van a second time. Reed emptied the pistol, and in the rearview mirror, I saw the other van swerve and come to a stop, air whistling out of the tires.

I laughed. "You did it!"

Reed pulled himself back in the car and went sheet white again.

"Watch out!" he screamed.

I looked up just in time to see the beach. We crashed over the partition guarding the driveway and went hurdling towards the ocean. I slammed on the brakes, but all the tires did was spin in the sand.

We screamed as the van landed in the waves, sinking several feet until it finally came to a stop. The nose pitched forward, sending Daniel hurdling into the back of my seat. Water poured in through Reed's open window.

"What the fuck is happening?" Daniel shouted.

"We're alive. We got rid of the other van," I breathed. "I also crashed this one. But we're alive."

"Speak for yourself," Daniel groaned, feeling his head. "Am I bleeding?"

"Um . . . guys?" Reed had curled himself up on his seat but the water was rising fast. It was nearly to his toes. I felt my legs going numb.

"We can swim out once the car fills up," I said.

Reed shook his head. "You don't understand." The water reached his shoes.

"Cut the act, we know what you are!" Daniel said. "Right? Did we come to that conclusion? He's merfolk? God my head hurts." The water reached Reed's torso. I let myself sink into the water and phased, grateful there wasn't any broken glass floating around. Above me, bloodcurdling screams filled the cabin.

Reed's body contorted, looking like he was the victim of possession in a horror movie. He clawed at the seat as he phased. His flesh tore apart and fused back together. Scales ripped from his skin, shimmering in the moonlight. His markings looked like someone had scribbled over the left side of his face with a crayon and then tried to erase it - blurry and disjointed.

Are you okay? I mouthed, but he wasn't looking at me. He curled against the back of the seat, gills flaring in and out. His entire body trembled.

Behind me, Daniel phased and felt around for the window. It refused to roll down. Reed was blocking the only exit.

I cautiously reached out and pushed his trembling body through the window. He winced as if my touch burned him. Daniel followed me out as I gently pulled Reed to the surface.

We crawled up on the beach to see all the lights spilling onto the sand from Atlantis. Small figures were running towards us.

Daniel and I phased, and I pulled Reed to the surface only for him to try to claw his way back to the water.

"No, it's too soon." He scarcely had time to drag himself back before his body contorted again. He writhed against the sand, screaming into the night as he phased back.

Norman skidded to a stop beside us, attempting to hold Reed down as he thrashed around. Beside me, Daniel wavered as if he was moments away from fainting. Blood stained his white hair. Reed moaned and finally came to a stop as he phased back to human form. Sweat plastered his hair to his forehead, and he gasped for breath.

Norman and the others helped us up toward the hotel. Reed collapsed on top of me as we reached Amy's office. His body wrenched and the stream of puke barely missed me. Amy did not look pleased.

"What happened?" Amy demanded.

"Someone tried to kidnap us," Daniel said, shoving Reed off me, hopefully not into the pile of puke. I could feel the terror cut through Amy like a knife. She shut the door behind us, leaving the other concerned adults and kids outside.

"What *happened?*" she asked, trying to still the tremors in her voice. I explained how Daniel and I had followed Reed – *which thank God we did by the way otherwise Reed would be toast* - ignoring the little curses under Reed's breath as I talked.

"Why on Earth did you think it was a good idea to leave at night?" Amy hissed. "Reed, I told you it's dangerous. All three of you are lucky to be alive right now."

"Yeah, I'm super happy we're all alive, but why the fuck is Reed Cursed?" I demanded. "Why aren't you being honest with us? What have you been hiding?"

Amy pinched her lips tight. "Are you three okay? Physically?"

We all muttered an affirmative, except for Daniel and Reed, who lied. I could still feel his body trembling beside me.

"Daniel, you're bleeding. Go tell Norman to take you to the nurse," she commanded. Daniel sighed and let himself out of the office.

"Reed, do you need to go to the hospital?" she asked. He hesitated and shook his head. "Grayson - you look fine. Go upstairs. Go to bed."

I clenched my fists. "I'm not going anywhere until you tell me what's going on!" I demanded.

"You need to let the adults handle this!" Amy shouted.

"Damn right I do, some adults just tried to kidnap us!"

"Who fucking cares?" Reed spat.

"Me! I care. So tell me what's going on!" I shouted. Amy slammed her hands down on her desk.

"Fine. Reed is Cursed. So are other human kids. There's an unknown group going around and Cursing humans. On purpose. Meanwhile, other people are kidnapping more and more merfolk to traffic them. Any questions?"

My mouth fell open. "Um yeah, like a thousand questions. Why would someone do that? That's super illegal."

Reed rolled his eyes but barely made it to the trash can in the corner before throwing up again. He groaned as he wiped his mouth.

"Why would someone be going around to Curse humans?" I asked.

"We don't know. From what we can tell, the victims are attacked personally. They would have to be - for the blood types to match."

"Why is he so sick?" I asked, pointing at Reed.

"The later in life one is Cursed, the harder it is on their body. Reed is the oldest one who's been Cursed so far. Hence - why he's having the hardest time of it," Amy said, motioning to the trash can.

"So . . . where are the other Cursed? Why hasn't anyone gone to the police about this?"

"Believe me, the police are involved. We're trying to keep this whole thing under wraps so no one panics. The other Cursed are currently living with their families." *More secrets*, I thought. *I thought we were done keeping secrets?*

"Why isn't he living with his family?" I asked. Reed seemed to deflate even more beside me. Amy inhaled sharply.

"That is a question Reed can answer himself if he wants to," she said shortly.

Norman insisted on checking me over for injuries before I was allowed to go up to my room. He was uncharacteristically quiet as I walked away. Reed followed me, still carrying his trashcan of puke. Daniel sat on my bed, his head bandaged.

"The nurse said I don't have a concussion," he said. I nodded and plopped down next to him. Outside my window, the flashing lights of police cars showed a tow truck attempting to drag the van out of the sea.

I can't believe that just happened, I thought. *This is insane.*

Reed sat on the floor, leaning against the wall.

"Are you okay, Reed?" Daniel asked.

Reed laughed bitterly. "Why do you care? Go ahead. Make fun of me. I got exactly what I deserve, right?" he jeered.

"I thought about it. But you already look pathetic enough curled around that trashcan full of puke," I snapped. He flicked me off.

"Dude, I'm kidding. Let me help you." I carefully took the trash can out of his arms and helped him onto the edge of my bed. Feeling like a dad, I took his shoes off and wrapped a blanket around his shoulders. His skin was still sweaty and clammy, but I wasn't sure if he could handle a shower.

"I'm sorry this happened to you," I whispered.

He scoffed. "No, you're not."

I winced. I forgot he could now read exactly what I was feeling. Heck, he had been able to read my emotions for days now, and I hadn't realized. Guilt blossomed in my gut. *Wow, I'm an asshole,* I thought.

He looked up, surprise written on his face. "You actually feel bad." He said it like a statement instead of a question.

I sighed. "I mean . . . you were an asshole before. But no one deserves to have their species changed without permission," I said.

He shrugged. "Too late now."

"I assume . . . your parents didn't take it well?" I asked.

"I'm living here, instead of at home, aren't I?" he said, stiffening. He recoiled as I tried to hug him.

"I know we're supposed to be touchy-feely, but touching other people makes me feel nauseous right now," he said. "God, I don't know how you things live your whole lives like this."

I chuckled. "I mean, I like being able to tell what other people are feeling. I like being this way. But then again, it's not painful for me. How exactly have you been staying hydrated?"

Reed laughed. "I haven't. They've been trying to get me to swim, but I'd rather be thirsty than feel every cell in my body rip apart." He shuddered, falling back on the mattress.

"Do you know why you were targeted?" I asked.

"Someone probably thought it would be funny."

"Were the other kids merphobic assholes too?" Daniel asked.

Reed shook his head. "All the police told me is that we have the same blood type. A positive."

I winced. That was my blood type. I wondered for a split second if Reed thought I had been the one who Cursed him as revenge.

"How did you get Cursed?" I asked.

"Someone broke into my house at night. Injected me. My dad took me to the hospital. The doctors had no clue what was going on until a mermaid nurse walked in."

Someone broke into his house? That takes some serious planning. What the hell is going on?

"That's insane. Why would anyone want to be Cursing humans?" I thought aloud.

Reed scoffed. "Isn't it obvious? You freaks are always complaining about how badly you're being treated. Maybe you're just trying to make more of you so you can freaking take over."

My jaw dropped.

"That's quite the conspiracy theory," Daniel chuckled.

"Are you serious? You think we're trying to take over the world by Cursing everyone who wasn't born merfolk?" I demanded.

"Why else would this be happening?" Reed asked. I bit my tongue. He was making it hard to be nice.

"As if I would ever want you to be part of my species," I muttered.

Reed sat up, dark eyes narrowed. "Yeah, keep making fun of me. When we find out who's been Cursing people, your whole species is going to be driven back to the ocean for good."

Data Log 6:23 AM

A mixed-species couple came in yesterday for genetic screening. The future mom allowed us to extract some of her eggs - and I confirmed that her eggs were infected - meaning their offspring would be merfolk. It has me wondering - are Amy's eggs infected? Not that she would ever let me check but it would be interesting to know.

It also makes me wonder . . . the vaccine . . . if her human partner was vaccinated, would her children be safe from the virus? Either way, I can't test it. And if Duncan finds out that I can't test it . . . he's gonna be pissed. Especially with what's going on right now. I can't believe human kids are being Cursed. Whoever's doing this needs to stop. I'm dead if they don't.

REED

I stumbled back to my room on the third floor and collapsed on my bed, every bone in my body screaming in protest. I groaned as my stomach lurched, and I clamped my jaw shut, refusing to throw up again.

I dragged myself to the bathroom and scrubbed my teeth clean until my gums bled. I avoided eye contact with the mirror. I refused to let my markings show, but I swore I could still feel them under my skin, writhing like bugs, burrowing into my flesh.

I should've known Grayson and his stupid friend would figure it out, I thought. *Can't keep his nose out of anyone's business to save his life.*

I lay in bed, the night's events repeating themselves in my head. I had never phased twice in one day, and my bones felt like they had disintegrated into dust. I wasn't sure what was worse - almost being kidnapped or hearing the sirens of the cops my parents had called on me.

My hands started to shake, and I slammed them down into the mattress. *What kind of stupid reaction was shaking when you were upset? Why couldn't I just cry like a normal person?*

Because I'm not a normal person. I'm a fish freak. I'm sick.

I knew I shouldn't have gone back to my family. I couldn't risk getting them infected too. But they knew damn well I couldn't infect them over the phone. They hadn't bothered to talk to me since I sprouted a tail that night in the ER. I had heard them talking about how disgusting and horrible merpeople were ever since I could remember. But *I* wasn't disgusting. I was their kid. I didn't *ask* for this. Just because I got sick didn't mean I was the same as those creatures.

I just want my parents back, I thought. *I want my normal life back. But at this rate . . . I'll be stuck like this forever. My parents won't want me around them ever again. At least the kidnappers wanted me.*

Amy had warned me about the mermaid trafficking problem soon after my arrival, telling me to be careful of my surroundings and fight like hell if anyone tried to grab me. She had used the weird albino kid as an example, but I hadn't believed her until a few hours ago. Humans kidnapping merpeople seemed ridiculous. Why would anyone want one of those things in their house?

Why would anyone want *me*? Better yet, how had the kidnappers known what had happened to me if Amy had respected my request to keep my new infection under wraps? Maybe it was one of the doctors at the hospital. Maybe the wrong person overheard.

I shivered suddenly, wrapping my arms around myself. If Grayson and Daniel hadn't been there to save my ass, I would be god-knows-where by then. Daniel looked like a freak, but even I had to admit that a blind kid running up to a kidnapper to save someone who hated him was pretty damn impressive.

Why even bother saving me? I wondered. If they had let those men take me, they both would've been one enemy free. I was almost tempted to thank them but remembered Grayson muttering about how he would never want me to be part of his species.

I eventually drifted off into a fitful sleep, where my subconscious replayed every detail of the previous night in enough quality to be a 4k movie. I woke up feeling more tired and stumbled downstairs.

I heard voices coming from Amy's office and hesitated down the hallway. I lingered by the corner and listened, almost grateful for my improved ears.

"How did the traffickers know?" a hushed voice whispered.

"I don't know," Amy whispered back. "But I'm worried. More kids are disappearing and more are turning up Cursed, but the police only seem concerned about the Cursed kids."

Oh yeah, how dare the police worry about humans getting infected with a disease that has no cure, I thought, rolling my eyes.

"I'm surprised it's not all over the news right now," the stranger muttered.

"I doubt their parents or victims want that information shared."

"How's the kid doing?"

Amy drew a sharp breath. "Don't. Just don't. You're not turning him into a science experiment to see if you can get rid of it." The sharp smell of anger and indignation floated down the hallway.

"I don't want to experiment on him. I'm just saying . . . you know what, never mind."

I jumped back as the stranger stomped out of the office. *Is that Sam?* I thought.

Extensive knowledge of all of the original Rebels lived rent-free in my head from the countless documentaries and conversations around the dinner table. Sam was the smart one - the one who had figured out their so-called species was nothing more than an infection spread by blood contact. I knew she worked for some biotech company and studied merpeople, but the tension between her and her adoptive mom was not something I had been privy to before.

I quickly turned and ran back down the hallway as Amy walked out in her huff of irritated energy. I walked to the cafeteria and plopped down at a table, my head spinning. Amy had jumped to the conclusion that Sam wanted to experiment on me . . . experiment on me to get rid of the virus.

Was that even possible? I wondered. I knew it was way too late for a vaccine, but could there be a cure? If it was possible, I would be more than happy to be an experiment.

But Amy would never let that happen, I thought, scowling. If Sam did figure out a cure to get rid of the mermaid virus . . . anyone could take it. Anyone *should* take it. And Amy didn't want her species to be wiped out. She couldn't give less than a damn about the Cursed kids if it meant her species was preserved.

Maybe I'll just call up Sam myself and volunteer, I thought. Amy can't stop me from doing that - right? Or could she?

My thoughts were interrupted as two more figures walked into the cafeteria. Norman and Emanuel noticed me immediately.

Emanuel was pretty easy to figure out. Out of the two of them, he seemed more concerned about trying to be nice and welcoming, even though I could feel the awkwardness he felt around me.

Norman was harder to figure out. The security uniform and gun on his belt almost looked too adult and heavy for his small body, but I had seen countless videos of him chasing fishermen twice his size and bringing down armed guards to rescue other merpeople. I knew a sharp tongue lurked in his mouth, and I had expected him to throttle me when he arrived with Amy and his partner at the hospital after my dad had peaced out. I had just tried to fry his honorary son in chlorine after all, but he had been shockingly not abusive and protective since my first ride home. It made me hate them even more. I didn't need any fucking sympathy. It was *their* kind's fault I was sick.

The couple stared at me for a minute before heading to the line for breakfast. I turned my attention back to the bare table in front of me, wondering what they would have to say about a potential cure for being a mermaid.

I jumped as Emanuel plopped down in front of me. He slid over another tray of breakfast food and offered his award-winning smile.

"How are you feeling?" he asked.

I shrugged, picking at the pile of eggs with my fork. "Alive," I muttered.

He nodded through a mouthful of food. "Alive is good."

"I think it might've been one of the doctors or someone at the hospital who's connected to the trafficking problem, or whatever," I said. "They were the only ones outside of you guys who knew about . . ." I trailed off.

"Amy thought of that last night. The cops are interviewing them today, searching for leads," he said. I nodded and attempted to swallow a spoonful of eggs. Whoever had made them had added too much salt. Maybe the merpeople liked them better that way.

"Don't worry. Amy's doing her very best to make sure you stay safe," Emanuel said. I snorted, and the eggs almost went down the wrong tube. *Protect me, right*, I thought. *If she wanted to protect me, she would be letting Sam try to cure me.*

"Yeah, whatever," I muttered, pushing the tray away. "Can you just take me to school?" Emanuel winced but got up. I didn't offer to carry my tray to the trash and waited impatiently in the garage. A few spots over, Grayson and Daniel got in a different car with Norman. Grayson stared at me like he couldn't decide if I was a lost puppy or a dog that needed to be put down.

Our ride to school was silent, and I prepared myself to pretend to be human in front of my old friends. No wincing at noises that weren't supposed to be loud, no sniffing the air to tell how someone was feeling, no quick reflexes. Just a boring, simple, ordinary human who wasn't sick. I had already lost my family. If my friends found out – I would have no one left but the circus brigade back at the hotel.

Dang, maybe I should have let myself get kidnapped.

I debated messing with Grayson during math class like I normally did, but hesitated. He knew what had happened to me. With his temper, it would be all too easy for him to slip and point out to the rest of the class that I was the same freak of nature as him. And then I would go to jail for killing him. So, I held my tongue.

I almost bit it off when my science teacher said that I would be working with Grayson and some other random girl for a class project. Grayson looked like the teacher had just killed his dog. *There's no way she's serious*, I thought. I raised my hand.

"Um . . . do I have to work with them?" I asked.

The teacher nodded. "Yes. All of you need to learn to work with people you don't like," she said. "You boys have had enough drama with each other. It's time to get over it."

Kill me, I thought. *I already have to deal with him at home, now here too?* I dragged my feet like they were made of concrete, and Grayson forced a bright smile on his face as I sat down. The other girl whose name I had already forgotten flounced down next to us.

"Okay, let me make one thing clear," I said. "I have an A in this class. I plan to keep it that way. So, you two are going to do exactly what I say so we don't get a bad grade on this project - okay?" Grayson saluted me.

"Aye, aye captain," he said through a shit-eating grin.

"Wait, you're a mermaid, right?"

Our heads both snapped up to stare at the blonde girl. I looked down at my arms to make sure my markings were still hidden and tried not to hyperventilate. *Holy shit, does she know? Can she tell?* I thought, my heart racing.

"Um . . . yes," Grayson said slowly. The girl's jaw dropped as if this was news to her, and she had never noticed she had a Merfolk classmate before. *Oh thank god, she was talking about him,* I thought. *Duh.*

"Okay, but are you like *actually* a mermaid? Because my dad says they're fake," she said. Grayson and I exchanged another glance.

"I mean . . . I'm sitting right next to you," Grayson said. "So obviously I'm real. Unless you're hallucinating."

She giggled. "Wait, so does mean like . . . vampires are real too?" she asked. I smothered a laugh behind my hand, and Grayson's eye twitched.

"You know what, why don't you pick out some pretty paper for us to start working on?" he asked, forcing sweetness into his voice.

"Okay!" She bounced out of her seat and Grayson leaned over to me.

"So we're both in agreement that she cannot do any part of this project, right?" he whispered. I nodded.

"I mean, most of you are stupid compared to me, but Jesus," I whispered. "*Are vampires real too?*"

Grayson cracked a genuine smile. "It was pretty funny when you started to panic back there," he whispered. I threw my pencil at him.

"Don't worry, I'm not about to out you," he whispered as Blondie started to return. "Now what do you want me to do for this project, o Wise One?"

SAM

I was elbow-deep in a sink washing beakers when someone knocked on the door. I turned around to see a middle schooler standing in the doorway of my office, his knuckles white on his book bag strap. His eyes flicked around nervously as if he were afraid of being seen.

"Can I help you?" I asked.

He nodded. "Yeah . . . I'm here to . . . volunteer for the . . . testing stuff," he said. I sniffed the air, and instantly realized why he wasn't showing his markings. *This must be the Cursed kid,* I thought. My previous heated discussion with Amy flashed through my head. *Was he eavesdropping on that conversation? Amy needs to watch her kids more closely.*

"Come with me."

273

I dried my hands, and he followed me behind a curtain and sat down on a gurney. I handed him a clipboard with all the options listed on it.

"You can donate blood, let us x-ray you, let us do an anatomical workup. You even get a sucker if you donate body parts." At the last one, the color drained from his face, and he almost dropped the clipboard.

"Of course, you have to have a guardian's consent for any of these, and Amy doesn't know you're here, does she?" I asked.

He scowled. "Amy doesn't give a shit about actually helping me. You can make a cure," he said. "You can fix this."

I sighed and pulled up a chair. "Viruses are complicated," I said. "We can make vaccines for them, we can come up with treatments that tackle the symptoms . . . but cures? You can't cure a virus like you can a bacterial infection or a broken leg," I said.

He shrugged. "Okay. So treat it."

"Treating your symptoms is you getting used to being merfolk," I whispered. He shoved his hands in his pockets.

"I can't stay like this forever," he said. "My parents abandoned me. Every cell in my body hurts. I can't eat. There has to be something you can do." I could feel the desperation wafting off him. I had been near some pretty anxious people before, but nothing like this. I slowly shook my head.

"I'm sorry. I wish there was more I could do," I said.

"Are you only saying that because of Amy?" he asked. I winced. *So he had been eavesdropping,* I thought.

"Even if I did turn you into a science experiment behind her back, it wouldn't work. There is no cure, there is no treatment," I said.

He crossed his arms. "What about a vaccine? You could at least stop this from happening to other human kids," he pointed out. My heart seemed to freeze in my chest.

You promised Duncan you would do it.

I debated how easy it would be to lie to this kid. Was he adapted enough to his new body to feel the emotions of other people?

"Developing a vaccine for this is above my pay grade," I said, standing up and crossing my arms. "You need to go home before Amy realizes you're gone. Otherwise, we're both going to be in trouble." He screwed up his face like he wanted to argue but hopped off the bed and stomped towards the door.

"Thanks for nothing," he muttered. I sighed as he slammed the clinic door shut. Mr. Duncan walked around from behind his desk, an eyebrow raised.

"What's wrong?" he asked.

"That was the Cursed kid," I whispered. "He wanted me to cure him."

Mr. Duncan chuckled. "Well, you've been close for a while now, right? At least we have a failsafe to stop this from happening to other people," he said. I nodded, thankful for the millionth time that he couldn't smell lies.

I had been "close" to creating a vaccine for almost a year. But in reality, I had spent the last five years studying anything else - bone structure, reaction time, our likelihood of developing cancer - things that would help the average merfolk. My community already resented me enough, but if I could prove that I was helping them, then maybe I wouldn't get so many dirty looks. What was the point of studying merfolk if it only benefited humans?

"How much more time do you think we have?" I asked.

"If human kids keep getting Cursed, the mayor is going to demand that the vaccine be released," Mr. Duncan said.

I nodded. The mayor and Duncan would both be furious when they discovered there was no vaccine to release. A few months ago, I wouldn't care how mad they would be. But seeing Reed beg me for a chance at being normal . . . maybe I didn't feel sick, but he sure did. Maybe the humans did need a vaccine.

And I was running out of time.

REED

The next morning, a loud banging on my door startled me from sleep. Norman stepped in, hair mussed and bags under his eyes. I tensed.

"Come on," he said shortly. I pulled on some clothes and followed him downstairs to the living room. Amy Wilson stood in the front of the room next to her husband, hands folded in front of her, jaw clenched. Several other kids sat on a couch next to her, staring down at the floor. They looked no older than ten. Grayson and Daniel sat off to the side, looking like they had also been dragged out of bed at the buttcrack of dawn. Amy cleared her throat.

"Good morning." She motioned to the three kids sitting on the couch. "As you know, an unknown person is Cursing human children," she said. "These are the other three Cursed." The kids on the couch offered a tentative wave. Grayson furrowed his brow, leaning forward as if he was going to sniff the newcomers like a dog.

"I know that none of you are thrilled about this," Amy said. "But I want to help you make the best of this situation, and unlike others, I know exactly what you are going through." *Bullshit*, I thought.

"There are beautiful aspects to being merfolk," Amy continued. "And I want to show you all what that beauty looks like. I have gotten permission from their parents to take them and you guys on a little field trip." Emanuel grinned and pulled a set of keys out of his pocket.

"We're going to the Sanctuary," he said.

. . .

I was not thrilled to be stuck with Grayson and all the other sick kids on a boat for three days. Meanwhile, I had never seen him so happy. He leaned over the boat's railing like a dog out a window, looking like freaking Rose on the Titanic with his hair blowing back in the wind. The rising sun caught his dirty blond locks, lighting them up like fire. He breathed deeply, and I could almost taste the salty air on his tongue for him. Meanwhile, my stomach lurched again, and I slapped my hand over my mouth. I stumbled back to the living room, groaning as I lay across the floor. I wasn't normally the type to get seasick, but the rolling of the deep waves combined with my general illness seemed like the perfect combination to kill me.

At that moment, Grayson chose to walk in and sniggered when he saw me curled up on the floor.

"Imagine a merperson being seasick," he said. Retorts bubbled up in my head, but I didn't trust myself to spit them out without spitting out some other things as well.

I'm not a merperson, I thought. *I'm sick. That's all. I'll never be one of you freaks.*

"Go away," I said, flicking him off. He laughed and disappeared. I could hear the muffled voices of him talking with the younger kids outside. I shuffled off towards the back bedroom and shut the door, curling up on the bed.

This is remarkably stupid, I thought. *They're trying to indoctrinate us, and I'm not having it. All I am is sick. Nothing more.*

Hours passed and my nausea refused to go away. I clamped my hands over my ears as I heard the others eating in the living room. By day two, I could feel Norman and Emanuel losing patience.

"That kid hasn't eaten in like . . . a day," Norman said. "Tell him to get his ass out here." Grayson knocked on the door.

"Go away!" I shouted. He opened it anyway.

"Dinner's ready," he said.

"Fuck off," I moaned. This time he didn't bother to make fun of me.

"Why don't you at least try to eat something?" he asked.

"If I eat something, I will throw it up all over this bed on purpose," I said.

"Fine, starve then." He slammed the door shut. I could hear him whispering to the adults despite myself.

"He's seasick," he said. "And I'm not cleaning up his puke." Emanuel sighed.

"Let's just leave him there," Norman muttered under his breath. Yeah, I thought. *Leave me there. You don't care about me. You just want me to believe whatever bullshit you're spitting.*

Mercifully, we reached the island without tearing each other's throats out or throwing someone into the ocean. The light nearly blinded me as I ventured out of the bedroom.

The air was hot and sticky, and my hair instantly stuck to my forehead. Calling the place an island was generous. It resembled a giant traffic cone if traffic cones were covered in rotting vegetation and merpeople wearing nothing but a reed of skirts around their waists. Many of them were holding spears and had spread themselves out along the beach, staring at us with narrowed eyes. All of them had their fins out, the poisonous needles glinting in the sun. An involuntary shiver traveled down my spine. *Are those guards? What's the point in guarding the island from us?* I wondered.

The beach came lurching towards me as I took my first steps on dry land. I scrambled to catch myself, and Grayson didn't bother to smother his laugh behind me. *I should've stayed on the boat,* I thought.

I balanced back to my feet and took a deep breath, gazing up at the giant traffic cone and its many guards. Though they all stood perfectly still, I could see how tense their shoulders were. They scanned the horizon, tanned bodies poised and coiled, ready to attack or defend. *What are they so nervous about?*

Behind us, Amy arrived and hobbled out onto the sand with surprising ease. Her husband followed her, scanning the beach with flitting eyes. They walked over to Norman and Emanuel, who also surveyed the surrounding waters as if they expected the Kraken from *Pirates of the Caribbean* to show up. Norman especially seemed concerned with standing up straight, his shoulders squared.

"You have your gun, right?" Norman whispered. Tom nodded, and I shivered. *Why would Tom bother bringing a gun here?*

My thoughts were interrupted as a skinny teenager with bronze skin and pink fringed hair ran out onto the beach, waving and jumping around like a little kid. Grayson grinned and waved back, and we followed him through a hole in the side of the traffic cone. We wandered in darkness for a minute before emerging into the middle. For a short moment, I stopped formulating insults in my head.

The reason the island looked like a cone was because it technically *was* one. I had seen pictures of the insides of volcanoes in science textbooks before, but none as beautiful as this. Gentle sunlight filtered in through the hole at the top of the structure. Moss dripped down the rocks, except in places where old carvings were etched into the stone. A sparkling blue pool shone in the middle, whooshing gently against the sand. It looked like a portal to another world, and for a split second, I wanted to go swimming.

I ran my fingers along the rocks, tracing over a set of carvings.

"What are all these?" I asked.

Grayson gently plucked my hand from the rock. "Probably shouldn't touch them. They tell our history. Our *actual* history."

I looked up at the walls, drinking in the images. The largest one depicted a sinking ship, and humans drowning in the water. A merperson had dragged a small child to shore and let their blood rain down on them, changing their life and DNA forever. Cursing them. If there was one thing I agreed with merpeople - it was that the human-born ones were truly Cursed.

A towering man with a large pole walked up to our group, smiling. He had the same dark skin and sunburnt hair as the teenager.

"Welcome to our home," he said. The smaller kids immediately took an involuntary step back. I crossed my arms.

"Guys, this is the Protector of the Sanctuary," Grayson said proudly. "That's his son, Caspian." The blond teenager waved again. The Protector smiled and extended his hand out. No one stepped up to shake it. His smile faltered as he drew his hand back. The tart smell of awkwardness overcame his previous smell of confidence.

"Well . . . Grayson, I'll let you show the group around a little bit, huh?" The Protector vanished, leaving Grayson with the rest of us. He turned to face our group, clasping his hands together a little too tightly.

"Alrighty then . . . I guess to start, I'll tell you guys a story." He sat on the ground, and the kids followed suit. I stayed standing, leaning against the rock wall.

"A really, really long time ago, all the merfolk in the world lived here, at this island," he started. "And they lived in peace with each other until ships full of humans began to pass by. Sometimes, these ships would accidentally run into the rocks and crash." The kids' eyes widened.

"But, the merpeople did their best to save the humans they could. They carried the children to shore and offered to turn them into merfolk so they could survive." He pointed up to the giant mural near the top of the volcano, showing the exact scene he was talking about.

"Out of these new merfolk, they appointed a Protector - one to watch out for crashing ships so they could go rescue whoever they could. Isn't that cool?"

One of the kids raised his hand like he was in school.

"Yes?" Grayson asked.

"What about the merpeople who drowned humans on purpose?" he asked.

"Oh . . . well that's a good question!" Grayson said quickly. "But that never happened. See - when more and more humans started traveling near here, it got more dangerous for the merfolk. Many of them decided to go to land and live amongst the humans, but to keep the others safe, they made up all these scary stories about Merfolk and the Bermuda Triangle in general so the humans would be scared to come here."

The boy raised an eyebrow. "So, they lied?" he asked.

". . . Yes, they did," Grayson admitted. "But it was for good reason." *And look where it got them*, I thought.

"Do the merpeople still rescue humans from sinking ships?" one of the girls asked.

"Well . . . ships don't sink like they did back in the day," Grayson said. "And merpeople don't Curse humans anymore." The irony of the statement echoed off the stone walls, and he suddenly went very quiet. The kids stared down awkwardly at the sand.

"Well . . . we're not supposed to be Cursing humans anymore," he muttered. "But . . . that just goes to show that just how humans can be good or bad, so can merpeople."

"Are they ever going to find who did this to us?" another little girl asked.

"I hope so," he said. "But I also hope that you guys will learn to enjoy being merpeople. We're pretty cool." The kids exchanged dubious glances.

"Any other questions?" Grayson asked.

"When are we going to get fins?" the little boy asked. I snorted as Grayson blushed. He looked like he wanted to throw himself into the abyss.

"Well . . ." he started. I smirked. One particularly interesting dinner conversation with my folks about how merfolk reproduced had given me plenty of ammo to use back at school when I had been normal.

"You can't tell them to ask their moms," I whispered. "Come on, explain it."

"When two merfolk love each other . . . your body changes . . ." Grayson started. The girl's giggles grew louder, and Grayson's blush grew redder.

"That's it," he finished. "When you fall in love, your body changes. Boys grow fins and girls can cry healing tears."

The boy's eyes grew big. "That's cool," he said. "Why don't you have fins?"

"Next question," Grayson said. The giggling girl tilted her head before raising her hand.

"So, you must not have a girlfriend if you don't have fins," she pointed out.

Grayson clapped his hands. "Okay, let's make something clear. It is very rude in merfolk culture to comment on someone's fins or lack thereof," he said.

"Why is it rude?" she asked.

"Do you want me asking you if you have a boyfriend?" he asked.

She crossed her arms. "I'm only ten! I can't have a boyfriend!"

Grayson's eye twitched. "Okay, let's talk about emotions. I want you all to close your eyes and take a deep breath." They did so, taking obnoxiously loud gulps of air.

"Now, I want you to focus on me. All of you can understand what I'm feeling. Some merfolk describe it more like a smell . . . like you smell worried or you smell happy. Others describe it as a gut feeling. Pay attention to me. What am I feeling?"

The girl sniggered. "You're frustrated that we keep asking you why you don't have a girlfriend," she said.

"Correct," Grayson admitted. "Isn't that cool? If you pay attention, you can tell what anyone is feeling." The little boy clutched his gut.

"It makes my stomach hurt," he complained.

Grayson sighed. "Okay, let's take a break."

GRAYSON

Well, this is going great, I thought. The kids scattered, walking around the cavern, running their grimy hands over the sacred carvings. Reed followed me around like a lost puppy as I paced. His smug energy felt like tendrils sticking themselves into my skin.

"What's wrong, Grayson? Frustrated they're not buying the rhetoric yet?" Reed asked.

"You think we brought them here to indoctrinate them?" I asked. "News flash, learning about your culture and history isn't indoctrination."

Reed scoffed. "You're still trying to make them like being merpeople."

"You would rather them be miserable like you?" I shot back.

"I'd rather be miserable than brainwashed," he muttered. *I literally do not have the energy for this*, I thought. *Now I understand why Daniel wanted to stay home.*

"Can you go be miserable somewhere else?" I asked.

He opened his mouth to snap back but hesitated. "You're my babysitter, remember?" Something in his voice was off. I turned around, narrowing my eyes. His skinny frame was tense, and his eyes flitted nervously. He was scared of something. *He doesn't want to be left alone with all these strange merfolk*, I thought.

"The boat is right where we left it," I said.

He shrugged. "Nah, I think I want to keep asking you questions about our culture," he said, grinning.

I rolled my eyes and kept walking. "Fine. What do you want to know?"

"Aren't you supposed to get Mated soon or whatever?" he asked. I stopped in my tracks, gritting my teeth. I had been uncomfortable when that kid asked me that question. Merfolk puberty was weird enough in itself, especially considering most of what I had been taught originally about Mates being permanent was never actually true. I didn't understand it enough to explain it to a random kid who had no clue how merfolk viewed loyalty or protection.

And Reed didn't care about understanding loyalty or protection.

"No . . . don't really want to have a Mate," I muttered.

He raised an eyebrow. "Why?"

I sighed. "I'm asexual. Probably aromantic too." I held up my finger as he opened his mouth. "And before you say anything - *yes* - I'm sure, at least about the ace part. *No* - it's not a phase. *No* - I don't need to try it before I'm sure. And *yes* - it is weird for a merperson to be asexual or aromantic because of how traditionally touchy-feely and emotional we are."

Reed crossed his arms. "I was going to say *cool*."

I lowered my finger. "Oh."

"My older brother is aroace," he said. "You're not special."

I deflated. "Sorry," I said. "I'm just used to getting a bunch of stupid questions about it."

"And because you thought someone like me would be homophobic?" he snapped.

I shrugged. "I mean . . ."

He rolled his eyes. "Look, just because I don't like merpeople doesn't mean I'm racist or homophobic," he muttered.

"Sorry. Forgive me for not assuming the types of people you're phobic about," I muttered. He spun on me, eyes narrowed, teeth bared.

"Don't!" he snapped. "The exact reason I don't like merpeople literally happened to me - so I don't want to hear it!" I stepped back, stung, but at a loss for words. *He technically has a point*, I thought. *But it shouldn't matter! You can't hate a group of people for something an individual might do to you.*

"Whatever," I mumbled. He continued to follow me around as I paced around the cavern. It was smaller than I remembered. If I concentrated enough, I could almost see the past ghosts of my family lingering in the pool or lounging in the sand. We had been terrified out of our minds, but at least we had each other. We were happy.

And then they had left us to fend for ourselves.

The sudden sour memory took hold of me, and I shoved my hands in my pockets. *I will not cry in front of Reed*, I thought. *Distract yourself.*

I looked at one of the guards and noticed his polished bone sword hanging by his waist. I walked up to him. "Hey man, can I borrow that?"

A few minutes later, I had gathered up all the kids again. I held out the weapon. *Surely the kids will think this is cool*, I thought. *Who doesn't love swords?*

"Any of you interested in learning how to use a traditional merfolk sword?" I asked. The kids exchanged uncertain glances. I motioned for the small boy to come forward, and he slowly walked up. His face went pale as I handed him the sword. It wobbled in his tiny hands, and I had to lunge forward to help him balance it. I curled his fingers around the handle and smiled, trying to shove my inner confidence into his small frame.

"There you go. Just like that."

He offered a shaky smile as I stepped away, but quickly went back to staring at the sword like it might bite him.

"Our ancestors have been carving swords and spears out of bones for hundreds of years," I said. Somehow, his face got even paler.

"This is a bone?" he cried, flinging it away from himself.

"Ew!" the girl shrieked, skittering away. The boy wailed, his fingers shaking as he curled in on himself. Even Reed had the nerve to look uncomfortable as I stared at the two kids, at a complete loss for what to do. I held up my hands, dragging the sword away.

"Hey, hey, it's okay! You don't have to touch it if you don't want to!"

"Did they kill the animals for their bones?" the girl asked, her eyes wide.

I clamped my mouth shut. "Um . . . no."

Her bottom lip trembled. "You're lying!" she accused.

I floundered. "Well . . . I don't know if they were killed on *purpose*. They might've just used the skeletons after the animal died of natural causes," I said.

She sniffed. "So . . . we don't eat fish, right?" she asked. Somehow, my heart fell even further.

"Well . . . we do actually," I said. The boy's wails got louder.

"But we're fish!" he cried. "We eat ourselves?"

My eye twitched. "You guys do know that like . . . sharks eat other fish, right? It doesn't make them cannibals . . . you know what . . . never mind." I turned on my heel and marched out of the cave. Reed stared after me.

"You're just leaving me with them?" he hissed. I threw up my hands.

"Well, I'm just traumatizing them apparently, so take your best shot. Tell them how brainwashed they are." I stalked back to the boat and burst into the living room. Amy stared like she was expecting me.

"Where are the kids?" she asked. I motioned angrily out to the volcano.

"Probably drowning because they don't know how to swim," I said. "I don't know what to do with them! I tried answering their questions, showing them all the cool stuff and they're just . . . they're just *repulsed* by all of it." My chest heaved.

"I don't get it," I said. "I mean . . . from what I've heard - you handled the transition way better than these freaking snowflakes." Amy cracked a smile and leaned back.

"Well, to be fair, I wasn't your average iPad kid. I was constantly getting into trouble, being places I shouldn't be, messing with things I shouldn't have been. It's exactly how I got myself Cursed to begin with."

"I don't know how to get them to appreciate any of it," I muttered. "They don't care. They don't understand. They're not real merfolk." I froze as I realized what I had just said. Amy raised an eyebrow, and I stumbled to apologize.

"That's not what I meant," I said. "I know *you're* real merfolk."

Amy scoffed. "Better damn well be." She took a deep breath. "Truth be told, those kids might never identify as merfolk, even if that's what they are. And we can't make them."

"It feels wrong that they get to be one of us without really being one of us," I said. "I mean . . . why can't people like Emanuel get Cursed? Or Tom? They would make good merfolk. Heck - Emanuel would love it."

Amy chuckled. "Just be patient with them," she said.

How patient am I supposed to be?

I walked back onto the beach, taking my time to make it to the cavern. Emanuel loitered by one of the entrances, and Norman walked up to him from the other direction.

"I'm sorry," Norman said softly. I stopped in my tracks and pressed myself against the rock wall, hoping they hadn't seen me. Norman *never* apologized. I couldn't mess up this moment.

Emanuel sighed. "I don't want you to feel guilty," he said. "I just wanted . . . I just want the world to know we're together. That we're linked. I can't biologically adapt to you like you can to me."

"Why didn't you just say that?" Norman asked.

"I don't know. I was being stupid. We don't have to get married for our relationship to be legit. Just forget I ever brought it up," Emanuel said. Norman hesitated a bit, and I could hear him digging in the sand with his foot.

"Well . . . it's kinda too late."

There was another moment of hesitation, and Emanuel gasped.

"Are you *actually* proposing to me right now?"

"I mean . . . do you want to get married or not? Adam already agreed to officiate, so I kinda need to let him know." Norman yelped as a smile broke over my face. *Finally*, I thought. *Looks like they both decided to listen to me for a change.*

"Put me down!" Norman protested.

Emanuel laughed. "Really, you decided to propose on the beach at sunset? How cheesy is that?" he teased.

"Blame your son for that one!" Norman shot back. I stuffed my hand in my mouth to keep my laughs from being heard.

"Babe, seriously. Are you okay with getting married?" Emanuel pressed. Norman took a deep breath.

"I love you. And I want to make you happy. Plus, maybe a ring on your hand will stop random strangers from flirting with you. I want everyone to know you're mine," Norman said. *That's adorable*, I thought. Emanuel sniggered, and the smells suddenly changed to something spicier.

"I could make you mine on this beach, right now," Emanuel purred.

Norman chuckled. "Is that so?"

Yup, time to dip out, I thought. I backtracked and used a different entrance to reenter the cavern. I saw Reed sitting by the opening, knees curled up to his chest. Across the pool, Caspian seemed to be entertaining the kids with little figures carved from wood. *Better let them have their fun*, I thought. I turned towards Reed. His skin was pinched and pale. I could practically see his veins fluttering under his skin.

"You look like you need to swim," I said.

He scoffed. "Nah, I'm good."

"Come on man, you need to. You'll only feel worse the more dehydrated you get," I said. He sighed but reluctantly got to his feet and followed me towards the center pool. He eyed the water like it was acid. He swallowed, and I could practically hear how dry his throat was.

"It's beautiful down there," I said. He sighed and took a deep breath before jumping in. I dove in after him.

The water was crisp and gloriously salty. It had a flavor the pool in the basement could never mimic. I stretched out as my body morphed, grinning as the cold water flowed through my gills. I politely averted my eyes as Reed phased behind me, his scream muffled. After the water went quiet, I turned around.

Reed's gills flared open and closed, but he remained curled in a ball. I swam up to him and tapped him on the shoulder. He peeked out from behind his arm as if he was ashamed to reveal himself. I shot him a smile, trying to propel my confidence towards him. He slowly unfolded, wincing as his tail drifted through the water.

Follow me, I mouthed. He raised his eyebrow but joined me as I swam down deeper. The water grew colder, the light quickly fading. Right before the sea descended into complete darkness, I stopped and pointed down towards the bottom.

Barely visible was a hulking skeleton of a whale. How it had ended up there, I had no idea, but I knew Merfolk had been mining its bones for years. During the Rebellion, I had dived down there and helped haul up the ribs I could carry.

Reed shivered behind me. He tried to speak, but the flow of bubbles obscuring his lips made it impossible for me to tell what he was saying. I pointed to my lips.

Talk like this, I mouthed. He shook his head and tried to talk again, more bubbles flowing up to the surface. *Can he not read lips?* I thought. *Of course he can't - he's human. He's probably never had to read lips before.*

I covered his mouth as gently as I could, pointing to my mouth.

Talk like this, I mouthed. His eyes suddenly went wide and he backed away from me, pointing behind me. I turned to see a shark swimming lazily along the rock wall, definitely minding its own business. I had heard Emanuel lecture on and on about how most sharks were more scared of humans (and merfolk) than we were of them. I know I would want to avoid a species that knew how to make weapons.

But Reed was already panicking. He shot off towards the surface, which was possibly the worst thing he could have done. His frantic swimming caught the shark's attention. It turned, focusing its beady eyes on my friend. *This day really can't get any worse*, I thought.

I showed my back to the shark, moving in front of his field of vision. It turned in the opposite direction, and I swam up slowly, keeping an eye on it until I reached the surface.

By the time I crawled onto the sand, Reed had already phased and was attempting to walk to the boat. His legs wobbled beneath him, and he fell to his knees in the sand. I ran up to him.

"Hey man, it's okay. Sharks know better than to attack merfolk. Some of us are poisonous, remember?" He shoved me away from him.

"Yeah, well I didn't know that, now did I? You weren't even listening to what I was saying. I thought we had like super-sonic hearing or whatever?" he snapped.

I recoiled. "You can't talk in a human pitch underwater. We read lips."

He threw up his hands. "Well, thanks for fucking briefing me beforehand." He clambered to his feet again, making it several steps before falling again. He drove his fists into the sand.

"I fucking hate this!" he screamed, spraying sand as he punched the ground over and over again. I stood silent and stunned until he ran out of steam, gasping for breath, the skin missing from his knuckles.

"I hate this," he said. "I want my old body back. I want my family back. I want this to be gone."

I swallowed. "I - I'm sorry."

He glared at me. "Just leave me alone," he demanded.

Data Log 7:45 AM

Most vaccines attack a specific part of the body using proteins on their surface, and technically, this one does too. It latches onto blood cells and spreads from there - which makes sense because the blood types have to match. It can't spread if the antigens on the surface don't match. But that makes me wonder how the virus evolved to begin with. Who was the first merfolk? What was their blood type?

I know that humans are being Cursed with A positive blood. I could technically pull a list of A positive people from the volunteer records – but that would be illegal. Besides, I doubt the merperson doing this would be the type to come donate their body.

DANIEL

I didn't get to talk to Grayson or Reed until the morning after they returned from their field trip. They shuffled like zombies into the garage, yawning and still smelling of the ocean.

"How was the trip?" I asked.

"Shut up," Reed muttered. *Whelp, that summarizes that,* I thought.

"I'll tell you about it later. Has anything been going on at school? Did you hang out with Avery?" Grayson asked. I tensed. I hadn't talked to Avery at all – in fact – I was pretty sure they had been ignoring me on purpose. The past few days had been very quiet. Peaceful.

"Um . . . a little bit," I lied. I didn't want Grayson to realize there was tension between the two of us.

Other footsteps entered the garage. "C'mon, all of you in the car," Amy said, unlocking the doors.

Reed scoffed. "Why isn't Norman taking them?" he asked.

"He's busy," Amy said, opening the car door. "Get in or walk."

Reed grumbled under his breath during the whole ride and refused to get out at the same time as us. Amy drove down slightly further down the line to let him out, and he speed-walked past us as if we were going to contaminate him by breathing the same air.

"The trip was awful!" Grayson complained as we walked through the front doors. "I think all I did was freak the kids out and made Reed hate merpeople even more. I just don't know how - " He was interrupted by the thudding of heavy boots.

"Are you Grayson?" a stranger asked.

"Yeah," Grayson said, his voice tense. "Why?"

"We just want to ask you a few questions about your friend, Avery."

"Grayson, who are these guys?" I whispered.

"Cops," Grayson whispered back. *Crap.*

"Who are you?" one of the cops asked. I switched my cane to my other hand and held it out.

"Daniel," I said. "I'm one of the foster kids living at the group home. I know Avery too."

"Might as well talk to both of you then. Step in here."

I followed Grayson and the cops down a hallway and into a room. We sat across from them, and I tried to still my pounding heart.

"What's going on with Avery?" I asked. *Did they tattle on me?*

"They've been missing for almost a week," the officer said. My heart settled in my feet. *Oh no.*

Grayson sucked in a breath. *"What?"*

Crap, crap, crap, I thought. I had told Grayson I had been talking with Avery while he was gone. Now he'll know I was lying.

And he'll know that he didn't notice I was lying.

"We've been searching, but haven't found anything," the cop said. "All we know is that they disappeared sometime after school last Wednesday. When's the last time you heard from them?"

"We both hung out on Wednesday during school," Grayson said. "I texted them the next day, but never heard back."

"Do either of you have any clue where they might be?" the cop asked. I shook my head.

"They've been kidnapped, haven't they?" Grayson whispered. "Someone took them?" My blood ran cold. Foggy memories flashed through my skull. Trapped between panes of glass, muffled voices, the guilt of escaping.

"We don't want to jump to any conclusions," the cop said slowly. "But . . ." His silence was all that was needed to answer the question.

"How are you going to find them?" Grayson demanded.

"We're working on that," the cop said. His words were just as empty as before. I gripped the edge of the couch, forcing myself to keep breathing. *They have no clue where Avery is,* I thought. *Just like how no one had a clue where I was. They could be locked in a tank somewhere, they could be in another country, they could be dead.*

And they couldn't do what I did to escape. They were a normal merperson.

"Do you have anything to tell us that could help us know where they are?" the cop asked.

"No," Grayson said, his voice hoarse. We left the office, and I heard Grayson grinding his teeth.

"You told me you had been talking with them," he seethed, grabbing my shoulder. "Why the hell did you lie to me?"

I winced. "I - I didn't . . . I just . . ."

"Do you know where they are?" he demanded.

"No, of course not!" I said. "Look - they don't like me. I don't know why. I said that we had been talking so you wouldn't think anything weird was going on."

Grayson deflated. "Yeah . . . yeah okay, that adds up," he admitted.

I raised my eyebrow. "Wait . . . you knew they didn't like me?" I asked.

"They told me the first day they met you that there was something off about you," he said. "Told me to stay away from you. I ignored them - of course - I don't know why they would say something like that. They're usually super nice."

I wanted to point out that it had been their idea to pretend to drown Reed and his friends, but I held my tongue.

"And you didn't tell me they said that because you didn't want to make things awkward," I realized. We stood there in silence for a moment.

"When you were taken, they didn't do anything bad to you . . . right?" he asked. "I mean, they just used you as a pet?"

I winced but nodded. "Yeah."

"Then maybe they'll be fine," Grayson whispered. I swallowed, remembering the cop's words to Amy the day I had been rescued. *Rare one like that, no wonder he was trafficked.*

Avery wasn't unique like me. And I could imagine things much, much worse than being a decoration in someone's house.

3:34: dude this is an emergency
have you seen my sister

3:34: no? shes like seven and
goes to a different school

3:35: fuck

3:35: bro whats wrong
3:37: hello???

GRAYSON

I went through the rest of the day in a fog. The men in the van played through my head on repeat. Had Avery been taken in the same way? How had no one noticed a bunch of vans going around snatching kids in plain sight? What were they doing with them?

Kidnapping an albino no one knew was merfolk was almost understandable. He was rare and anonymous, no one would know why he was taken. But Avery? Everyone knew what they were. They were your normal, traditional, average merfolk. They had their original biological family - a rarity in today's world. What was the point of kidnapping them to put on display? Then again, why kidnap Reed? How did the kidnappers even know Reed was merfolk? Something wasn't adding up, and the cops didn't appear to know anything. Were they in on it?

I collapsed in the car at the end of the day, my head pounding with a headache and my patience running thin. Reed raised his eyebrows as he finally joined us.

"Who died?" he asked.

"Shut up," I snapped.

Amy turned around in the backseat. "Everything okay?" she asked.

"When were you going to tell us that another kid had been kidnapped?" I demanded.

Amy deflated and turned back around, pulling out onto the road. "I didn't know another kid had," she muttered.

"But you're not surprised either," I retorted. "How many other kids have been taken that you haven't bothered to tell us about?"

"What would the point be?" Amy muttered. "It'll just scare everyone."

"At least we would be prepared," Reed pointed out. "We almost got kidnapped ourselves."

"Yeah, and whose dumb fault was that?" Daniel muttered. Reed shoved him, and Daniel faked a loud cry.

"Wow, beat up the blind kid," Daniel winced.

"Oh please, spare me the dramatics," Reed shot back.

"All of you, shut up!" Amy shouted. I settled back and crossed my arms, gritting my teeth. We rode the rest of the way home in silence.

As soon as the car pulled to a stop, I stomped off towards the pool in the basement, nearly running Norman over on my way there.

"Whoa, why are you so mad?" he asked, putting his hands on my shoulders to steady me. I glared up at him.

"Avery was taken. But let me guess, you didn't tell me because you didn't know?" I seethed.

His face fell. "That's who got taken? I knew another kid had but . . . I didn't know it was your friend."

All my anger promptly evaporated, replaced with heaviness. I hated being kept in the dark. My best friend was missing, no one had a clue where they were, and no one but me seemed to care.

Norman put his arm around my shoulder and steered me towards the pool. "Let's talk for a bit."

We found ourselves in the shallow end, draped over some boulders. I tried to relax, but my entire body felt like guitar strings pulled tight. Norman listened as I ranted about all of my frustrations, everything from the Cursed kids not understanding our culture to the police not caring about the trafficking to stupid Amy keeping her secrets.

"I know you don't like feeling lied to," Norman said. "But you're just a kid. You shouldn't have to be worrying about any of this."

I snorted. "You were barely older than me when you started leading the Rebellion," I muttered. Norman blinked as if he hadn't previously considered how young he had been.

"I mean . . . I was almost sixteen," he said. "I was sixteen by the end of it all."

"Dude."

He flipped over on his stomach and looked at me, close enough that I could see his pupils under his blue eyelids. "Believe me, I didn't feel like a leader of any Rebellion," he said. "I was just a scared kid, trying to do what was right." He reached out and grabbed my hand.

"I know I'm not your real dad or brother," he said. "But I want you to have the childhood that got taken from us. So please, let us worry about this stuff. Let us handle it. But I promise I won't keep any more secrets from you." *I guess that's better than nothing,* I thought.

"So, you don't have any other secrets to spill?" I asked. Norman flushed but shook his head. I raised my eyebrow, a smile breaking over my face.

"So, you and Emanuel aren't getting married?" I asked.

Norman's jaw fell open. "How did you know I proposed?" he sputtered.

"I might've been in the right place and time to spy on you at the Sanctuary," I said.

Norman rolled his eyes. "You're a nosy brat, you know that right? But anyway, soon I hope. We talked more, and we don't want a huge fancy thing. Just a little ceremony on the beach with all of you heathens," he said, ruffling my hair.

"When are you going to announce it?" I asked.

He shrugged. "Emanuel told his mom this morning, so it's only a matter of time. I think she wants to go shopping for flowers later."

"Awwww."

He stuck his tongue out at me. "If you're so excited, you can come flower shopping with us after dinner," he said.

"Deal."

We went back to lounging in silence until Norman suddenly went tense.

"How . . . long were you eavesdropping on us?" he asked.

I wiggled my eyebrows. "Don't worry, I left before you two defiled the beach."

He flushed bright red and shoved me off my boulder.

That night at dinner, all was quiet. We ate in silence, the only sound was the scraping of the forks against the plastic plates. The weight of Avery's absence made the little food I ate sink like a brick into my gut despite the comforting conversation I had had with Norman. Meanwhile, the adults ate at their table, eating normally, with no stress locked in their shoulders. The little kids chattered excitedly at their table. They smelled like flowers, carefree and vibrant. They had no clue what was going on.

My thoughts were interrupted as the doors to the cafeteria burst open.

"Mi ninos!"

Norman and Emanuel both flushed as Emanuel's mom threw her arms around them, happy tears streaming down her face. Amy and Tom scooched over as the rest of the family streamed in around them, hugging and jumping up and down in excitement.

"Why did you wait so long to tell me you had gotten engaged?" Emanuel's mom demanded.

"We've been busy?" Emanuel offered. She playfully swatted his head and wedged herself between them, taking out her phone.

"Well, we have a lot of planning to do," she said. "We need to pick a venue, we need to pick the color scheme -" Norman gave Emanuel a violent look, and Emanuel gently covered up his mom's phone.

"Mami, I know you've always wanted to give me a big wedding. But Norman doesn't want that," he said. "We just want to do a small ceremony here on the beach, with friends and family." Emanuel's mom stuck out her lower lip.

"You've got two other boys to throw big weddings for," Emanuel reminded her.

She sighed. "Very well. But we are still going to look at flowers tonight, right?" she asked. Norman cracked a smile and nodded. She clapped in excitement and took her phone out of Emanuel's hands. Meanwhile, his younger siblings wandered over to our table as his dad followed around the two merfolk toddlers they were fostering.

"You guys look like someone died," David said. I resisted the urge to punch him in the face. *Avery might as well be dead*, I thought.

After dinner, I hopped in the car with Norman, Emanuel, and his mom. We walked into the flower shop and Emanuel's mom made a beeline for the front. As she chatted with the desk lady, Emanuel and Norman browsed through the rows of arrangements.

"So, which one of you is carrying the bouquet?" I teased.

"Watch it or I'll make you be the flower girl," Norman shot back with a smile. Another lady in the next row over turned to look at us.

"Aw, who's getting married?" she asked. Emanuel grabbed Norman's hand.

"We are," he smiled. The woman instantly stiffened.

"And is that your child?" she asked pointedly, looking down at me through her glasses. Emanuel and Norman exchanged an amused look.

"No, we just found him outside," Emanuel said, winking at me. The woman pursed her lips.

"Well, I just don't think that sort of thing should be allowed," she muttered.

"The gay part or the mixed species part?" Norman asked. She turned and glared.

"Both." She disappeared around the corner, and we dissolved into giggles.

"I vote we keep following her around and make out as grossly as we can," Norman said, wiping tears from his eyes.

"If she causes any more trouble, my mom will handle her," Emanuel said. "Come on, let's keep looking." Emanuel and Norman continued to browse, and I settled myself by an ancient TV perched in the corner. It was the local news station, and I instantly grew bored and started scrolling on my phone until something the newscaster was saying caught my attention.

". . . several human children have been infected with the merfolk virus . . ." My head snapped up, and I saw the mayor on the screen, clutching the podium and looking grim.

"We will not be releasing names at this time, but multiple children under the age of eighteen have indeed been infected with the virus. This has not happened by accident. All of the victims were attacked in their homes, between the times of one and three AM. All children have type A blood. Our police department is working around the clock to find who is doing this, but in the meantime, make sure you are locking your doors and keeping your children safe," the mayor said. *What about the children who are being kidnapped?* I wanted to scream. *What about them?* Cameras flashed and a dozen reporters raised their hands.

"Do you have any idea of who would be doing this? What their motive is?" one of them shouted.

"At this time, we have no additional information," the mayor said. Something in his tone made me think that he had plenty of additional information to spare. *He's hiding something.*

"What is being done about the children who are already infected?" someone else asked. At this, the mayor gave a heavy sigh.

"At this point, there is unfortunately nothing to be done. The children are being cared for as best they can, but there is no vaccine to stop the virus from spreading," the mayor said. Norman and Emanuel walked over to me.

"What's going on?" Emanuel asked.

I swallowed. "They're finally coming clean about one thing," I said. *Why isn't he addressing the trafficking issue too?*

"Are there any efforts being made to create a vaccine or a cure?" another one asked.

"At this time - no."

A chill ran down my spine. *At this time? Does that mean there's about to be someone working on a vaccine?* I wondered.

The phobic lady walked over, and suddenly her dirty looks felt a lot more venomous.

"I knew your kind was trouble," she snarled. Norman gritted his teeth and opened his mouth, but Emanuel grabbed his arm and sent him a warning glare.

"*We* haven't done anything," I snarled on his behalf.

"Sure, you haven't," the lady sneered. "You never should have come back from the ocean. I hope that vaccine wipes all of you away."

Daniel was waiting by the door to grab me once we arrived home. He dragged me into his room, which I thought was ironic considering how much he hated being pulled around. Reed was already sitting on his bed, staring down at the floor with a furrowed brow. Daniel shut the door and locked it.

"You heard what was on the news, right?" Daniel demanded. I nodded, then kicked myself for forgetting he was blind for the millionth time.

"Yes. Like . . . what the hell? Why speak up about it now?" I said.

"At least he didn't give any names," Reed muttered. "But I'm pretty sure I know how he found out."

"I just don't understand why he wouldn't talk about the trafficking problem too," I said. "I mean - that's just as bad if not worse!" Daniel raised his hand, silencing me, and turning back to Reed.

313

"What do you mean you think you know how the Mayor found out?" he asked. Reed flashed through a variety of emotions, before settling on reluctance.

"The Mayor is my uncle," he muttered. I blinked in surprise.

"That makes a lot of sense," Daniel said, almost laughing. "I'm assuming hatred of merfolk runs in the family? That's why he's more worried about the Cursings than the trafficking."

I shook my head. "You know he like . . . founded this entire hotel for us, right?" I asked. "He can't hate us that bad."

Reed fiddled with his fingers. "Yeah, well, I've sat across from him at Thanksgiving, and he hates merpeople," he said.

"If he doesn't like us, then why did he fund the group home?" I asked. "I've never heard him say anything bad about us on TV before."

"He plays both sides so everyone will vote for him," Reed said. "He also thought it would be better to keep you guys segregated away from the other human kids in group homes."

My jaw fell open. "He used the word *segregated*? In this century?" I repeated.

"Color me surprised," Daniel muttered.

"I mean, aren't you happy to have your own place?" Reed snapped. "Would you rather be here or in some home with random human kids?" I opened my mouth to retort, but nothing came out. He had a point, other group homes probably didn't have a luxury saltwater pool in the basement, but that didn't make the word *segregated* feel any better.

"But *why* does he hate merpeople?" I pressed.

"He was rightfully worried about the infection spreading. Which is *exactly* what's happening right now," Reed said.

"We're getting off-topic," Daniel said. "I want to know what the hell is going on with the trafficking."

"And how do you propose we do that?" I asked. "Amy will barely talk about it, and it doesn't seem like the cops have figured out shit. And the Mayor doesn't care about it either."

"I don't know," Daniel admitted. "But it's driving me crazy not knowing."

"What if it's a revenge thing?" Reed asked. "Like . . . one human gets Cursed for every merperson that's kidnapped? The trafficking problem started first, after all. Maybe one of you got mad enough to start getting revenge."

"But the traffickers going after Cursed kids too," I pointed out. "Why make more if they're only going to disappear?" I winced at the callousness of my words.

"At first I thought it was a person at the hospital - they would be the only ones who would know about the Cursed kids. But the cops said that was a dead end," Reed said.

"Maybe it's a cop?" Daniel suggested. I scoffed.

"The only merperson I know who vaguely resembles a cop is Norman," I said. "And he's definitely not going around Cursing people."

"You sure? He seems like the type who would enjoy a revenge quest," Reed said.

315

I threw up my hands. "Nice theory, but Norman is O negative, so his blood couldn't have infected you," I shot back. "So try again."

"Guys, we won't get anywhere if we keep arguing," Daniel snapped. "And Reed, like it or not, you're a merperson now. This involves you as much as it involves us." Reed pursed his lips. We lapsed into silence.

"Well, first thing first, let's try to figure out how many kids have disappeared. We need to know how big this problem is, or if it's happening in other towns too," I said.

"How do we do that?" Daniel asked.

I shrugged. "Google?"

We spent the next few hours hunched over our phones, looking for articles about missing merpeople. Turns out that they were buried in the backs of digital newspapers. My heart sank once more as I recognized Avery's face among the pictures.

I mean, I get not wanting to scare the little kids, I thought. *But surely it would be safer for all of us to know? How are we supposed to protect ourselves if we don't know what the threat is? How are people supposed to watch out for the kidnappers if no one knows they're there?*

"According to my count, I have five kids missing," Daniel said.

"There's ten more missing the next town over," Reed said. "And their mayor is doing something about it. Increasing patrols, alerting citizens."

I scoffed. "And of course, our mayor hasn't done anything," I muttered. I looked down at my phone. "Well . . . let's see if he has to say anything about it," I said. I stood up and paced as I copied and pasted the phone number from the city's website. The phone started ringing.

"You're *calling* him?" Reed demanded. I held up my finger as someone picked up.

"Hello? This is Mayor Lawson' office."

"Hi there, my name is Grayson. I am a . . . local citizen concerned about some things, and I was wondering if I could speak to the mayor about . . . those things." I winced at my awkwardness. Reed rolled his eyes.

"Um . . . may I ask what the concern is about?" the secretary asked.

"It's about . . ." I cleared my throat. "It's about the recent kidnappings of merfolk kids in the area. I want to know what the mayor is doing to address the -" The line went dead. I slowly pulled my phone away from my ear, stunned. Daniel crossed his arms, his jaw clenched.

"Told you," Reed said.

. . .

As the days went by, no more clarification bothered to show her head, but everyone made sure to freak out about the Cursings. It felt like before the Rebellion again, everyone questioning everyone else's true identity. Other kids at school who had previously been nice to me now avoided me. I could hear the suspicious whispers as I walked down the hallway. It bothered me, but I was too angry about being hung up on by

317

the mayor's secretary to care much. Avery was still gone and no one bothered to care or notice.

But if Avery had been a human kid who got Cursed, everyone would be up in arms. Human kids were more important than merfolk kids.

Reed joined in on the suspicious bandwagon, teasing and insulting me like normal as we worked through our group project. Unlike previously, he at least had the nerve to feel a little guilty about it.

On the way out to the bus loop, a kid shoved me as he walked past, then pretended to spasm and fall to the ground.

"He Cursed me!" he wheezed before dissolving into laughter. The other kids around us stopped to join in. Concerned parents looked out their car windows. Some pulled out their phones. Daniel sighed and lifted his cane into the air like it was a baseball bat.

"Fuck off!" he shouted. "We haven't Cursed anybody!" The crowd scattered, and Norman shot us sympathetic looks as we piled into the backseat. *This day literally cannot get any worse*, I thought. We trudged into Atlantis to see that Amy had everyone gathered in the living room. She stood in front, hands clasped, lips pinched in a thin line. She stared at the floor.

"What's going on?" Reed whispered. Norman sighed, and for the first time, I noticed how tense he was.

"You'll find out," he muttered. We took our seats near the front. Amy cleared her throat once we were settled.

"In light of recent events, Tom and I have had to make some difficult decisions." She sighed. "As some of you know, merpeople are being kidnapped. Mostly kids. As of now, there are five missing kids in our town alone," Amy said. The younger kids exchanged glances, faces going pale.

"We have upped security, but we can't follow all of you around everywhere you go to keep you safe, especially in the ocean. And currently, the town seems more preoccupied with all the Cursing stuff going on, so we have decided to take things into our own hands and implement some new safety precautions," Tom said.

"Starting now, no one is allowed in the ocean," Amy said. A chorus of complaints rose from the crowd, but a sharp look silenced all of them. "All of you will remain in your classrooms at school until one of us arrives to pick you up."

"We are also going to be putting trackers in all of you. So even if you are taken, we'll know where you are and can find you," Amy said quietly as if the words physically hurt her to say. I jumped up from the couch, curling my hands into fists.

"You're putting trackers into us? Like we're dogs?" I shouted. She narrowed her eyes at me, but I refused to sit down.

"This is to keep you safe," she said. "If it makes you feel better, Tom and I will be getting them too." It did not make me feel better.

"What makes you think the kidnappers can't hack into whatever program that tracks the implants? What if putting these inside us only makes us easier to find?" Daniel protested.

"They can't be hacked. We made sure of that. The only way to disable the tracker would be to cut it out of you," Tom said. I turned to Norman and Emanuel, who stood off to the side with their arms crossed.

"Why are you letting them do this?" I hissed. Norman refused to meet my gaze.

"It's for the best," he whispered. My jaw fell open. *Is he serious?* I thought. *How is this okay?* Emanuel gave me a pointed look.

"You and your friends have been worried about what could be done to protect you guys. This is what we've decided on," he said. "Be grateful." *Be grateful? Be grateful to have zero privacy ever again? This is bullshit.*

As much as I wanted to scream and throw a tantrum like a little kid, I knew there was no getting out of it. We were lined up and injected one by one. The needle was thick, and a little trickle of blood fell down everyone's ankles as they walked away. I let Amy inject the tracker without protest, only feeling slightly more like a caged animal than I had the previous weeks.

The thought of being kidnapped and made to do god knows what was the only thing that scared me more than having to be monitored.

Data Log 7:45

The virus starts in the lysogenic stage, which then forces the cell to inject the DNA into other cells without lysing. Normally lysogenic viruses like that aren't expressed until they go into the lytic stage, but these genes are expressed almost immediately. It's incredible.

I'm continuing to organize what genes do what in the virus. Unsurprisingly, most of them are triggered by water, but what happens to the cells themselves is fascinating. The skin cells morph into something different once the genes get turned on. When the cell is dry, it changes back.

Usually, viruses mutate - which is why it's so hard to find cures for them - if at all. But of all the strains of this virus I've seen are almost identical. And it's a huge virus, with over 2000 genes. Why does it not mutate? Does it not need to? If it doesn't mutate, wouldn't that make it easier to defeat? Have we finally found the organism that won evolution?

REED

Amy and countless others had assured me my body would get used to the transformation. They said it just took time. It took practice. My body would adapt.

My body was not adapting.

I could go three days without swimming before the virus locked in my DNA compelled my body into the water. And every time, it was agony. My bones twisting, my muscles turning to goo before solidifying. Screaming, throwing up, and exhaustion, every time.

Amy, who had been the most persistent of them all, was starting to lose hope. I could see it on her face as she helped pull me out of the pool in the basement. I collapsed on the ground, shivering and groaning. Emanuel stood beside her, not looking much more optimistic.

"Amy, it's been weeks," he whispered. "We need to figure out how to help him."

"What do you think I've been trying to do?" she snapped.

I lay on my back on the concrete, gasping for breath. "Just kill me," I muttered.

"Maybe Sam has some ideas of how to stop the transformations? Or make them less painful?" Emanuel asked. Amy shook her head.

"I've already talked to her. Unless he gets severely injured and his body goes into stuck mode, there's nothing that will stop it."

"What the hell is stuck mode?" I asked.

Amy tapped her cane on the ground. "If you get severely injured in one form or another your body gets stuck in that phase until you're healed enough to switch back again. When my leg got injured, I got stuck for weeks. When Adam got shot, he got stuck for a few days."

"Cool, so just break my leg," I said.

"Might not be a bad idea," Emanuel said.

"Except it's not permanent," Amy pointed out. "And as soon as his leg heals, what will he do? Break his other leg? Just keep switching what leg is broken? That's no way to live." *Neither is this*, I thought. I got up, wincing as my knees wobbled beneath me.

"Well, let me know when you care enough to do some extra research," I muttered, stalking back up the stairs. On the way up, I almost bumped into Daniel. He looked like a ghost with his white skin and white

T-shirt. He stared in my direction with those pink eyes, and I shivered involuntarily. *Jeez, this guy is creepy,* I thought.

"Scuze me," he muttered, stepping around me. As he walked past, I spied the black barcode tattooed on his shoulder through his shirt. *Why hasn't he gotten that removed yet?* I thought. *I would've clawed it out of my skin if it were me.*

I continued walking, only to be grabbed from behind. I turned around to see Daniel's fist buried into my shirt. His pink eyes were wide.

"You're gonna wanna see what's on TV right now," he whispered. *Jeez, his hearing is that good?* I thought. I followed him down the hallway and into the living room where the others had gathered. The blue glow of the TV cast shadows across their faces. Amy gripped the back of Grayson's chair with white knuckles.

Sam stood next to a man in a white lab coat, hands neatly folded in front of her. She walked up to the podium with the grace of a ballerina and closed her eyes as if she were saying a prayer.

"In light of recent events, my team has decided the best course of action will be to proceed with creating a vaccine to inoculate human children against the merfolk virus," she said.

All the air seemed to be sucked from the room. Amy's eyes widened, her jaw falling open. Grayson's face had gone pale.

A small weight was lifted off my heart, not that the announcement meant anything to me. It was a little too late for the ones already Cursed, but if it could help other humans, that would be wonderful.

The Sam on TV kept droning on, but everyone was too busy whispering and exchanging wide-eyed looks to hear. A knock sounded on the door, and the evil scientist in question walked into the living room. She sighed when she saw the others gathered around the TV. Amy and the others turned to face her, eyes narrowed like they wanted to tear her apart with laser vision.

"I was hoping I would be able to talk to you before you saw that," she said quietly. Amy opened her mouth, but Tom grabbed her arm.

"Why don't we talk about this over dinner?" he suggested.

A few moments later, we all sat at a table in the cafeteria. I picked at my food as the others ate in silence. The waves of tension rolling across the table were almost enough to make me puke again. I forced myself to hold it in as I tried to drown out everyone else's feelings.

It wasn't working.

Sam was the only one who seemed to be eating without letting the others get to her. She occasionally tucked her braids behind her ears as she chewed, thoughtfully staring into space. Amy seemed intent on melting her face with her glare. Tom looked up at the ceiling as if he were praying for a higher power to intervene and end the dinner.

Sam finally broke and met Amy's gaze.

"You can be mad at me all you want. But this has to be done. Things are getting out of hand," she said.

"Even if you were to make a vaccine now, it wouldn't help those already Cursed!" Amy muttered.

"You'd rather have a complete cure? That's worse!" Grayson blurted.

"There is no such thing as a complete cure for a virus. There are treatments, sure, but no such thing as a cure. Vaccines are the only way to stop this from getting worse," Sam said.

"You know exactly what will happen if you make a vaccine. The government will make it mandatory," Amy argued.

"And it won't freaking matter because you can't vaccine someone who's already sick!" Sam shot back.

"We are not *sick*," Amy growled. "That's like saying everyone should get vaccinated from having red hair. Being merfolk has never hurt anyone!" This time, it was my turn for my jaw to drop. Before I could spit out my reply, Sam did it for me.

"Are you serious?" she whispered, motioning in my direction. "Your ward came to me begging me to make him a cure because of how much pain he's in!" Several heads turned toward me, and I sunk in my seat.

"Thanks for ratting me out," I muttered, a flush crawling over my cheeks.

"Arguing about this isn't helping," Tom interrupted, glaring at his wife and Sam in turn. "If you're going to scream instead of talk, can you not do it in front of the kids?" I bent my head, suddenly self-conscious. *If I had been nice to merpeople in the first place, would I even be in this mess? I* wondered. *Or was I just a randomly generated name on a long list of kids with type A blood?*

Grayson grasped my hand in his, and I jumped in surprise. I could feel his worry the same way I could feel the heat coming off an oven. I knew Merfolk held hands to help regulate their own emotions, but I couldn't understand how feeling all of my panic was going to help Grayson feel any better.

Still, I let him as the adults argued. Amy was out of her chair, pointing an accusing finger at Sam.

"After all we did to earn our freedom back, you just want to throw it all away?" she shouted, finger trembling.

"I'm not throwing it all away!" Sam shouted, her fingers trembling. "I'm just trying to keep everyone safe. What do you think humans are going to do when they keep losing their loved ones to the virus? They'll take away our rights and drive us out all over again!"

Something shifted. Amy's nostrils flared, and sweat beaded on Sam's forehead.

"Why do you smell guilty?" Amy growled. For the first time, Sam tensed. "What is going on?" she demanded.

"Nothing," Sam said quickly. "But if I don't make a vaccine - this situation could get a lot worse. It's for the best."

"You're lying. You're trying to hide something," Amy whispered.

More sweat beaded on Sam's forehead. "N-no I'm not," she protested. Grayson leaned forward.

"Tell the truth, Sam," he said.

She hesitated and sighed. "The only reason that Mayor Lawson let you build this place is because I promised to make a vaccine," Sam said.

The icy tidal wave of shock that washed over me from Grayson was almost enough to make me gasp.

Wait, *what?*

Amy's face drained of color. So did Tom's.

"What?" Tom whispered. Sam looked up to glare at him.

"Don't act like you're so shocked. Duncan made you promise him some things too," she spat at Tom.

"How do you know about that?" Tom demanded. Amy turned her gaze to her husband, who withered.

"Tom, what is she talking about?" Amy demanded. Tom took a deep breath.

"I knew that the mayor would make showing markings in public be mandatory. And . . . I had to . . . reduce the numbers of refugees."

Ha! I thought. *I told them my uncle never cared about helping merpeople, but did they listen?* Beside me, Grayson went ridged. Amy's eyes flitted from her adopted daughter to her husband, her expression dissolving from furious to devastated.

"So, you both have been lying to me this entire time," she echoed. Tom's face turned from pale to pleading.

"Amy, it was the only way this would work." He tried to hold her hand, but she tore it away from him, stumbling backward. "He promised to give us all the funding and resources we would ever need if we made the deal."

"And let me guess, you called Mercer to come take away the ones who wanted to leave?" Grayson asked, his voice icy.

Tom threw up his hands. "Of course not!" he protested.

"But you still let them leave," Grayson hissed. "My parents abandoned me because of you!"

This all makes sense, I thought. *My uncle doesn't like merpeople any more than my father does. He saw an opportunity to sabotage merpeople and took it.*

"It was the only way. If we hadn't made that agreement, he would've chased every single one of us back to The Sanctuary!" Tom argued.

"You didn't even talk to me about this! You lied to me!" Amy cried.

"Yeah, well we both knew that if we asked you, you would've said no, and we would've been screwed," Sam said. "We did what we had to." Amy laughed, the bitter noise echoing through the cafeteria.

"Yeah, just like how this vaccine is what you *have* to do. There's never another option, is there?" Amy shouted.

"We can't all just make up our own rules whenever we feel like it!" Sam shouted.

"Amy, please try to understand." Tom reached out for his wife once more, but she shied away.

"Don't touch me!" she snapped. Tom's face fell. Grayson's grip on my hand tightened. Amy grabbed her crutch, hands shaking so badly she could barely hold it. She made to move away from the table but stopped as the back door was flung open. We all stared as a skinny merfolk stumbled into the entryway, pale a ghost.

"Who is that?" I whispered.

"My brother," Grayson said, eyebrows furrowed. The brother forced a smile and an awkward wave.

"What's up, guys?"

He promptly fell to the floor. Grayson jumped up and ran to him, pulling him to his feet and settling him in a chair. Tom hurried over, pressing the back of his hand against his forehead.

"Will? What's wrong? You're really pale."

Will weakly tried to push Tom's hand away.

"I'm fine. Don't worry about it."

Grayson frowned and held up Will's arm, which was wrapped in a bright pink bandage.

"What the hell is that?" Amy asked. The room grew silent. Will withered visibility.

"Nothing," he whispered. *He's hiding something*, my gut told me. *Why else would he have come through the kitchen door and not the front? He was trying to sneak in.*

"*Will*," Amy growled.

He swallowed. "I was . . . donating."

Tom frowned. "Donating blood? Where would you have been donating blood?" he asked. For a split second, I wondered if it was Will's blood that had Cursed me. Amy turned her glare back on Sam, but this time she seemed more scared than angry. Sam's eyebrows were furrowed.

"Will, why are you donating blood?" Grayson demanded.

He sighed. "Because I need the money, okay?" he muttered. Amy stared at Sam.

"You promised me that Duncan wasn't providing any benefits or bribes to his volunteers," Amy whispered.

Sam shook her head. "He - he told me he wasn't giving any reimbursement," she whispered, staring down at the table.

"Will, how long have you been donating?" Tom asked.

"A few months," he mumbled.

"A few *months*? Why have you been selling yourself for months? I thought you had a job!" Amy asked.

"I do, and it's not enough, okay?" Will snapped back. "I can only make so much lifeguarding."

"We could have helped you - you shouldn't have to be selling -"

Will slammed his hands down on the table, almost falling out of his chair in the process.

"This is exactly why I didn't tell you!" he shouted. "Because I knew you would freak out about it! I don't want to live off your handouts!" He pushed himself up from the table, wobbling dangerously.

"How much did they take?" Grayson asked, trying to steady him.

"They pay more the more I give, so I give as much as I can," Will said, pushing Grayson away and stumbling towards the door. "And I'm going to keep donating, and you all are going to keep your fins out of it!" He vanished from the room. Amy stared after him, stunned.

Sam swallowed. "I'm going to talk to Duncan," she said. *If she convinces him not to give out payments, then merpeople like Will are just going to be more screwed,* I thought. *Which is worse? At least he can make some money this way. Regular humans sell plasma all the time.*

Amy scoffed. "Yeah, sure you are."

"This isn't my fault!" Sam protested.

"Well, the vaccine you're making is your fault. And it'll be your fault when our species is gone," Amy spat, stomping from the room.

We gathered in Daniel's room after the dinner fiasco. My body felt strange as if it were no longer connected to the planet. Grayson's knuckles were white.

"It's got to be him," Grayson said.

"Sorry?" Daniel asked.

"It's the mayor. He's the one Cursing the random kids. He's creating the problem so he can have an excuse to make a vaccine and get rid of all of us," Grayson accused.

I laughed. "So, my Uncle Cursed me on purpose? I mean, I was never super close to the guy, but I didn't think he hated me that much," I said.

"He's got a point," Daniel said. "That seems a bit conspiracy-theory-ish."

"This whole thing is conspiracy-theory-ish!" he protested. "And it makes total sense!"

"I seriously doubt he would want to sacrifice humans like that - even if it meant getting rid of merpeople for good," I said. "Besides, what Sam said earlier is right. Even if there is a vaccine made, it's not like it's going to make you guys extinct. You can't give a vaccine to someone who's already sick."

"Well, what if a human-merfolk couple wants to have a baby?" Daniel asked. "They couldn't. I mean, they probably could. But it would be human."

"No, it wouldn't. Parents can't pass vaccines onto their kids," Grayson argued.

"Moms actually can pass antibodies to their kids in embryo," I muttered.

Grayson threw his hands up. "Well, aren't you so smart! So, the vaccine *can* wipe us out then?" he snapped.

I shrugged. "I don't know! Genetics are weird. They probably won't know until they start testing it on people. But I really don't think it's going to wipe you out like you think it will," I said, my brief meeting with Sam flashing back through my head. "A cure - yeah - that would wipe you out. But Sam is right - you can't just cure a virus. It's not that simple."

"So, you're saying that all the mayor is doing is try to keep his human population safe?" Grayson mocked. "That it's not because he hates merpeople at all?"

I rolled my eyes. "Whether or not he hates merpeople is irrelevant. The vaccine only affects humans. Someone needs to explain that to Amy," I muttered.

"How much money do you think they're giving Will for his blood?" Daniel asked.

Grayson shrugged. "I have no idea. It's not like he talks to me - ever," he muttered. I frowned. Sam hadn't looked guilty when Will stumbled in - she had looked confused. *If all the volunteers go through her - she would've seen him there before*, I thought. But she looked just as surprised as the rest of us. Maybe he was donating somewhere else that was paying him?

"Maybe Mr. Duncan was paying him instead of Sam," I mused out loud. *But why would Duncan or anyone need to pay for merfolk blood? Why did they need it that bad if Sam was already collecting donations for free?*

No one appeared to hear me. Grayson's fists were still clenched, his body coiled like a spring, so I closed my mouth. It was something I could bring up later - if ever.

In the meantime, I wondered what would happen if they really could cure the virus. Would the government make it mandatory? Would they wipe the species out of existence?

. . .

The mood at Atlantis had turned poisonous. The kids no longer ran around, laughing or cracking jokes. They stared solemnly at each other as if mentally preparing themselves for their future funerals, or for the kidnappers to barge in and whisk them away at a moment's notice.

Amy and Tom barely looked at each other, let alone talked to one another. The only ray of sunshine was Emanuel's mom flouncing around with her wedding plans, shoving sample flowers in everyone's faces, and asking their opinion between white or off-white.

As the big day loomed closer, more and more people pretended to put on a happy face. I did my best to buy into the good mood, if anything just to make Grayson stop moping. It didn't help.

Two days before the wedding, an Uber pulled into the driveway, releasing a tall lanky man. Grayson grinned the first genuine smile I had seen in days as the man, all smiles and freckles, ran towards us. Grayson joined him halfway, grabbing him in a hug.

"I'm so glad to see you," Grayson said.

"Yeah . . . heard things have been pretty . . . intense while I've been gone," the redhead said.

"Who is that?" I whispered to Daniel.

"How should I know? What does he look like?" Daniel asked.

"Tall. Red hair."

"Oh. Probably Adam. I heard he's officiating the wedding," Daniel said. *Adam? Why does that name sound familiar?* I wondered. My question was answered as Adam pulled a cutlass from his bag and offered it to Grayson. *The fencer*, I thought. I had seen countless videos of him on YouTube, running into chaos barefoot with nothing but a sword carved from bone. Even back then I had to admit his daring was impressive. I occasionally saw news stories about the controversial merfolk fencer on the Olympic team. Grayson's eyes went wide as he grabbed the sword.

"Right now?" he asked. Adam nodded, withdrawing another sword.

"Remember the lessons I taught you?" They both instantly lowered themselves to the ground. Adam's ears morphed, pressing flat against his head. He stuck his other hand out, balancing on his toes. The two circled each other like dogs rearing for a fight.

I jumped as they lunged for each other. The sword clashed and sparks flew in the setting sun. Adam made quick work of Grayson, toying with him for several strokes before disarming him. The sword flew several feet away, landing neatly in the sand like a javelin. Grayson stood up, wiping sweat off his brow.

"Not as bad as I thought you would be," Adam grinned, straightening back up. I could feel Grayson beaming across the beach. I rolled my eyes. *Suck up.*

Adam suddenly turned his green eyes on me as if he heard my sarcastic thought. He pulled the fallen sword out of the sand and offered it to me.

"You wanna try? I promise I'll go easy on you," he said.

I took a step back. "No thanks." There was no way in hell I was going to risk fighting a merperson with enhanced literally everything.

I smothered the other little voice that reminded me I also had enhanced everything.

"Wimp," Grayson said. I grit my teeth. I knew he was baiting me. And it worked. I stomped forward and grabbed the sword, surprised by how light it was. I gripped it awkwardly with both hands, unsure of how to hold it. Adam rearranged my fingers, casting one hand to the side.

"There you go. Try to hit me," he said, lowering himself into his stance. *This is stupid*, I thought. But I lunged forward, trying to catch him off guard. He blocked me but smiled.

"Keep trying. Aim for the vital organs." I swiped wildly, aiming for his ribcage, but he continued to dance around me as if I were a kitten trying to bat at him. *This isn't fair*, I thought. *Even if he was human he would beat me. He's on the freaking Olympic team!*

Adam's foot suddenly swept underneath me, knocking my feet out from under me. I yelped as my back hit the sand. He grinned down at me.

"You fight like a human," he said. I huffed.

"I am human," I muttered under my breath.

"Then of course this fight is unfair," he grinned. I paled, suddenly wondering how much Grayson had told him about me. Did he know about my rant that merpeople shouldn't be able to compete with humans? Was he about to skewer me to the sand as revenge?

He extended his hand and after a moment of hesitation, I took it. He pulled me to my feet, and I brushed the sand off of my back.

"I don't think it's fair either," he said. "But the news doesn't care about what I think."

"You - you don't think it's fair?" I echoed. "To fight against humans?"

He shook his head. "Generally speaking, no. Don't get me wrong, humans have beaten me in fights before. But it gets a lot more fair when I dull my senses."

"A lot of merpeople think you deserve to compete against anyone," I muttered.

He shrugged. "Well, they can think what they want, but I think differently than most merpeople."

"Why bother telling me?" I asked, crossing my arms.

"Because I want you to know that it's okay to feel the way you do about things," he said. I blinked in surprise. Not a single merperson here had ever offered a consoling word or an apology about what happened. It was always just *this is who you are now, better get used to it. Embrace the culture. The pain will go away, suck it up.* The closest thing I had ever gotten to an apology was Grayson feeling guilty for making fun of me. My fingers unexpectedly trembled, and I quickly shoved them into my armpits.

"You don't mean that," I muttered. *I hate merpeople*, I thought. *Even if I technically am one.*

"You know who else also lowkey hated merfolk?" he asked. He pointed across the beach to where Amy leaned against her cane, staring into the sunset. *She doesn't count*, I thought. *She only hates the sect of merpeople that tried to use her.*

"I know you don't like being stuck here," Adam said. "But I hope for your own sake that you learn to embrace it. There's more than one way to be merfolk."

GRAYSON

The next day, Atlantis was alive with stress, but a happier kind.

Adam had dragged Norman into a different bedroom for the night and fussed over making sure his tux didn't have a wrinkle or stray hair anywhere near it. Emanuel's siblings set up folding chairs and bouquets on the ends of the rows. Tom set up the trellis at the end.

Meanwhile, I hung out with Emanuel on the other side of the house, dabbing sweat off his forehead with a cloth as he tried to look like he wasn't about to throw up.

"It's stupid to be this nervous, right?" he chattered. "I mean, we've been Mates for five years."

I chuckled. "I think everyone is nervous on their wedding day," I said. "Just try to relax."

A few hours later, everyone was seated in their chairs. I plugged in my phone and began playing the music Emanuel's mom had picked out. It trailed softly over the speakers, and Adam motioned for everyone to stand.

There had been much arguing over who got to walk down the aisle first, and Norman ultimately won over an intense game of *Phase Ten*. Norman came down first, accompanied by Emanuel's father. He was already the same color as the red rose pinned to his front lapel.

Emanuel's father gave him a firm handshake at the end of the row and took his seat in the front. He tried to wipe his eyes casually, but everyone noticed.

Next, Emanuel came down accompanied by his mom, who was not trying to hide her tears. She beamed and gave her son a wet kiss on the cheek at the end of the row before sitting next to her husband.

Norman and Emanuel faced each other, hardly daring to make eye contact like they were shy kids again. Adam playfully scooched the two closer to each other, and the audience laughed.

"We are gathered here today to witness the union of Norman Davis and Emanuel Reyes," Adam said. "I have known these two losers for . . . what feels like forever." The crowd laughed again. "They have written their vows and would like to say them now."

Norman cleared his throat and held up a piece of paper, his hand shaking.

"Emanuel . . . when we first met, I was in a really dark place," he whispered, so quiet I could barely hear him. "I was so scared and full of hate. I didn't ever want to fall in love again, but you made it so damn hard to not fall head over heels for you. And you know how stubborn I am, but you have also shown me that you must conquer fear to enjoy love." Emanuel's mom cried harder, blowing her nose loud enough to startle a seagull.

Emanuel wiped his eyes. "Believe me, I know how stubborn you are. But I also know that you are the bravest person I have ever met. And I am so incredibly happy that you chose to take a chance on me," he said. "I love everything about you, and I promise I will never betray your trust."

My eyes inadvertently strayed to where Amy and Tom were sitting in the crowd. I had yet to see them touch since the big argument. *Did they say similar things in their vows?* I wondered. *Are they ever going to make up?*

"Norman, do you swear to take Emanuel as your husband, to have and to hold for better or for worse, for richer or for poorer, in sickness and in health, to love and to cherish?" Adam asked.

"Through hell or high water," Norman said, letting Emanuel slip a simple silver ring onto his finger.

"Through hell or high water," Emanuel repeated, letting Norman do the same.

"Then by the power invested in me, I now pronounce you husband and husband!"

The audience cheered as Emanuel scooped Norman into his arms, dipping him dangerously low and securely planting his lips on his. The chairs were quickly whisked away so people could dance to my wedding playlist.

Daniel stood off to the side, tapping his foot along to the music. I sidled up beside Reed and nudged him.

"You wanna dance?" I teased.

He rolled his eyes. "I thought you were aroace?" he muttered.

"Jeez, I asked for a dance, not to marry you."

"Fuck off."

I shrugged it off and went around looking for someone else's toes to step on, but instead noticed a figure pulling themselves out of the ocean. As soon as they got to their feet, they screamed. The sound washed over the crowd like ice water. Everyone's dance came to a screeching halt as they turned to stare at the water. The smell of blood traveled over the breeze. I ran towards them as the guards went for their guns.

"Caspian?" I asked. More figures emerged from the ocean behind him. Capsian looked at me, and my stomach twisted. His left eye was swollen. His lip was split. He clutched the Protector's staff in both hands like it was about to fly out of his grasp. His hands were shaking. The others behind him didn't look much better. Their fear filled the beach with the smell of sewage. Amy hobbled up beside me, face pale.

"What happened?" Amy whispered.

Caspian swallowed. "We were attacked. They . . . they killed my parents. They killed anyone who wouldn't join them or flee."

And just like that, the wedding was over. Everyone hurried back inside, leaving the decorations stranded on the beach.

My faith that Amy Wilson, Tom, Norman, or Emanuel had a truthful bone left in their bodies evaporated. I knew the vibes had been weird during our field trip at the Sanctuary. I knew Caspian had been visiting more for more reasons than just to say hi. And even after Norman promised not to keep any more secrets from me . . . he obviously had.

The guards ushered the refugees into bedrooms. The ones with injuries were sent to the nurse. The line trickled down the hallway and into the living room. Merfolk waited silently, their hands shaking as they held their broken body parts.

And I was screaming at the adults.

"What the fuck is going on?" I screamed. For once, Reed seemed to be on my side as he glared at the adults we had cornered. They all exchanged glances.

"It's Mercer," Tom finally said. "He's been causing trouble at the Sanctuary for a while now. Showing up, demanding that people join him, or there would be consequences."

My world fell out from underneath me. For the most part, I tried to keep Mercer's sect buried deep in the back of my brain. Just thinking of him made me remember how my parents had abandoned us.

And now, I knew that my parents had just helped Mercer raid the Sanctuary and kill our kind. And they were only there because Tom had let them leave.

"Whoa, wait, who the hell is Mercer?" Reed asked.

"Why didn't you tell us?" I whispered.

Daniel scoffed. "They're liars," he said.

"We just didn't want you to-" Amy started.

"Didn't want us to *what?*" I snapped. "Worry? Be scared? You guys must truly be the dumbest people on the planet because guess what? We're already worried. We're already scared. Our friends are disappearing, humans are trying to get rid of us, and now the fucking Sanctuary has been taken over by the worst merfolk on the planet!"

Daniel grabbed me to keep from lunging at them, and Emanuel's eyes filled with tears.

"Grayson, please," he started. I jerked away from him, chest heaving.

"You're all a bunch of liars!" I screamed. "A bunch of hypocrites! I thought when we were freed we would finally stop lying. You've been lying to us this entire time!" I spun on my heel, racing upstairs, my hands trembling violently.

I burst into my room to see Caspian sitting on my bed, his wounds freshly bandaged. My rage instantly faded as Daniel and Reed ran up behind me. We all silently stepped in and shut the door behind us.

"Do you want a hug?" I asked finally. Caspian nodded. I sat beside him on the bed and let him sink into my arms. I concentrated on any positive emotion I could muster up and tried to project it toward him like I could numb his pain. He trembled against me.

"I don't know what to do now," he whispered. "It was all I could do to get as many people out as I did but . . ."

"It's not your fault," I said. *It's fucking Amy's fault*, I thought. *If she had told us the truth, we could have protected them. If Tom hadn't let Mercer take merfolk away . . .*

Reed suddenly stood.

"Where are you going?" I asked.

"None of your fucking business."

He slammed the door shut behind him, and Caspian winced at the sound. I sighed, wondering if it would be worth it to chase after him. *I'll go find him later*, I thought. *Caspian needs me right now.*

By the time Caspian and Daniel had drifted off to sleep, Reed still hadn't returned. I covered Caspian with a blanket and slipped out, sniffing for Reed. The hallways were empty. So was the living room. By the time I discovered that even the basement was empty, I started to panic.

Why would Reed pick tonight of all nights to run off? I thought, opening the front door, and scanning the darkness for annoying skinny shapes. Where could he have gone? He wouldn't go swimming in the ocean - would he?

I should go get an adult. I should go get Norman, or Amy, somebody. Maybe I'm just overreacting and he's in the bathroom or something. It would be dumb as hell to go looking for him by myself with everything going on.

Fuck it, I was still too mad to ask any of them for help. I peeked outside to make sure the guards weren't looking and ran for it. I pumped my legs as fast as I could and looked up and down the street. *Maybe he tried to go back to his parents' place again*, I thought. I did one more scan and saw a small figure standing in the darkness by the bus stop. My heart sank.

What an idiot, I thought. *Why would you go back to the place where you were almost kidnapped?*

Reed's eye twitched as he saw me. He jumped off the bench, mouth falling open as I gasped for breath, pointing back towards Atlantis.

"You're . . . not . . . supposed . . . to be . . . out here . . . by . . . yourself . . . Idiot," I gasped.

He crossed his arms. "Neither are you! Although, I'm surprised to see you didn't tell an adult on me."

I scowled as I grabbed him and attempted to pull him back down the street. "Believe me, I thought about it."

He dug his heels into the asphalt, yanking his hand out of my grasp.

"What the fuck do you think you're doing, seriously?" I shouted. "You choose tonight of all nights to run off to do god-knows-what? Do you understand what just happened?" My hands began to shake, and I shoved them in my pockets.

"Exactly!" Reed hissed. "A lot is going on, and no one will tell us shit! I'm tired of being lied to - I'm tired -" He took a deep breath. "I'm going to find answers on my own." I blinked several times before I understood.

"You are the absolute dumbest person I have ever met."

He opened his mouth to protest, but I shouted over him. "You're trying to get yourself kidnapped?"

"I want to know why they're doing this. Besides-" he tapped his ankle. "Amy will know exactly where I am. She'll be able to find me - and find all the others too. It's foolproof."

"This is idiotic!" I hissed. "You have no clue what they're doing to them! They could be dissected, or dead!"

"I want answers!" Reed protested.

"So what, your plan is just to wander the same bus stop where you almost got kidnapped before and hope they show up to take you?"

"That's what happened last time, isn't it?" he said. "You need to go back."

"If I go back, I'm telling on you!"

We glared at each other.

"Look," I said. "I know you want answers. I want them too. But intentionally trying to get kidnapped to find those answers? It's . . . it's *crazy*. Do you know what Amy and Norman and the others would do if *another* kid got taken?" Reed's shoulders softened the tiniest bit.

"Are you kidding me? They'd probably all be thrilled that I got taken. Perfect karma, right?" he muttered. I resisted the urge to roll my eyes and grabbed his hand once more.

"Argue with me about it later. It's late. You're tired and emotional. Let's go home." I finally succeeded in dragging him a few steps only to bump into another figure. I turned around to see what looked like a homeless man. The blankets draped over his shoulders smelled musty, and something was growing in his patchy beard. I held my breath.

"Sorry, sir, scuse us." I walked around him, pulling Reed behind me like a reluctant dog. I tried not to scream as his weight suddenly tripled like he had decided to sit down.

"Reed, will you just come *on!*" I turned around to see him lying facedown on the asphalt, a dart sticking out his back. The homeless man stood behind him, a tranq gun poking out from his blankets.

My heart stopped beating as I stared at him, suddenly very aware that my markings were showing. My legs refused to move as he held up a cell phone to his ear, his eyes black and beady.

"There's another one with him."

"Reed, wake up," I whispered. He didn't move - of course, he didn't - *he's tranqed, you idiot.* I finally forced my legs to move, and I scrambled to pick him off the ground. His limp body felt like it weighed a thousand pounds. The man nodded and put his phone away. Whoever was on the other end must have given him an affirmative answer because he pointed the gun at me and pulled the trigger.

The world faded to black before I hit the ground.

Part Three

"True belonging doesn't require that we change who we are. It requires that we be who we are."
~ Dr. Brene' Brown

Data Log 1:14 AM

I finally came clean about not researching the vaccine. Duncan is disappointed, but the mayor is furious. He's threatening to pull all the funding from Atlantis if I don't have a vaccine on his desk in a month.

So now I've got to figure out how to kill it.

I started wondering if there's something in an adult's immune system that prevents the virus from taking over . . . maybe that would be the best place to start, but nothing. Tests have shown that it's not the adult's immune system that kills the virus, the virus simply . . . gives up once it realizes its in an old body. Doesn't even attempt to spread. It kills itself. It's like it knows its host won't survive. I've got to try something else.

But one more thing is bothering me . . . I told Duncan about Will donating his blood for money. He claims to know nothing about it. He must be donating to a different blood bank or hospital, but I've never heard of one paying for merfolk blood before . . .

GRAYSON

The world came into focus slowly, although there wasn't much to focus on. Wherever I was - it was dark and cold. The surface I was on was hard and slippery. It smelled musty and coppery.

I tried to sit up only to be pushed back down. I cried out as my skull hit the ground.

"Damn it, he's waking up," someone complained. Thick hands pushed down on my shoulders, pinning me down to the ground.

"We've got to hurry."

"I need a light."

I recoiled as someone turned on their phone's flashlight. In the beam, I saw Reed in the corner guarded by several other men. His face was

351

the color of glue. He had his knees pulled to his chest. His fingers trembled. The men around him had guns strapped to their waists.

What the hell is going on? I wondered, trying to make my brain cooperate.

I woke up very quickly as soon as I remembered.

Fuck fuck fuck fuck.

Wait, the trackers! They can still find us. We'll be just fine. We just have to survive whatever messed up thing they're going to do to us and wait. Surely it can't take them that long? I thought, sweet relief making me go limp.

One of the men standing over me scanned me with a metal wand. When it reached my ankle, it beeped.

"This one's gotta tracker too," he said. My relief vanished. Reed hid his face behind his knees as another man knelt over my ankle, a rusty knife in his hand.

Oh no.

It took several more men to pin me down as I thrashed and screamed. Several minutes later, blood poured from a hole in my ankle as the man smashed my tracker to dust under the heel of his boot. They yanked me to my feet and made me walk back to a rusty ice cream truck. On another day, I would've thought it was pretty ironic that my kidnappers were using an ice cream truck to kidnap kids. I thought that only happened in movies.

They shoved Reed and me inside, but not before they bound our hands behind our backs. The truck rumbled to life as it sped down the road.

Part of me wanted to scream and kick, but the amount of despair radiating off of Reed made me pause in my panic.

This was all his idea. And it failed in the most spectacular way possible. But I don't need to tell him that, I thought. *He already knows. What we need is to get out of here.*

I scooched over and grabbed his bound hands in mine, trying to soothe him. *We'll get out of this,* I thought. *We'll be fine. Amy and the others will still find us.*

Yeah, right, how are they going to find us if our trackers are dust?

The truck rumbled on for what felt like hours. My stomach growled, and my throat itched for water.

And I had to pee.

The truck suddenly screeched to a halt, nearly sending us into the back doors. Someone ripped them open and dragged us out. I looked around, trying to see where we were, but all I saw were thick trees draped with Spanish moss.

Okay, we're either still by the coast or they took us south, I thought. *How long were we in the car? One hour - two? Could we be in Florida?*

We were dragged towards an Amazon warehouse. Well - the ghost of one anyway. The little smirk had long faded out from beneath the letters, which stared blankly into the sky. Vines grew over the dirty windows. Broken glass and graffiti decorated the outside.

The stench of blood and decay hit my nostrils like a brick as the door opened. I forgot to walk, my body going stiff.

There must've been fifty kids - all in rusty cages. They sulked in their dirty clothes, huddled in the corners of their cages. Foul-smelling buckets adorned each one. They ignored us as we were dragged in.

"Where should we put these two, boss?" the henchman holding me asked. A large man in a pinstripe suit not meant for this environment turned, balancing on a thin black cane. He grinned at us through a cloud of cigarette smoke but frowned when he saw me. He leaned close to my face, blowing his smoke directly into my eyes. He grabbed my chin with his sausage fingers, inspecting me like a prize horse.

"Not pretty enough. Stick him with the others."

Not pretty enough?

"Prettier than you," I muttered. He laughed as he straightened back up.

"A spicy one, huh? We'll see how long that lasts, sweetheart," he sneered.

I bared my teeth as we were dragged away. The human holding me cut off the ties on my wrists right before shoving me into a cage that smelled like a musty Doberman. I nearly upset the bucket in the corner. Beside me, Reed was tossed into his cage. Our kidnappers locked the doors behind us before securing the keys back on their belts.

"Enjoy your stay," one of them laughed before walking away. I fumed, silently calling them every name in the book as Reed trembled beside me.

Mafia man said I wasn't pretty enough, I thought. *I wonder if that means the attractive merpeople are shipped off to personal zoos like Daniel was. Was Daniel held at this same spot? How could he not remember this?*

If they're not selling us off to be in personal zoos, then what are they doing with us?

I looked around at the other merfolk around us. They all stared at the floor, eyes clouded over. They were all covered with bruises and cuts. One trembled as they held a mangled arm to their chest.

"Psst, hey! What are they doing with us?" I whispered to my neighbor. He looked up at me as if he wondered why I bothered asking. I had to squint to make out the details of his face, but once I did, my heart dropped even further.

They were Cursed.

I swiveled around, staring at the other kids, my heart dropping further and further. At least half of the kids around me were Cursed.

"Kid, come on, talk to me. What's going on?" I asked.

"Just don't lose," they whispered.

. . .

The next morning, I woke up with a sore back and a stomach that was growling even louder. *What do we have to do to get some breakfast around here?* I thought. *Would it kill them to feed their captives?* I glanced over at Reed, who had his knees pulled up to his chest. He stared at the other kids, hardly blinking. I forced my wrist through the thin bars of the cage and reached for his hand.

"How are you doing?" I asked. He didn't respond. *This is insane, I* thought. *I mean, we knew that human kids getting Cursed was a problem, but there are dozens of Cursed in this room. Why were we only able to find a few missing people in our Google search?*

Maybe they're Cursing the kids after they've been kidnapped.

The thought made my stomach roll. I scanned the room, but none of the faces were familiar. *Avery isn't here, I realized. Where the hell are they? Were they taken by different people? Are they in a zoo somewhere?*

The two humans from earlier strode through the rows before stopping at my cage. I flicked them off with my free hand. They only laughed and dragged my cage onto a flat lift. Reed stared after me with wide eyes as I rolled through another set of double doors. The room was filled with gigantic saltwater tanks divided in half with a partition. Others stuck in their cages lingered around the room.

I was brought to one in the left corner. Another merperson in a cage waited on the right side of the tank. He couldn't have been more than ten years old.

The door opened, and the human dragged me out, forcing me up the stairs to the top of the tank. The lid had been opened on either side. The boy's handlers made him do the same thing, and he stared at me from his perch. His right eye was swollen so much I couldn't see the whites of his eye. He flexed his fists like he was getting ready for a fight.

What the hell is going on? I thought.

"You have thirty seconds to phase."

With that, the human pushed me into the cold water. I phased instantly, my dry skin grateful for the hydration. I relaxed for the briefest of moments before I heard screaming from the other side of the partition.

It didn't sound as bad as Reed when he phased, but it still made me wince. I wondered how well the kid could see underwater with his eye like that.

The partition in the middle slowly rose, and the little merperson flung himself at me, slamming me against the wall.

The fuck?

I tried pushing him away, but he clawed at every inch of my body he could, his remaining eye wide with desperation. I shoved him away from me, trying to swim away, but it was like trying to swim away from a mosquito. A very angry, desperate, large mosquito. The humans laughed as they watched us fight.

Is this kid drugged? Why is he attacking me? What does he want with me? Is he trying to kill me?

I had an advantage. I was bigger, and my transformation hadn't hurt me. I wasn't already injured. I could've attacked him back, but there was no way in hell I was beating up a ten-year-old.

I eventually stopped trying to defend myself. The kid grabbed me by my hair and pushed my face down to the bottom of the tank. I winced as my nose was smushed against the glass, but he had at least stopped clawing at me.

The humans outside clapped, and the kid promptly let me go, swimming back up toward the surface. His captor pulled him out, and I turned away from his screams. I reluctantly swam up to the top and pulled myself out.

"What the hell was the point of that?" I demanded. The human ignored me as he locked me in my cage again and pushed me back to my spot. Reed was gone, as were several others. I sat in the corner, still numb and smarting in random places. My stomach growled.

This sucks. But at least I'm not being dissected, I thought. I perked up as I saw Reed being brought back. He groaned as they let his cage fall back onto the ground.

"Reed, are you okay? What did they do to you?" I demanded.

"They put me in a tank and made me fight this crazy son of a bitch," he gasped. "My legs are killing me." He turned over and dry heaved before curling into a small ball.

"They did the same thing to me," I said. *What on Earth is going on here?* I thought. What's the point of kidnapping kids just to make them fight each other? Surely there are more important things they could be doing with us? There wasn't even anyone watching. Usually with dog fights - there's an audience to watch and place bets. Could they have been recording us? Were they selling the videos? Who would want to pay to watch merfolk kids fight?

We lay in silence for what felt like hours until another man came walking by, carrying a rusty bucket. He pulled out a long fish and dropped it between the slots of Reed's cage. To my surprise, Reed started eating it, sinking his teeth into the flesh and tearing off chunks like he had been doing it for years. The man kept walking, and I pounded against the bars.

"Hey, where's mine?" I demanded.

He turned around, smirking. "Only winners get fed. Try harder next time."

My jaw fell open as I gawked at skinny Reed. My neighbor's words from earlier suddenly made sense. *Don't lose.* Reed paused in his eating to shrug at me.

"I won my fight."

There's no freaking way, I thought. *How could Reed win in a fight against another merperson? Was it a younger kid, or an older kid?* I decided I didn't want to know.

He ended up sharing his fish with me when the humans weren't looking. It wasn't the freshest gourmet fish I had ever had, but it prevented my stomach from digesting itself any further.

This is so messed up, I thought. You only get fed if you win your fight? What happens if you never win? Do they actually let you die? How do they expect you to have enough energy to win if you're weak from not eating?

The thought of having to hurt another merperson just to get fed made me want to throw up what I had just eaten. *This isn't fair!* I thought. Merpeople stick together. They don't hurt each other, no matter what.

Except I wasn't fighting Merfolk - I was fighting Cursed who knew nothing about Merfolk culture. And not even all merfolk were good. The

Sanctuary had literally just been overrun by Naturals wanting control. Those merfolk certainly didn't care about hurting their kind.

Mafia Man walked by, his black cane clicking on the floor. He tsked at me when he didn't see any bones in my cage.

"Shame, I thought you would have an advantage," he said. I glared at him, wrapping my fingers around the bars.

"Merpeople don't hurt their kind," I hissed.

He shrugged. "You'll learn to or end up like the others."

I raised my eyebrow. "Like what others?"

He smirked and brought his cane closer for me to look at. My heart dropped for the millionth time that day as I saw what it was actually wrapped with.

Merperson scales. They glittered in the low light, sending little blue rainbows flickering over the concrete floor. I covered my mouth, scrambling backward in my cage as the man laughed, his big belly bouncing over his belt.

Oh my god. That *is* what they do with the losers. They make us fight until we're dead.

And then they skin us.

That must be how they're making their money, I thought. Who knows how much someone would pay for a purse made of merfolk skin? Maybe people are grinding our bones into medicine like they do to rhinos. Maybe our flesh is a delicacy.

I dug my nails into my legs, as if doing so would keep my skin attached to my body as Mafia Man walked away, his laughter echoing off the walls. Reed had dropped what was left of his fish, looking green.

"There's no way," he whispered. "Merpeople are too valuable for that." His words faded to silence as my fingers trembled. He was right – why of all things would merpeople be used for fancy purses? Surely there were more important things we could do – like be dissected for science.

But it didn't matter. I either had to start winning my fights or die.

NORMAN

We stared down at the blood-slicked floor of the abandoned gas station. I swore, driving my fist into the wall as Emanuel's eyes filled with tears. The cop beside Amy attempted to offer a sympathetic look.

"I'm sorry. This is all we found. The blood is definitely theirs," the cop said. Another investigator walked by, two plastic bags clutched in his hands. Tiny fragments of the trackers Amy insisted on being injected into their bodies glimmered in the low light.

Tom attempted to hug his wife, but she brushed him off. She still smelled furious, even with everything else going on. I wanted to tell her to get over it, but every time I thought of doing so, Grayson's anger raced back through my head.

You've been lying to us this entire time.

My heart splintered, and Emanuel grabbed my hand. I barely felt it. My son was gone and the last words he said to me were calling me a liar. *I should've been more honest with him,* I thought. Why did I let Amy talk me into keeping everything a secret?

For a moment, I was on Tom's side. Maybe doing everything Amy's way wasn't the best course of action after all.

"Have you found anything else?" Emanuel asked.

The cops shook their heads. "We're lucky someone saw the van here and reported them. We have some footage of them on the highway headed south, but they must've gotten off on some backroads and traveled from there. But we're looking as hard as we can," he assured me. I wanted to get in the car and drive down every road in the country until I found the boys but gone were the days where we could disappear on a heroic mission. The kids and Caspian's band of refugees needed us at Atlantis.

We piled back in the car and drove home, the air reeking of despair. By the time we arrived at Atlantis, another familiar figure waited on the steps. Amy gritted her teeth as she stood up, wringing her fingers.

"I heard about what happened," Sam said. "I'm so sorry." At that moment, all I saw was the little girl Tom had rescued all those years ago. *She's only eighteen,* I thought. *Barely older than us when all this started. She's just a kid. She was trying to do what was right.*

All at once, the angry energy drained out of Amy. Her fingers shook as she reached forward and gingerly embraced her adopted daughter as if she would shatter into glass if she squeezed too hard. Sam stiffened as she did so, but slowly relaxed, resting her head on Amy's shoulder.

"I'm still super fucking pissed," Amy said. "And you and Tom for lying to me. But I understand why you did it."

"I don't want to make a vaccine," she said. "But I don't know how else to stop this from happening. The mayor threatened to pull all funding from Atlantis if I don't." Amy nodded. They separated, and I took a deep breath.

"Okay, where do we go from here?" I asked.

"From now on, no one leaves Atlantis - not for school - not the doctor - not anything. We have to keep the kids safe," Tom said. I nodded in agreement. We filtered into Amy's office and sat down on the floor in a circle.

"Do we actually think the police are helping?" I asked. "Because according to the news and social media, people only care about human kids getting Cursed. There's been no mention whatsoever of the trafficking."

"Everyone seems to think it's a merperson Cursing the kids . . . but why would a merperson be Cursing kids just for them to get kidnapped? It doesn't add up," Sam muttered.

"So, you think it's a merperson kidnapping the kids?" I asked.

She shrugged. "I don't know. This would all make more sense if we knew why they were being taken."

My fingers shook again as I thought of Grayson – alone, scared. Who knew what these people were doing to him?

If we didn't figure this out, I would probably never see him again.

Data Log 1:14 AM

There are three strategies to make a vaccine. Weaken the virus so it can't reproduce, kill it with toxins, or cut it into pieces. Weakening it hasn't worked, so I've tried cutting it into pieces. That doesn't work either. I'm having to use my blood as samples. The volunteers have all but disappeared with recent news. Everyone is mad at me. And I can hardly blame them.

But I don't figure this out, Atlantis loses all of its funding, and everything Tom and Amy worked for will be for nothing. Humans will hate our kind even more. And we no longer have The Sanctuary to go in case the humans drive us out again. I have to figure this out.

REED

I thought for sure that Grayson would put effort into winning his fight the next day after seeing the man's cane made of scales, but at dinner time, he didn't even look up as the man came around with the bucket of fish.

I resisted the urge to roll my eyes as I passed him chunks of flesh through the bars.

"You're going to die if you keep this up!" I hissed. *And I'll starve too if I keep having to share with you.* Grayson took the chunks, chewing slowly.

"I can't just beat up some random kid," he whispered. "Merpeople stick together. We don't hurt each other."

"I don't know if you've noticed, but these aren't your traditional merpeople!" I said. "We're humans who got stuck in a shitty situation. They'll tear you apart."

Grayson winced. "Yeah, I know."

I could already see bruising forming on his right cheekbone, the skin swollen and red. *This is ridiculous*, I thought. *He's wasting his advantage. He doesn't have to spend thirty seconds feeling every cell in his body rip apart before he has to fight someone.*

I wanted to tell him that if he was just going to lose on purpose, that only meant I for sure had to win if I wanted to keep both of us alive. I didn't see any other Cursed feeding their cage-mates. But how long would we both last going like this?

Every cell in my body screamed at me. So far, I had won my fights out of pure desperation and rage. It was my entire fault Grayson and I were here, and I would be damned if I didn't get us out of it. It didn't matter what the cost was.

Even if that cost was some kid slowly starving to death and getting skinned.

I shivered as the memory of the man's laugh ricocheted through my head, but something still didn't add up. If they only wanted us for our skin, what was the point of the fighting? Logistically speaking, wouldn't that only damage their product? If they wanted the skins to be healthy, they would kill us peacefully and skin us right away.

I was still struggling to interpret the emotions of the people around me, but I couldn't shake the feeling that something else was going on. And I was going to get to the bottom of it.

But first, I had to figure out how to escape before it was too late.

For the next several days, I paid close attention to the fight pairings. It seemed that they tried to put together the kids who would be evenly matched - and they started the newcomers off easy to give them a chance.

The first kid I had fought had been scrawny like an elementary schooler. They had tried, but it was pretty easy to overpower them and smush them down. My second opponent had been harder. He looked closer to my age and had given me a few scrapes and bruises before I wrestled him down. My third opponent had almost torn my arms off.

This one looked to be an actual high schooler, bulky and long with the traces of a beard on his blue-tinted skin. I marveled at how he had even survived being Cursed for approximately two seconds before he dug his fingers into my throat. He instantly pinned me against the bottom of the tank, but since my actual face wasn't pressed against the glass, he wasn't done yet.

I screamed as I clawed at his fingers, trying to pry them away. I wondered if you got extra food if you killed your opponent in battle. How on Earth I was still breathing? *Wait, duh, we're underwater. I don't need my throat to breathe. I have gills.* He couldn't suffocate me like this. Crush my windpipe maybe - but not suffocate me.

I remembered that I had a tail and flung it at his face. I blinded him, diverting his focus for a few precious seconds. I wriggled out from underneath him and bolted to the other side of the tank, massaging my sore throat as he turned, flexing his fingers. The muscles in his arms literally bulged as he stalked me. Where did they find this guy - a wrestling tournament?

I ducked out of the way as he tore after me again. The humans booed as I raced around the tank, barely staying out of his grasp. *So sorry we're not being entertaining enough for you*, I thought.

I definitely couldn't beat this guy physically. His muscles were the size of my head, but maybe I could use my speed as an advantage.

I shot towards the bottom corner of the tank and waited until the last possible second to dart out of the way. As he hurdled towards the bottom, I curved and slammed my tail into his back. His cheek touched the bottom.

I raised my hand and pointed. *That totally counts!* I mouthed. The humans side-eyed each other before shrugging and walking back up the stairs. The merperson glared at me as he swam back to his side.

You look like you've never lost a fight, I thought. *You can miss a meal.*

As I was taken back to my spot on the floor, I scanned the room for cameras. I saw nothing other than other merpeople being pushed toward their fights. *There's got to be a better reason for this*, I thought.

"So . . . how much are you guys getting paid?" I asked. They ignored me. I wondered briefly if we had the same blood type. How would they feel if they suddenly found themselves in our shoes?

After the guards left, I surveyed the others around me. Grayson was gone, but I could see his neighbor in the cage next to him.

"Psst," I whispered. "Hey! Do you know why we're in here?" The little kid ignored me, eyes plastered on the floor in front of him. I turned my attention to a girl across the way.

"Hey kid, talk to me. How long have you been in here?" I asked. She turned her head away from me. I huffed and leaned against the bars. Guess there was no point in making friends if you just had to battle them for food later. And after receiving my fourth fish, the looks got dirtier.

They're going to keep putting me with harder and harder opponents until someone beats me, I thought. *Maybe I should start throwing some fights so they go easier on me.*

Grayson showed back up a little while later, looking just as dejected as he normally did. His injuries were getting worse. I could see his ribs poking out from under his shirt.

I opened my mouth to voice my concerns, but he silenced me with a glare. When I offered the chunks of fish, he refused to take any.

Across the floor, someone started screaming. We both perked up and craned to see what was going on. Several cages were being loaded onto a cart, but instead of being wheeled out to the tank room, they were wheeled out the front doors that we were first brought through. All the kids in the cages looked dead.

The fish in my stomach suddenly lurched upwards, and I forced myself to swallow the vomit. *So the kids aren't being skinned here,* I thought. *They take them somewhere else.*

Beside me, Grayson dry-heaved, his hands shaking. As the days passed, he looked worse and worse. Whenever he wasn't fighting, he lay in the bottom of his cage, staring at the ceiling, not moving. He shivered as the temperature dropped every night. I noticed more and more cages were being taken out of the front doors and returned empty.

No new plans for escape had crossed my mind. There was nothing to pick the locks on the cages with - and even if there were - humans constantly walked around to make sure we weren't getting up to no good. Several of them carried guns, and I was sure they would feel little guilt if they had to shoot someone.

That day when I was pulled to fight, my heart sank. The teenager on the other side had fins.

Oh, I'm fucked, I thought. *One nick of those poisonous needles, and I'm done. They'll have to fish me out with a net. I won't be able to move even if they do decide to feed me out of pity.*

Wait. Needles.

A plan formulated in my head as I was pushed into the water. As the partition lifted, I took a deep breath and prayed my plan would work.

I halfheartedly swam around the tank for a few minutes, dodging the poisonous spikes. After it looked like I had given an effort, I let the merperson stab me.

Numbness instantly spread through my arm, but before he could pull away, I grabbed the needle with my free hand and ripped it as hard as I could. It broke off in my hand, and my attacker howled in pain. I shoved the needle behind my ear, hoping it would still be there when I phased back as the rest of my body went numb.

I sank like a rock towards the bottom, and my human grumbled as he fished me out with a net. He carried me and shoved me in the cage, stuffing my tail behind me. I lay there, unable to adjust myself or phase back into human form as I was dumped back into my normal spot.

Out of the corner of my eye, I saw Grayson clutch at the bars of his cage.

"Reed? What happened?"

I couldn't reply, but I could feel his panic growing.

"Reed!"

One of the humans smacked the top of his cage. "Quiet!" The human walked away, and I prayed that the other humans wouldn't assume I was dead and skin me before I could enact my plan.

"Did you get poisoned? Why the hell would they put you with someone who's poisonous?" Grayson asked. He slumped as he realized I couldn't respond.

"You better not be dead," he muttered, curling his knees to his chest. I wondered if he was beginning to regret throwing his fights.

Hopefully, it won't matter, I thought.

Hours passed. The human skipped the both of us with the fish bucket. I could hear Grayson's stomach growling. I could see the sunset through the narrow windows. After what felt like years, I was able to make a finger move.

Then my hand. Then my arm. I phased back to human form.

I had always heard that merperson poison took days or weeks to wear off - but maybe that was just how it affected humans. Either my Curse or sheer force of will was making it go away faster because I was able to sit up and move my legs by the next morning.

Grayson looked so relieved he could cry. I felt along my hair and clamped my jaw shut so no one would see me smile. Before I was carried to my next fight, I tucked the needle under the waste bucket. As I suspected, they put me with an easier opponent this time. I won and resisted the urge to tap my fingers as I waited for the fish man to come by with the bucket.

As he began to make his rounds, I fished the needle out and held it in my palm, making sure not to poke myself with it again. I refused to think of what would happen if this didn't work.

It had to work.

The man dropped the fish through the bars at the top of my cage. I lashed out, stabbing him in the calf with the needle. He yelped in surprise, dropping the bucket as his body went stiff. He staggered away and fell to the ground, his face frozen in shock.

I clawed at his ankles and dragged him back. I grabbed his keys on his belt loop and after a moment of fumbling, succeeded in unlocking my cage. I jumped out and immediately started searching for the key to unlock Grayson's cage.

"You are fucking incredible," he said, staring at me slack-jawed.

"Don't praise me just yet." I cursed under my breath as key after key failed. A human shouted in the distance, and I froze in fear.

"Go, just go while you have the chance! Get help!" Grayson whispered.

"I-I can't just leave you here!" I protested. The shouting grew louder.

"Just go!" he said, shoving me away from his cage. "Go get help!" I scrambled to my feet and booked it for the window. Holding the needle in my teeth, I pulled myself up and shattered the glass with my elbow. Cheers rang out from the cages as I pulled myself through and dropped to the ground. The sensation of grass on my bare feet almost made me want to cry.

The humans exploded out the door behind me, shouting. I yelped as gunshots decorated the ground around my feet. I looked around me. There were no other buildings in sight as far as I could see. Running down the road with them shooting at me would be suicide.

I bolted into the woods across the street. Branches whipped my face and vines attempted to trip me as I forced myself to move as fast as I possibly could. All I could hear was my heart pounding in my chest.

How far do these damn woods go? I wondered. *I better not get fucking lost in here. Please tell me merpeople have some sort of magical tracking ability.*

I risked turning around to see the humans still chasing me. Yellow flashlights tore through the darkness.

I skidded to a stop, gasping for breath, the world tilting around me. *I can't keep this up*, I thought. *I need to hide.*

I clamored up the first tree I could find. Bark scraped my skin, and the branches bent dangerously under my weight, but I kept climbing until the flashlight beams below were tiny. I flattened myself against the trunk, trying to make myself as small as possible. I barely breathed, hoping against hope they wouldn't find me. I couldn't very well avoid the bullets in a tree.

I stayed there for what felt like hours, trying not to cry out every time I heard a twig crack or heard a human shout. The temperature dropped lower and lower, but I refused to shiver. At some point, a spider crawled across my face and took a nap on my cheek before disappearing.

Eventually, the humans left. I still refused to move. The night slowly morphed into sunrise, the bright sun turning the sky pink. When I realized how high I had climbed up, I nearly fainted. If I had slipped - I would have died for sure. The ground looked like it was a hundred feet away.

I am not afraid of heights. I am not afraid of heights.

I slowly climbed down, biting back screams as branches creaked underneath me. I made it to the ground, but my legs were shaking so badly, I could hardly stand. I let myself catch my breath before forcing myself to run again. I had no clue where these woods ended, but there was no way in hell I was running back toward the warehouse.

I ran, the world becoming more and more lopsided as I maneuvered through the thick vegetation. Thorns scratched my skin. Blood dripped down my legs. My stomach growled.

I was seconds away from lying down in the dirt and letting myself decompose into the leaf litter when I spotted a sign of life. A building glowed with soft yellow light in the distance. I smelled waffles. I ran harder, afraid that at any moment, a human would shoot me and drag me back.

I broke out of the woods and ran across a street filled with potholes. A Waffle House logo with half of the bulbs flickering welcomed me. I cried out in relief as I made it to the front doors. I stumbled inside and everyone looked up, various expressions of confusion crossing their faces.

I let myself fall on the front counter, praying that none of my captors had decided to have lunch at this particular restaurant. The waiter stared at me, horrified as I leaned against the counter, trying to suck some oxygen back into my lungs.

"Can you call the police for me?" I gasped.

Turns out, people who hung out at Waffle House were the best. The waiter - Kai - called the police as a heavyset guy wearing an ankle bracelet made sit down and cooked me as many waffles and hashbrowns as I could choke down. It felt a little too early to celebrate by eating, but I was starving, and the sound of police sirens in the background filled me with relief.

Soon Grayson will be here eating hashbrowns with me and reminding me of how much of an idiot I am, I thought. *And I'll deserve every word of it.*

A pair of cops walked in and immediately started to interrogate me. I answered between bites of food, telling them everything I remembered.

"Where are we?" I asked once they were done. "Have you told Amy? Does she know?"

"You're in Florida, and yes, we've informed her that you were found as soon as we were called. She's on her way, but it'll take about two hours for her to get here."

"Have you got my friends out?"

"We've got the building surrounded. No one's getting in or out. We'll have your friends soon." My fingers shook with relief, rattling against the plate.

Amy burst in some time later, definitely sooner than two hours. *How fast did she speed to get here?*

I smiled at her, expecting her to respond with a grin and perhaps a small trophy for being so brave. But all she did was frown when she saw me. The hashbrowns sank in my stomach as she motioned me towards the door.

"What's wrong?" I asked.

"Son, are you sure it was the old Amazon warehouse?" one of the police officers asked me. I nodded, the hashbrowns sinking lower and lower. I got into the car beside Amy as she drove us there.

Dozens of cop cars surrounded the building, lights flashing. I looked around to see if they had arrested any of the humans, but I saw no one sitting in the back of their cars. I saw no merpeople getting treated for their wounds or crying in relief. I followed the cop up to the door. I nearly threw up when he opened it.

The warehouse was empty.

"How many merpeople did you say were here?" he asked.

"Like, fifty," I whispered. I ran inside, scanning the gigantic room. There was nothing. Not a leftover cage, bucket, or puddle of water. The only thing that remained was the smell and faded spots on the concrete where the cages had sat. My fingers trembled. I sank to my knees.

"No. They were all just here. THEY WERE ALL JUST HERE!" I shouted. I turned around, poking my finger in the cop's chest. "Did you check the other rooms? The ones with tanks? Where are my friends?"

Amy gently pulled me away from him as I sank to the ground, trembling. The cop frowned and turned to whisper in his partner's ear.

"It's okay, Reed," Amy said. "Breathe." I tried, but I couldn't. I had gotten Grayson into this mess only to abandon him. I had lost him all over again. I hadn't been fast enough. I had never even considered the possibility that they could pack up their stuff and move somewhere else.

We were back to square one. We had no clue where they were. Or if they were still alive.

"I know. We'll find them. They can't have gone far. This brings us a step closer. You're so brave," Amy said. I wanted to shake my head and tell her no - that this was all my fault - but all I could think of was where the fuck they had taken my friend.

GRAYSON

I should have known that Reed escaping was too good of news to last. When the humans returned empty-handed, they immediately got to work stacking our cages onto carts and whisking us out of the pair of double doors.

I didn't have enough energy to protest as they shoved me into the back of a much larger truck with the others and sealed us in the darkness. Some kids screamed and pawed at the bars, but most sat quietly, hands quietly shaking or not moving at all. The brief hope that had washed over the captives as Reed escaped had vanished like a candle in the wind. The stench of despair was ten times stronger.

Where are they taking us? I wondered. *To another abandoned warehouse to make us fight? Or are they going to take us to wherever they take the dead kids to skin us?*

At least Reed was safe.

A few hours later, the doors opened up. They unloaded our cages in what smelled like a parking garage before ushering us inside a building that reeked like bleach.

We all squinted as we were dropped in a room with the lights turned up way too bright. Or maybe they were just normal lights, and we were too used to being held in the darkness.

This room was pristinely clean. The floor glistened. We were the dirtiest things in there. Humans in white lab coats wandered around the cages, jotting things down on clipboards.

One of the kids next to me cried out, reaching a hand out to someone in a cage across the room. The other merperson responded with a weak grin. I recognized them as one of the merfolk who had been wheeled out of the doors - presumed dead.

Wait . . . they're not dead, I realized. Although, they hardly looked better. Their markings looked even more jagged and blurred than before. A few weak strands of hair clung to their head. Instead of regular clothes, they wore a hospital gown with a plastic bracelet around their wrist.

As I looked around the room, I noticed more and more of the supposedly dead merpeople. They all looked the same - hospital gown, thin hair, skin and bones.

Mafia Man lied, I thought. *They weren't waiting for us to die so they could skin us. They were waiting for us to die so they could send us here . . . wherever here was.* I wanted to feel better, but the haunted expressions of the kids in gowns made me hesitate. Did they wish they were dead?

Wait, is Avery here?

I looked around as much as I was able, sniffing the air, and searching for their familiar scent. I eventually found it. I nearly cried out in relief. They looked like they were asleep, but I could see their stomach rising and falling out. Like the others - their markings looked blurred and disoriented. But at least they were alive.

Thank god.

I was so distracted I barely noticed the man who came and stood in front of my cage. He tapped a pen against his clipboard, analyzing me through a pair of glasses.

Is this the part where I get dissected? I wondered. The man surprised me by unlocking my cage and pulling me out with a much gentler touch than the other humans had. I debated punching him in the face and running, but he very purposely flashed me his tranq gun before escorting me down a hallway.

I was led to a bathroom and given my own gown.

"Shower and change," he said. I looked around for a curtain and saw none. I sighed as I reluctantly stripped and showered as quickly as I could. The man stood guard as I scrubbed myself clean. I pulled the gown over my head and let him lead me to another room.

It looked like the nurses' office at Atlantis. I sat down on the bed covered with tissue paper and watched as he typed some medical jibberish into a computer. I didn't have the energy to protest as he collected blood samples and clicked away at his machine.

He eventually got back up and fished out a bottle full of clear liquid out of his pocket. He filled a syringe with it and motioned for me to hold out my arm.

"Relax," he said. He held my arm almost gently as he inserted a needle into my arm. He pushed the plunger down.

"What are you injecting me with?" I asked, almost too tired to care.

"You'll find out soon," he said.

Data Log 3:14 AM

Mr. Duncan and an entire team are helping me work on the vaccine. We've been trying different toxins. Whatever we throw at this virus, it throws it back. It has a mind of its own, and it does not want to die.

Mr. Duncan keeps saying that I look terrible and that I need to rest, but I can't. If Atlantis gets shut down because of me, I'll never forgive myself. I have to keep going. I have to figure this out.

REED

Atlantis was in chaos.

The remaining children were confined to the building - not allowed to step a toe outside the doors even for school. Armed guards - Norman being one of them - surrounded the building and even roamed the hallways. Everyone was scared and on edge. Amy looked like she hadn't slept in days. Norman and Emanuel were inconsolable.

Meanwhile, Caspian and his refugees had all but taken over the basement pool. The room radiated with energy. Not the kind of positive energy one might need to finish their homework but the kind that would motivate someone to commit arson.

Caspian stalked around, clutching the Protector's staff in his clenched hands, seething. The happy-go-lucky teenager I had met at the Sanctuary was gone.

Everyone looked at me like I was a ghost. I answered the same questions a million times. I waited in vain for something to happen. For my parents to call and apologize for wanting nothing to do with me. For the cops to call and say they had found the captives. For Mercer to call and say that he had changed his mind and was giving the Sanctuary back.

Nothing.

Daniel was my only point of normalcy, but even he was tense and paler than normal. He flinched whenever someone tried to touch him. He barely spoke. We had started sleeping in his apartment. Neither of us wanted to be left alone.

One night as we sat in silence, someone knocked on the door. Daniel immediately reached for his cane, his pink eyes going wide.

"Who is it?" I asked.

"Me."

I raised my eyebrow and opened the door. Sam stood in the hallway, face drawn and dark circles under her eyes. I hadn't seen her since the dramatic fight at dinner. She smelled like rotting garbage and didn't look much better.

"Who let you in?" I asked.

"Norman," she said. "Can we talk?" Daniel scooched over on the bed, but she remained standing after she shut the door behind her.

"I know you've probably been asked, but I need to know *everything* you remember," she said. I sighed and repeated my story.

"They used this wand thing to find our trackers and cut them out. Then they took us to this old Amazon warehouse where they kept us in cages and made us fight. Whoever won got to eat that night. The others were eventually taken out and skinned. The head guy had a cane with merfolk skin on it," I said. Sam nodded, frowning.

"That doesn't make sense," she said. "I mean . . . of all the things to do with a mythical species . . . dog fights and skinning them?"

"I was thinking the same thing," I said.

"Daniel, I know you don't remember a lot of what happened to you . . . but does any of what Reed's describing sound familiar?" Sam asked.

Daniel shook his head. "The only thing that's been remotely familiar was the smell of that van that tried to kidnap us the first time," he said. He pulled down his t-shirt, showing us the barcode that was still tattooed into his shoulder.

"And Reed, you didn't see anyone else being tattooed or held in a tank, right?" Sam asked.

I shook my head. "When we first arrived, the head guy said something about us not being pretty enough," I said. "I guess if we had been, we would've ended up like you, Daniel."

"I think there's something to this that we're not seeing. You said that almost all the captives were Cursed, right?" Sam asked.

I nodded. "What if it's the traffickers that are Cursing the kids?" I asked, surprised as the words crossed my tongue. Sam crossed her arms as Daniel shrugged.

"I thought you were positive it was a merperson doing it?" Daniel asked.

I flushed. "I mean . . . that's what I thought originally. But all it's done is made things worse for you," I pointed out.

Daniel and Sam both winced.

"No, you're right," Sam said. "It would make sense that humans would be the ones doing the Cursing. It makes the trafficking business more profitable, it makes merpeople look bad, and it made the vaccine become a thing. Whoever did this was very smart and thought very far ahead."

Who would want to do something like that? I thought. *I mean, plenty of people don't like merpeople and see them as a threat . . . but to sacrifice other humans to get rid of them?*

"So . . . the mayor?" Daniel asked. "I mean . . . he bribed you years ago to make a vaccine. What if he started Cursing people so he would have an excuse to make you do it?"

"Well, Duncan was the one who originally brought up the vaccine," Sam muttered. "But there's no way Duncan would do *this*. He thinks merpeople are too valuable to treat this way."

"So . . . the mayor?" Daniel repeated.

"I would believe it," Sam said. "But we don't have any proof. And if anyone tried to accuse him . . . it probably wouldn't go well for them."

"Even if it is my uncle who started this - how would he have gotten enough merfolk blood to Curse so many kids?" I asked. "How did he find out who has what blood type?" *Why would he sacrifice me?* I thought.

"I mean, he's the mayor. Maybe he bribed other people to get the information he needed. Bribed people to Curse the kids for him," Daniel said. Sam sighed again.

"How would we prove it?" she asked.

Data Log 7:13 AM

I can't sleep at night. I keep worrying about Grayson and the others - why they've been taken. Maybe I should be concentrating my efforts on reversing Daniel's amnesia. If he remembered more - maybe he could help us.

I wish my sister was here. She would see something I'm missing. She would be smart enough to figure out what was happening to the kids.

GRAYSON

I never got the chance to try and talk to Avery. As soon as I was returned to my cage, exhaustion poured over me like concrete. I fell asleep and stayed that way for what felt like days. When I finally did wake up, they fed me, and I scarfed down every bit of it. I threw it up a few hours later. The other kids around me were faring about as well.

Still, I had more energy than I had in days. When the scientist came to take me back to his office, I made his life as difficult as I possibly could, dragging my feet, trying to bite him, you name it. His responses were calm and infuriating.

"This is going to help you. It'll all be over soon," he whispered as he wrestled me down onto the bed and strapped my rebellious limbs into submission. He took blood and injected me with the same mystery liquid before returning me to my cage – where the same exhaustion hit me once again.

The next day, my energy did not come back. I wanted to scream and thrash, but my body refused to listen. The most I could do was call the scientist every dirty name in the book, but he ignored me like I was a whiny child and continued his work.

The days passed in fogs of sleep and disorientation, and their words seemed more and more like lies. Nothing was helping me feel better and it certainly didn't seem like it would be over soon. I didn't know what they were injecting into us, but it made me feel like my cells were disintegrating into dust. I threw up whatever food they tried to give me. I was freezing cold despite the blankets they wrapped me in. The very air seemed to sting my skin, and the ache settled deep into my bones and stayed there. They hadn't let me swim since my arrival, and my skin felt like paper. My brain felt heavy and sluggish. I didn't have the energy to wonder who was doing this or why. Or how.

At the end of what I guessed was a week, a man lifted me from my cage, carrying me like a baby over to a different room. A tank of water leaned up against the wall. I was too weak to walk, but I almost laughed in relief. *Oh thank god*, I thought. *They're finally letting me swim.*

My body hit the cold water with a splash. It enveloped me, soothing my burning skin. I relaxed and waited for energy and strength to pour back into me, but all I did was sink to the bottom. My lungs began to tighten, and I realized with a start that I couldn't breathe. I hadn't phased.

I clawed at my throat, accidentally inhaling a mouthful of salt water. My nose and lungs burned, and my body twisted as it coughed, spewing bubbles into the water. I tried to swim to the surface, but my legs felt like rocks.

I stared down at them, blinking several times before realizing they were barely visible. *I can't even see*, I thought. *And I never learned how to swim. Great. I'm going to drown.*

I kicked, finally gaining some movement. My lungs tightened even more. The corners of my blurry vision started to go black. Something grabbed me by the wrist and yanked me to the surface. I gasped for air, coughing up water. As the man dropped me to the floor, my legs crumbled beneath me. I lay on the tile, pinned down by the weight of my wet clothes as the scientists above me laughed and hugged each other, cheering and congratulating themselves.

"This is the best trial by far."

"We need to see if it will stick this time."

Stick this time?

I stopped breathing, my brain clear for the first time in days. I hadn't phased. I hadn't been able to see. I hadn't been able to hear. These men, whoever the hell they were, were trying to *cure* me. And I had been their best trial run.

That's why they've been kidnapping kids, I realized. They never cared about who won the fights. They were just trying to weaken our bodies so we were more susceptible to whatever this cure was. Or maybe they were seeing how strong we were, so they knew how much medicine to give us. It can't be a merperson that's Cursing the random kids. It's a human.

A human who wants to get rid of us forever.

Rage lit fire in my veins. I launched myself off the ground, unsteady on my feet but too furious to care. I dug my nails into the arm of the scientist closest to me, shaking him.

"I am merfolk!" I screamed. "You're not going to take that away from me!" He pushed me backward, and I fell back to the floor in a heap. The others grabbed my arms and dragged me to my cage, ignoring my struggling and screaming. The other merfolk barely looked up as I beat the bars until my knuckles bled and screamed curses until my throat felt just as cracked and bloody as my fists.

I eventually sank to the floor, spent. One of my neighbors looked over.

"Why are you so upset?" they asked. "Don't you want to be normal? Don't you want to get better?" *I am normal*, I thought. Why most of the victims were Cursed suddenly made perfect sense. People like Reed were probably happy to volunteer themselves to make a cure. So they could be *fixed*.

I shoved my hands under my armpits, but they didn't shake. Instead, hot water streamed down my cheeks. My world got even blurrier.

I reached up and felt my face, surprised to feel tears staining my cheeks. I followed the trail up until I touched my eyes.

Oh my god, I'm crying, I thought. *I'm actually crying. Merfolk can't cry.*

The tears grew stronger, and liquid from my nose joined it. My neighbor looked away as I turned on my side, covering my face with my hands.

I cried until there was no more water in my body to leak out.

. . .

The next day, I forced myself to pay more attention. The bastards had said something about *hopefully it'll stick*, meaning that whatever had disabled the virus wasn't permanent. If it wasn't permanent, that meant it could be reversed. And I was going to figure out how.

True to my prediction, they stopped injecting me with the mysterious liquid but continued throwing me in the pool once a day. It was a struggle to swim with human legs, but I had to force my body into the strange motion if I didn't want to drown. And I couldn't drown. I couldn't die before I was back to normal.

As every day passed, I felt more like my old self. I could see farther across the room. I could hear distant conversations. I stopped throwing up my food. My legs felt familiar the familiar pre-morphing numbness whenever they threw me in the tank.

Until one day, maybe a week after my last injection, my legs finally twisted into my old body. I grinned and huddled at the bottom of the tank, flicking off the scientists as best as I could with webbed hands as they glared and bickered over their clipboards.

"It's still not sticking," one of them said.

The other one shrugged. "Up the dosage. It'll work eventually."

I braced myself for a fight. I had been too tired to resist before, but not this time. I had some energy back. I hadn't thrown up for a day and a half. There was no way in hell I was going to let them inject me with any more of that stuff.

They tried to fish me out of the tank with a fishing net. I yanked it from their hands, and the scientist holding it almost fell into the water with me. I had dark thoughts about what I would've done to him had he fallen in.

They returned with fancier nets - loops of rope on long poles. They surrounded me. *I won't be able to avoid all of those at the same time*, I thought. I braced myself, pressing my tail against the floor. As soon as they pushed the poles towards me, I shot to the surface.

I came out of the water swinging, teeth bared. I told myself they hadn't erased everything about me, that I still had my old reflexes and enhanced senses. I caught them off guard and managed to push one off the platform before the others dropped their poles and lunged for me.

I phased, but it took longer than normal for my tail to morph back into my legs - like my body was an old computer that hadn't been updated in a long time. I swung for the one closest to me, completely confident that my rage would be more than enough to knock them senseless. When the scientist caught my hand and pushed me back to the floor, that hope quickly died.

They barely hid their sniggers as I struggled to get to my feet, my head already spinning. *They must be sucking the oxygen out of this room, I* thought, holding up my fists again. I lunged again, but they pushed me back too easily. It felt like I was trying to fight trapped in a giant cube of Jello. All my punches seemed to be in slow motion.

They finally grew tired of playing with me. The tall one reached into his pocket and drew out a syringe. With too much ease, he stabbed it into my arm as I hit him one last time. My body instantly went numb, and I collapsed to the floor, limp. I swore I could feel the chemicals seeping through my veins. I instantly felt exhausted and nauseous.

This can't be happening to me, I thought. *I am merfolk. They can't steal that from me.*

But there they were. Stealing it from me. Stealing my life from me.

"I'm not sick," I mumbled, my world quickly fading. "I'm not sick. I'm not -"

DANIEL

I lay awake, our conversation with Sam about the mayor Cursing the children replaying itself over and over again in my head.

How would we prove it?

If the mayor was responsible for all of this, surely there would be records of some kind in his office - in his email or hidden in a secret compartment on his desk. Maybe a list of evil henchmen or a diary outlining his conspiracies would be on his desk.

I knew how we *could* prove it, but we would never get away with it. It would require sneaking out and breaking into the mayor's office, but we would never make it past the front door with the guards Amy had in place.

We could in theory get another person to do the breaking in for us, but I wanted to go myself. I wanted to smell the papers on his desk.

If any of it smelled familiar, I would know exactly who had been keeping me in a tank as a *pet*.

Hell, if I could just talk to the mayor . . . I might be able to force him to tell the truth. I knew I could lie, but I had never tried to force anyone else to speak their dirty secrets. However, something deep in my gut told me it would be easy.

"Jeez, whatever you're thinking about, can you stop?" Reed muttered from his sleeping bag.

I winced. "Sorry." I heard him shuffle around in his bag, but my thoughts refused to leave me alone.

"Do you think if we asked Sam to break into the mayor's office to search for incriminating papers, she would?" I asked.

Reed groaned. "Dude, it's like . . . two in the morning." He trailed off, then I heard him sit up. "Actually . . . maybe? But he's probably got cameras and stuff in there. She'd get caught. And in her situation, that would look really bad."

"True . . ." I muttered. "Do you think anyone here would do it for us?"

"Emanuel or Norman, maybe? They're upset enough about Grayson that they'll do anything to find him," Reed said. "They don't technically run Atlantis, so it wouldn't be the end of the world if they got caught."

"Let's ask them," I said. Reed yawned.

"Can we ask them at a not-ungodly hour?"

Once the sun had risen, we ventured down to the cafeteria. The place was bustling with the addition of Caspian's refugees. I could feel the apprehension of them picking at the strange human food they weren't used to. Their cloud of emotions made it hard to focus on the bouncing sound waves I normally used to navigate. I eventually held onto Reed's elbow to make my life easier. I swore I heard him smirk.

"What, the supersonic ears not working this morning?"

He yelped as I kicked him in the back of his right knee. "Shut up and find them!" I hissed.

"Find who?"

We turned around, and I smelled someone familiar, although I couldn't quite place it.

"Oh, hi. You're . . . Grayson's brother, right?" Reed asked. I vaguely remembered the older brother crashing the already dumpster-fire dinner the night the vaccine was announced. What was his name again?

"Yeah, I'm Will," the brother said, the sharp smell of guilt staining the air. I sniffed again. *Why does he smell so familiar?* I wondered. *It must just be because he's related to Grayson.*

"Have you seen Norman or Emanuel? We need to talk to them," I said.

"They're both on guard duty. Why, what's going on?" he asked. I felt Reed tense. Could we trust Grayson's brother with this sort of information? I mean, I knew that Will was his legal guardian, but I had barely heard Grayson talk about him. From what I understood, Will was mostly absent in attempting to get enough money for them to survive. Hell, he had been selling his blood. Surely he would care enough to help?

Plus, he was an adult. He was allowed to leave Atlantis. He wasn't famous or connected with the original Rebellion. It would be way easier for him to sneak into the mayor's office than Norman or Emanuel.

"You might be able to help us with something," I said.

Half an hour later, he debated our plan upstairs in our new shared room.

"So let me get this straight," he said, clasping his hands together. "You guys think that the mayor has been behind the Cursing this entire time this entire time because he secretly hates merpeople and wanted a reason to force Sam to make the vaccine? And he's also in cahoots with the trafficking people because having more victims makes more money? Am I understanding this right?" *It does sound rather preposterous when said like that*, I thought.

"Yes," Reed said.

"And you guys want me to break into his office . . . a government building . . . to look for evidence?"

"You got it," I said.

Will blew through his lips. "I don't know guys . . . this sounds awfully risky," he said, nerves spewing from his breath.

"We know. But we think we might be onto something here," Reed said.

"And what happens if I get caught?" Will protested.

I shrugged. "Don't get caught."

"You want to help your brother, don't you?" Reed pressed.

Will sighed. "Fine. I'll do it."

That night, Reed and I huddled around my phone. Will wore a Bluetooth receiver across town. I could hear him panting as he jogged to the mayor's office downtown.

"No cars here," he whispered. "I'm going up to the window now." I held my breath as the window creaked and slid open. I waited for alarms to go off, but none sounded.

"Doesn't appear to be an alarm," Will said.

"It might be a silent alarm," Reed said. "Hurry." Will grunted and his feet slapped down on what sounded like an old hardwood floor. For the next few minutes, we listened to his breathing as old drawers slid open and closed. My heart fluttered in my chest. Sweat beaded on my forehead. *God, I hope we're right about this.*

"I can't find any incriminating papers or hidden drawers," he said.

"What about his computer?" Reed asked. Air whooshed out of an old chair as Will sat down, and a ding sounded as he opened up a laptop. We listened in silence as I counted down the seconds.

"Yeah . . . doesn't appear to be anything crazy here either. It's all just legal . . . political garbage. Stuff about the Cursings, but nothing else. I'm sorry guys." His voice was tense. Reed sighed.

"At least we tried. Get out of there before the cops show up," Reed said before picking up a pillow and screaming into it. I rubbed his back, my mind spinning. I had been so confident it was the mayor secretly behind everything that now I had no clue what else to think.

Maybe all of his sketchy stuff is at his house instead of his office, I thought. *Maybe we should've searched there first.*

I thought about asking Reed if we should send Will on another adventure - just to make sure - but Will had already seemed stressed and worried enough about breaking into the mayor's office. I wasn't sure if he could handle anything else - and the mayor was much more likely to have a security system at his house versus his office.

Let it go, I told myself. *You were wrong.*

Shouting sounded from downstairs, and we both jumped. My blood ran cold as worst-case scenarios ran through my head. Had the traffickers broken in? Was someone else being taken?

"Will, we gotta go, something's going on," Reed said.

"Huh, what's going -"

We hung up on him and dashed downstairs. The living room was in chaos. I pressed my hands over my ears, trying to block out the cacophony of noise. Reed grabbed my hand. He was sweating.

"You're not stopping me!" Norman's voice rang out from the din. I lifted my palms off of my ears and heard Emanuel crying.

"They'll kill you if you go out there!" he screamed.

"I'm not scared of them!" Norman shouted.

"What the fuck is going on?" I whispered. "Go where?" Another set of hands grabbed us, trying to pull us away from the commotion.

"What the hell are you two doing down here? Go back to bed!" Amy snapped.

"Tell us what the hell is going on!" Reed demanded.

"Caspian has the refugees in a frenzy. He wants to go back to the Sanctuary and take it back by force," she muttered. Reed tore away from both of us, and I lost track of him in the crowd. Another set of footsteps came up to us, and I recognized Will's scent.

And something else too.

"Hey, what's going on?" Will asked. I sniffed, just to make sure, and I nearly fainted.

He smelled like the kidnapper's van.

REED

Norman and Emanuel were facing each other. Emanuel wasn't embarrassed at the tears that were falling down his face. He clutched the front of Norman's shirt.

"I just got you," he protested. "You're not leaving me. They will murder you - you know that!"

Norman gritted his teeth. "I know how to fight. Every second they stay there is a second too long!" he seethed. "I'm not letting Caspian go by himself!"

"What about Grayson?" I demanded, inserting myself between the two of them. "You're just going to leave him?" The adults stared at me, mouths open. I scanned the crowd for Caspian, and I saw him standing on one of the coffee tables, the Protector's staff held high in his hands, his markings glowing like war paint. He was riling up the crowd like a Baptist preacher. Violence shone in his eyes.

"Those *animals* don't deserve our home!" he screamed. "They killed our friends! Our families! And I'm not going to stand for it!" The crowd around him shouted, lifting their fists in approval.

Meanwhile, Amy had marched up to Caspian on his coffee table and looked ready to punch his lights out with her cane.

"You are not going to come into my house and rile up my kids for a battle that can't be won," she seethed. "This is stupid, and you know it."

"They stole everything from me. And you just want me to sit here and do what? Wait for them to give it back? Ask nicely? It's been weeks already!" Caspian seethed.

"I get it - okay? But marching in there without a plan - with no armor, no weapons, no nothing is going to get the rest of you murdered - and then what?" Amy argued.

"She's right!" Emanuel snapped. Norman's eyes flashed between Capsian and his mate.

"If you die in a stupid battle, Grayson will never forgive you," I said. "Why don't we solve one problem before we tackle another one?" At that moment, someone grabbed me and pulled me away. I spun around to see Daniel, his face somehow paler than normal.

"I think I know where Grayson is," he whispered. I almost laughed at the absurdity.

"Doesn't freaking matter - all the adults are about to go kill themselves in the ocean!" I said.

"I know. That's why we're going. We need to steal a car."

Steal a car? Who does he think is gonna drive it? He pulled me down the hallway and towards the garage. He felt around for the door and opened it.

"Are you going to tell me why you think you know where Grayson is?" I demanded as he shut the door behind us.

"I'll explain on the way. Can you drive?"

I thought back to the last time I was forced to drive in a life-threatening situation, and my stomach flipped. I looked around the mass of cars and smirked as my eyes landed on Tom's fancy motorcycle gleaming in the moonlight.

"I'll do you one better."

Daniel followed me, felt what I was talking about, and groaned.

"Are you sure you can't drive? A car feels safer than this thing!" he complained.

"I'm sorry, do you remember what happened the last time I drove a car? I at least know how to drive a motorbike!" I snapped.

He raised an eyebrow. "Is that even the same thing as a motorcycle?" he demanded.

"It's close enough! Or would you rather attempt to drive a car for us?"

After a few moments of jerky starts and stops, we cruised down the road, the wind making my eyes tear up. Daniel clung to my back, fingers knitted into knots.

"You gonna tell me where we're going?" I shouted.

"Biosyn," he shouted back. After a few moments, I screeched to a halt on the first floor of the parking garage. Daniel flung himself off the back, scraping his cane along the ground. I clamored after him, my mind still trying to catch up.

"So, you definitely didn't explain on the way here," I said.

"It's Will. The first time I saw him -"

"You mean heard him?"

Daniel hit me with his cane. "Saw, heard, *whatever* - he smelled familiar - but I thought that was just because he was a relative of Grayson. But tonight, after he got back, I smelled the same thing." Daniel took a deep breath as if the next words were harder to spit out.

"I don't think he went to the mayor's office. I think he came here. He said he's been donating here, that someone was compensating him." Daniel paused and sniffed the air.

"The smells match," he said. "I think the kids are being kept here."

I blinked, my brain still struggling to keep up. "Wait, you think Will is the one that's been Cursing the kids?"

Daniel turned to face me. "Your blood type is A positive. So is Grayson's. I bet Will's is too." I swallowed. I had originally been so positive the perpetrator had been Merfolk, but the thought of it being a person so close to Grayson made my stomach turn.

"Look, all I know is that the kidnapper's van smells like this parking deck. And Will just came home smelling like the kidnapper's van. And he's been selling his blood here. So I'm going to find out if I'm right."

He turned and continued walking. I ran after him, quickly realizing how stupid this idea was. We weren't armed. No one knew where we had gone. My body barely worked, and Daniel's body was fucking blind. The last time I had pulled something this stupid, I had gotten Grayson and myself kidnapped and tortured.

We are so going to die, I thought.

"Why don't we get an actual adult to help us?" I asked.

"Because I don't fucking trust a ton of adults right now," Daniel growled. "How could Sam have not noticed a bunch of kidnapped kids being shuttled here? Maybe she's in on it too."

I was just about to bring up that merpeople couldn't lie when Daniel resumed his sniffling once more and turned towards the wall, where an old door with peeling paint stood by itself. He kicked it open with a sudden bang, and I yelped in surprise. Daniel started down the hallway.

Yup, definitely going to die, I thought. As we continued down the corridor, the smells changed from musty and dusty to bloody and bleachy. A faint light appeared on the left, and I shoved Daniel behind me as I peered through a window. My stomach dropped.

"What do you see?" Daniel whispered. I ignored him as I opened the door and walked in. Thin faces from cages stacked around the room looked up to stare at me, but I only cared about the one I saw in the back corner.

I ran across the room, sliding to my knees, and crying out in relief. Grayson leaned against the back of his cage and offered me a weak smile. I could almost see the bones through the skin on his face.

"Son of a bitch," he whispered.

"Where are the keys?" I asked. He pointed to a hook on the wall behind him. I grabbed them, unlocked his cage, and threw the door open.

"What are you doing here?" he asked, taking his time to crawl towards the door. I grabbed his arms and pulled him the rest of the way through, wincing as I felt how thin he was. *He's only been in here for a couple of weeks*, I thought. *How could he have lost so much weight?*

I helped him to his feet only for his knees to buckle and take him back to the floor. I knelt as he wrapped his arms around his chest, shivering.

"Dude, what's wrong?" I asked. He looked up at me, and my blood ran cold.

"What happened to your face?" I whispered. His blue markings were almost gone. It looked like someone had gone in with an eraser and made the majority of them vanish, leaving random splotches. He smelled like death.

"Th-they've been trying to cure me," he whispered. Tears filled his eyes, which only made my heart drop lower. Merpeople couldn't cry.

"With what? I thought there was no cure?" Daniel demanded.

"I don't know what it is. They keep talking about making it stick." As Grayson talked, a chunk of his hair fluttered to the ground.

"Okay, we've got to get you out of here," I said, wrapping my arms around his chest and trying to heave him to his feet again. Daniel grabbed my shoulder, and his wave of fear hit me like an ice pick to the stomach.

"Guys," he whispered. We turned around. Grayson blinked in confusion.

"Will?" Grayson whispered.

Will stood in the doorway we had just come through. He lowered his gun enough to look his brother in the face. He almost smiled. "It's working. You're turning into a human," he whispered. The tears brimming in Grayson's eyes dripped to the floor. He struggled weakly against me.

"I-I don't understand," Grayson stammered.

"I'm sorry. But I had to do something. We would all be so much better off if we were human," Will said.

"So you decided to infect a bunch of strangers and kidnap them so you could make a cure?" I demanded. "What kind of sick plan is that?"

"What the hell else was I supposed to do!" Will shouted, swinging the gun haphazardly. "If things keep going the way they are - we'll never find jobs - we'll never find houses - we will be nothing."

"Why not just fuck off back to the ocean then?" Daniel demanded. "Merfolk is who you are. Why would you want to give that up?"

"Daniel, he has a gun," I warned.

"I'd rather be fucking normal and be treated as such!" Will growled. "Now put my brother down and back away."

Grayson sobbed. I held him tighter as Daniel stepped in front of us. I could've sworn his pink eyes were glowing.

"Put. The. Gun. Down," he said. His words were calm and quiet, but I suddenly had the overwhelming urge to drop a gun I didn't have. The color drained from Will's face as the weapon wavered in his hands. Daniel took a step forward and stretched out his hand.

"*Down.*"

It clattered to the floor. Daniel knelt and felt for it, quickly emptying the bullets onto the ground. *How did he just do that?* I wondered. *He totally just made Will drop the gun just by telling him to.*

Will blinked slowly, looking at the bullets on the floor like he didn't know what had just happened. Hell – I didn't know what just happened – but I didn't have much time to care. We were safe. Now, we just had to free the rest of them and get the hell out of -

No sooner had the thought passed my mind than Will seemed to snap back to his senses. He cried out, diving for the weapon. He tackled Daniel, slamming his body into the concrete. He drove his fist into Daniel's head, and Daniel went limp, the gun rolling out of his hands.

I jumped up and skittered backward, but by the time I had Grayson standing again, Will had the gun reloaded. He turned his dark eyes on us.

"Get in the cage," he said, pointing the gun at my face. "Both of you."

Grayson whimpered. *There's no way he would shoot his brother*, I thought. I shifted Grayson in front of me, holding my ground.

"Now!" Will shouted.

"I hate you," Grayson spat. *Not as much as I do*, I thought. This guy broke into people's houses and injected them so crazy scientists could make a cure. He wasn't trying to take over anything. He was trying to make himself *normal*.

And somehow that was worse.

I mean . . . I did want to be normal. My kind of normal – which was being human. Grayson's normal was being merfolk, but that didn't make *his* normal any less than *mine*. I hadn't broken into people's houses trying to change them into something I wanted to be.

I dropped Grayson, walking right up to the traitor. I could see the surprise in his eyes.

I didn't feel much more merfolk than I had a few weeks ago. But I knew buried deep down in my DNA were sharper reflexes, better eyesight, and a whole lot more bravado. And I really needed it to kick in right now or I was going to get shot.

I swooped down and grabbed Daniel's cane, screaming as I swiped. It thwacked him right across the face, leaving an angry red mark across his cheek. The second hit broke the cane in half, leaving me with a jagged plastic point. I remembered Adam's very brief demonstration of merfolk sword fighting, and I sent my makeshift weapon hurdling towards Will's chest.

Will ducked out of the way, but he was slow. He clutched the gun like a baseball bat but seemed hesitant to use it on me. That gave me plenty of time to dance my way around him, swiping. In the background, I saw Grayson crawl to Daniel and fish his cell phone out of his pocket.

"How fucking dare you!" I shouted, trying to keep Will distracted as Grayson spoke to the 911 operator. "Were you even donating your blood? Or just draining yourself so you could Curse random human kids? Who came up with the whole skinning idea? Was this all you?"

Will kicked me in the stomach, sending me sliding into a different row of cages. I vaguely recognized one of the trapped figures as Avery.

"These kids are happy to participate in finding a cure!" Will seethed. "The only ungrateful ones are the ones who were born this way."

I rolled as bullets pinged against the concrete. I prayed none of them had hit the kids behind me as I scrambled back to my feet.

"If they're so willing, why are they all in cages?" I challenged. He scowled, and the next bullet scraped my arm.

"You know - I thought one of you freaks was behind this the whole time - but I never thought any of you would be this crazy," I hissed.

Will laughed. "You're telling me that you wouldn't take a cure? I thought you just hated being like this," he jeered. I hesitated, and he used the moment to knock me to the ground. He tore the broken cane from my hands and pressed it against my throat as I struggled beneath him.

"You should be grateful!" he hissed. "You hate merpeople! You hate being like this! Why does it matter that this was the cost?" *He has a point*, I thought. *But was a cure worth all of this? Cursing kids, kidnapping them, turning them into science experiments?* This was exactly what Amy had been so afraid of. If I survived to tell her that, she would rub it in my face for the rest of my life.

But at least I would be alive. As the cane pressed harder against my throat, I wasn't sure if I would make it long enough to tell her she had been right the entire time. There was just one question lurking in the back of my mind.

If the mayor had commissioned a vaccine, why was this other group so intent on finding a cure? Had my uncle not been behind this entire conspiracy theory? Had he been acting in the best general interest of the public? Who was behind finding an actual cure?

I resigned myself to wondering that question as my last act on earth as Will was suddenly yanked away from me. I gasped for breath and sat up to see that Avery had grabbed Will by the back of his shirt and now had him pressed to the front of their cage. Will struggled, but Avery had clamped on with a vengeance. I grabbed the cane again as faint sirens filled the air. Will's face drained of color.

"You're fucked now, Little Fucker," Avery whispered in his ear. Will grit his teeth and sent his elbow back into Avery's fingers. They hissed and let go. I brandished my sword as Will pointed the gun at me once more.

"You should've helped me!" he said. Cops flooded the room, shouting and pointing their weapons at Will. He slowly put his hands into the air and sank to his knees. I dropped my cane, relief making my knees go weak. Several cops rushed forward to handcuff Will as another figure pushed their way from the crowd.

Norman slid to Grayson and grabbed him in his arms, hugging him fiercely as Grayson sobbed into his chest. I sat back down on the ground as the other officers started letting the other merpeople out of their cages. An EMT grabbed me by the shoulders and started looking at my throat.

"How did you guys get here so fast?" I rasped.

"Tom has a tracker on his motorcycle," one of the cops said. "He knew something was up as soon as it disappeared." *I guess it is a good thing we didn't steal an actual car*, I thought. Another EMT loaded Daniel's unconscious body onto a gurney. Norman lifted Grayson in his arms and carried him outside, his fingers trembling.

They didn't go to the Sanctuary, I thought. Thank god.

GRAYSON

I watched endless bodycam footage of my brother's arrest on the small TV in my hospital room. At that moment, I was feeling a grim sense of satisfaction watching him get shoved into the back of a police car, but a few moments ago, I had been crying. *Actually* crying.

I didn't know how humans dealt with literal water coming out of their faces whenever they were upset. It was so much harder to hide than shaking fingers. Tears somehow made your nose run too - and then you had to buy tissues - it was such a mess.

My entire body felt like a dumpster fire. The doctors had been pumping me full of water and nutrition, but my stomach felt like it was stuck in a permanent state of nausea. My skin felt like paper. Half of my hair was missing in random patches.

All because of my stupid brother.

According to Reed and Daniel, Will had been the one Cursing the kids. He had somehow gathered a list of local kids with type A blood and their addresses. He broke into their homes, Cursed them, and let the traffickers take over from there.

The traffickers had never cared about skinning us. Their only job was to take our bodies to the breaking point with the fights and starvation and despair. And then when our immune systems were running on fumes, they sold us to Will's crew so they could pump us full of experimental cures.

All because Will wanted me to be *normal*. All because he was sick of being treated like a *freak*. He had decided being Merfolk was worse than being anything else and used me and everyone around him to exterminate us. A vaccine wasn't enough for him. He wanted us *gone*.

I clenched my fists, my chest rattling. Merpeople were supposed to be loyal above all else. We kept secrets for hundreds of years, even going so far as to threaten people with death and exile if they dare breathed a word or hell - even had the nerve to want a divorce from a partner. There had never been an exception to loyalty.

But none of that mattered anymore. Will was trying to destroy the species, and Mercer's gang of islanders were perfectly fine with murdering any merpeople who dared disagree with them.

More tears pushed against my eyes, and I winced as they rolled down my cheeks.

I love being merfolk, I thought. *I love the idea of being part of a group that is always there for each other. But that group was never real.*

I wasn't even sure if I was going to get my body back. Even after days of laying in the hospital – I didn't feel any more merfolk than I had before I was kidnapped. Reed's horrified look upon rescuing me was more than enough to tell me how badly I had been ruined. The last dosage of chemicals they had forced into me seemed pretty *sticky*.

The only light at the end of the tunnel was that I could still pretty easily pick up on what others were feeling. Holding hands still made me feel better. But my sharp senses were gone. Everything felt dull and slowed down. I couldn't eavesdrop on conversations from across the hall or read the tiny print on the IV bags. Water no longer felt magical. My markings were barely visible.

I hope you're fucking happy, Will, I thought. *You got what you wanted after all. I'm* normal.

"Sup, loser?"

I perked up to see Reed leaning against my doorway, familiar faces behind him. A ring of purple bruises decorated his neck like a choker. *Haha get it - choker?* I nodded, hastily wiping my nose.

"Hi guys," I said. Seeing Reed made me want to burst into tears all over again. *Why does he get to be merfolk when he doesn't even want to be? I* thought. *It's not fair.*

Reed invited himself in and sat down on the edge of my bed. Sam and Mr. Duncan followed, pulling the curtain closed behind them.

"How are you feeling, Grayson?" Sam asked. I shrugged. She attempted to do the head-ruffle thing Emanuel always did, but her fingers felt cold and sterile. More tufts of my hair floated down to the floor - which didn't help me hold back my tears.

"I should probably wait until Norman and Emanuel are back to discuss this with you," she said. *Oh great, she has plans for me*, I thought. But all I did was nod.

Norman and Emanuel walked back in like they were being summoned. They had barely left my side since my rescue. To my surprise, they smiled at Sam as they walked in. I guess they had worked out their issues in the weeks I had been missing. Emanuel handed me a bag of McDonalds. I left it on the side table as Sam cleared her throat.

"I am optimistic that Grayson will return to normal," she said. My heart leaped into my throat, and a smile broke over my face.

"Wait, really?" I whispered.

"Why?" Norman asked.

"So, we've been running tests on the chemicals they were injecting you with. Turns out - it was chemo," Mr. Duncan said.

I blinked. "Like . . . cancer stuff?" I asked.

Sam nodded. "See - chemo is traditionally used to destroy DNA. You inject it into the problem area and hope that it kills more bad cells than good cells. What those men were trying to do was fill up your whole body with it - hoping that it would eradicate the virus - but that's not what happened.

"It damaged a lot of your body for sure. Chemo usually is the harshest on cells that reproduce more often - hair, skin, intestines - which is why you've been throwing up, hair falling out, all that stuff. However, your cells that don't reproduce often or at all - like your brain cells - seem to be fine. That's why your empathy is still working," Sam explained.

"So, why can't he phase if the virus wasn't killed?" Emanuel asked.

"You know how merfolk can get stuck in one form or another when they're sick or injured?" Sam asked. "It appears that the chemo made his body get stuck in the human form. Without many of your cells able to reproduce normally, it decided to shut down," she said.

"We've been taking samples of your blood. It's slow - but it appears that as the chemo wears off, his healthy cells are replacing the damaged ones. If the cycle continues, he should be back to normal in a week or so," Mr. Duncan said.

This time, tears did slip out as I laughed in relief. "I'm not going to be stuck like this forever?" I asked.

Sam smiled. "You shouldn't be - no. And that brings me to the other side of our problem," she said, motioning towards Reed. "My team and I have been going through the other's research with their chemo treatments. And according to their data . . . they seem to have been onto something." My blood ran cold once again.

"Don't get me wrong - they were incorrect with the whole notion that they could wipe out the virus from your entire body. They were looking for a complete cure, not a treatment, but . . . they did manage to create something to weaken the virus. We think there might be a way to balance the negative effects of the chemo while also letting it inhibit the virus enough to stop certain symptoms," Sam said.

"So, what are you thinking? A smaller dosage?" Emanuel asked.

"Small doses every day." Sam looked up at Reed. "I wanted to ask Reed if he would be willing to try it," she said.

Reed glanced at me, eyebrows bent. "Um . . . this just sounds like I would trade one set of side effects for another," he said. "How do I know taking the chemo won't make me feel worse? No offense man, but you look terrible." I stuck my tongue out at him.

"We don't know, that's why we would have to try," Sam said. "But if it does make you feel worse, we can always take you off of it. It's not permanent."

"The chemo probably won't get rid of all your abilities, but it should damage the virus enough that your body will go into stuck mode," Mr. Ducan said.

At this, Reed perked up. "So I wouldn't phase in water, but I would still have all the emotional stuff?" he asked.

"At the moment, it seems that way, but again, this is all hypothetical," Sam said.

Reed looked down at the floor, twisting his fingers. "Okay," he said finally. "Let's try it." Sam grinned.

"We'll start right away, but please keep this under wraps," Mr. Duncan said. "Right now, the world thinks that there is still no vaccine and no cure. We want to keep it that way. If this works, there won't be a need for a vaccine or cure." Reed nodded. *More secrets*, I thought.

"Come to the lab tomorrow, and we'll begin treatment," Sam said. "Grayson, we'll let you get back to resting."

The adults got up to leave. Norman crushed me in a hug on his way out, his fingers trembling.

"I'm so glad you're going to be okay," he said, squeezing me so hard my back popped.

"Yeah, you would hate me as a human," I joked.

He rolled his eyes. "I would love you either way. But I'm happy that you get to keep being you."

More tears threatened to spill over as he left. *Jeez, how do humans deal with this?* I thought. *How are they not constantly crying?*

Reed remained on my bed, wringing his fingers once again.

"I'm sorry about your brother," he said after a moment. I turned in surprise. I didn't think I had ever heard him apologize.

"I'm happy that you're going to get treatment," I said.

He scoffed. "No, you're not."

I shook my head. "I should be happy; I know I should. If I hate feeling this human, I can't imagine how much you hate feeling like a merperson. I just wish . . ." Another lump rose in my throat and a tear ran down my face.

"You just wish your brother's fucking conspiracy theory hadn't been the thing that allowed a treatment to be found?" Reed finished. I nodded, the heaviness in my chest traveling back down into my fists.

"How could he do that to us? To me?" I asked. "If he hated being merfolk that bad, he could've experimented on himself. He didn't have to drag anyone else into it. And now he's in jail, probably going to be stuck there forever, and I don't know what I'm going to do by myself," I whispered, hugging my knees to my chest.

I was fourteen, years away from being a legal adult. I doubted CPS would be cool with my only legal guardian being in prison. I would have to move my stuff from our apartment to one of the bedrooms and wait for a rare family to foster me or just wait until I was eighteen.

But I shouldn't have to do any of that. I *had* a family already. I had Norman and Emanuel, Amy and Tom. I knew I wasn't their technical family, but they had always been there for me. I didn't want to be adopted by random people.

"I don't know what's going to happen to your brother," Reed said. "But I'm glad the treatment isn't permanent."

I cracked a smile. "Do you think your folks will let you come back home once you're all cured?" I asked.

Reed shrugged. "I don't know. The more I think about it, the more messed up I realize they've been acting. I mean . . . who kicks their kid out of the house for getting sick, you know? Even if I am technically contagious?"

"Who kidnaps random kids so they can be tortured and then experimented on to create a cure for your existence?" I echoed. "I guess humans and merpeople are pretty messed up."

He cracked a smile and punched me in the shoulder. "Hey, don't be so hard on yourself. You don't suck. You're one of the real ones," he said.

Data Log 3:49 AM

They did it. They found a treatment. I thought it was impossible.

If anyone gets accidentally infected, they can go back to being human if they want – but if they like being merfolk – they can keep it. It's the perfect compromise. Now, I won't have to make a vaccine – which means Amy and the rest of them can't be mad at me anymore.

Part of me is extremely excited to go through the research we found. The other part of me wished it had never been created. Every time I look through it, I see Grayson crying.

REED

It was Amy who drove me to Biosyn for the first round of treatment,
which I found incredibly ironic considering her bad history with science
labs. I could smell the sweat gathering on her armpits.

"You know, Norman or Emanuel would have driven me," I said.
She white-knuckled the steering wheel.

"They need to be with their son," she muttered. I chuckled. The
car came to a stop in the parking garage. The very one I had barely escaped
from.

"You were right," I said. "You were right about being worried that
we would all be turned into science experiments to get rid of the species."

Her fingers wobbled on the steering wheel. "No, I wasn't," she whispered. "I was afraid that Sam was being manipulated . . . I never thought that one of our own . . ." She trailed off. "I owe Sam a huge apology," she said.

"I mean . . . probably," I said. We got out of the car and started walking towards the main building. A nice lady at the front desk escorted us to Sam's lab. It was decidedly less creepy than the old room the kidnapped kids had been trapped in. Sam sat at her desk, a single bottle and a syringe lying next to her laptop.

Nerves suddenly shot through me. What if the chemo only made me feel worse? Then I would be stuck feeling nauseous, still phasing, *and* having my hair fall out.

Amy put her hand on my shoulder, and the surprise of it made me jump.

"If this is really what you want, go for it," she said quietly. I nodded, wondering if, even for a moment, the famous Amy Wilson would ever want to change back to the human she used to be.

The injection was very anti-climactic. I sat down in a folding chair, Sam flicked the syringe, injected me, and gave me a pink band-aid to cover the wound. Then, we went back home. I felt no different. I began to wonder if Sam had measured out the chemicals correctly. Then again, it was supposed to be small doses every day. Maybe I wasn't supposed to feel different yet.

Later that night, I went down to the pool by myself, just to see if I would phase. I did. And it still hurt like a bitch. But I held out hope. I told myself that Grayson and everyone else's suffering couldn't have been for nothing. Something good had to come out of it.

I went back upstairs and scrolled through TikTok on my phone, unable to sleep. Daniel was still in the hospital, along with Grayson and the dozens of other kids who had been rescued. I occasionally found myself wondering how Daniel was able to make Will drop the gun. Maybe Will's resolve about making a cure had faltered for a moment. Or maybe Daniel just looked super freaking scary.

News about the incident showed up almost constantly. People were stitching various news reports, either talking about how messed up the situation was or talking about how they had wished Will succeeded.

I skipped over most of them until I landed on one from my uncle. I bit back a scowl as I watched him smile at the camera.

"I am so relieved that the missing children and merpeople have been found and are now receiving treatment." *Uh-huh, sure,* I thought. "I hope that all the perpetrators will soon be found and apprehended for their actions." *All the perpetrators?* I wondered. I guess the scientists doing the actual experiments and the humans running the torture rings hadn't been caught yet. Would Will rat them out? Maybe they would lessen his sentence if he cooperated. What crime would he be charged with, exactly? Breaking and entering? Accessory to kidnapping?

"Any person found having information about the merpeople responsible, please come forward."

Just merpeople? Nah, there were plenty of humans helping too, I thought. *Merpeople aren't the only ones to blame here.*

I briefly flashed back to the mafia man with the cane supposedly decorated with merfolk scales. In hindsight, I doubted they were real. It was probably just meant to scare us. My first impression was right. They wouldn't waste merfolk scales on a decoration - they were too rare and valuable.

Funny how merpeople were considered rare and special creatures but treated so terribly. Humans were lowkey kinda of the worst.

After my injection the next day, I started to feel different. I couldn't smell or see every tiny little thing in my field of vision. The world no longer felt overwhelming.

In my excitement, I ran downstairs to the pool and jumped in, hoping that two doses would be enough. It wasn't.

By the time I pulled myself out of the water and caught my breath, I had a visitor. Caspian looked down at me, his fuzzy eyebrows furrowed.

"I thought it would take a while for the medicine to start working," he said. I sighed from my place on the floor.

"I was hoping," I said. He chuckled, and I sat up. He sat down next to me, looking very tired.

"I wanted to say thank you," he said. "Daniel realizing where your friends were being held captive was what stopped us from making a very irrational decision."

I shrugged. "I mean . . . I get it. If these crazy people took over my home, I'd want to kill them all and take it back too," I said.

Caspian winced. "I . . . I am very angry with Mercer and his followers. I want to destroy them. But they are still merfolk," he whispered. "I think my parents would be disappointed with me if we resorted to such violence."

I rolled my eyes. "You things are obsessed with loyalty," I said. "Don't you think you take it a little too far sometimes? If someone is trying to kill you - don't you deserve to treat them the same way?"

Caspian shrugged. "That is a very human way of thinking," he said. "But perhaps you are right. Something will need to be done - and soon. But taking care of our family on shore is more important right now. Once Grayson and the others are out of the hospital, then we will decide," he said.

GRAYSON

After a night in the hospital, I was awoken by a phone call. I fumbled for my cell and answered it with a yawn.

"He - *ahhh* - llo?"

"Grayson, it's me," Will said. My blood instantly ran cold. The panicked voice on the other end rambled on.

"Listen - I know you don't want to talk to me - but there's something important you need to know. The men behind the trafficking - the ones who started it -"

I hung up the phone, throwing it across the room, seething. *How dare he call me*, I thought. *How dare he call me and try to blame this on someone else? He was the one who broke into people's homes and Cursed them with his blood. He's the one who let them get kidnapped. He's the one who let me get kidnapped. He's the one who let them be turned into science experiments.*

I hope he rots.

Norman walked into the room carrying a tray of breakfast food. He frowned at the phone on the floor.

"Everything okay?" he asked. I forced myself to nod. He ignored the lie and watched as I tried to force down the food.

"When can I go home?" I asked.

"Hopefully soon. When all the drugs get out of your system," Norman said. "Want me to bring you anything? Books, movies?"

I shook my head. "Actually . . . there is one thing. Is my friend, Avery, here?" I asked.

He shrugged. "I can check."

"If they are - I'd like to go see them," I said. He nodded. Emanuel joined us, and we lingered in silence, flipping through the channels on the TV that weren't news about the trafficking. I eventually drifted off to sleep, and when I woke up, a familiar face was poking into my room. I grinned and sat up.

"I heard your weird friend saved the day," Avery said. Tears clouded my eyes, and I hurriedly wiped them away. All over again, I saw Will shove Daniel to the floor, heard his head crack open, all while I lay there too weak to stand.

But before Will had gotten the upper hand, Daniel had convinced him to drop the gun. No, not convinced. He had just narrowed those pink eyes of his - *wait, they had definitely been red* - and told Will to drop the gun.

And he had done it. Just like that.

My blood ran cold again. Too many things were still not adding up.

I realized that Avery was waiting for a response and cleared my throat.

"I just wish he could've been a little quicker," I said. They sat down on my bed and squished me in a hug.

"I'm so glad you're safe," they whispered. I squeezed them back.

"Me too," I said. A familiar tapping sounded down the hall, and the aforementioned weird friend tiptoed into my room. I winced as I saw yet another set of bruises decorating his face.

"You look terrible," Avery said.

Daniel smirked. "Good thing I'm blind."

Avery got up and squeezed my hand. "I'll let you two catch up," they said.

Daniel slid out of the way as they walked back to their room, and then awkwardly sat down on the edge of my bed, fumbling with the handle of his new cane. The silence oozed by as I tried to figure out how to ask him all the impossible questions swirling around my head.

Multiple people had commented on how Daniel smelled different. Merpeople's eyes certainly didn't *turn red* like his. And his performance with Will made me suspect how he had actually escaped from his captors – the story he had kept hidden.

"You're . . . you're not merfolk. Are you?" I asked.

Instead of getting defensive or yelling, he only sighed and shrugged. "I don't know," he whispered.

"You made that guy drop the gun," I said.

He shook his head. "I can't *make* people do things." He placed a cool hand on my arm. I was suddenly filled with peaceful images that made me wonder why I was even worried or upset. The feelings vanished as soon as he removed his hand.

"But I can make them feel whatever I want. And it's pretty easy to make people do what you want when you can make them feel how you want."

I shivered. Making people feel things was definitely *not* a merfolk trait.

"How long have you been doing it?" I asked.

"I didn't know I could for the longest time. I think I realized something was up when I escaped from the people who kidnapped me. I just remember wanting my captor to be careless, to forget about me so I could slip past unnoticed. And he did. When kids started getting Cursed and kidnapped . . . I started practicing," he said. *Ugh*, I thought. *What had he made people do while he was practicing?*

"I kinda made Reed go with me to track you down," he admitted.

"Dude!" I protested.

"I know, I know. It wasn't right. But I was scared to go by myself. And no one else was listening to me," he said. I softened. Making people feel things without their knowledge was definitely shitty, but it was the reason I was alive. Maybe I should be grateful.

Maybe he was just making me feel like it wasn't a big deal.

Okay, now you're just being paranoid.

"Did you know that your eyes glow? Like, not the iridescent shimmery thing our eyes do, but like literally glow? I could see your irises in that dark room. They were bright red," I said.

He blinked and reached a hand up to his eyes as if to inspect them. "No. No, I didn't."

We sat in silence for a few moments.

"Are you going to tell anyone?" I asked.

He snorted. "In the beginning, humans assumed we could brainwash them or control them. We had to fight so hard to get rid of that myth. I am *not* going to confirm some creatures actually can."

"Good point," I said.

He squirmed on the bed. "I'm being released today. And after the whole Sanctuary thing is solved, I'm going to go back to the ocean. I need to try to find my mom or figure out who my dad was. I'm tired of hiding. I want to know exactly what I am," he said. *Don't bring your answers back here,* I thought. *If there are really some mythical creatures out there who can mind-control people, I don't want to know.*

And the humans shouldn't know either.

He stood up and turned towards the door.

"Can you lie?" I asked.

He turned, raising an eyebrow. "Sorry?"

"If you can control how people feel . . . can you lie? Can you just make us feel like you're trustworthy?"

He smiled. "I guess you'll never know." He chuckled and disappeared out of the room. I shivered again, hugging my arms to my chest. The thought of Daniel having possibly been a liar this entire time made the hair rise back up on my neck. Who's to say that he didn't know exactly what he was? Who's to say he had amnesia?

If there are other mythical creatures out there, why haven't they helped us? I wondered. Why would they have not joined with Amy and Tom to fight for our rights? Then again, if they were the monsters humans thought we were, maybe it was best that they had stayed hidden. If they could lie undetected, who's to say they hadn't been working behind the scenes? How many of them were there? Why had we never met them before? Were they all pretending to be merfolk? What did they look like with regular pigment?

I thought back to how Morris had been obsessed with killing us because we were dangerous. According to Tom's stories, their father had spun stories about the same thing. What are the odds that Tom's family had merfolk mixed up with these other creatures?

Daniel's last words echoed through my head.

I guess you'll never know.

. . .

I was discharged the next day along with Daniel and the others. All of Atlantis cheered as we walked through the doors. Reed crushed both of us in rib-shattering hugs, and I made a mental note to tease him about being sentimental later. Adam came up next, fingers shaking.

"Glad you're okay little man," he whispered. The kids came up next, throwing their arms around us. Amy finally shooed them all away, and Daniel, Reed, and I found a couch to sit on.

"Heard you broke my cane," Daniel said dryly.

Reed shoved him. "Well, I had to do something since you decided to get yet another head injury," he teased. Daniel grinned back.

"So, how are you two feeling?" Reed asked.

"Less dead," I admitted. "How are your treatments going?"

Reed grinned. "Slowly but surely. Sam's picking me up in a few minutes for my next shot. She thinks this might be the dose that gets me stuck, so wish me luck!" Reed left out the door, leaving me with Daniel. Daniel whom I loved, but still creeped me out immensely after his confession. He glanced towards the door as if he could hear my inner thoughts.

"Are we allowed to go swimming in the ocean now?" he asked. "I sure could use some actual salt water."

I forced a laugh. "Go ask Norman, he's on guard duty." Daniel tapped from the room, and I settled for watching TV over the little kids' shoulders. Part of me wanted to go with him, but I wasn't sure if I could handle the rejection of not phasing. I wanted to wait until I was sure I could morph again.

I had barely started paying attention to the show when Daniel came bursting back through the door, gasping for breath, hair still dripping salt water.

"They're coming," he gasped. "Mercer - they're coming!"

At that moment, Amy's cell phone rang. She answered it, and her face immediately turned to stone.

The words on the other end blurred together. All I knew was that I saw red and ran into the garage while everyone else was distracted. Daniel attempted to chase after me, and I told him something about how I would tell everyone his secret if he tried to stop me. He faltered, and I peeled out of the garage on Tom's motorcycle before he could change his mind.

REED

The cold grate above the swimming pool bit into my bare feet. The water churned beneath me. Sam and Mr. Duncan stood to the side, clipboards in hand.

"Reed, whenever you're ready," Sam called out. I took a deep breath. I was starting to feel the effects of the chemo. My hair shed way more than normal, and eating had become massively difficult. But if I could dive into this pool without every cell in my body ripping apart, I would take what I could get.

I stepped off the grate and hit the water. I let myself sink towards the bottom, bracing myself for the onslaught of pain I had become so used to.

But nothing happened. I opened my eyes and everything was blurry. My lungs started to tighten and burn. My arms and legs instinctively kicked, trying to keep my body upright. No cells ripped apart, no gills grew, no scales pushed out of my skin.

I yelled in excitement, promptly swallowing a mouthful of salt water. I coughed, sending bubbles up towards the surface. I pushed up and pulled myself out of the tank to cheers from below. I coughed and wheezed, trying to force the water from my lungs as Sam raced up the ladder and hugged me. However, I assumed she was more impressed by her scientific achievement than me as a person.

"It worked! It worked!" she crowed. I grinned, shaking the water out of my thinning hair and ears. I was able to stand without my legs going wobbly. I wasn't aching in pain from a violent transformation.

I could still easily pick up on what others were feeling, but as far as the water was concerned, I was human. Sam's treatment had worked.

My body was mine again.

Tears clouded my eyes – actual tears – and I whooped in celebration, almost slipping into the puddle of water I had made. For a split second, I wondered if my parents would let me back in the house again, but I quickly buried the thoughts. I didn't know if they deserved to have me back.

Mr. Duncan handed me a towel, and I realized that I probably should have changed into swim trunks before attempting this. I hadn't wanted to jinx it.

"So, what now?" I asked. *I can't wait to tell Grayson!*

"We'll keep monitoring you, keep adjusting the dosage as needed. We want to give you the lowest amount possible to minimize the negative symptoms," Sam said. I nodded, too elated to pay much attention.

"We can begin treating the other Cursed kids," Mr. Duncan said. "This is going to change everything." Relief crashed over me. *Thank god, I thought. It's finally over.*

The door suddenly flew open, crashing into the wall. A skinny man stood in the hallway, smelling like salt, his markings splayed out from his nose. Beside me, Sam went rigid. Her clipboard fell to the floor. The man walked into the room, shutting the door behind him as he lifted a gun. *Who the fuck is this?* I thought.

"You're going to change nothing," he hissed.

Sam stepped forward, holding up her hands. "Markus?" she whispered. "What are you doing here?"

Several more men trickled in behind him. They carried gallons of gasoline. The harsh smell immediately flooded my nostrils, even from across the room. They stalked towards us and started dumping the contents on the floor, surrounding us in a ring.

"Markus, what are you doing?" Sam repeated. Her calm demeanor had vanished.

"Who the fuck is Markus?" I whispered.

Sam's eyes flashed with anger. "He's Mercer's son," she whispered. "The son of the asshole who invaded the Sanctuary." Markus smirked. *Fucking dammit,* I thought. *Things were just going back to normal.* The men cast the empty jugs aside and stood by the border, holding flickering lighters. If they so much as twitched, the lighters would fall on the gasoline and incinerate us. I was suddenly very grateful to have soaking wet clothes on.

"Sam, get out your phone and call Amy," Markus said calmly. "Put it on speaker."

Sam did as she was told and fought to keep her voice steady. "Hi, Amy. I'm at the lab with Duncan and Reed. Markus decided to pay us a visit."

I heard Amy suck in a breath on the other end.

"Markus, what do you want?" Amy asked. Markus' grip tightened on the gun.

"You have two options. You and everyone in that building can leave land right now and join us at the Sanctuary, or I can burn your friends and their precious lab to the ground," he said.

I don't like those options, I thought.

"Why are you doing this?" Amy asked.

"You know exactly why," Markus said. "You have ten minutes to decide or it's lights off. My father is waiting just off the coast."

Sam swallowed, and I looked around the room, debating my options. I wasn't technically merfolk anymore after days of taking the treatment. My enhanced reflexes and senses were gone. On the plus side, I could probably handle a little fire better than the average aquatic creature - right?

Amy's probably calling the police, I told myself. *They'll be here any second. They'll get us out of this. They're trained on how to deal with* hostage situations. At the worst, we'll leave here with some third-degree burns, but we'll be alive. Right?

We had been through too fucking much to die now. I probably should have been scared, but I was so used to having my nerves fried with terror that the situation seemed almost comical. Part of me wanted to laugh at the irony of another catastrophe right after things were just starting to go well.

And that's when it dawned on me.

I had started to suspect my uncle being behind all of this – his hatred of merpeople made him an easy target. But who else hated merpeople with a burning passion?

"You're the ones behind the trafficking," I said suddenly, looking directly into Markus' eyes. "You're the ones who made Will start Cursing people for you. You were the ones trying to create a cure. You wanted to wipe out everyone on shore who wouldn't join you."

Markus smiled. "Smart boy."

"Bitch," I growled. "Who helped you?"

Markus sneered. "Who do you think? This plan's been a long time coming," he whispered. The truth settled over me like concrete. For a moment, I was so mad my senses winked out on me like a fuse blowing. *I was right! Dammit.*

"Aw, don't tell me you're surprised," Markus crooned. "Your precious uncle never liked our kind, but he was willing to work with us when he saw we had a common enemy." The world swayed around me. It all made perfect sense.

I could imagine it. Mercer and my uncle sitting in his office, brainstorming schemes to get rid of us as quietly and naturally as possible. *Pay for their group home to make it seem like we're on their side but get rid of the adults first. Curse human children so we have an excuse to force Sam to make a vaccine. Use the vaccine as a smokescreen to cover up the trafficking. Use the trafficking to make a cure. Use the cure to get rid of the ones that won't go back to the ocean.*

Mr. Duncan took a step forward.

"Gentlemen, let's talk about this," he said. "There is no reason that Amy and these others need to join you in the ocean. Take the Sanctuary. Let the other merpeople stay here." *Fat chance in hell Caspian will stay on land after this,* I thought.

Sam shifted her weight ever so slightly, and I noticed that she was slowly inching towards the man at our backs. I took the hint and started shifting to my right, towards the guy holding the lighter. He was approximately double my size, with a huge scar across his chest that made me think he had battled much scarier things than me.

I was the one who bolted first. Screaming, I hurled myself at the stranger, tackling him and grappling for the lighter. He dropped it, and I grabbed it in the palm of my hand, barely feeling the burn before I flung it away from the circle of gasoline. In the background somewhere, the gun popped, Sam screamed, and I felt something wet tickling down my body.

I looked down to see blood pouring from my leg. *That's probably not good,* I thought.

Meanwhile, the stranger had untangled himself from me and was staring down at us, barely concealing a smile. I turned around to see Sam on her knees, holding her hands against her bleeding abdomen. Mr. Duncan was facedown on the floor, his gut leaking blood in a giant puddle underneath him.

Oh my god, we're all going to die, I thought. *After everything that's happened, this is how we go. At least I'm in too much shock for it to hurt that bad.*

"I suggest not trying that again," Markus said. "Amy, you now have two minutes. Hurry up."

I gritted my teeth, slipping in the gasoline as I tried to hold my hands against the wound on my leg. Sam's hands were shaking, and I was ready to end this prick's life.

"You know - a real merperson wouldn't feel the need to get rid of everyone else that didn't live the same way they do," I spat. Markus turned the gun back on me, and I was certain I was about to get shot again for my insolence. I closed my eyes and held my breath. A loud bang sounded, and I waited for the burst of pain and blood, but after a moment of feeling nothing, cracked an eyelid open.

Grayson stood in the doorway. I had spent a lot of time making him mad on purpose, but I had never seen fury radiating off him like this before.

He held a merfolk sword in his hand, and his webbed ears were pushed back against his head. His bared teeth shone in the fluorescent lights. His eyes gleamed with rage.

"*You.*"

The single growled word was enough to make Markus pause and turn around. Grayson stalked across the floor, eyeing Markus like a cat would eye a mouse.

"*You.*"

Grayson swiped with the sword, and Markus shouted as it cut him across the face. Blood seeped through his fingers. He seemed to completely forget about the gun in his hand as Grayson glowered down at him.

"You stole my life."

Grayson stabbed the sword towards Markus' heart, but he moved out of the way just in time. Markus finally seemed to remember he had a gun and pointed it at Grayson, not that Grayson cared in the slightest. He pointed the tip of his sword against the tip of Markus' nose with all the confidence of Adam.

"You were never real merfolk," Markus rasped. The other men stepped forward, but Markus held his hand up.

"He's mine," he spat. The guards slunk away. Grayson's eye twitched, and I recoiled from the carnage spilling from his lips.

"Real merfolk die to protect themselves and others. Real merfolk do not hate. You have betrayed and dishonored us for the last time. You are not true merfolk."

Grayson raised his sword for the killing blow, but the gun was faster. I screamed as the bullet popped, but Grayson barely winced. The sword crashed down into the meat of Markus' shoulder, and blood sprayed across the floor.

Markus yelled and dropped the gun. The wound on Grayson's shoulder wept, but he was still on his feet. He kicked the gun away from Markus and turned to face the other men, who were now ignoring Markus' orders and attacking. With a swiftness I had never seen before, Grayson hacked away at them, blood decorating the tile floor and his face like a confetti cannon had gone off. In moments, they were all slinking away, clutching their wounds.

Grayson dropped his sword as he bolted over to me, running his shaking hands over my face.

"That bastard shot you," he growled, helping me to my feet. I cried out as my leg collapsed underneath me.

"He got Sam too," I slurred. He looked over to her. The puddle of blood underneath her was much bigger than it had been a minute ago.

"Get her first, I'll be fine," I said. He hesitated, but then dropped me back to the floor and started pulling Sam towards the door. In the distance, I heard police sirens. *Thank god, we're saved,* I thought.

I tried dragging myself across the floor, pausing for a moment to debate if I should try pulling Duncan along with me. A quick look behind me proved what I had already suspected. He wasn't breathing.

I used my good leg to shove my body across the floor, silently admiring the irony once again. Even if I hadn't started the treatments, my body would be in stuck mode now.

448

Grayson ran back into the room, the sound of sirens much louder now. The bloodstain on his shirt was growing, and he stumbled as he bent down to hook his arms underneath mine. He dragged me, smearing more gasoline along the floor, the foul smell making my head pound.

Markus suddenly lashed out and grabbed my ankle. Grayson lost his grip and slipped to the floor. I screamed as my leg was wrenched, and Markus' fingers found my throat. Grayson reached for the sword he had left several feet away on the floor, realized he didn't have it, and lunged for Markus, clawing at every inch of him he could reach.

Markus screamed, and I joined the fight, desperately trying to kick and squirm away from him, but he was stubbornly strong. Grayson finally grabbed onto the closest weapon he could - a lighter. Markus' eyes went wide.

No, I thought. *Don't you dare.*

Grayson kicked me away from Markus before he flicked the lighter on.

The room exploded in flames. The *woosh* flooded the room. The fire alarm screamed, reverberating in my skull. Heat seared my skin. I couldn't breathe. I couldn't see. *Oh shit, I just went blind,* I thought.

I realized that wasn't true as the darkness wavered. It was smoke.

I looked up to see flames surrounding us. The only reason I wasn't currently on fire was because of my wet clothes. I flashed back to what every teacher in elementary school drilled into our heads.

Stop drop and roll.

I crawled along the floor, groping for what I couldn't see. I grabbed what I prayed was Grayson and started heading for the exit as fast as I could. I lifted my shirt and covered my mouth and nose as best as I could, but my lungs and exposed skin were still burning. My eyes watered, and my leg screamed at me, but I forced myself to move.

As I crawled into the light, I saw fire trucks and ambulances decorating the parking lot. Sam was on a gurney, a respirator over her mouth. The paramedics all but attacked me as I dragged ourselves outside.

Someone shoved an oxygen mask over my mouth and ran gloved fingers over my body. They shouted questions at me, but all I could do was stare at Grayson's body as the other paramedics stripped away his smoldered clothing and held fingers to his throat. A respirator was put over his mouth and one of them started CPR. The song to match the beat started playing in my head.

Stayin alive, staying alive, ah, ah, ah, ah, stayin alive.

I counted the repetitions, waiting for Grayson to take a gasp of air and wake up. But he didn't.

The paramedic giving him CPR stopped and shook his head. The other looked at his watch. The third lifted a sheet over his head.

No, I thought. *He was just here. We've been through so much. He can't be . . . he can't be . . .*

The shouting around me intensified as my world faded to blackness.

DANIEL

The call Amy was on came screeching to a halt. The last thing we heard was a loud *whoosh* before the line disconnected. The phone crunched as Amy hurled it against the wall, and Caspian shouted something about going into the damn ocean to finish this.

I should've gone with Grayson, I thought. *I should've made him stay behind.*

Norman and Emanuel let me ride in the car with them to the lab. All I could hear was the screeching of ambulances and police sirens. The air smelled like burnt flesh and blood. Someone was screaming.

"Stay by the car. I'll be back in a minute," Emanuel said, ditching me for the chaos. I swallowed and leaned against the car, unable to tell who or what anything was in the cacophony of noise. Paramedic radios rang out.

"Three DBs. Two GSW. On the way to the hospital now."

Right as I was about to ignore Emanuel's instructions and run into the burning building to find my friends, he returned. He held me against his chest. He was barely breathing. Tears dripped onto the top of my head.

"Reed's okay," he finally choked out. "He and Sam are on their way to the hospital."

"What about Grayson?" I asked.

Norman's scream was all I needed to answer my question. Emanuel's quiet tears turned into sobs.

My world wobbled beneath me, but my hands didn't shake. The din in the background turned to silence. My heart forgot to beat. I sat in the backseat in silence as we drove to the hospital. We lingered in the waiting room until one of the nurses said Reed and Sam could receive visitors.

I tapped down the hallway in a fog. I couldn't see Reed, but I could smell the bloody bandages on his leg and the burned skin trapped under the aloe vera. For a very brief moment, I thought it was funny that Reed was now the one suffering burns after pushing Grayson in a chlorine pool that one time. It was only a few months ago, but it seemed like ages.

He was barely conscious, but the reality of what had just happened came crashing down on me as I sat down on the edge of his bed and held his hand. Clear as day, I felt the pain, the terror, the panic, the desperation.

The loss.

My hands finally began to shake, and Reed sobbed as he lay there. The sobs eventually turned into sentences. *I want him dead. They all deserve to be dead. I fucking hate merpeople.* All I did was hold his hand and listen.

And plot how to murder Mercer and the others myself.

. . .

The rest of the day passed in a blur of tears. No one left when visiting hours were over, and the nurses knew better than to try and make us. I slept in the chair next to Reed, my body too exhausted to be uncomfortable.

By the next morning, Reed was done crying. He grabbed my hand the second I walked over to him, and this time, he felt pissed.

"Get Norman and close the door," he hissed. I stepped into the lobby and smelled around the room until I found him curled up on a bench. I gently woke up. I couldn't see the man, but holding his hand felt fragile like one gentle breeze might tear his flesh apart. He wordlessly followed me until we stood across from Reed's bed.

"All of this is the mayor's fault," Reed rasped. His voice sounded like he had been smoking for thirty years. I selfishly was grateful I was blind so I didn't have to see the wounds on his body. "Markus admitted to everything. My uncle was the one collaborating with Mercer from the beginning. And they're not going to stop until all of you are dead."

I heard Norman grind his teeth. "Those bastards are going to pay for this," he growled.

"Is Markus . . ." I asked.

"Dead," Norman muttered.

"Mercer's going to lose it when he realizes," Reed said.

"So, what do we do? Attack first?" I asked.

"If it came to a fight, we're about evenly matched in numbers. But we have better weapons," Norman said. "We could easily take them out."

"But the mayor is never going to stop trying to get rid of you," Reed pointed out. "We need to do more than just get rid of Mercer and his minions."

"Like what? If we say that the mayor has been the one behind all of this, no one will believe us," I said. "We need proof."

"We need to talk to Will," Reed said.

Half an hour later, Norman stood in the corner of the jail's visiting room. The echoes of my cane tapping on the floor made the room feel thick and enclosed – like we were trapped inside a giant coffin. The cold metal chair bit into my butt. It took me a moment to grab the phone and tell Will his brother was dead. I sat there silently as he sobbed. I could hear his fingers tearing at his hair through the protective glass.

After a few minutes, he gathered himself back together enough to talk.

"Reed told me that Markus admitted to everything about working with the mayor," I said.

"Yes," Will whispered. "I tried to call Grayson and tell him the same thing, but he didn't listen." He swallowed. "Right after the Rebellion, Mercer made a pact with the mayor that he would try to get rid of as many merpeople as he could. Mercer gave him the idea for the trafficking and the vaccine and the cure - all of it. He sent his son and several others up to run the experiments, but they didn't figure it out in time."

I leaned across the table, my nose almost pressing into the partition separating us.

"Listen to me very carefully," I said. "You're going to tell me how I can find proof of everything you just said. Real proof. Something that'll hold up in court. It is the very least you can do for me. For Grayson."

Will hesitated. Dark impulses surged through my veins, and I grit my teeth.

The only person who knew my secret was gone. I could easily hack my way into Will's brain and force him to tell me whatever I wanted. Stretch my brain into his, toggle whatever switches in his psyche that would make him feel at ease, comfortable, willing to share, and listen to the secrets spill from his lips. It would be so easy. I had made excuses for myself before. No one would believe Will if he said my eyes were glowing red. Hell, I could always go straight to the source and force the mayor to spill his secrets. The thought of playing puppet master who murdered my friend made me smile.

But I had felt how disturbed Grayson had been when I admitted to what I could do. I could feel the relief that hit him when I told him my plans to abandon the land and figure out what my parents were. How desperately he had wanted me to not come back with answers. Answers that could spell even more disaster for his kind.

But I was so mad I almost didn't care. What would Grayson do - haunt me?

"There's a burner phone under my pillow at the house" Will whispered. "It's got texts with my instructions on it. Records of all the kids with Type A blood."

"Thank you," I said.

Norman walked up behind me. "I sure hope you're telling the truth," he said. "Because Mercer just gave us another ultimatum."

"The world reels over the shocking events that happened yesterday. Four people were held hostage at *Biosyn* by a rogue merperson from an unknown ocean tribe. Two are in the hospital being treated for their severe injuries. The other three unfortunately didn't make it . . .

"Rumors spiral as detectives and police try to piece together what happened Tuesday night. Who exactly is this group of merpeople from the ocean? And why are they attacking merpeople who live on the surface? One thing is for sure - merpeople are more dangerous than they told us they would be."

~ XYZ Nightly News

Mom Against Mermaids

I knew it! I knew these things were going to cause trouble! They should go back to the ocean where they belong!

45 People liked your post

Mom Against Mom Against Mermaids

Let me guess, this includes all the cursed kids?

178 People liked your post

Mom Against Mermaids

There's a cure now. If they don't want to be cured of their illness, they can leave.

55 People liked your post

4:03: Dude no fucking way
are you watching the news?

4:05: Yeah man kinda busy rn.
We're with my baby sister at the
hospital

4:05: Wait . . . was she one
of the . . .

4:06: Yeah. She didn't want
anyone else to know she got
sick. But she's safe now.

4:07: Why didnt you get cursed
too?

4:07: Different blood type I guess
I got lucky

REED

My uncle stopped in his tracks when he saw me sitting at his desk. I didn't bother to sit up and take my feet off his mahogany table as he gawked at me.

"My friend died," I said.

He quickly shut the door. A vein near his temple throbbed.

According to the news, I was still recovering in the hospital, but the news didn't know about the surprise field trip I had convinced Norman to take me on. He had been loathe to let me leave the hospital in my crispy condition, but with Mercer only giving an hour's notice he was about to come demolish Atlantis, I had gotten my way.

"I mean, I don't know if I would really call him my friend. We kinda hated each other - he was super annoying. But he *died*," I said.

My uncle started to open his mouth, but I continued.

"And he didn't just like . . . die in his sleep all peaceful or die so quickly he didn't feel it. He suffocated in a fire. His stupid lungs probably look like beef jerky."

I took my feet off the table and stared at the sweating man, my wounds smarting under the bandages.

"What happened to that young man is very unfortunate -" he started.

"Save it," I snapped. "I know what you did."

He dared to laugh. "And pray tell, what did I do?"

"You collaborated with Mercer's group to eradicate the merfolk on the surface," I said.

He finally had the common sense to go pale. I explained what Daniel and I had figured out.

"That's quite a conspiracy theory," he said. "Got any proof?"

"Will told me everything," I said.

"And people are going to believe the words of someone who Cursed their children to further spread the mermaid disease? I doubt it."

I held up a copy of the flash drive Norman and Daniel had quickly copied from Will's burner phone.

"This flash drive contains all the evidence people will need," I said. His smile quickly evaporated.

"Allow me to put this into words even you can understand," I said, twirling the flash drive around my fingers. "This gets posted on YouTube and sent to several news stations unless you do exactly what I tell you. Oh - the police get a copy too. Pretty sure it'll illegal to commit genocide."

The color drained from his face. "What do you want?" he whispered. I held up four fingers.

"You're going to take away the rule that merpeople are required to show their markings in public places. You're going to continue funding Atlantis. Whatever they want - they get - no questions asked. And you're going to start punishing parents who abandon their merfolk children. Make them pay child support, charge them with child abandonment, something."

"You hate merfolk. You offered yourself up as a guinea pig to find a treatment," he said. "Why are you interested in helping them?"

"Because if they're okay with being sick, they shouldn't be punished for it," I said.

He crossed his arms. "Another scientist will make a cure," he said. "An actual cure. It's only a matter of time."

I shrugged. "It won't matter. Merpeople will always exist. We won't let you eradicate us."

He gwaffed. "Us?"

For the first time since being Cursed, I let my markings slither into view. They were barely visible. It looked like someone had smeared blue paint over the left side of my face and then tried to wipe it off. But they were still there. The virus was still in my blood, even if it was temporarily paralyzed. And after seeing what Grayson had sacrificed, I was no longer willing to hide it.

"Yes, *us*. True merfolk are more loyal than any human I've ever met," I said. "They didn't have a good reason to let me live in Atlantis after what I did, but they still welcomed me. They tried to help me, and I refused to understand why until now." I stood up.

"Then why take the treatments?" he asked.

"I don't need a tail to be merfolk," I said.

He rolled his eyes. "Fine. I'll do what -"

I held up my finger. "I'm not done," I said. "Mercer is still intent on destroying the rest of the merpeople on the surface. They're coming any second now to kill everyone in Atlantis. And you're going to stop them."

OG Soccer Mom <3

Fuck off Karen no one cares what you think. If you hate merpeople that much maybe move so you never have to see one again. You should be ashamed of yourself.

208 People liked this post

Turing Machine

Lol boom roasted

14 People liked this post

NORMAN

Amy sat in a lawn chair in the very front of the beach, her gun sitting on her lap, her cane lying in the sand. Her husband stood beside her, his gun tucked into the back of his shorts, his hand on her shoulder. It was the first time I had seen them touch since the big fight in the cafeteria.

The adults and members of Caspian's tribe lined the sand as the wind howled around us. Caspian stood in the middle, the Protector's staff clutched in his hands like a javelin. His young face was twisted with rage, teeth bared, eyes locked on the sea. Emanuel stood beside me, but not too close to risk getting impaled on my fins. Inside, Adam guarded the kids with his swords. After a brief argument over what had happened the last time he had killed someone, he begrudgingly agreed to be the last resort.

Despite the wind and thunder, the world seemed oddly quiet and still, as if the globe had forgotten to spin.

I glanced over at Emanuel, who drew steady breaths. I could smell how worried he was. For the millionth time, I felt for the flash drive in my pocket. We had agreed to let Reed blackmail the mayor for help, but we remained skeptical. If his plan failed, I was prepared to do anything to defend my family.

A figure emerged from the ocean, carrying his twisted version of a staff. I tensed, but Emanuel only squeezed my hand tighter.

"I love you," he whispered. Careful to keep my fins away, I leaned over and kissed him on the cheek, hoping desperately it wasn't the last time. Mercer had made no secret that Amy, Tom, Emanuel, and I would be the first targets. We were the ones who dared to love humans. We were the ones who ruined the sacred mating system. We were the true abominations. We deserved no salvation, no mercy.

But he had killed my son. He killed Caspian's parents. It was Mercer who deserved no mercy.

"Step on this beach and die," Amy said calmly.

"You killed my son," Mercer said.

"Karma's a bitch, huh?" I shouted. Mercer turned towards me, and there was no end to the depths of rage contained in his black eyes. I smiled and shot him the middle finger.

Behind him, other figures rose from the ocean like zombies out of a grave, water streaming off of their clothes, smelling of blood and brine. They all held weapons, spears, and knives carved from the bones of ancient monsters. I looked through them, wondering if my parents were among them. Which ones were Grayson's parents? I wondered if they knew or even cared that their son was dead because of their precious leader.

Mercer held up his staff, and they flooded the beach, charging towards us with an animal cry.

I bolted for the chaos, my poisonous fins fully extended. Amy squinted and began firing into the crowd, her husband matching her shot for shot. In a previous life, she might've hesitated or tried to compromise, but I had watched her change from a scared teenager to a pissed mom. She had taken life for lesser sins before. Caspian bolted straight for Mercer, fire in his blue eyes.

I let the rage fuel me as I pierced anyone who dared get close to me, imagining each one to be the bastard who had killed my son in cold blood.

I never got the chance to help Caspian fight Mercer. I was yards away when helicopter blades sounded in the distance. Everyone paused to look up. Several of the giant machines flew over the house, lights blazing down on the sand, guns peeking out from the doors.

"STAND DOWN."

Humans wearing body armor descended from the sky, sending up clouds of sand as they landed. I ducked to the ground as tranq darts rained on the enemy from the helicopters above. In moments, Mercer and his followers were lying unconscious in the sand.

I retracted my fins, slowly standing and surveying the damage. The Atlanteans stared at the bodies with slack jaws and lowered weapons.

Reed did it. That was easier than I thought it would be.

Emanuel broke the stillness, tackling me in a hug, relief pouring off him in waves as he sobbed into my shoulder. Around us, cheers from Atlanteans rose into the sky. I decided not to be salty that I didn't have a chance to stab Mercer as cops pulled up onto the beach and started dragging the unconscious bodies into the cars.

"I'm so glad you're safe," Emanuel whispered into my ear. I wrapped my arms around him, weight disappearing from my shoulders as I felt his love pour into me.

"It's over," I said. "It's finally over. Reed saved us all."

REED

Several days after I was discharged from the hospital, we arrived at the Sanctuary. Caspian and the others met their old home with cries of glee, running their fingers over the old carvings, relieved to see they were still intact.

Norman, Emanuel, and Daniel helped me carry Grayson's coffin to the inner pool. After some debate, I insisted we bury him at the place he loved most – in the traditional Merfolk way. He had already been cremated enough. We placed him gently on the sand. The others gathered in a solemn circle. Caspian stood on the other side.

"Reed, may I say a few words before we say goodbye to our friend?" he asked. I nodded and stepped behind the coffin. Daniel held my hand. Caspian lifted his chin and pounded his staff against the ground. The cavern instantly quieted as everyone turned their attention to him. It took several times for him to clear his throat.

"In light of recent events, there has been much discussion over what constitutes real merfolk," he started. His fingers trembled.

"Our beautiful Sanctuary, as well as our brothers and sisters on land have been under attack by merfolk who claim to be the true ones. But we know they are not true. They have sought to eradicate us for associating with humans and rejecting the lies of our ancestors.

"Those merfolk who wanted to hurt us are now gone. But I sense there remains confusion for many of us as to what counts as a true merfolk. I have met and mingled with all types of merfolk and humans these past few weeks, and now feel ready to answer this question once and for all.

"Merfolk can be born or Cursed. Merfolk can be able to phase or not. A special few can even be human." A slight chuckle rose from the crowd at that. Norman elbowed his husband, who blushed. Caspian smiled.

"But merfolk will never abandon their kind. Merfolk will never use their heritage as an excuse to hate. Merfolk will use their abilities to protect those around them - human or otherwise. Merfolk are kind, understanding, merciful, and empathetic. Any creature willing to abide by these is true enough merfolk for me," Caspian finished.

Around the pool, merfolk shouted in agreement. Caspian turned his blue eyes to me and nodded. I took a deep breath and let go of

Daniel's hand. I opened the coffin and gingerly lifted the body of my friend. The people at the morgue had sealed him in a white waterproof body bag after telling us the coffin would float.

The sea was pleasant and cool, the small waves almost friendly. I stopped as the sand dropped off into the depths.

The tears came suddenly, but my hands were too full to wipe them away. They dripped down my nose and fell onto Grayson's chest. All around the cavern, hands shook.

"I'm so mad that you died," I whispered. "But I'm sure you're glad that your death solved some problems." I could imagine him laughing in agreement.

Well, I better not have died for nothing.

"I hope you're happy, wherever you are. I'll do my best not to call you guys fish freaks anymore."

You're a fish freak too, don't forget.

I grinned. "I'll miss you. But I'm glad I got to fight with you. No matter what, I'll stand with you. Through hell or high water," I whispered.

I let go of his body. He slowly sank into the darkness. I walked back to the beach and fell into Norman's arms.

"Grayson would've been proud of you," he said. I laughed, hiccupping. Daniel inserted himself in, squeezing my ribs.

"He would be making so much fun of you being all sad and sappy," he said. I laughed, nearly choking on my tears.

"Yeah, he would be. But seriously. You have honored him in a way no one else could have. He would be happy," Norman said. "You saved all of us."

Out of the corner of my eye, I saw Amy and Tom walk up and join in. More weight piled on me until I could barely breathe, but I didn't mind. Even with the chemo treatment running through my veins, I could still smell their love. I didn't know if I would ever move back in with my parents, but I knew I had a family elsewhere that would always accept me - tail or no tail - Cursed or not Cursed. I let their love and acceptance burn into me until it felt seared into my skin, my blood, my everything.

For the first time since getting Cursed, I truly understood what it felt like to be Merfolk.

And I wouldn't trade it for anything.

. . .

We returned to land, and things were shockingly normal. We were the only ones not surprised when the mayor suddenly renounced several of his previous decrees - that human parents were no longer allowed to abandon their merpeople children without repercussions - that merfolk were allowed to choose if and when they wanted to show their markings in public. Mercer and his followers were awaiting trial for their crimes. Sam was back in her lab, studying whatever it was she had left to figure out about merpeople.

There was just one more thing nagging at me.

Will. He was in jail - as he honestly should have been - but he was about to take the fall for the entire trafficking operation when it was mostly my uncle's fault.

I kept the flash drive containing all the evidence from Will's burner phone on my nightstand. I took it out that night, twisting it in my fingers.

I went downstairs to the library and sat down at one of the computers. I plugged the flash drive into the USB port and found the email address of one of the local news stations and the local police station.

Dear whoever reads this, I think you'll find the following files very interesting ;)

I had told my uncle that I would keep the flash drives out of the public eye if he did what I said. But what kind of merperson would I be if I didn't lie at least once?

I attached the contents of the drive and clicked *send*.